Praise for the novels of
DONNA FLETCHER . . .

Wedding Spell
A *Magical Love* Romance

"I was bewitched by *Wedding Spell*. It is light, bright, and entertaining. There are no broomsticks, cauldrons, or black cats in this tale, only sophisticated witches that are handsome and beautiful . . . so enchanting . . . I flew through the pages."

—*Rendezvous*

Whispers on the Wind
A *Haunting Hearts* Romance

"Donna Fletcher's ghostly romance is a treat for those with a taste for the spectral world. The main characters are 'lively,' passionate, and engaged in a fine adventure."

—*Affaire de Coeur*

"*Whispers on the Wind* is an exquisite mixture of suspense, fantasy, and blazing passion. The plot is fresh and the characters are remarkable. This is a magnificent book that is worth another read."

—*Rendezvous*

The Buccaneer

"Donna Fletcher has written a joyous adventure on the high seas that will delight all her readers. The witty characterizations, unique situations, and swashbuckling action combine to make a terrific fast-paced romance that is thrilling to the very last word. This sensuous romance is a delight—right down to the very last sigh!"

—*Affaire de Coeur*

"*The Buccaneer* is a grand adventure and a sexual romp on the high seas. Fast-paced and well-written, it sizzles!"

—*The Paperback Forum*

Magical Moments

DONNA FLETCHER

JOVE BOOKS, NEW YORK

MAGICAL LOVE is a trademark of Penguin Putnam Inc.

MAGICAL MOMENTS

A Jove Book / published by arrangement with
the author

PRINTING HISTORY
Jove edition / November 1999

All rights reserved.
Copyright © 1999 by Donna Fletcher.
This book may not be reproduced in whole or in part,
by mimeograph or any other means, without permission.
For information address: The Berkley Publishing Group,
a division of Penguin Putnam Inc.,
375 Hudson Street, New York, New York 10014.

The Penguin Putnam Inc. World Wide Web site address is
http://www.penguinputnam.com

ISBN: 0-515-12681-0

A JOVE BOOK®
Jove Books are published by The Berkley Publishing Group,
a division of Penguin Putnam Inc.,
375 Hudson Street, New York, New York 10014.
JOVE and the "J" design
are trademarks belonging to Penguin Putnam Inc.

PRINTED IN THE UNITED STATES OF AMERICA

10 9 8 7 6 5 4 3 2 1

*To two very special friends, Johnnie and Tracy,
who understand and practice the true meaning
of magic.*

Magical Moments

One

~

"She is a disgrace, sir."

Dagon listened with his eyes closed and his head resting back against the plush gray velvet seat of the old Rolls-Royce. Alastair, his steadfast chauffeur and a spry, wiry man for his one hundred years, started complaining as soon as Dagon had asked how things were at the castle.

A question he now wished he could rescind. He was tired from his long flight from the States to Scotland. And presently he wanted nothing more than to take a shower and slip into bed for several hours of much needed sleep.

He should have used his powers to transport himself across continents, thus saving himself the affects of jet lag. After all, he was a witch. A three-hundred-year-old witch with tremendous powers at his disposal. But a last-minute business venture forced him to take a normal flight with the mortal businessman he was presently in negotiations with. And now, like a mortal, he required sleep.

He could recharge his energy in other ways. The blond stewardess had made her interest clear, and a passionate romp in bed would have more than restored his depleted energy.

He had given her blatant invitation considerable thought

and reluctantly declined her offer while graciously accepting her phone number. He had personal business at his ancestral castle that required his immediate attention, and he could put it off no longer. The matter had already suffered enough unexpected delays, an urgent business deal in Athens and an important wedding in the United States to be precise.

Now, however, after listening to Alastair's continuous complaints, he wished he had accepted the shapely mortal's lusty offer and lost himself in a night of passion.

"She barely has any powers and she attempts to tackle her chores as a mortal would," Alastair said with disdain. "It takes her forever—that is, if she doesn't break something first or injure herself."

"Injure? How can she injure herself? She's a witch," Dagon said, confused. His whole household staff consisted of witches to one degree or another. All witches were not equal in power and skills, even though most mortals erroneously believed them to be. Some witches possessed great powers, others only one or two particular skills, and some a mere sprinkle of power, but even the least skilled witch was able to complete a task much faster than any mortal.

"It's a shame, a disgrace," Alastair lamented, shaking his head. "She goes and cuts herself while dusting in the dining room, and she can't even stop the bleeding." He shook his head harder. "She attempts to stop the blood with her apron and makes more of a mess."

"What could she possibly have cut herself on in the dining room?"

Alastair cringed, his narrow shoulders hunching up. "The broken James V vase."

"What?" Dagon said, bolting up straight.

Alastair hurried to explain. "She accidentally dropped the antique while cleaning."

"Why didn't she prevent it from hitting the ground?"

"She doesn't seem to have sufficient powers."

"Which means she didn't have the skills to return the vase to its original condition," Dagon said and dropped back against the seat, releasing a hefty sigh. "Well, at least Bernard will see to its repair."

Bernard had been his butler for the last two hundred years. He was a tall, dignified man with startling white hair and a penchant for fine clothes. He took his duties seriously and ran Rasmus Castle with the precision and skill of an accomplished general. He and his wife Margaret, the housekeeper, had served Dagon well, and he didn't know what he would do without them. His various business dealings often took him away for months at a time and he was grateful he had the efficient couple to depend on.

"Now, there's the strange part," Alastair said and reluctantly continued. "It seems no one can right her wrongs. If she breaks something, it stays broken."

This time Dagon sat up slowly. "Are you telling me that the vase presented to my father by James V is beyond repair?"

Alastair delivered the bad news in a single word. "Shattered."

Dagon growled beneath his breath and once again sank back against the velvet seat. "What is this incompetent witch's name?"

"Sarina."

That brought a chilling laugh from Dagon. "Well, she certainly doesn't live up to her name—peaceful and serene."

"That, sir, I can certainly attest to. Why—"

"No more," Dagon ordered. "I will take care of the matter when we arrive."

Alastair nodded along with a "Yes, sir."

Dagon glanced out the window. It was autumn in Scotland and the heather was in full bloom, spreading across the countryside wherever one looked. He had left on a business trip in the spring when the rhododendrons had burst into full glorious shades of pink, red, and violet. He had hoped to return in the summer when the fuchsias were spilling their exceptional colors from the bushes that grew abundantly in the country gardens.

He had to smile, recalling the reason for fuchsias being

so prevalent in the countryside. In days of old the bush was believed to ward off witches, another misconception by humans but one that at least produced a beautiful result.

And then there was *the gloaming,* a stunning sight to behold during summer. After the sun set, hours of twilight remained and the sight of the land in such ethereal splendor simply stilled one's heart.

This was the Scotland he loved and carried with him always. This was where his roots were firmly planted and where he would one day raise his own family. Another reason he had returned home. It was time to settle down, find one of his own kind to commit to and mate with.

He supposed it was his recent visit with Alisande that made him think so strongly on marriage. Ali was like a sister to him. They grew up together, she spending time here in Scotland and he spending time at her family's estate just outside of Washington, D.C., in Virginia.

He had gotten her out of many a difficult situation through the years, and this most recent one had given him pause to think. Ali had fallen in love with a mortal male and wished to mate with him for life. He couldn't understand her choice, but after meeting Sebastian Wainwright, he discovered he liked the courageous mortal. And he envied the deep love the pair shared. It had taken some wise maneuvering to bring the two together, especially since his hands had been tied as far as his powers were concerned. But he had managed to use his wit just before he had left the States and it had worked. He recently had the honor of being the best man at their wedding.

The wedding had started him thinking more seriously about a lifemate.

While he never lacked female companionship, he recently felt the need for a more solid, binding relationship. One bound by a strong commitment of respect, admiration, and equal powers.

Mortal females were out of the question as were witches with limited abilities. He desired a witch as powerful or even more powerful than himself. Two strong powers uniting would create strong baby witches, and he wanted a slew of them.

He had his sights set on one particular witch. She was called the Ancient One; legends said she was born with the dawn of time and that her powers were limitless. There were few witches who knew her. She kept to herself and chose those she would teach or befriend. It was also believed that she had loved but once, and since losing that great love she refused to love again.

Dagon intended to change her mind, and he had no doubt that he could. He was far from conceited where his looks and abilities were concerned, though he wouldn't deny he possessed an air of arrogance. He simply understood himself and his unique capabilities.

It would be foolish of him to deny that women found him attractive. He couldn't walk into a room without females turning their heads in interest or men shaking theirs in envy.

He walked with pride and confidence and an intimidating arrogance that appeared to rankle mortals. Of course, he was well aware that his looks commanded attention. His long shiny black hair fell past his broad shoulders, his well-defined body remained in top shape because he worked to keep it that way, and his face?

He smiled to himself. He was grateful to his parents for his handsome features. They had chosen wisely when they mated and their physical beauties blended well when they conceived him. Women forever commented on his good looks.

Therefore, he was certain he possessed all the attributes a witch of this old one's caliber would be searching for in a mate. He also knew a witch who was once her student. Ali's aunt Sydney, and he intended for Aunt Sydney to introduce them.

He yawned, his weary eyes drifting closed. First, he would see to this dilemma at the castle. This Sarina had come highly recommended by old friends, the MacDougals. Unfortunately, the couple were presently on an extended vacation, and he wasn't able to question them in regards to her background.

It didn't matter, though. If the woman was as incompetent as Alastair claimed, he would simply release her from her contract and be done with it.

Dagon was drifting off into a peaceful slumber when the Rolls turned up the long driveway and came to a stop at the castle's front door.

Alastair barely had the car door open when a thunderous crash was heard followed by female screams.

Alastair shook his head. "She's at it again."

Dagon raced up the stone steps and flung open the heavy wooden door.

Chaos reigned in the large foyer. A tall wooden ladder lay toppled on its side on the white marble tile floor. Two screeching maids pointed trembling fingers toward the ceiling. Bernard was yelling, his head tilted back and his wide eyes fixed where fingers pointed.

Dagon stared up in utter confusion and surprise at the woman who dangled overhead from his centuries-old chandelier. Her hands gripped the brass bars while hundreds of crystal teardrops harshly chimed against one another. Her shapely legs swung back and forth as she obviously attempted to gain control of her precarious situation, and she was minus one black shoe.

Her slim black skirt had managed to inch its way up her slim thighs from her constant wiggling, and Dagon caught an unexpected glimpse of black lace panties. He couldn't quite catch sight of her face, but her dark brown hair was falling loose from the pins that held it, leaving several strands falling past her shoulders.

The shouts and screeches continued, no one having noticed his entrance over the chaos.

He delivered his order sharply and loudly. "Enough!"

Silence immediately followed.

"Sir—"Bernard began only to be cut off by Dagon's raised hand. The butler obeyed his silent command without hesitation.

Dagon walked to stand directly beneath the dangling woman. "Sarina, I presume."

"Yes, sir," came the much too soft reply.

"Sarina, if you would be so kind as to float down here."

Gasps sounded in the foyer, and Dagon saw Bernard shake his head in weary disgust.

"I can't do that, sir."

Her gentle voice quivered and Dagon sensed her fear. "You don't possess the energy?"

"No, sir," she answered on a gasp. "And I don't think I can hold on much longer."

Dagon didn't hesitate. She obviously was in immediate danger. Her apprehension assaulted him full force, and sensing her urgent alarm only irritated him all the more. He released a low, annoyed mumble and with no difficulty floated up to her swaying body.

When he was directly beside her, he reached out and slipped his arm securely around her slim waist. She instantly anchored her arms around his neck and buried her face against his shoulder. Her slender body trembled, and he moved his other arm protectively around her back to hug her to him and calm her nervous tremors.

"You're all right now. I have you," he assured her softly.

He slowly drifted down to the ground, and when their feet touched the tiles, he felt her body sag against him in relief. He kept a firm hold on her, though his one hand sought her chin to draw her face away from his shoulder so he could speak with her.

"Are you—"

He stopped, his breath stolen from him as he looked into her eyes, their color a nondescript pale blue, but within their depths shined an age-old wisdom so profound it momentarily stunned him speechless. In the next second it was completely gone, and he suddenly wondered if he had simply imagined it.

Dagon kept a firm arm around her waist. "Are you all right?"

Sarina barely confirmed his query with a nod, though her body continued to tremble against his.

"I think tea and brandy would serve you well right now." He then turned to Bernard and ordered, "See that this mess is cleaned up and bring tea to my study. I will speak with you later."

Bernard nodded respectfully and immediately began issuing orders to the servants.

Dagon lent a steady support to the quivering woman until he was finally able to sit her on the beige silk striped settee by the large hearth in his study. He quickly saw to getting her a brandy from the cherry wood cabinet that housed his personal stock of liquor.

Bernard entered the large room that housed an impressive collection of books, several being first editions, as Dagon handed the crystal glass to Sarina.

She reached for it with shaking hands and Bernard cringed.

She cast the intimidating butler a nervous glance then she grasped the Waterford crystal in both hands and carefully brought the trembling glass to her lips.

Dagon watched the exchange and grew annoyed. "Leave the tray."

Bernard attempted to protest. "She is not capable of serving tea."

"I will not repeat myself," Dagon said authoritatively.

Bernard did as directed, arranging the silver tray that held delicate china cups and saucers, a silver teapot, a creamer and sugar bowl with small elegant silver tongs for the tiny cubes, on the small table in front of the settee and then he quietly left.

Dagon returned to the cherry wood cabinet to pour himself a glass of brandy and allow Sarina time to calm her nervous tremors. The brief time also allowed him to study her, and his findings surprised him.

Though he could not term her beautiful, she possessed a face that captured attention. Her features were strong, high cheekbones leading to bold, large eyes and full lusty lips that tormented a man. Her silky brown hair, half pinned up and half falling down, was a few inches past shoulder length, and she wore it parted in the middle with a wisp of bangs that ended just past her eyebrows and down along the sides of her temples. She had small breasts that looked as though they would fit quite nicely in the palm of his hands. Her waistline curved over slender hips that molded—

He closed his eyes for a moment, recalling her firm and perfectly curved backside.

He shook away the enticing memory and downed a good portion of his brandy. Whatever was the matter with him? While he found most females attractive in their own special ways, he would not think of involving himself with an incompetent witch. The absurd notion was simply out of the question, even if she did possess a backside that he itched to touch.

"Behave yourself," he whispered to himself in warning and then turned and joined her on the settee.

"Feeling better?" he asked.

"Much," she answered, her voice soft and much too sensual, to Dagon's annoyance.

He took another generous swallow of brandy.

Sarina continued to hold tightly, though with one hand, to her brandy glass. "Thank you so much for rescuing me."

Dagon wished to question her about her spell-casting problem but thought better of it. She seemed to no longer tremble, and he did not wish to further upset her.

"Would you like some tea?" he asked.

Sarina looked at the elegant tea service with trepidation.

Dagon instantly relieved her fears. "I shall do the honors."

Her face brightened. "Thank you. I would love a cup of tea."

Dagon poured two cups from the silver teapot and turned a questioning glance to Sarina.

"Just one lump of sugar, please."

He dropped a tiny cube in her teacup, placed a silver teaspoon along the saucer, and handed the cup to her. Her fingers looked steady as she reached out to take it, and when he was certain she had a firm hold on it, he let go to turn and reach for his own cup.

Sarina moved forward to place her brandy glass on the tray, and as she moved back in her seat her hand holding the teacup collided with Dagon's, and both cups went toppling over, spilling the hot contents all over the both of them.

Sarina yelped, Dagon gasped, and she immediately reached down to retrieve the fallen cups and saucers. Her hands fumbled over him in the most intimate place, and he silently cursed her inept hands. She made matters worse when after placing the china on the tray, she reached for a white linen napkin and attempted to pat him dry.

She apologized profusely while pressing the napkin along the zipper of his black wool trousers.

His annoyance wasn't the only thing growing, and he hastily reached for her wrist and drew her hand away from him. "Clean it up the proper way."

While he attempted to keep the irritation out of his voice, her wide, apprehensive eyes and her full, quivering lips cautioned he had not succeeded.

"I cannot," she admitted, her trembling voice warning she was on the verge of tears.

Two

The unshed tears that glistened in her gentle blue eyes upset Dagon in a way that irritated him. He favored spirited women, ones who would defend themselves against the greatest of odds and with the greatest of courage. And here he sat with an inept witch without a lick of courage, who fought tears that pooled dangerously close to spilling over, and yet he felt a tremendous urge to comfort and protect her. And worse yet was the fact that he had an insatiable desire to make love to her.

Jet lag. A good, sound reason for his strange response to a witch he would not ordinarily find appealing. And of course there was his depleted energy that could very well be boosted by a pleasurable hour or two in bed with her. Another sane and sensible explanation to his unbridled and unexpected passion.

He spoke more calmly than he felt. "I will take care of this mess. Do not upset yourself." He waved his hand over his lap and the surrounding area where the spilled tea lay staining the antique wool carpet. And to his surprise and annoyance nothing happened. All remained the same.

Two more waves of his hand followed as did a deep grumble before he turned suspicious eyes on Sarina. His annoyance immediately melted when he caught sight of her distraught features and disheveled appearance. She bravely continued to fight the tears, though one had managed a fast escape and was hastily running down her flushed cheek. She chewed nervously on her bottom lip that was already enticingly plump enough, and several strands of her silky straight brown hair fell wildly around her face while others remained pinned sedately to her head. And there was that button on her white blouse that looked about to slip open and reveal her breasts, and while she was merely average in size, he could not help but wonder if her soft white flesh would fit his hand perfectly.

He groaned more loudly than he had intended, and she slowly slid away from him to safely tuck herself in the corner of the settee.

"I think it would be best if you returned to your duties," he said, reaching for a white linen napkin on the table.

"I can clean this up," she offered softly.

"I will see to it," he answered and told himself that by keeping his eyes from her she would understand his disappointment in her behavior, though his own emotions cautioned that his reason was purely selfish. If he looked he just might want, and dallying with the help was not something he deemed appropriate, especially when that want bordered on a lusty urge. "You are dismissed and please tell Bernard I wish to speak with him."

"Yes, sir," Sarina said and cautiously moved off the settee. She stood a moment as if indecisive and then spoke. "Thank you for rescuing me. It was most gallant of you."

He watched her walk out of the room and wondered over her age. Her response spoke of another time, perhaps a time she favored and found herself more comfortable with.

Bernard entered almost on Sarina's departure. Dagon had no doubt that his meticulous butler had hovered near in expectation and his expectations proved accurate.

"I expected much worse," Bernard said, immediately seeing to cleaning up the mess.

Dagon stood, dropping the napkin on the silver tray and brushing at the damp spot on his trousers as he walked over to the cabinet to pour himself another brandy. "Tell me about Sarina."

The look of relief on Bernard's face warned Dagon that he was in for an earful. He filled his brandy glass and took a seat near the window that looked out on the stone terrace and tiered gardens.

With a dramatic sigh and a tug of his gray vest over his belted gray trousers and a brush of a minute speck off the lapel of his black jacket, Bernard was ready to tell all. "Her credentials are impeccable. I was relieved and immensely pleased to have her join our efficient and remarkable staff, and I must say she seemed pleased and most anxious to accept the position."

"Then you had no reason to suspect that her work would be inadequate?" Dagon asked.

"Absolutely none, sir," he answered with a firm shake of his head. "I check all references personally and put an applicant through a thorough interview. In my estimation Sarina possessed more than adequate experience for the position. I had her sign the usual contract committing herself to at least a year of service which she did without delay, and the very day she began her duties the trouble began."

"The very same day?"

"The very first hour," Bernard said with a hefty sigh. "She broke a glass in the kitchen, and Margaret, my blessed, patient wife, told her not to worry, to just clean it up. Which she proceeded to do with a broom and dustpan. Margaret thought her nervous about starting in a new place, and she gave her the benefit of the doubt only to have another glass break and another and another."

Dagon watched Bernard's face turn red with annoyance.

"Needless to say a new set of glasses was needed to be purchased by the end of her first day. On her second day Margaret discovered why she continued to work as a mortal would. It seemed that not only her powers were insufficient to clean up after herself, but no one else's powers were capable of righting the wrong her messes made."

"Your reaction to this discovery?"

"It alarmed me," Bernard admitted. "There could be

many reasons for her dysfunctional abilities, and I did not care to think that I might have unwittingly brought a problem into the castle. But then I thought of her references and Mrs. MacDougal's penchant for helping the less fortunate, and I reached the sad conclusion that the woman was attempting to aid an inept witch in securing a good position for herself."

Dagon nodded. "Mrs. MacDougal was aware that you could not release her from the contract without my permission. And the woman was also aware that not only she and her husband would be away for several months, but so would I."

"Precisely," Bernard agreed. "And perhaps in that time she had hoped Sarina's skills would have improved and she would remain part of the staff. Unfortunately that was not the case, and the ordeal I and the rest of the staff have had to contend with has been unacceptable. I request that she be discharged immediately."

Hesitation was not what Bernard expected nor hoped for. Quick dismissal was the only answer. To Bernard's chagrin Dagon did not agree.

"Perhaps we should give her another chance."

Bernard almost choked on his words. "Ano—another chance?"

Dagon smiled and sipped at his brandy.

"She has been given more than sufficient time to prove herself and has failed to do so. She continues to perform her duties inadequately which provides ample cause for dismissal."

Dagon retained his patience. "Have you attempted to see how Sarina handles various household duties?"

Bernard answered reluctantly. "I thought it best to keep her where she would cause the least problem."

Dagon chose his words carefully, not wanting to alienate Bernard, whose exceptional services he could not do without. But then he did not wish to see Sarina be discharged of her duties. He found he wanted to learn more about this witch who seemed to be powerless, and besides, he felt the need to protect her. Where would she go and what would she do if he dismissed her? The thought that she would roam aimlessly with no way of adequately surviving or protecting herself left him feeling distressed.

"Perhaps she would work well on the laundry staff," Dagon suggested. "I doubt she could cause much harm there."

Bernard disagreed with a brief shake of his head, though he answered, "As you wish."

Sarina returned to her room in the west wing where all servants resided. Her room was of ample size containing a single bed, a dresser with a mirror, and a small writing desk and chair. A window over the desk looked out on an expanse of green land and rolling hills that captured the eye and stole the heart. The view was especially breathtaking now in the fall when the purple heather covered the hills and the mist kissed the hilltops. Rasmus Castle was in Trossachs and bordered Queen Elizabeth Forest Park, a stunning land complimented by ash, willow, oak, and stika spruce. Weasels, deer, and wildcats roamed the area, and sparrow hawks and golden eagles could be seen if one had the patience to watch for their flight.

Sarina loved this land of her birth. She had traveled much in her younger years, but she always found herself returning home to Scotland. Recent years had found her more of a homebody. She had studied and perfected her skills and used them to help others. Unfortunately, her desire to help had gotten her into more trouble than she had ever thought possible. And now she guarded her secret carefully for fear of discovery and guarded her privacy just as fiercely out of necessity.

She sighed and shook her head as she pulled the pins from her messed hair and ran her silver-handled brush through the silky brown strands. She gave it a vigorous brushing, feeling the intense bristles scratch her scalp. She then twisted up the thick strands that fell past her shoulders to the middle of her back and tucked in several pins to hold the heavy strands to the top of her head. Her bangs covered her full eyebrows and along her temples and she ran a touch of blush over her pale cheeks.

Dagon Rasmus had exceeded his reputation. The staff had gossiped like any staff was want to do, and she had listened silently when the female servants had commented over his good looks and his worldly arrogance that they all admired. She had thought they had embellished the stories and, therefore, was shocked to learn they had spoken the truth, though she felt their words had not done the man justice.

Dagon Rasmus was simply gorgeous. His looks went far beyond just good. His handsome features captured the eye, and his confident arrogance easily intimidated. And to add to that he was a powerful witch who could perform more than the ordinary feats. He was a witch who had earned and demanded respect and not one to match skills with, especially when one's skills were less than adequate.

Sarina checked the buttons on her white long-sleeve cotton blouse, tucked it securely in her waistband, and made certain that her slim black skirt was free of lint or dust, then she hurried off to the kitchen to see if Margaret required help and perhaps discover her fate, for which she had little hope.

She hurried down the steps eager to speak with Margaret. The tall slim woman was the first to befriend her when she had arrived. Her dignified manner belied her position. To look at her one would expect to find her behind a desk and in a position of high authority; instead she was housekeeper and cook at Rasmus Castle, feeding an appreciative staff with a talent that would put the finest culinary chef to shame.

Margaret greeted her with a wide smile, her hands buried deep in soft dough that would soon be turned into an apple cinnamon bread that would tempt the staunchest dieter. Two loaves were already baking in the double wall oven and the delicious smell assaulted the nostrils and salivated the tongue.

"Sit," Margaret said with a warm smile. "You know how much I love company when I bake."

Sarina enjoyed visiting with Margaret while she worked. The room always smelled heavenly, and the professional stainless-steel appliances and stark white cabinets, though modern for the castle environment, looked at home in the large room. Of course Margaret had added her own personal touches, which happened to be her love of cows. They were everywhere one looked, from the teakettle, to potholders, towel racks, a clock, pitchers, and framed pictures that crowded the walls. It was simply a delightful place to share friendly conversation and a spot of tea.

She took the chair closest to the fresh-baked loaves that sat cooling on a wire rack on the rectangular oak table. "Delicious," she mumbled and sniffed the air.

"As soon as I finish these two loaves we'll share a slice or two and a nice hot pot of Earl Grey tea."

Sarina nodded enthusiastically.

"I heard that your morning did not go well."

Sarina had to laugh; if she didn't she would have cried— something she was not in the habit of doing, though of late she found her unusual circumstances bringing her closer to tears. Perhaps it was the fact that she felt her life spinning out of control, and any effort she made to grasp hold and right it simply failed. "I not only made a fool of myself yet again, I did so in front of Dagon Rasmus and probably sealed my fate."

"Don't judge so quickly."

Sarina stood. "I'll put the kettle on. You tell me about Dagon Rasmus."

Margaret smiled. "A handsome one he is, there's no denying that."

Sarina sighed as she filled the cow-spotted kettle. "He surely is, though he will find love where he least expects it."

Margaret nodded. "Your spell skill should match your sight skill."

Sarina silently admonished herself. She had repeatedly made the mistake of predicting future events for several of the staff, and they all thought her accuracy was remarkable. Lately many had sought her advice, and while she gave it freely she watched her tongue. It would do no good for those at Rasmus Castle to learn the truth about her.

"I'm practicing," Sarina said with a weary smile. "Dagon's skills appear powerful."

Margaret cast her a cautious glance. "More powerful than most know. He takes his heritage seriously and he is wise in his use of his skills. That is why he has survived and thrived. He knows when his skills are necessary."

"Does he ever think of marriage?"

"He will marry one who he feels will be worthy of mating with. Her energy will need to equal or surpass his. He has no tolerance for mediocre witches. He requires a woman of extraordinary power and intelligence to deal with the likes of him."

Sarina took two cow mugs from the row of hooks that ran beneath the cabinet beside the sink. "I best stay out of his way then."

Margaret wiped her hands on her black-and-white spotted apron, the bib being a cow head. "Lord Dagon—" She stopped abruptly and shook her head. "I sometimes forget what time I am living in, and Dagon did make a wonderful lord. He is kind and considerate of others, especially those less fortunate."

"Like clumsy witches?"

Margaret offered a comforting pat to her hand after Sarina placed the filled mugs on the table. "He will give you another chance."

Sarina sat on the chair tucking her one leg beneath her and sipped at the hot, soothing tea. "I would appreciate his tolerance, but how long will he be tolerant with me?"

"I think that depends on you," Margaret said, sitting down after slicing two healthy slices of the apple cinnamon bread and fetching the honey butter from the refrigerator.

"I need to focus on my work."

"Your skills," Margaret corrected. "Your energy is weak causing your powers to be less than sufficient. Have you considered mating with a strong witch?"

"We both know that is not my problem," she said. "My powers are completely depleted."

Margaret agreed with a nod. "That could explain why your mistakes cannot be made right. If you allowed your energy to dwindle near to extinction, then it would be hard to retrieve even a small amount."

Sarina spoke honestly though cautiously. "I was foolish."

Margaret pushed the tub of honey butter to Sarina. "We are all foolish when we are young. Why, I bet you are barely a hundred years old."

Sarina smiled and again spoke in a broad sense. "I feel like a child."

"You will learn, my dear. In our youth we make many mistakes, and Dagon understands youth. He was a wild one himself."

"I doubt he lost his powers."

Margaret folded the sliced bread to lock in the honey butter that dripped from the sides. "He wisely protected himself at all times."

"Then he was not foolish."

"No, no one could ever call Dagon foolish."

Both women grew silent while taking bites of the delicious warm bread.

Sarina worried over her future. What if Dagon was not tolerant with her? What if he dismissed her? Where would she go and what would she do? She was not accustomed to mortal living. She was barely accustomed to her present surroundings.

"Do not worry," Margaret said with another comforting pat. "All will go well. You will learn and your skills will grow."

Sarina managed a smile, though she knew full well that her skills could not be learned. It was a far more complicated problem than any imagined, and even she herself wondered how she would ever solve it.

"I thought Mr. Rasmus ordered you to return to your duties?"

Sarina was so startled by Bernard's unexpected entrance that she knocked over her half-filled mug. She immediately reached for the nearby towel to wipe up the spill and knocked over the butter tub. Margaret wisely took the towel from her hand and saw to cleaning up the mess.

Bernard sighed and shook his head as he walked into the room. "I do not understand why he insists on keeping you on at Rasmus Castle, but Mr. Rasmus says you are to be given another chance."

Sarina sighed with relief.

Bernard continued. "I myself think you have been given sufficient chances to prove yourself and have failed every one."

Sarina could do nothing but apologize since she agreed with him. Bernard had been tolerant of her ineptitude, and she could easily understand his frustration with her. "I am sorry."

A mordant glance and tightly pursed lips from Margaret caused her husband to alter his attitude and speak with a less biting tongue. "Perhaps you will find your new duties less difficult."

Sarina was ready for anything. She intended to work hard and be extra careful even if she had to work twice the hours of the other staff members. She would show everyone that she was capable of attending to her assigned duties. She would be diligent and self-reliant even if she had to resort to mortal tactics. Perhaps she was not learning witching skills, but she certainty was learning about mortal abilities more and more each day. Why, she rarely broke a glass anymore, and she was getting the hang of using a ladder. If she had been extra careful this morning, she would never have lost her balance on the ladder and accidentally kicked it over, leaving herself dangling in thin air.

No, whatever her duties this time, she would pay close attention and make certain she made no mistakes.

"You will be assigned to the laundry staff," Bernard informed her.

She smiled with delight. She could handle the laundry. After all, what damage could she do washing and drying clothes?

Three

Dagon felt wonderful. After a good, solid night's sleep and a generous helping of Margaret's French toast sprinkled liberally with powdered sugar and a hint of cinnamon and her stubby homemade sausages that tingled the tongue, he felt better than his usual self. He was ready to tackle anything. Which was why he took himself off to his study to make a long-distance phone call.

He was pleased with the peacefulness that pervaded the castle. No loud voices had been raised, the staff quietly went about their work, and Bernard had made no complaints. Which lead Dagon to believe that Sarina was working out quite nicely in the laundry room. Of course it was barely noontime, but still, things did seem as if they were working out well.

Dagon closed the door behind him as he entered the room he felt most comfortable in. Many years ago when titles were of importance he was called a lord and this his solar, but over the years the room had become a place of solace to him. This room housed the many objects he collected over the years, and while some items were priceless, others held no monetary value at all, though they were priceless to him.

Two tall windows draped in dark green velvet drapes and trimmed in heavy gold cording flanked a large stone fireplace along the back wall. The plush drapes were drawn back with the same thick gold cording leaving a breathtaking view of the mermaid pond—an eye-catching creation of three tiers of mermaids holding up a large shell over their heads with the top lone mermaid sprouting water from the partially closed shell she held in her arms and the surrounding area a carpet of thick green grass and shade trees.

Floor to ceiling bookcases covered two other walls with a sliding ladder that ran along both for easy access to the far top shelves. An ornate French desk dated somewhere in the seventeenth century was positioned near the windows with a perfect view of the pond. Chairs covered in a beige silk and thin dark green stripes along with a solid beige settee from the same period as the desk sat grouped before the fireplace whose intricate brass fireguard was a work of art. Two antique Persian rugs whose colors had retained their charm and blended perfectly with the decor covered a good portion of the polished wood floor.

The entrance door was on the fourth wall and was surrounded by paintings of various family members throughout the centuries. One painting in particular caught Dagon's eye, and with a smile he sat down at his desk and reached for the phone.

It would be early morning in the States, but he was certain Sydney Wyrrd would be up. She always greeted the dawn, an old habit of hers and one she never broke. She was a remarkable woman for her six hundred years, and she held a special spot in Dagon's heart. And he remembered when that particular portrait was painted of her in the late sixteenth century when he was but a mere lad. She was as beautiful and charming now as she was then, and she had been a constant in his life of which he was forever grateful. He was certain she would not deny his request. Well, almost certain.

Asking Sydney to introduce him to the Ancient One was actually asking quite a large favor. There wasn't a witch who did not wish to meet her or one who would not be honored to be educated by her. Sydney had been chosen as rare few are by the Ancient One herself to be a pupil of hers. Certain conditions had to be met, and one was that the student would not violate her privacy. Her identity and whereabouts would always be held in strict confidence. But Dagon wanted only for Sydney to extend an invitation to the Ancient One for him and her to meet. What harm could there be in that?

"No," Sydney said quickly.

Dagon had chattered for a good thirty minutes before proposing his favor. He had learned that the newlyweds Alisande and Sebastian were having a delightful time on their honeymoon in England and Ireland, and she wouldn't be surprised if they stopped by to see him before returning home.

Sebastian was having some difficulties with his newly acquired skills, though he was thoroughly enjoying his unexpected powers. Alisande thought otherwise since it was she who usually ended up the worst for wear from one of his attempts to demonstrate a spell he thought he had perfected.

Dagon couldn't help but enjoy a brief laugh over that bit of information since he had purposely failed to advise Sebastian of the consequences of the spell he needed to cast to unite Alisande and himself. He could only imagine the look on Sebastian's face when the man learned that he was now a bona fide witch. Sydney did assure him that Sebastian intended to discuss his unexpected abilities with him when next they met, and Dagon laughed once again having expected nothing less from a man as practical and dynamic as Sebastian Wainwright.

But now with that discussion done and his request presented he found himself facing a response he had not expected, and he asked simply, "Why not?"

Sydney sounded her usual patient self. "Need you really ask? You know full well the Ancient One does not like to be disturbed. She chooses her own friends. And, my dear boy, she would never be interested in you as a mate."

"Why not?" he asked again, though he sounded more

like a petulant child who was disappointed he was not getting his own way.

"Dagon, she is far more powerful than you could ever imagine. She was born with the dawn of the earth, and her wisdom is limitless. And besides, she is not looking for a mate."

"You have spoken to her?" he asked anxiously.

"All her students remain in contact with her, and we all respect her privacy."

"I do not wish to intrude on her privacy. I only ask that you mention that I would like to be introduced to her. What harm could that do? Perhaps she would find me to her liking."

"I am sure she would find you a delight to speak with," Sydney said, "but mating with is another matter. And besides she loved once and lost that love and has sworn to never love again."

"Not to sound arrogant, Sydney, but I think I could make her forget him."

Sydney retained her patience. "You know not of what you speak, Dagon, and I suggest you forget this foolish idea."

"If this was nothing but a whim I might, but I am determined to meet the Ancient One. I feel we would be well suited for each other, and once united we could create powerful and beautiful children."

"I have no doubt you would," Sydney agreed. "But I am telling you as a close friend to beware of what you ask for."

"I know exactly—"

A rapid pounding on his door interrupted Dagon. "Excuse me, Sydney." He held the phone away from his face. "I am on an international call."

Bernard's anxious voice penetrated the closed door. "There is a problem in the laundry room."

Dagon shook his head. "Can't you handle it?"

"No, sir, it is imperative that you come at once," Bernard insisted to Dagon's surprise.

"Sydney," Dagon said, returning the phone to his ear.

"I heard," Sydney said with a laugh. "I will leave you to solve your dilemma, and, my dear boy, I will give your request some further thought."

That brightened Dagon's disposition. "Thank you. I knew there was a reason why I loved you so much."

"And I love you," she echoed, "though give my words thought."

The line went dead and Dagon felt a tingle rush over him. Sydney had a way of teaching without instructing, and if he was wise he would pay attention, for he had the feeling that she had just given him a lesson.

He replaced the phone on the receiver and called out to Bernard, "I'll be right there."

Bernard was waiting at the top of the stairs for him, and they both hurried down the two flights to the laundry area. No words were necessary. Dagon could tell by their destination and the perturbed look on Bernard's face that the problem could be none other than Sarina.

The two men heard giggling as they turned the corner, and they both stopped dead in their tracks. The corridor was a mass of suds, and two female servants were standing on the perimeter, their hands digging into the white sudsy mass and playfully tossing thick puffs into the air.

"Return to your duties at once," Bernard ordered.

The two young woman jumped, startled by his sharp command.

The one young woman spoke for them both. "Our duties are in there." She pointed at the thick mountain of suds that seemed to grow larger by the minute. "Ellen and I went to gather the remaining laundry and left Sarina to tend the machines."

"Sarina is in there?" Dagon asked with concern.

Both women nodded and kept steady eyes on him.

Bernard shook his head. "Go assist Margaret in the kitchen."

The two women obeyed immediately but not before casting quick admiring glances at Dagon.

"Sarina is not capable of the simplest—"

Dagon's curt remark stopped his complaint. "Not now."

Bernard wisely offered assistance. "Perhaps I should contact a plumber."

"Yes, I suggest you do that," Dagon agreed and stepped toward the high wall of suds.

"Sir, your clothes," Bernard warned.

Dagon glanced down at his black wool trousers and his white cotton knit long-sleeve sweater that covered a black turtleneck. He spent a goodly sum on his clothes, his appearance being important to him, but at the moment Sarina's safety meant more.

He did at first attempt to make the suds disappear with a wave of his hand, but just the opposite occurred, the sudsy mountain thickened.

Bernard shook his head and left Dagon to deal with the mess.

Dagon, though concerned for Sarina's safety, was also irritated. She was a witch with limited abilities and limited sense. She did not seem to belong in either the world of witches or the world of mortals. And he wondered where it was she came from.

Wishing to bring this dilemma to a speedy end, Dagon plunged into the wall of suds pushing the lightweight obstruction out of his path and finally reaching the door. He grabbed hold of the brass knob, his hand slipping several times before he grasped it firmly enough to open it.

Water and suds hit him like a wave rushing to the beach, knocking him down on his backside. The water washed over him, the suds sticking here and there to his soaked clothing and his face. He sputtered and spit the suds away from his mouth and wiped angrily at his face to clear his eyes.

He stood with difficulty, slipping several times before he managed to get to his feet. And no amount of magical powers would help him. He had no choice but to deal with the situation as a mortal would and that irritated him all the more. His temper mounting, his clothes wet and uncomfortable, especially his wool trousers, he shouted for the culprit who caused this disaster.

"Sarina!"

"Help," came the squeaky and fearful reply.

He sensed her confusion and fright, and his heart tumbled in his chest. Without thought to his actions he plunged into the suds-filled room like a warrior charging into battle.

He called out her name again to determine her where-abouts. "Sarina."

"Here. I'm here," she called back, her voice quivering and sounding as if it came from far back in the room.

He took careful steps, the stone floor slick with water and suds. "Stay where you are. I'm coming for you."

"I only used half a box of detergent," she said in way of an explanation.

Dagon chuckled. "Were the clothes that dirty?"

Her gentle laugh sounded tearful and again tore at his heart. He hurried his steps, slipping several times but managing to keep himself on his feet.

He found her braced against the back wall, her eyes wide and her slim body trembling.

He mumbled beneath his breath and reached out to wrap her in his arms.

"You're wet," she said, her arms instinctively going around his neck.

"A wave greeted me as I opened the laundry room door," he explained, his arms tightening around her waist and holding her close as if reassuring her safety.

She laid her head on his shoulder. "I could not stop the machine from spewing suds or water. It seemed to possess a will of its own, and I didn't know what to do to stop its strange antics."

"Next time try pulling the plug," he suggested.

"Plug?" she asked curiously.

He shook his head. "Never mind. Let's get you out of here. You're as wet as I am and shivering."

"I am cold," she admitted and pressed herself closer against him.

His wet clothes may have chilled him, but her slim body heated him fast enough and it was best for them both if he got them out of this situation fast. He attempted to use his abilities once again, but nothing happened. All remained the same and his irritation returned.

She felt his body tense and offered a whispered apology. "I'm sorry."

He lifted her in his arms, and she looked at him with sorrowful eyes. Her hair hung in her face, her long wet lashes stuck to one another, and a white sudsy mustache tickled her upper lip. Gobs of suds clung to her cheeks and her hair, and his only thought was to kiss her. To bring his lips to her plump ones and capture them in a senseless, mind-drugging kiss that would heat her chilled skin and cause her to dampen intimately.

He silently cursed his sensuous thoughts and purposely averted his eyes from her face, though where his glance landed did not help the already tense situation. He stared at her hard nipples straining against her wet blouse.

That was it. He had to get her out of his arms, and then if he was smart he would call that stewardess and see to relieving this relenting ache. And again he silently cursed his thoughts when he recalled how well endowed the beautiful blond was and how instead of his desires being focused on her luscious full breasts, he could think of nothing but Sarina's small breasts and hard nipples that teased him from beneath her wet blouse.

"Foolish," he admonished himself and started toward the door.

His feet suddenly lost their balance on the slippery stone floor, and he slid toward the open doorway, some of the suds having dissipated, providing him with a clearer view of his destination.

Sarina yelped and buried her face against his chest.

Dagon spewed forth several spells, but none offered help. He and Sarina simply sailed through the door and landed with a solid thud on the wet floor directly outside the laundry room.

Sarina lay on top of Dagon, whose arms remained locked around her waist. Her head remained on his chest and her legs rested between his.

He took a minute to get his breath, having tried yet again

a spell to help repair this mess and again nothing happened. His head and backside continued to ache from the sudden fall, and he momentarily lost his breath when he went down, the impact of Sarina's body knocking the wind out of him.

"Are you all right?" he finally asked.

"I am fine," she answered, lifting her head to look at him. "And you?"

Why did she have to feel so good there on top of him? His hands had instinctively ran up and down her sides attempting to determine any injuries until they finally came to rest on her firm backside. Damned but if she didn't make his skin itch. His only thought was to slip his fingers beneath her skirt and roam her wet bottom.

"Are you all right, sir?"

The *sir* part shocked him back to reality as did the fact that he had moved his lips much too close to her face and those tempting full lips of hers. "I'm fine," he assured her, returning his hands to her waist.

Sarina moved off him to stand and found herself slipping on the wet floor. Dagon got to his feet with less difficulty and grabbed hold of her yet again.

"You're forever saving me," she said with relief and wrapped her arms around his neck once more. "I am grateful."

Those sensuous lips of hers sat much too close to his, and temptation tapped him hard on the shoulder. He in turn attempted to ignore it, a difficult feat to say the least. "Let's get you to safer ground."

He swung her up in his arms and took careful steps both in where he walked and where he looked. He kept steady eyes on his path, and with a strong sense of relief washing over him, he turned the corner and stepped on a dry floor. The feeling so overwhelmed him that he realized it was not only his sense of relief that flooded him but Sarina's as well, and the idea that he could so strongly sense her emotions disturbed him.

He should have immediately deposited her on the floor, but the urge to protect her and make certain she was all right lingered, and he carried her to the kitchen where a stunned Bernard and Margaret greeted him with wide eyes.

"Hot tea and dry clothes, please, Margaret," he said and placed a shivering Sarina on a chair near the table. He kneeled in front of her and rubbed her chilled arms. "You'll be fine."

She nodded, her lips quivering.

Margaret put the kettle on and hurried off to return shortly with a large blue terry-cloth robe. "Out of those wet clothes with you."

Dagon stood in haste and backed away from Sarina, whose wide eyes remained on him. "I am truly sorry for the mess I created."

"Do not worry, the damage is minimal," Dagon assured her and wanted once again to comfort her in his arms.

"Out with the both of you," Margaret ordered as she hurried to unbutton the shivering woman's wet blouse.

Her helplessness stabbed at him and the urge to order Bernard and Margaret from the room and see to her care himself so overwhelmed him that he grew irritated with his irrational feelings. And yet when he watched Margaret begin to unbutton Sarina's blouse, he grew annoyed that it was not his hands at work on her clothes.

"Bernard," he snapped and marched out of the kitchen with the startled man on his heels.

Once they reached the foyer, Bernard took over. "I will run a hot bath for you, sir, and see to taking care of those clothes, though I do not know if your wool trousers are salvageable."

Dagon nodded, his thoughts in turmoil, which seemed to be a constant since he met Sarina.

He was out of his wet clothes and into a long black silk robe only minutes after entering his bedroom. Bernard already had a hot bath running and was seeing to selecting dry garments for him. He in turn paced back and forth before the stone fireplace that Bernard had lit upon entering.

This section of the castle he had updated several times throughout the years. A smaller adjoining room had been made into a large bathroom and a dressing area with a closet that boasted ample space for his generous wardrobe. His own bedroom was tastefully decorated in a style befitting a man of station and wealth. Soft blues, greens, and beiges with a touch of gold blended remarkably well as did the mixture of antique furnishings from various periods. His oversized four-poster bed was draped in pale blue damask drapes with matching bedcovering, and the numerous pillows were touched with a hint of gold. A two-step footstool helped a person of smaller height climb into the high bed, though Dagon did not require its assistance.

"Sir," Bernard said, holding out a snifter of brandy.

Dagon stopped pacing and accepted the glass without hesitation. "Tell me, did the MacDougals say who previously employed Sarina?"

Bernard thought a moment. "I don't recall."

Written records were never kept on any witch; oral records were relied upon. A practice that was started far before Dagon was born and continued to this day. It was meant to protect their kind, and it had saved many a witch's life throughout the centuries.

"I do recall Mrs. MacDougal being adamant about her skills. When I spoke with her, she continually boasted about Sarina's exceptional skills. Of course, I took the woman at her word. I saw no reason not to. References are always exchanged truthfully, I have never known one to intentionally misfeed information. That is why I cannot understand this perplexing dilemma."

Dagon sipped at his brandy. "The one thing that disturbs me is that her wrongs cannot be made right."

"There are a few explanations," Bernard offered.

"Very few," Dagon said, sitting on the beige silk-covered bench seat at the foot of the bed. "Her power could be so depleted that she is unable to perform the simplest of magic."

Both men shook their heads.

"She would have some power even if minute," Bernard said.

"You're right," Dagon agreed. "Unless she never possessed full power to begin with."

Bernard appeared stunned. "I cannot believe Mrs. MacDougal would intentionally lie about Sarina's skills. We rely on the truth to protect us—"

Dagon interrupted. "Exactly what skills did she say Sarina possessed?"

Bernard gave his question thought and appeared to have a difficult time finding an answer.

Dagon proposed another question while Bernard continued to ponder the previous one. "What were Sarina's duties at the MacDougals?"

Bernard didn't hesitate to respond, though his response died before reaching his lips, and it was with a shake of his head he answered, "I don't recall Mrs. MacDougal ever actually mentioning Sarina's duties. She continually spoke of her skills and abilities but never detailed them. She assured me repeatedly that I would find it an enlightening experience to have Sarina part of the Rasmus staff. Of that I can agree with her."

"How did you learn of Sarina?"

"She simply appeared at the front door one day asking if there were any positions open. Ironically, that morning Josephine had informed me she would be leaving to join her sister in France and that she would stay until a replacement could be found even though her contract did not require her to do so."

Dagon sipped at his brandy before asking, "And naturally she had references."

Bernard grew uneasy.

"I should amend that to one reference?"

Bernard seemed annoyed with himself. "It was my own fault, sir, I was so impressed by Mrs. MacDougal's glowing reference, I did not think to verify a previous employer. Though I do now recall the woman mentioning that all who knew Sarina were pleased with her skills."

"So she did have a previous employer?"

"I would assume so."

Dagon seemed annoyed himself. "Then why the mystery? Why didn't the woman simply provide a list of references? Why did she give you only one? It is almost as if she is hiding something, and if I didn't know any better I would say so was Mrs. MacDougal.''

Bernard appeared to agree. ''It does seem strange that the MacDougals left on an extended vacation only two days after Sarina arrived at Rasmus Castle.''

Dagon grinned after finishing his brandy. ''We have a mystery on our hands, Bernard.''

Bernard caught the note of excitement in Dagon's voice and almost cringed. ''Yes, sir, a mystery.''

Dagon handed his empty brandy glass to the frowning man. ''Cheer up, Bernard, we'll get to the bottom of this in no time. In the meantime I intend to chase this damnable chill from my bones in a hot bath.''

With that announcement Bernard took his leave, and Dagon took himself to the tub.

Steam rose from the black marble tub, and Dagon slipped with a grateful sigh into the hot water. The black-and-white colors of the room would have been stark if not for the generous amount of gold that softened, blended, and joined together the opposing hues so perfectly.

He rested his head back and allowed the heated water to warm and soothe him. He still had many questions, actually too many questions pertaining to Sarina. The one that especially tormented him was the fact that her wrongs could not be made right by another witch. Even an incompetent witch could have her spells corrected by a more skillful witch.

But was Sarina incompetent or powerless? And if that were the case, then why couldn't another witch see to righting things for her? And if she was powerless, then why?

Was she more mortal than magic?

He sighed, the answers eluding him. He enjoyed solving a good mystery, and this dilemma certainly proved mysterious, so, therefore, he should enjoy the challenge, but one thing disturbed him.

He could not explain his heightened sensitivity toward her. He was well aware and attuned to emotions. It was a skill most witches possessed to one degree or another and one that offered them protection. But his sensitivity to Sarina went beyond the ordinary. And what was even more perplexing was that her senses triggered his own.

If she felt fearful, he felt the need to protect. If she needed comforting, he felt the need to console. If she needed shielding even from her own doubts, he felt the need to offer her his strength. And he had done so without hesitation.

He had literally leaped before looking, something he had never done in his life, and the idea of doing something so out of character alarmed him.

What surprised him all the more was the intensity of his concern for Sarina. He had just met her, and yet he felt an overwhelming desire to protect her, not to mention his lusty appetite for her.

He shook his head. How long had it been since he felt such a strong urge to have a particular woman? He had never lacked for female companionship. And he had had many companions through the years, some more favorable than others. But it was a rare woman whom he lusted after.

He frowned. "Lust?"

Did he actually lust after Sarina?

He sighed and groaned and wished he could get the bumbling witch who was driving him insane out of his thoughts.

Four

Sarina woke from her nap still wrapped in the blue terry-cloth robe Margaret had tucked her in. After having stuffed her with hot tea, scones, and homemade leek soup, which was so delicious Sarina devoured two bowls, Margaret had ordered her to take a nap, insisting that a short slumber would make her feel better.

Unfortunately, the short nap replenished her body but did little to ease her concerns. Sarina was worried and rightly so. She had been given a chance to prove her worth and had failed miserably. She had always been praised for her intellect, and yet she could not perform the simplest of laundry tasks.

What now would happen to her? And why did she forever seek Dagon's help? She could not understand this uncontrollable desire to reach out to him. Why did she feel so safe and protected in his arms? Why did she feel the need to have him hold her? Why did she ache to be close to him?

A soft knock interrupted her troubled thoughts.

"Sarina, it's Janey. I need to speak with you."

Sarina sat up in her single bed, ran her fingers through her tousled hair, and went to open the door.

"I'm sorry to bother you," the young woman said, slipping past the partially open door to enter the room.

Solitude was something Sarina cherished. Her moments spent alone were important to her. They allowed her time to sort through her problems and search for solutions. But of late she found her time was not her own and that was something she missed, but there was no point in complaining. Action was necessary.

Sarina shut the door and turned to look at Janey, who stood in the middle of the room wringing her hands. She was tall, slim, and quite pretty and only one hundred years old. Much too young to have worries.

"Please, I've heard you have excellent sight and I need to know something," Janey said anxiously.

"My sight is no less or more than another," Sarina said, not wishing anyone to know the extent of her extraordinary skill. It would lead one to answer questions and possibly search for explanations. Explanations she was not yet ready nor willing to give.

Janey smiled. "The castle staff knows full well your exceptional ability, and we also know that you wish none to know of it. We all respect your privacy and will say nothing. Our only request is that we are able to seek your skill on occasion."

Sarina nodded her agreement, knowing once a witch gave her word it was to be trusted. She feared no gossip related to her talent, though her ineptitude was a different matter. "What is it you wish to know?"

Janey sighed. "I've met a man."

"A mortal."

Janey nodded. "Yes, and he is wonderful."

Sarina smiled. "Lucky for you that is the truth." She went on to detail the mortal male's attributes and his weaknesses and then predicted their future together. By the time she finished, Janey was thrilled and relieved.

"I knew he was the one," the young woman said with a happy grin.

"Only if you proceed with caution," Sarina warned. "He is not yet ready to rush into a relationship."

"I'm not in a hurry," Janey insisted. "I enjoy the times we spend together. The walks we take, the talks we share, and the time we take to come to know each other. I do not want to rush. It is too much fun getting to know him."

"You are wise for your young years, this is good."

Janey gave Sarina a hug. "Thank you. You are wonderful."

Sarina opened the door.

Janey seemed hesitant but spoke anyway. "If you need help with anything, please feel free to ask me."

Sarina couldn't help but laugh. "I need help with *everything!*"

"Whatever I can do," Janey offered and hurried out the door.

Sarina dressed quickly slipping into her usual attire of black skirt and white blouse. She tied her soft brown hair back with a white ribbon and hurried to the kitchen to see if Margaret needed assistance.

Margaret was glad for her help and the company.

Sarina worked well with the older woman, and any mistakes she made didn't seem to bother Margaret. Sarina simply cleaned up her messes as a mortal would. And she was becoming quite proficient with a peeler. Carrots and potatoes no longer had large chunks missing, but suffered a mere nick or two.

Dagon was served his supper in the dining room, and Sarina commented on how lonely it must be for him in that large room all alone.

"Old habits die hard," Margaret said. "And don't you worry about him. He is rarely lonely."

Sarina ate the evening meal with the staff, but she and Margaret enjoyed dessert alone, a bread pudding with rum raisin sauce that had Sarina licking her lips in appreciation.

"I could never cook such delicious dishes," Sarina said.

"Of course you could," Margaret insisted.

Sarina shook her head. "My power is limited."

"Do you see me use my power to prepare meals?"

Sarina looked startled. "You cook as a mortal."

"Most don't realize that fact unless I point it out. At one

time it drove Bernard crazy, but he's come to understand that I enjoy the task of preparing and creating appetizing dishes. It takes skill and creativity to be a good cook and I enjoy the challenge.''

"Did it take you much time to learn the fundamentals of cooking?''

Margaret laughed and poured them both another cup of Earl Grey tea. "Time was not a question nor a problem. I made the acquaintances of many a noted chef and many who never achieved notoriety but possessed exceptional talent in preparing food. I have learned much from them.''

"I wish I could say the same.''

"Nonsense," Margaret scolded gently. "You are young and therefore inexperienced in many areas. In time you will learn all you need to know. We all have a time in our lives when we find our heritage difficult to handle. It is how we face that difficulty that counts.''

"Did Dagon?" Sarina asked.

"Dagon has always been determined, and he allowed nothing to stop him from acquiring the knowledge he felt essential. I often think of him as an exception to the rule. I have known so many witches who at one time or another found themselves faced with a difficult problem they thought impossible to handle.''

"Perhaps Dagon has yet to face a true challenge," Sarina suggested.

"I can't imagine a problem Dagon could not handle and successfully.''

"But don't we all think that until proven wrong?''

Margaret grinned. "Now you speak more like a wise witch. Are you older than I think?''

Sarina provided Margaret with a response though not an answer. "I have much to learn.''

"As long as you are willing to do what must be done.''

"Willing, yes," she said and laughed. "Able is another matter.''

Margaret patted her hand. "You'll do fine. Now take yourself off and enjoy the rest of the evening. Tomorrow and your laborious chores will come soon enough.''

Sarina did as she directed, Margaret refusing to let her help clean up the dessert dishes. She hurried to her room and slipped on a large white cotton cardigan, then returned downstairs and made her way outside to wander the gardens.

She took the pebble path to the rose garden, where a few stubborn blooms retained their petals regardless of the chill. And though the night's air was crisp, the tenacious petals looked as though they intended to hold on until winter's first frost.

She favored being outdoors and would love to help tend the beautiful gardens that surrounded most of Rasmus Castle. But in her present condition she feared she would do more damage than good.

The cool crisp air stung her flushed cheeks and made her feel more alive than she had in the last few months. Her dilemma had proved more difficult than she had thought and was proving even more difficult to solve. Her attempts had taken her far and wide and only managed to return her to her starting point without an ounce of success. She was beginning to think she would never find the answer to her problem and what then?

"Your thoughts trouble you?"

Sarina jumped and released a startled cry as Dagon emerged from the shadows. He appeared a shadow himself dressed all in black from his wool trousers to his knit sweater that just barely hugged his neck. He wore his long dark hair loose, the silky strands falling over his shoulders to rest on his chest. And his handsome face was a portrait of perfection.

For a brief moment Sarina grew alarmed, for he reminded her of a mighty warlock.

He stepped toward her. "Something troubles you?"

"Why do you ask?" she asked, annoyed that her quivering voice betrayed her nervousness.

"You frown."

She forced a smile. "Wandering thoughts that hold no credence."

"All thoughts hold some credence." He extended his hand toward the bench, offering her a seat.

She accepted, though a small voice warned her to run. He sat beside her, *much* too close beside her. She thought he would pursue his line of questioning and was therefore surprised when he asked, "What brought you to Rasmus Castle?"

Her response was quick. "I heard a position was available."

"Who informed you of this?"

She shrugged. "I don't recall."

He pursued his inquiry. "Did Mrs. MacDougal mention the possibility?"

Sarina had spent enough time on the staff to learn that the employer was the last to learn of a employee's intended departure. "No, I think it was one of the staff who informed me."

"So you appeared on my doorstep."

"In hopes of acquiring the position," she reaffirmed and thought of that fateful day when she knocked on the door, hoping she wouldn't be turned away and hoping her stay at Rasmus Castle would give her the time and energy required to tend to her awkward situation.

Dagon leaned back and stretched his arm along the back of the bench directly behind her. "Tell me about yourself, Sarina."

Her response surprised him. "Why?"

He laughed. "Why not? Do you have something to hide?"

"No, nothing, but what do you wish to know? I have already interviewed for the position."

"I am not conducting an interview, I am simply curious about you."

She didn't know whether to feel relieved or alarmed. Why was he curious? And why did he sit so close to her? She could sense the steady rhythm of his heart and almost feel the rush of his warm blood racing through his veins. He was alive and vibrant with the heat of passion, or was part of what she felt her own racing blood and desire?

"There isn't much to tell," she said, attempting to evade his question.

He thought otherwise. "Where did you grow up?"

"Not far from here."

"Do you have a large family?"

"No."

"Friends?"

"A few."

Her brief answers did not seem to disturb him, though his next question stunned her. "A lover?"

She did not trust her answer to her quivering voice, so she shook her head.

He leaned closer and brushed his thumb over her lips. "It's as though you dropped out of nowhere into my arms."

She shivered, his touch much too sensuous, or was it her own sensuality that startled her? She had to be careful, so very careful. She could not make a mistake. So much depended on her making a wise decision, and yet she found herself attracted to Dagon Rasmus.

Still, caution was called for. "I dropped off a chandelier into your arms."

His hand fell away from her lips and he laughed. "That you did, Sarina, though you did make my return home a memorable one."

She took advantage of the moment. "Were you away visiting family?"

"A friend who is like a sister to me and her aunt, whom I admire, respect, and love."

"And your own family?"

He didn't seem to mind her probing questions. "My mother and father travel extensively, though they keep a permanent home here in the far north of Scotland. They are presently enjoying an extended visit with friends in Greece."

"Friends?" she asked, mimicking his questions though curious just the same.

"Many, though of late I find myself seeking solitude and contemplation."

"Problems?"

He laughed softly. "A mystery."

She didn't care for the direction the conversation was taking and hastily asked a question she would never have thought of asking if she had given herself time to think of the consequences. "A lover?"

His smiling laugh turned serious. "Are you interested in the position?"

Her answer surprised him. "I don't think you could give me what I need."

"I'm quite skilled." He grew irritated with his answer. He sounded as if he was interviewing for the position of *her* lover.

"I have no doubt you are," she assured him, her hand offering a comforting touch to his arm. "But I require more than I think you wish to give."

Her rejection annoyed him. Why, he did not know. He had no intentions of taking a lover. He was looking for a lifemate. And she certainly didn't possess the skills or qualities he was searching for in a mate. She was actually the opposite of what he desired.

His irritation had him saying, "Perhaps you expect too much from a lover."

"No more than I would give myself," she answered softly and slowly moved her hand off his arm.

He felt her heart race along with his and sensed the tingle of desire ignite low in her stomach. His own lust grew and would be apparent if not for the dark night and the pale light of the half-moon. He felt a strange connection with her. Her breath was his, his heartbeat was hers, and one could not survive without the other.

An insane thought.

He had connected on an emotionally intimate level with all his lovers, and that was what made him so skillful a lover. He could sense their desires and satisfy their every need. And while he sensed Sarina's desire, he also sensed a deeper emotional tug that connected him so strongly to her that he found it difficult to comprehend.

Disappointment filled her soft voice. "I am not whom

you seek, Dagon, and you are not whom I need.''

"You sound certain of this.'' He was irritated that she should dismiss him so easily. Did she not feel what he felt? The idea that he alone felt this intimate tug between them irritated him all the more.

"Lately, I am not certain of anything.''

His tone took on that of lord of the castle. "If it is your position you fear losing, then I will calm your fears. I do not intend to dismiss you because of your inadequacies''

Her own tone was that of a penitent servant. "Thank you, I will attempt to do better.''

He stood. "Your attempts only manage to get you into further trouble. I would suggest practice for one so young and inexperienced. And I suggest you return to your room and get a good night's sleep. You will need your energy for the new chores that will be assigned to you.''

She had done nothing to warrant his testy attitude and thought to tell him so, but she remembered a wise witch's words. *In silence there is knowledge.* She chose knowledge and remained silent.

He seemed disappointed by the lack of her response and turned to walk away.

Surprisingly, she shared his disappointment, and suddenly she didn't want him to leave. His name anxiously escaped her lips. "Dagon.''

He turned his bold blue eyes on her and waited silently.

She had called out to him to keep him near, but how was she to do that?

He took several steps toward her, and she watched his long legs move with grace and his body with pride. There was arrogance in his stride, but there was also an integrity that could not be denied. And as he drew close she found herself speechless.

"What is it you want, Sarina?''

What did she want from him? The question troubled her for she could find no answer, though of late answers seemed to elude her.

He reached out and gently brushed a stray strand of hair

away from her eye. "Be truthful with yourself and the answer will come."

Truth is what got her into her present situation, but still she could speak nothing less. "Thank you for giving me another chance."

He made a point of keeping his arms firmly to his sides, so great was the urge to reach out and wrap them around her. And he chose to offer encouragement when his thoughts wondered who would ever save her from her inept skills if she were allowed to go off on her own. "I expect you will do better."

Sarina nodded, unable to take her eyes off his brilliant blue ones. The intense color captivated, cautioned, and caressed. And at that moment she wanted nothing more than for him to kiss her.

Her desire was palpable and his passion was raging. He warned himself to walk away, to turn and not look back, and he did. With a brief departing nod he turned and took several slow steps as if his legs refused to obey him or cautioned he was making a mistake.

He heard her sigh of regret. It sounded like a steeple bell clanging in his ears, though it was but a whisper on the night wind. And again he warned himself to walk away, to run if necessary, but his ego would not allow him a coward's retreat.

He turned back around and walked straight toward her.

Sarina's eyes widened, her heart beat rapidly, and her stomach fluttered in sensual chaos.

His arms wrapped around her, and his lips came down on hers in one sweeping move. Her response equaled his. Her arms locked around his neck, and her lips settled on his with the same lusty urgency. And they were both lost.

Their kiss was a mutual sharing of emotions, a bounding of kind that demanded acknowledgment. And they acknowledged it in a primal, natural way. They tasted, they sampled, they savored.

He didn't disappoint, he was as skillful as he claimed, perhaps more so, and she lost herself in the magic of the moment. She could go on tasting him all night, feeling the heat of him, aching with the need of him.

Her arms tightened around his neck and his arms locked more securely around her waist, drawing her more firmly up against him. There was no denying his potent desire, and her tenacious clinging proved she was where she wanted to be.

Her sensuous sigh tickled his mouth, and his hungry groan sent goose bumps rushing over her, and it was at that moment they both realized that they desired more than an erotic kiss.

They broke apart and stepped away from each other.

Sarina's fingers instantly flew up to touch her lips as though attempting to capture the memory of his kiss.

His tongue traced his own lips, savoring her taste and committing their heated exchange to his memory.

He then, without a word spoken, turned and disappeared into the shadows of the night.

Five

~

Bernard rarely smiled. That was why his wife looked so startled when he entered the kitchen shortly after breakfast. He was grinning from ear to ear and looked quite pleased with himself.

He approached Margaret with a bounce to his step and kissed her soundly. "A good day it is, Margaret!"

Margaret smiled, delighted her husband was in such a fine mood, even though the weather itself was foul, storm clouds having moved in with the dawn to deposit a steady flourish of rain. "If you say so, Bernard."

"Oh, but I do, I do," he insisted. "I am on my way to the study, a summons I have been waiting for and looking forward to. I think that His Lordship has finally come to his senses and intends to dismiss Sarina."

Margaret disagreed but did not wish to deflate her husband's good mood any sooner than necessary, though she felt the need to warn him. "Dagon has a kind heart. He may wish to give her another chance."

Bernard's smile vanished. "Don't be ridiculous."

Margaret shrugged. "Dagon does not judge people lightly."

"That I can agree with, but he is also no fool, and it

would be foolish of him to retain her useless services.''

"He may find something appropriate for her to do.''

"Heaven forbid," Bernard said on a dramatic sigh. ''I don't think there is a chore she can do without causing a problem.''

"She is young and requires patience.''

"I have had all the patience with her that I can stand," Bernard insisted. "My staff here at Rasmus Castle is skilled and efficient in their duties, and I will not have a novice ruin its reputation.''

Margaret shook her head at her husband's stiff, retreating back.

"You wished to see me, sir?" Bernard said, his smile having returned and his demeanor pleasant upon entering Dagon's study.

"Yes," Dagon said, slipping several papers into a folder on his desk. "I have decided that Sarina would serve well on the first-floor staff primarily in the small receiving parlor. I don't think she could get into much trouble there or cause much damage.''

Once again Bernard's smile vanished. "I disagree, sir.''

Dagon expected resistance from Bernard and handled the man with patience. "I understand your reluctance to keep Sarina on the staff. But I think we should give her another chance.''

"I have given her more than sufficient chances, and she has repeatedly proved she is not skillful enough to handle her duties—any duties, for that matter.''

"Still I feel the need to give her more time to prove herself or at least show improvement.''

"We are not a teaching center, sir.''

Dagon cast a sharp look on Bernard. "No, we are not, but we are witches, and witches see to the care and safety of other witches. I will not turn a clumsy witch out on her own.''

Bernard realized he had spoken out of term and softened his tone. "I am sure I could find her an appropriate position elsewhere.''

"I am sure you could," Dagon said, his irritation apparent in his intense blue eyes. "But I wish for Sarina to remain in my employment until I direct otherwise."

Bernard knew his place and kept his tongue. "As you wish, sir."

Dagon stood and walked from behind his desk. "I understand how she must have tried your patience, and I regret the disturbance she has caused at the castle, but my decision is final."

Bernard nodded. "Perhaps I should place some of the parlor antiques in storage for the next few days."

"I don't think that will be necessary."

"I will see to directing her to her duties," Bernard said and turned to leave.

"Bernard," Dagon called to him and he turned. "Perhaps you should see to the removal of the older antiques."

Bernard nodded once again, and as he turned around to leave he smiled.

"You will dust every item in this room," Bernard instructed, handing Sarina a feather duster. "With fine-toned skills it would take little time to complete this chore, but since your skills need improving I intend to give you more than adequate time to finish."

"I appreciate your patience," Sarina said, nervously glancing around the room that held a variety of breakable and expensive items.

"Do not rush. I prefer the chore be done properly instead of inadequately."

"Yes, sir," Sarina said and stared at the collection of paperweights that graced the glass-top sofa table.

"Let me know of any problems," Bernard instructed.

She nodded and was finally left on her own.

She walked around the room carefully admiring the beautiful ceramic pieces that she was aware dated to the eighteenth century, and then there were the crystal bowls and the fragile lamps hand-painted with the most stunning pictorial scenes.

The furniture was a beautiful blend of soft velvet mauves with gentle greens and beiges. The colors worked well in the print of the plush sofa and the solid mauves on the Queen Anne style chairs enhanced the setting. It was a warm welcoming room that frightened Sarina.

Her hands trembled just thinking about touching one of the priceless items or knocking over one of the charming lamps or breaking a crystal vase that had survived more years than Dagon.

She sighed and stared at the duster in her hand. "If only my powers were as they should be, this room would be dusted in a flash, far faster than the witches on staff could possibly manage."

Procrastination was not something Sarina prescribed to, so she got right down to the matter, though with gentle hands and careful steps, and soon felt more at ease as she proceeded to succeed at her chore without a problem.

Her thoughts turned inward to her own home not far away. It was not large by any means though to her it was a castle and she missed its warmth and comfort. The last few months had been difficult. She had first attempted to solve her problem without leaving familiar surroundings, but as it grew obvious that approach would fail her, she made the decision to travel in hopes of finding a solution. So far she had not been successful, though she had enjoyed her travels, but now her journey was seeming endless and that was unacceptable.

What was also proving unacceptable was the feelings Dagon's kiss had stirred last night. When she returned to her room, she could think of nothing but Dagon and the way she had felt at home in his arms and the taste of his lips so sharp and tangy and full of passion. She shivered at the memory.

While her sight worked well for others, it failed her and she could not turn to it when in a quandary. And she certainly was confused, and it didn't help that her powers had dwindled near to vanishing.

She felt on the verge of tears. She had never expected a spell to be cast on her. She had never harmed another witch, offering accurate guidance to those who sought her talent.

Her mistake had been offering that guidance when it had not been asked.

Last night, in her fanciful dreams, she had thought perhaps it was Dagon whom she had been waiting for and who would provide the solution to her problem. But in the light of day she realized that her words of the previous evening rang true.

He was not whom she needed, and she was not whom he sought.

And he had not sought her out since last night, proving he felt the same as she did. The dark night, the sweet fragrance of the last blooming roses, and lusty desires all added to temptation and were the reasons they had kissed.

Her mind so heavy in thought caused her to almost drop a delicate antique candy dish, and she sighed with relief when she finally righted it in her grasp.

"Are you all right?"

Dagon's unexpected voice startled her, especially since he had just been in her thoughts, and the fragile dish once again fumbled in her hands.

His first thought was to direct his finger to the slipping dish, then realizing his magic powers would not work, he hurried over to her side and caught the dish before it hit the carpet.

He placed it on the sofa table.

"I'm sorry," she said, upset that those words were so constant and necessary to her vocabulary.

"Nonsense, my unexpected appearance startled you and caused the dish to slip from your grasp. You have done well here."

Sarina gave the room a quick glance and realized that she had done well. Not a speck of dust touched the many pieces she first had been afraid to touch. The room actually sparkled and she smiled.

"You are comfortable with this chore?"

"Yes," she answered eagerly. "The room welcomes and the pieces are so beautiful. You collected them through the years?"

"Some were gifts, others I purchased myself in remembrance of special moments. I placed them in this particular room for, like you, I feel it welcomes."

Her eyes had traveled over him with interest as he spoke. He looked quite splendid in dark gray trousers and a light gray sweater. His long hair was pulled back, accenting his gorgeous blue eyes and handsome features, and Sarina couldn't help but admire his fit form and good looks.

"Yes, I welcome you," she said without thinking and quickly amended her slip. "It welcomes you. The room welcomes you."

He smiled. "I have disturbed you enough. I will leave you to finish your duties."

"Yes, yes, I have much to do," she agreed, knowing her thoughts would never settle nor would her nerves if he remained close by.

He was about to walk out the door when he turned. His smile teased. "Do you intend to walk in the gardens tonight?"

Was he daring her to? She had no intentions of finding out and creating a worse situation than she was already in. "No, I intend to spend the evening reading in my room."

"The gardens no longer hold an interest to you?"

His probing held a hint of enticement she found hard to ignore. "The gardens proved very interesting."

"I thought so myself," he said and with an intentional sweep of his sensual blue eyes over her body his smile broadened. "Although a feather duster could prove even more interesting." His soft laughter trailed him out of the room.

His suggestive words froze Sarina in place, her eyes closing as a shudder racked her body. He certainly could work magic with those titillating eyes. She could only imagine what he could do with a feather duster.

"Margaret requires help in the kitchen." Bernard's command startled her and the feather duster went flying up in the air.

Bernard didn't stay around to see where it landed, he simply shook his head in disgust and walked away.

•   •   •

Dagon relaxed in his bed that evening, a book in hand and a glass of red wine on his nightstand. His mind could not focus on the words he had been attempting to read for the last fifteen minutes, and he closed the book finally giving up.

He had been busy all day with international business calls and working on his computer. He had several deals pending that needed his constant attention, and he saw that his mind remained cleared to handle them. But come suppertime, a rather late one since his business took him past his usual supper hour of eight, his thoughts began to drift toward Sarina. And there his thoughts had remained for the rest of the evening.

He had purposely sought her out during late morning, convincing himself he wanted to make certain she was doing well at her newly assigned chore. It was a poor excuse and he knew it. Bernard always saw to the staff and he had preferred it that way, and while he was familiar with his staff members he rarely, actually he never directly dealt with them. Bernard had all the power where that was concerned, that was, until now and Sarina.

Dagon reached for his wineglass and sipped more than a mouthful. Ever since their kiss in the garden he couldn't get Sarina off his mind. No matter how much he chased her from his thoughts, she would hurry back and torment him.

He recalled in vivid detail how she tasted, a sweetly tart raisin-and-rum mixture, a perfect flavor that had him wanting a second helping. And feel—lord, but her body felt good pressed flat against his. Soft curves, gentle angles, and smooth roundness just aching to be stroked.

He downed another generous swallow of wine before returning the near empty glass to the nightstand. All those vivid details had come rushing back to haunt him as soon as he laid eyes on Sarina in the small parlor.

The standard black skirt and white blouse for female staff members never caught his eye before, or perhaps it was that the plain garments fit Sarina so well. And her shiny brown hair looked as if it was forever falling from the pins that attempted to keep it in place. Even the low-heeled black pumps she wore on her feet, while plain and non-descript, did wonders for her slender legs.

"Damn," he mumbled. He tried to convince himself it was that he was simply in need of a woman. He needed to vent his energy, and yet when he thought of several women he could call that would eagerly oblige him, he found himself uninterested, his thoughts returning to the bumbling witch on his staff.

He punched his pillow several times, turned it over, then over again, and plopped his head down on it while slipping his naked body farther under the soft cotton comforter. He would rise early and take himself off to Edinburgh for the day. There was some banking business he needed to attend to and a friend or two he could call on, and a day away from Sarina would do him good. His absence from the castle and her presence would give him a better perspective on the situation.

And who knew, he just might decide to stay overnight if a generous and interesting invitation presented itself.

Sarina stood at the parlor window and watched Alastair close the door of the Rolls-Royce right after Dagon had entered it. Dagon had looked exceptional in a black wool suit, a white-and-black finely striped shirt, and a red tie with the finest of black lines running through the silk material. His black cashmere overcoat served to keep him warm on a cold autumn morning and added to his tasteful attire. His long hair had been pulled back in a pewter clasp that looked to have been an antique, and she wondered over its origin.

She didn't think there was ever a time Dagon did not look good, and she laughed recalling the day gobs of suds covered him from head to toe.

"You have duties to attend to," Bernard said from the doorway. "There's no time to dally when you take longer than most to finish your chores."

Sarina smiled, pleased with the initiative she had taken. She had set her alarm clock for five-thirty and had started her chores at six hoping to be done with her chores at a more reasonable time. That was why she was so pleased to announce, "I'm all finished."

Bernard looked doubtful and made his way around the room, running his hand over every piece of furniture and every item from the lamps to the paperweights. "So you are, and a fine job you did."

Her smile widened. Bernard might be staunch in his demeanor, but he was fair. If a job was well done, he saw that compliments were given, and if one excelled in her duties, rewards were generous.

He came to stand in front of her. "Since you did so well and have free time, there is a chore that requires attention, though I must warn you it is not a pleasant one."

She knew he was testing her—she could read it in the rigid expression on his face—and she had no intentions of failing this one, but first she wisely inquired about the chore.

He explained. "The hearth needs sweeping out. The old ashes must be shoveled and removed to the bin outside and new logs stacked for a fire. Do you think you are capable and willing to do this?"

Sarina did not mind dirt. She had played often in the woods as a child, and she still loved digging her hands in the earth and feeling her energy. A little soot would do her no harm. "I think I can do it."

"Fine," Bernard said, "but if any problems arise, I want to be notified immediately."

"I won't hesitate, sir."

He nodded, pleased with her minor progress, though certain of no miracle.

Sarina didn't waste a minute. She went straight to work. She spent extra time in preparation, spreading canvas cloths around the surrounding area and moving any furniture or items that could be damaged by any accidental spillage of ashes. She obtained several old sheets from Margaret to spread over the chairs and furniture closest to the hearth. She was taking every precaution to assure the room suffered no damage in case of a mishap.

A tin bucket sat on the canvas cloth and a long handled-brush and shovel lay against the stone fireplace. A shorter-handled brush and dustpan waited near the bucket, and she had changed her white blouse to an old gray flannel one. All set to work she reached for the long-handled brush and shovel.

Dagon loved Edinburgh, especially the old town where cobblestones still paved the streets and the slim alleys between buildings gave way to small restaurants with exceptional menus and a variety of shops that attracted tourists. He often toured Edinburgh Castle knowing more about the huge stone edifice than any tour guide or recorded tour cassette could furnish.

It was the memories that drew him there and to various places throughout Scotland, never failing to strongly touch his emotions. But today he had no time for the castle. He had a meeting at the Bank of Scotland and then lunch with a business associate. And if there was time he hoped to get to the National Galleries of Scotland.

He was well acquainted with an assistant curator there, and he thought he would stop by and pay her a visit, perhaps even see if she was free for supper this evening. There was no rush to return home, and he intended to enjoy himself.

Sarina wiped her sweaty brow with the back of her hand, not realizing she left a trail of soot on her forehead. But then the streak went well with the soot that dabbed her cheeks and settled in the corner of her mouth. Her appearance did not concern her, her chore did, and a fine job she was doing.

The hearth area was swept clean, the andirons wiped off, and all looked ready for the new stack of wood. At least she thought it was when a small spat of soot fell from within the chimney to dirty one andiron.

She frowned and bent her head slightly as she entered the mouth of the large stone hearth. She then could stand straight and cast a curious eye up the dark chimney. Her hand touched the sides, though it was too dark to see anything, and when she removed her hand she shook her hand. Her palm was completely black.

She stepped out of the hearth and grabbed the long-handled brush. She was determined to do a good job and make certain this hearth was clean. She returned to her position inside the fireplace and began to carefully brush at the soot-covered walls of the chimney. She reached higher and higher as the soot began to fall away, and when she could reach no further, she retrieved an old step stool and continued.

How she managed to work her way up the chimney walls she didn't recall; perhaps it was her determination or her lack of sense, but by the time she realized how far up she had climbed, she was wedged good and tight in the chimney.

Every attempt she made to free herself only managed to wedge her in tighter, and soon her shoulders and arms began to ache from the constriction of the harsh stone walls. All her wiggling and tugging did nothing to help, it only hindered her predicament.

She thought to call out for help and stopped. She felt like a fool. A complete and utter idiot who could do nothing right. How many servants got themselves stuck in the chimney? What was she to do?

A sigh only managed to make her cough from the soot that spilled into her mouth. She could wait and see if anyone came to check on her, or she could swallow her pride and call out for help. The thought of Bernard hearing her pitiful pleas kept her silent, and she prayed fervently for a miracle.

Dagon waited for Linda to finish for the day. All had worked out so perfectly for him that he wore a generous smile of anticipation. His business meeting went better than he had expected, lunch proved even more fruitful, and when he entered the National Galleries, Linda—a blond and beautiful mortal—stood right inside the doorway.

Her pleasure at seeing him and his invitation to take her to supper brought him a soft peck on the cheek and whis-

pers of how much she missed his occasional visits. All leading him to believe he just might receive an invitation to
spend the night.

To continue to keep his mind as busy as it had been all
day and off the witch who persisted in haunting him, he
browsed the galleries, enjoying the distinguished works of
art. He lingered over the French neoclassical landscape
paintings of *Francois-Xavier Fabre* and then moved on,
wanting to view *J.M.W. Turner*'s work.

Dagon walked into the next viewing room, and Linda
approached from the opposite entrance, coat in hand and a
wide sexy smile on her pretty face.

It was then his cell phone rang.

Six

Dagon materialized in the castle foyer and tossed his overcoat to a waiting servant. When first informed of the disastrous situation at the castle, he grew angry. But by the time he made a hasty apology to a petulant Linda and instructed Alastair to drive home alone, Sarina's predicament had settled in his thoughts and his anger had turned to concern and then worry. What if she was hurt? And surely she was frightened being stuck in the tight, dark chimney.

He entered the receiving parlor and stood staring at the chaotic scene. He had hoped that by the time he reached the castle, Bernard would have found a way to extricate Sarina, but that was not the case. Bernard stood instructing two male servants whose only visible parts of their bodies were from their waists down. They stood on small ladders apparently attempting to free Sarina.

Several female servants hovered in front of the hearth, and Margaret calmly stood to the side, but all eyes were steadfast on the fireplace.

"Bernard."

His deep, direct voice had all heads turning.

"I see you have not been successful in freeing her," Dagon said and joined everyone in front of the hearth.

Bernard wiped his perspiring brow with his white handkerchief. This alarmed Dagon, for he never saw the man perspire.

"I have tried everything from spells to potions to simple mortal means, and we cannot dislodge her."

The male servants, hearing Dagon's voice, removed themselves from the ladders and stood to the side along with the other servants presently waiting further instructions.

"Is she all right?" Dagon asked Bernard.

He lowered his voice to answer. "I think she grows tired and she suffers more discomfort than she will admit. She was not found until late afternoon and has been stuck there since early morning. She most certainly must be feeling the effects of her confinement."

Dagon swore silently as he entered the large hearth, bending his head until he could stand straight and lift his head to look up. This time his silent curses became mumbles as a lone lantern cast a harsh glow up the chimney. He had a full view of her slim body wedged a good distance up along the bricks that narrowed with the climb. Her stockings were torn, her legs scraped, and her shoulders and arms were wedged tightly. Angling his head in an odd position, he could see that a good amount of soot covered her face not allowing him to determine any further damage. She looked to be asleep. Her head rested back and her eyes were closed.

Sarina," he said softly and she glanced down as best she could, opening wide eyes to him. The white pupils looked enlarged against her sooty face and made her appear terrified, startling his own emotions all the more.

"Dagon," she said as though relieved by his presence. "I'm so glad you're here."

Her relief washed over him along with her weariness. She was completely exhausted, and he realized he had to free her as fast as possible.

"I'm afraid I became too overzealous in my attempt to complete my chore," she said in way of explaining her strange predicament.

"We can discuss that another time. What is important is that we get you out of here."

She sighed. "That would be nice. I am growing tired."

"Hold on tight, I'll be right back." Dagon reluctantly left her side and joined Bernard, who spoke quietly with Margaret.

"No spells or magic works?" he asked the couple.

"None," Bernard answered. "And I am worried. Without our powers I don't know how we will be able to dislodge her. We already attempted to pull her free but it was quite a chore, and I think our useless efforts cost her to suffer dearly."

Dagon rubbed his forehead in thought. "We must use mortal wit. It is the only way."

"Sir," Bernard said with obvious concern. "We are witches; how are we to ever think as commonly as mortals? It will take us forever to find a solution."

"I think I may have one," Margaret offered.

"Tell me," Dagon said anxiously.

"I have a special solvent I created for various chores. It is thick and greasy and once spread over her body may just be able to slip her out of there."

"It's worth a try," Dagon said, eager to try anything instead of standing there while she continued to grow more weary.

"I'll have John and Ben see to it immediately," Bernard said.

"No," Dagon said so abruptly that Bernard looked as though he had made a grievous error. Dagon wanted no one touching her. He tried to rationalize it by explaining to Bernard that he felt responsible for her dilemma since he had ordered her duties confined to the receiving parlor. But he was fully aware that the thought of John and Ben spreading grease all over Sarina's body sent his blood boiling. He would have no one, absolutely no one but him touching her.

He finished with "Therefore, I think it best that I see to taking care of this myself."

"As you wish, sir," Bernard said, "though I would suggest a change of clothes."

Dagon agreed and hurried to his quarters, insisting Bernard stay and help Margaret with the solvent. He hastily changed into jeans, an old gray sweatshirt, and sneakers and rushed back to the parlor, where he dismissed all the servants.

He entered the hearth to see how Sarina was and noticed tear tracks running through the soot on her face. He swore yet again beneath his breath and used his powers to float up as close as he could to her. He managed to get near her hips and placed a reassuring hand to her waist.

"You're going to be all right," he told her and gave her slim waist a gentle squeeze. "I'll have you out of here in no time."

She sniffled. "I am a fool who can do nothing right. I make a mess of everything. I lack simple common sense, which makes me wonder how I survived all these years."

"How old are you—one hundred, perhaps one hundred and twenty-five years old? Why, you are barely grown."

She kept silent, knowing the truth would not at all please him.

"This will all be over soon."

She sighed. "You forever rescue me, Dagon. And how do I repay you? By being even more incompetent than before." A sudden cramp caught at her neck and she cried out.

"What's wrong?" he asked, moving his hand to grasp at her stiff one and growing more concerned when he realized just how ridged her body had grown.

Her tense fingers were barely able to wrap around his. "I'm afraid my muscles are protesting my prolonged confinement."

He attempted to comfort her. "A steaming hot bath after all this is done should set things right for you."

She sighed and in her weariness and need to remain alert she teased him. "You tempt me yet again, my lord."

He laughed softly, admiring her ability to joke in this

awkward situation. "I have not even begun to tempt you, Sarina."

"The solvent, sir," Bernard called out.

"I'll be right back," he said, and with a gentle stroke of his hand to her waist he floated down.

"Dagon," she called to him anxiously. "Please hurry back."

His feet touched the stone when he said teasingly, "Miss me already, do you?"

"I miss you terribly," she said on a whispered sigh.

"I'll rescue you, Sarina, on that you have my word," he said with a chivalry that seemed long since gone.

"If only you were the one who could," she whispered softly and sniffled back her tears.

Margaret warned him that the solvent had to be dissolved in hot water that was sprinkled with a liberal mixture of herbs. She advised him that she would prepare a tub to soak Sarina in once she was removed from the chimney.

Bernard raised an eyebrow, though Margaret did not find it odd when Dagon ordered her to prepare *his* tub for Sarina. She immediately took herself off to do as directed. Bernard remained with Dagon to help him.

Dagon had assessed the situation while he had talked with Sarina. He knew exactly where the solvent needed to be rubbed on her to free her, and he wasted no time in sending the bucket upward with the crook of his finger.

He instructed Bernard to remain close by and then floated up near Sarina. He managed to work himself close enough to her to be able to reach the pertinent areas and he quickly dipped his hands into the thick greasy mess that thank goodness did not smell as bad as it looked.

"I'm going to coat your body with this solvent and slip you right out of here," he said, making sure she understood why his hands were about to become intimate with her. "Ready?"

"I trust you," she said without hesitation.

Her simple remark affected him much more than he was prepared to admit, and he made a concentrated effort to focus all his attention and emotions on the task at hand. He worked his goop-covered hands up the front of her blouse, scraping his knuckles on the rough bricks that held her prisoner. He coated her ribs and placed gobs of the solvent on her breasts, massaging the thick goop over every inch of her chest.

He repeatedly sunk his hand into the bucket to retrieve more solvent and continued to concentrate on his chore. He worked the solvent over her stiff arms, and she occasionally moaned when he touched a sore muscle.

"I'm sorry if I hurt you," he said, having moved himself closer to her so that his hand could reach farther up. His head now rested on her hip while his hand worked a thick portion of goop over her tightly wedged shoulders.

"You're not hurting me," she reassured him. "Actually, your hand feels quite good on my—" She paused a moment as if weighing her words. "Stiff muscles."

He tried not to think of how good her breasts felt in his hand. The soft mounds fit his palm just perfectly, but this certainly was not the time for such sensuous thoughts. He was rescuing her not ravishing her. But still, she did feel so very good.

He focused on her shoulders and down her back, which was the most difficult part of her to reach. His hands worked their way down a little more roughly than he intended, and she moaned.

It was not a suffering moan. It was a responsive moan, one that responded most satisfyingly to his touch.

He ignored the soft ache that issued from her lips and ignored his own lusty ache. He worked heavy gobs of the solvent again over her shoulders and down her arms. He massaged a good portion over her neck to protect her skin when he attempted to dislodge her.

Then his hand fought his way up her backside, squeezing the firm flesh harder than he had intended. His intimate action elicited another moan that left little doubt to either of them that his hands were causing her sensual havoc.

He worked as fast as he could, warning himself that she was exhausted and in her fatigued condition her body instinctively responded without thought or reason. He didn't bother to consider that his own body had responded out of plan, old-fashioned desire.

"Almost finished," he said and roamed his hand slowly over her body, making certain the solvent covered all the necessary places. It was a methodical task, though it took on the intimacy of a lover acquainting himself with a new partner, and this time they both moaned.

"Please, hurry, Dagon," she pleaded. "This ordeal has become unbearable."

He had to agree with her, though he remained silent and finished the task with a hasty hand that titillated all the more. He promised himself he would free her and leave her in Margaret's care. He swore he would, he vowed he would, *he damn well knew he wouldn't.*

"Sarina," he said gently. "I'm going to slowly ease you down toward me. If I tug too hard or you feel any pain, let me know."

"I'll be fine," she said, her voice sounding a bit stronger, though it quivered.

With a swipe of his finger he sent the bucket to land gently on the ground and wiped his goop-covered hands on his sweatshirt. He then positioned his hands below her hips on her thighs were there wasn't as much goop and tugged slowly. He had trouble getting a solid hold and grew annoyed. Knowing his only choice was to grasp on to something solid and free of the solvent, he ran his hands beneath her skirt.

"Sorry, but I need to get a good hold of you," he said, explaining his intimate intrusion. His fingers rushed up her legs and caught on the edge of her lace panties. He cursed his fumbling fingers and the lusty thoughts that invaded his senses and finally grabbed a solid hold of her thighs.

"Please do whatever you will," she pleaded softly.

Her words begged for release, and he pressed his forehead to her hip as he took a calming breath. Only this bumbling witch who haunted his every thought and intruded upon all his senses could turn a difficult situation into an erotic one.

With a groan of annoyance Dagon gave a gentle tug and

he felt her slip. Only slightly but still her body moved. He tried again, and again her body slid a little way down the wall.

He called down to Bernard. "It's working! Tell Margaret and be ready with the blanket."

"Yes, sir!" Bernard shouted, and Dagon heard him rush out of the room.

He then directed himself to Sarina. "This may take a little time. I don't want to rush and hurt you."

"I'm all right, really I am. I'm just very tired and stiff."

"Margaret has a hot bath waiting for you, keep your mind focused on that."

She sighed. "Oh, yes, I will do that. A hot bath, how wonderful."

Dagon worked her down inch by inch, moving slowly down the chimney with her. He heard Bernard return, and he hastily told him that all was in readiness for Sarina.

Dagon kept himself focused, a difficult task since as they made their way down, the chimney widened and she began to slip down his body. Her limbs were rigid from her long confinement, and she could not move them at all.

"I feel so helpless," she said when finally she was free and her head came to rest on his chest.

His hands had forced her skirt up, and while he wished her no further embarrassment, he could not push her skirt back down. He needed to keep his hands around her waist and besides the solvent already had her bunched-up skirt stuck together.

When he finally had her down in the mouth of the hearth, he lifted her as easily as he could into his arms, and Bernard didn't waste a minute draping the blue cotton blanket over her.

"Margaret waits upstairs, she will see to her care," Bernard informed him.

Dagon nodded and hurried out of the parlor and up the stairs.

Sarina continued to rest her head on his chest. "My arms, I cannot move them."

"Your muscles are rigid from being wedged in so long.

It will ease once you soak in the hot water.''

Her voice held a touch of panic as though she just realized she could do nothing for herself. "Margaret will help me?"

Dagon knew he couldn't turn her over to Margaret's care. He had to make certain she was all right. He wanted to see for himself with his own eyes, and he wanted his hands to be the ones who took care of her. He didn't understand why he felt the need, but it was an urgent need and one he didn't intend to ignore.

He refrained from answering her as he made his way down the hall to his quarters.

Realizing her whereabouts, she asked anxiously, "Why are you taking me up here? I thought Margaret was to look after me?"

He answered her honestly. "I ordered the bath prepared in my quarters. The tub is large and will be more comfortable for you."

Sarina shivered. "Suddenly I'm cold."

"A normal reaction to your ordeal," he assured her and entered his bedroom, walking straight for the bathroom. "You'll be in that hot bath in no time."

Margaret's presence sobered him fast and made him realize he had no choice but to leave Sarina in her care. Reluctantly he lowered her feet to the floor, but her legs gave way before he released his hold on her.

After several minutes it was obvious that Margaret was not going to be able to handle Sarina's care on her own. Between her stiff limbs and the gobs of goop, there was no way Margaret had the strength to hold her and undress her, never mind lift her into the tub.

Dagon spoke softly to her. "I think it would be best if I helped you into the tub."

Sarina was so embarrassed she buried her face against his sticky sweatshirt.

Margaret was the one who eased the situation. "Dagon has the strength, patience, and honor to handle what must be done. I think it is best if I go fix you a hot pot of tea and something to eat."

Margaret didn't wait for any acknowledgments; she made a hasty exit.

Dagon slipped the blanket off Sarina. "I promise to be a perfect gentleman."

A weak smile teased her lips. "I was afraid you'd say that."

Seven

Dagon worked at the buttons on Sarina's blouse. Trying to hold her and undress her at the same time was proving difficult. While her legs had grown weak her upper body had remained rigid and he worried about causing her discomfort.

He looked about to see if there was anyplace he could place her that would make disrobing easier for him and less stressful for her, but nothing proved adequate. There was a small vanity bench with a soft cushion top against the wall near the door, but that would not prove entirely useful.

If he were able to use his powers, this task would already be accomplished, but no matter how many times he attempted, his skill failed him. He knew his talent would work on anything not connected with Sarina, but she herself remained impervious to a witch's magic.

He finished unbuttoning her blouse and managed with tender care to slip the gooey garment off her. His eyes could not help but stray to her black lace bra and her hard nipples that protruded against the sheer material.

She moaned when he slipped the gooey garment off her shoulders, and he winced when he caught sight of her bruised and scratched skin.

"Did you struggle to free yourself?" he asked, more concerned with her immediate condition than his lust-filled thoughts. He tossed the blouse on top of the discarded blanket and surveyed her bruises.

Sarina rested her head on his chest. "At first I did, but I think my futile attempts only worsened my situation."

Dagon ran gentle fingers over the scratches. "The water may sting these abrasions."

Sarina attempted to ignore the flutter in her stomach. His touch was incredibly tender and caring, not to mention it tingled her skin. "I'll manage."

"I'll tend to them after your bath," he informed her and moved his hands to the button on her skirt. He wanted to afford her as much privacy as possible, if privacy was possible in this awkward situation. He thought to rid her of her outside garments first and then remove her bra and panties last, leaving her feeling the least vulnerable as possible.

He eased her skirt down along with her black silk slip and swore silently. The woman obviously had a penchant for black lace undergarments, and he had to admit her choice was exceptional.

The skirt dropped down around her ankles when he worked it past her thighs, and his glance dropped right along with it. She wore the slimmest, sheerest, scantiest pair of black lace panties he had ever laid eyes on, and he had viewed his share. The wisp of black lace hugged her skin beneath beige-colored panty hose, and he wondered if he could keep his eager hands from appearing too anxious of divesting her of the intrusive stockings.

He hoped her head continued to remain resting on his shoulder because if she ever glanced in his eyes she would see how his passion for her raged much too close to the edge.

He slipped his fingers beneath the panty hose waistband and began easing the garment down over her hips. She was slight of build, her waist narrow and just a hint of a curve to her slim hips, and her stomach, though relatively flat, possessed the most charming little mound where his hand now rested.

He ran his hand back and forth across her stomach, working the stockings farther and farther down and feeling every inch of her incredibly cool soft skin. When he worked the stockings down near her knees, he slipped his sneakers off, kicking them away, and lifted his bare foot to yank the stockings down to her ankles.

"Almost done," he said when he felt her shiver. She did not respond and her head did not move off his chest. She most certainly must feel uncomfortable with him undressing her and especially with being so dependent on him at the moment.

And yet he liked the feeling her temporary helplessness gave him, and that thought disturbed him. He always liked strong, independent women, and yet here he was enjoying looking after a totally inept, dependent witch.

He shook his head at his crazy thoughts and gently lifted her into his arms and carried her to the tub. He sat her on the edge of the black tub and balanced her with one arm around her waist as he knelt on one knee to remove the panty hose bunched at her ankles. He then stood her up once again, quickly unhooked her bra, tossed it to join the pile of discarded garments and then with the same haste removed her panties.

He could not allow himself to think at this moment or look at her with the eyes of a man who found her incredibly desirable. He had to remain a gentleman—he simply had to.

One gentle scoop had her back in his arms, and with care he eased her down into the steaming water. Her groan and cry startled him, and he realized the steaming water had penetrated her scratches.

"I'm sorry," he told her softly, "but it is better you remain in the heat of the water. It will help ease the stiffness from your joints."

She agreed with a nod and closed her eyes, relinquishing her complete care and safety to him. And he had every intention of seeing that she was looked after and carefully tucked into a soft welcoming bed for the night.

He released his hold on her and took a brief second to

remove his sweatshirt, the arms having gotten a thorough soaking clear up to his elbows. She looked serene lying there with the steaming water lapping over her. Her taut nipples bobbed to the surface every now and then as her body floated contentedly in the water.

She did not possess a perfect body, but then perfection could never be truly seen, only felt, and what he felt when he looked at her was perfection at its most extraordinary.

He forced his attentions to return to the matter at hand and kneeled in front of the tub near her head. Not wishing to frighten her he warned her of his presence. "I'm going to see to getting you cleaned up."

She still did not open her eyes. "Can it not wait for a moment? The hot water feels so good."

His stamina as a gentleman was being tested, and he was afraid failure was much too feasible, especially if his hands remained idle. "At least let me see to your hair and face."

"I do suppose I look frightful."

Dagon smiled and cast an appreciative eye over her naked body. "Frightful doesn't quite fit you."

Her eyes drifted slowly open, and she attempted to move her arms and groaned in the process.

"Don't," he ordered curtly, not wanting to see her suffer needlessly. "Let the hot water soothe your joints before you attempt to move them."

The water licked at her soot-covered face, and her eyes appeared two bright moons in the darkness. He noticed her lashes were thick and long and her eyes steady on him. She studied him from face to chest and back again, and he did not mistake her look of admiration touched perhaps with a twinge of desire.

She made no move to speak and he did not trust his own voice, so he reached for the washcloth that lay on top of the stack of white towels next to the tub. He soaked the cloth, and with a firm hand to the back of her head he brought the cloth to her face.

He was gentle and methodical in his care, wiping away the soot until her face was near clean. Then he lathered the cloth with the rose-scented soap and softly ordered her to close her eyes.

Sarina thought herself in a dream. His tame strokes betrayed his gentleness, his understanding, his character. He could take full advantage of her in her present condition, and yet he treated her with respect and saw to her care as only a gentleman would. Then why was she so damn disappointed? Even in her weariness she ached for a more intimate touch and was fully aware that his aches matched hers.

Why was she so attracted to this man? Physically he was appealing, that could not be denied, but physical appearance meant little to her. Her friends varied in shape and size, and she had never chosen any for their outward appearance. It was the inner self that always attracted her. There was where one found the qualities and character of an individual, his true nature.

Dagon caused any woman to glance more than once at him. She had found she often took several admiring peeks at him whenever he passed by her. But it was his strength of character and conviction that she most admired. No matter how inept a witch she was, he would not toss her out. He continued to be patient and put up with her bumbling skills. He was a special man, and if she were not careful she could easily lose her heart to him.

He rained water over her face, chasing away the lather, and then he wiped it clean before saying, "Keep your eyes closed and I will see to washing your hair."

She feared this forced intimacy might prove too difficult for them both and she wondered which of them would be the first to surrender to their emotions.

His hands worked magic after lathering her hair. His fingers massaged and scrubbed with a force that was simply heavenly. And when he stopped, she sighed in disappointment.

"You liked that?" he asked, his whisper sounding strained.

"Very much," she admitted, her eyes remaining closed as he rinsed her hair clean.

"The water will cool fast enough, we best get you finished."

He sounded rushed, almost anxious, and Sarina slowly opened her eyes.

He stared down at her with heated eyes. He was doing his best to control the passion that raged wild within him, and it was that contained passion that struck Sarina full force and jolted her own alert hormones.

She moved her arm in an effort to show her capability of seeing to her own care. Unfortunately her arms were still protesting and she winced.

"I told you not to move," he snapped, forcing her arm still with his hand. "Give the hot water time to work. There is no hurry."

"There isn't?" she asked cautiously.

He took a deep calming breath. "I am not a schoolboy incapable of controlling himself."

How did she admit that she was more worried about *her* control than *his*? She ached for him and in the most intimate places. Places that had been dormant for much too long and now raged near out of control.

She sighed much too invitingly and he laughed softly.

"You'd better behave."

She was feeling better and couldn't help but tease. "Must I?"

He teased back. "If I must, you must."

Her response surprised not only him but herself. "Then maybe we both should surrender."

He reached for the washcloth and lathered it. "Be careful of what you say, or the consequences may be more than you can handle."

Wise and truthful words, and ones she wished she had heeded months ago, for then she would not be here with him. A thought that suddenly brought a pain to her heart.

He lifted her with one arm while his hand proceeded to scrub her clean. She kept her eyes closed, fearing if she glanced one more time into those sensually blue depths, she would be lost.

He in turn worked with the speed and verve of a madman. He had to finish, had to end this madness now, or he would go entirely insane. He avoided all intimate areas except for her breasts, they were unavoidable. The gooey solvent had penetrated her blouse and bra and now stuck to her soft mounds and hard nipples. He forced himself not to linger and forced himself to disregard just how much he liked the feel of those taut nipples brushing over his palm.

He would not surrender to his lust-filled desires. He would remain a gentleman, damn but he would.

Dagon praised himself when finally he lifted her from the tub and went to wrap her in a soft terry towel. Exhausted from her ordeal and totally mindless by this point, she barely could stand and instinctively leaned against him.

A big mistake for them both. Her warm flushed breasts connected with his cool hard chest and it was like two live wires touching. His arms wrapped around her, her arms went around him, and their mouths claimed each other.

The room was charged with heated passion; the mirrors were steamed, a mist hovered overhead, and two lovers were locked tenaciously in each others arms. Their kisses demanded, and each one gave willingly and wantonly.

His hands moved to cup her backside and urge her up against him. She advanced on him most generously and cherished the feel of him pressing hot and hard against her. They were hungry, starved for each other, and they feasted like two lovers long denied.

Without taking his mouth from hers he scooped her up into his arms and marched into his bedroom, dropping down on the bed with her. He stretched out over her, and they continued their frenzied feeding.

Dagon thought he would erupt with the want of her. He had never felt this strong a passion for any woman. It was as though his desire raged out of control, out of his reach, out of his powers.

And she responded just as mindlessly, feeding his own crazy actions.

He ached to explore her, roam her body with his hands until he was familiar with every inch of her flesh, and then he would taste her, taste until he was drunk with the flavor of her. Then they would mate like only witches could.

His senses came hurdling back and he drew his mouth off hers though returned several times before grudgingly relinquishing her swollen lips. "If it is intimacy we are to share, then it will be a magical moment for us both."

He then moved off her, stood, pulled the comforter that had been drawn back over her, and left the room.

Tears sprang instantly to her eyes, and she shook her head in disbelief. She had traveled so far, searched in vain, and he was here in Scotland all this time. She found her discovery almost impossible to believe, but he had spoken the words she waited to hear.

Magical moments.

She had sought solace and a modicum of peace when she came to Rasmus Castle. She had wanted to gather her thoughts and make decisions, difficult ones if necessary, but she had never thought to find her answer here. She had never even given Dagon Rasmus thought. Why should she? She was far beyond his years and wisdom.

And yet now she realized he was the one who would help release her from the spell and make her whole again.

Margaret's entrance intruded on her thoughts.

"You, my dear lady, have been ordered to remain abed for the remainder of the night," Margaret said, placing the serving tray filled with more food than Sarina possibly could eat on a table near the window.

"Wouldn't it be best then if I returned to my room?" She thought to slip from beneath the cover, when she realized she was naked. Her face turned quite red.

Margaret ignored her blushing and pulled back the comforter to slip the white flannel nightgown she had draped over her arm over Sarina's head. After maneuvering sore arms into the sleeves, Sarina was once again settled beneath the covers.

And Margaret finally answered her. "You are to stay in this bed tonight."

She shook her head and grabbed the cover to pull back.

Margaret was faster and stayed her hand. "You are to sleep here alone. Dagon thinks only of your comfort. You will have a more comfortable sleep in this large bed than in your cramped single bed. And besides, he will not have it any other way.''

In no time Margaret had her braced against a mountain of pillows with a lap tray placed over her legs. She was then served a generous meal of fruit, juice, soup, biscuits, tea, and a baked apple of which she ate heartily to her surprise.

Margaret left her snuggled beneath the warm comforter, a fire burning low and exhaustion slipping over her. She was so tired her mind could barely form a coherent thought, but she managed. She managed to recall Dagon's words.

Magical moments.

She held the words close to her heart as she drifted off to sleep, knowing Dagon would save her. He would always save her.

Dagon listened to several minutes of scolding from Sydney before he spoke. ''I apologize again for calling you at this late hour, but it was necessary.''

''Is something wrong?'' Sydney asked, alarmed.

''Very wrong and I need your help.''

''Anything, my dear boy,'' Sydney offered graciously. ''You know you can always count on me.''

He felt like sighing in relief but contained his reaction. ''I was hoping you would say that.''

''Dagon, you can ask anything of me. If it is in my power to grant it, I will.''

He was probably taking advantage of their long friendship, but then at the moment he needed a good friend. ''Sydney, I really need to meet the Ancient One.''

She didn't seem at all surprised by his repeated request, she simply asked, ''Why?''

He answered honestly. ''I wish to mate.''

''You do not even know her.''

''I know of her,'' he said. ''She is all that I am looking for in a mate. She is powerful—''

Sydney didn't let him finish. ''Far more powerful than

you. Could you cope with a wife whose powers surpass yours?''

Dagon dropped down in his desk chair, tired of pacing the floor and just damn tired. Again he answered honestly. ''I would like to think I could, though I am not certain.''

''Good, at least you are being honest.''

''Does that help my cause?'' he asked with a weary laugh.

''Possibly,'' Sydney said, ''though I find that when witches attempt to dictate their lives, problems arise.''

''Like Ali?'' he asked, recalling the turmoil she had put herself through after insisting she would mate with a mortal.

''You are waiting for me to say yes so that you can counter with the obvious, that the situation worked out well,'' Sydney said with patience. ''But if you recall she suffered dearly and thought all lost because of her stubbornness.''

''Agreed, but I know better,'' he insisted.

Sydney laughed. ''We all think we know better.''

Dagon argued, ''I *know* that I know better.''

''Listen to me, Dagon,'' Sydney said with the voice of a concerned teacher directing a headstrong pupil. ''Some things in life are better left to magic.''

He remained obstinate. ''I intend to direct my own fate.''

''That isn't always possible, my dear boy.''

''Will you help me secure an introduction to the Ancient One?''

''Will you accept the outcome?''

He laughed. ''I already know the outcome.''

''Be careful, Dagon,'' Sydney warned. ''You do not now what you deal with.''

''I can handle myself,'' he assured her. ''You will speak with her?''

''I will make contact with her; the decision is hers.''

''Again I apologize for waking you,'' he said sincerely, ''and, Sydney?''

''Yes, Dagon.''

"Thank you for being there for me even when I am being an arrogant pain in the ass."

"You do know," she said with a light laugh and a quick good-bye.

Dagon sat staring at the phone. He didn't know what possessed him to call Sydney and her phone was already ringing when he realized the lateness of the hour in the States.

He felt as if his life had suddenly reared out of control and that was not an acceptable emotion. He always prided himself in his ability to handle any situation no matter the degree of difficulty. That was why he couldn't understand the irrationality of his emotions concerning Sarina.

That he desired her was obvious, but damned if she wasn't everything he *wasn't* looking for in a mate.

Mate?

When did he suddenly regard her as a possible mate? An affair perhaps or a night or two of shared passion, but a mate?

He shook his head not understanding his own thoughts. He had known numerous women in his three hundred years and had adored many of them, perhaps loved a few, but never had he felt this overwhelming need to protect, care, and make love to a woman. She seemed a part of him, an intricate part that he could not do without. She was like the beat of his heart, the rush of his blood, the breath he took to breathe.

He stood and paced in front of the window, raking his fingers through his hair. "Damn."

What was the matter with him? He should just make love with her and satisfy his and her lusty desires. And yet something warned him against it, something nagged at him to learn more about her and particularly to learn why her wrongs could not be made right.

Who was Sarina?

A good question, and he intended to find the answer.

Eight

~

Dagon rose early the next morning in a good mood. Even the gray skies and a light rain that shadowed the dawn did not sour his pleasant disposition. He had surprisingly enjoyed a restful sleep in one of the many guest suites and had assumed he owed his fine slumber to the fact that he had once again resumed control of his life.

He showered and dressed in black wool trousers, a black wool turtleneck, and added a gray sports jacket to keep the chill of the castle off him. A pewter clip held his hair back, and he slipped a black silk handkerchief into his chest jacket pocket. He was ready for the day.

He intended to speak with Bernard regarding Sarina, finding a more appropriate place on the castle staff for her. And he intended on solving this puzzling dilemma with a bit of research.

It was with a light step and an eager appetite that he entered the dining room. Margaret was just setting his place at the head of the long table.

"Up early this morning, sir; couldn't you sleep?"

His beaming smile answered her query, though he confirmed it with, "A most sound sleep. I hope Sarina slept as well."

"She still sleeps soundly, sir. I thought it best not to wake her, she needs rest to recover and I imagine her body will be quite sore today."

"I think a few days off will suit her well," he said, realizing he had no intentions of instructing her return to work until she was fully recovered from her ordeal.

Margaret nodded. "As soon as she wakes, I'll move her to her own quarters and see to it that she rests."

"No need to rush. I will be busy in my study for most of the day." He didn't want Sarina's peaceful sleep disturbed. He had actually thought to check on her before he came down for breakfast, but decided it was best he didn't see her in his bed, snug beneath his covers, her familiar body warm and tempting. No he didn't want to see Sarina anywhere near his bedroom again.

"I'll have Bernard bring you coffee directly and your breakfast will follow shortly," Margaret informed him, placing the morning newspaper beside his plate.

"I have a taste for one of your delicious omelets this morning," he said with a grin that charmed a smile and a blush from Margaret.

"Along with my angel biscuits and my blueberry bourbon preserves?"

Dagon licked his lips like an eager boy in a candy shop. Margaret's biscuits were so light and tasty that they could only be called angel biscuits, and her preserves won numerous awards. There wasn't anything he wouldn't do to keep her on his staff, and besides, he cared for her as he would a favorite aunt.

"You've brought sunshine to a dreary day," he said and she dismissed his compliment with a smile and a wave of her hand as she walked from the room.

Dagon settled in his seat to read the paper and await his meal.

Bernard appeared only moments after Margaret left and poured him a cup of steaming coffee.

Dagon felt this was the perfect time to discuss Sarina with him and placed his paper aside. "I have informed Margaret that Sarina will have a few days' recovery time before she is expected to return to her duties."

"I assumed so," he answered cautiously, this time prepared for battle. "I have already reassigned her chores."

"Good," Dagon said, dropping a dash of milk into his coffee. "I think we should find more appropriate duties for her."

Bernard cleared his throat and stood straight and stiff. "I assumed that would be your intention."

It was obvious the man was annoyed, and Dagon attempted patience. "I know how trying her ineptitude has been for you."

"We have more than sufficient grounds for dismissal, sir."

"I am well aware of that, Bernard, but she deserves a chance." He almost cringed at his own words. Sarina had been given more than her fair share of opportunities to prove herself and had not only completely failed but created havoc in the process. Any sane employer would dismiss her without regret. He could not. He wondered if he had just crossed the line to insanity.

"Shall I remind you of her many chances?"

"That won't be necessary. I understand how you feel."

"No, sir, you do not understand or you would not ask this of me. She possesses no powers and lacks even the simplest mortal skills. Whatever am I to do with her?"

"I am sure we can find a spot in the castle where she will be safe."

Bernard smiled. "I know the perfect place."

"Where?" Dagon asked anxiously, eager for this problem to be solved.

"Your private chambers."

It was a good thing Dagon had not sipped the coffee from his raised cup or he would have choked on it. "Impossible."

Bernard shook his head slowly. "I don't think so, sir."

Dagon's tone turned forceful. "I know so, Bernard. She will not be assigned to my quarters."

Bernard remained calm as he announced, "Then I am sorry to inform you of my resignation and of Margaret's, and Alastair mentioned that if I left he would join me."

Dagon sounded none too happy when he replied, "That's blackmail, Bernard."

"No, sir, it's called survival."

Dagon attempted to negotiate. "There must be some-place that—"

Bernard would have none of it. "No, sir, there is no-where in the castle where she will not create havoc. And if you insist on her remaining on staff, then I think it is only fair that the havoc she creates be in your own private quarters."

Dagon shook his head. He could not allow Bernard, Margaret, and Alastair to leave. They had been with him far too long and were like family to him. But he also could not turn Sarina out, at least not yet. Not until he was sure she could survive on her own. He had no choice. He had to allow her to be assigned to his quarters.

His blue eyes settled on the patiently waiting man. "I won't forget this, Bernard."

Bernard's grin bordered on a laugh. "I'm sure you won't, sir."

Sarina woke with a yawn and a lazy stretch. A steady rain tapped at the windows, and a blazing fire cast a welcoming warmth into the room. She smiled and snuggled deeper be-neath the thick comforter. She was home and it was a lazy rainy day. She would sit before the hearth and tell Lettie, her cat, and Podges, her dog, of her journey and of the special man who rescued her and stole her heart.

She bolted up in bed, her glance quickly sweeping the room. This was not her room, or her home, and she had yet to be rescued and she had yet to lose her heart. Hadn't she?

She threw herself back against the pillows and moaned. Why couldn't life be simple like it once was? She had lived many years without any major, earth-shattering problems and now suddenly she was in the throes of a full-fledged catastrophe.

She shook her head and that was when she realized she

was in pain. She hadn't noticed it before when she sat up, but after falling back on the pillows her body protested and loudly. Her shoulders and arms ached badly, and the rest of her felt as if every muscle decided to revolt in unison.

If she were her normal self, she would go to the woods that surrounded her house, plant her bare feet firmly in the soil, and allow the earth's energy to restore her. But she wasn't herself. She was at this moment more mortal than witch, a frightening prospect.

Not that she didn't respect and admire mortals, she did. It was just that their growth was slow and laborious. They fought their own inherent abilities and ignored the obvious, making life more difficult than was necessary.

An issue she was experiencing herself and one that was not going as easily as she had expected. She supposed she should think of this dilemma in her life as a lesson. The question was what was the lesson attempting to teach her?

A yawn slipped slowly from her mouth, and she felt the urge to return to sleep and forget her problems, her protesting limbs and muscles, and all lessons. But that would be running away, and she had never run away from difficulties before. She had faced many a problem with strength and courage and managed to emerge victorious, a little battle worn, but still victorious.

But at those moments she had been a witch of tremendous power and wisdom, and there weren't many who could match her skills. Now she was near to mortal, her only remaining power being her sight, and that didn't work for herself, only for others.

She scolded herself. "Stop feeling sorry for yourself, Sarina."

She was on her own with no one to help her. With limited skills she would have to rely on her wit and strength. She may have lost her powers, but she had not lost her intelligence.

Last night Dagon's words had proved to her that he was the one who could help her break the spell and she needed to concentrate all her efforts on doing just that. His participation could not be forced or contrived. And what she required from him could not be asked for, but must be given freely.

And then there were her own doubts and fears, but she had no choice, she had to take the chance regardless of the consequences. Losing her powers was one thing to contend with; dealing with a broken heart was entirely another.

Sarina forced herself out of bed, her body protesting every move and step she made, but she was determined. She couldn't lose her position here at the castle. Her destiny was here, and here was where she had to remain.

"Whatever are you doing out of bed?" Margaret asked with concern and hurried over to Sarina, who looked about to topple over.

She stood leaning against the doorjamb, her white flannel nightgown skimming her bare feet, her face turning pale, and her shiny brown hair uncombed and unkempt.

It had taken most of her strength to make it down the stairs and to the kitchen, and Sarina didn't think she had enough stamina left to make it to the chair. "My duties," she attempted to say, but her labored breath mumbled her words.

Margaret shook her head and slipped a supportive arm around her to help her walk to the chair at the table and sit. "You need time to recover. You have been relieved of your duties for the next few days. At which time you will be assigned new duties."

"He's not dismissing me," Sarina said on a sigh.

"Heavens, no," Margaret said. "Now let me help you to your bed, and then I'll fix you breakfast."

Sarina barely managed to shake her head without a neck muscle cramping. "Please just let me sit here for a few moments and regain my strength."

"A hot cup of tea should help set you right," Margaret offered and received a gratifying smile from Sarina. "And another hot bath might ease those aches."

Sarina thought of her last bath and blushed, her cheeks burning with color.

Margaret attempted to ease her discomfort. "I'll prepare my tub for your use."

A nod sent a muscle spasm to Sarina's neck, and she cried out, her hand going to her painful neck.

"What are you doing out of bed?" came the terse remark and caused Sarina to jump and her muscles to further protest.

Dagon stomped into the kitchen and went directly to Sarina, whose eyes filled with tears from the unexpected jolt of pain.

"You were to remain abed until feeling sufficiently recovered," Dagon said and brushed her hand aside, his fingers running gently over her strained neck muscles.

She winced and bunched her shoulders when his fingers began to knead her taut neck muscles. His fingers steadily worked at her tight muscle urging it to relax, and it was with relief she felt the tense cramp lessen.

Margaret placed a hot cup of tea in front of her on the table, and Dagon, to her disappointment, slowed his kneading until he stopped completely.

Sarina leaned forward to fix her tea, depositing a teaspoon of sugar in her cup. She slipped her finger through the handle and raised the cup when a muscle in her shoulder locked in a spasm. She held on to the cup but it toppled over and spilled the entire contents on the table.

Margaret immediately took the cup from her hand and threw a dish towel on the hot liquid to sop it up. "It's bed rest you need."

"She needs more than that," Dagon said and pulled her chair away from the table. He reached down, scooped her off the chair, and looked to Margaret. "Hot towels when you get the chance and bring them to my bedroom along with a breakfast tray for her."

"I can—"

"Do nothing but obey," Dagon said sternly and marched out of the kitchen with her snug in his arms.

He placed her on his bed and arranged the comforter over her up to her waist. He then removed his sports coat, taking it to hang in his closet. He returned pushing up the sleeves of his black wool sweater.

"I'm going to make sure those muscles relax, and you,"

he said, coming to a stop beside the bed and looking down at her intently, ''are going to stay in bed until I order otherwise.''

''I have my own bed,'' she said, though knowing any disagreement was futile. He was determined, and one did not argue with a determined witch.

''A cramped and confined single bed which will cause you more ills than you need. You will stay right here at least for another full day.''

One day wasn't so bad. She could manage a day in his big, soft bed, not to mention the cozy fire and the rain that steadily drummed at the windows. And she was already growing sleepy tucked in the welcoming softness of the bed.

''If you insist,'' she said on a sigh.

''I insist.'' Dagon sat down beside her on the bed. ''Turn over,'' he ordered.

She looked at him through droopy lids, sleep beginning to invade her weary body.

He pushed the covers down from her waist, and with a tender touch he eased her over. ''I'm going to massage your neck and back while we wait for Margaret to bring the hot towels.''

Her reply was mumbled, her face partially buried in the soft down pillow.

Her relaxed repose told him she had no objections to his intentions, and he slipped his hands under either side of her ribs and worked his way up to the ties of her nightgown.

His fingers skimmed her breasts and her nipples puckered against his palm, but he ignored their instant response and his own body's quick betrayal. He intended to see to her care and that was all. He would massage her painful muscles, apply hot compresses, and see to it that she rested. He was after all in complete control of himself.

He released the ties, removed his hands, and slipped her nightgown down over her shoulders to her waist. He wasted not a minute. His hands immediately went to work on her muscles, kneading, massaging, and forcing them to surrender.

Sarina thought for certain that his hands possessed magic, for she hadn't expected anything to work on her warring muscles. She thought herself doomed for days until the muscles finally wore themselves out and surrendered.

She sighed and a yawn followed.

"I assume that means my touch pleases you?"

Her reply was a simple, "Mmmm."

Margaret soon appeared with the moist, hot towels and informed Dagon she would return shortly with breakfast for Sarina.

"Mmmm," was again heard when Dagon applied a hot towel to her neck and shoulders.

"Is that all you can say?" he teased, massaging her lower back while the towel worked its magic.

Sarina turned her head slowly so her reply would be clearly heard. "You would make a wonderful mate."

His question came before thought. "And do you look for one?"

Her response came on a whisper. "A special one."

He wondered what she considered special. What were the qualities she looked for in a mate? "How special?"

"One special enough to accept who I am and not allow it to trouble him. One special enough to be there for me no matter what the situation, and one special enough to rescue me even from myself."

"Rescuing you alone would keep him awfully busy," Dagon said teasingly.

She laughed softly in return. "Yes, he probably would have his hands full, though I would richly compensate him."

"How?" he asked curiously.

"I will love him with a love that is rare. A love he has never experienced before and even thought to exist. A love born with the dawn of time, encompassing space and the heavens above. A love that fills dreams and creates fantasies. A love that he will feel in my every touch and kiss. A love that will be uniquely ours."

Dagon sat speechless, his hands stilled at her waist. *A rare love.* He had often wondered if such a love existed and she was right. It was a love born of dreams and fantasies. One forever searched for but rarely found.

Was that why in his search for a mate he had not considered love? Did he favor a rare love and believing it impossible to find did he decide on a more practical choice? Was he settling for less because he thought he would not be able to find more?

A rare love.

Was it possible?

Dagon looked down at the bumbling witch asleep in his bed and shook his head. He removed the now cool towel and she shivered. He immediately replaced it with another hot towel, spreading it farther down her back, and she sighed and snuggled her head farther under the pillow.

He peeled the corner of the towel back to check on the abrasions she had suffered. The scratches needed more ointment and should be covered with a bandage. He would see to that after he finished applying the compresses.

He brushed her hair away from her neck and gently massaged the muscles. How had she managed to invade his senses? He still didn't understand it. Never had a woman infiltrated his emotions so easily. Never had he allowed one to. But Sarina gave him no choice. She charged full speed ahead, and in her chaotic entrance she bridged his defenses and captured his emotions.

He leaned down and kissed along the back of her neck.

"Mmmm," once again filled the room.

She always responded to him without hesitation, without thought, with complete candor. There was no need for surrender, for she surrendered before they touched or kissed. Her capitulation was there in her eyes and in all honesty it was he who surrendered to her and with an eagerness that alarmed him.

He kissed her neck once more, and her predictable response filled the room.

Was it possible?

Rare love.

Did it exist?

Rare love.

He wanted to know.

Nine

"His private chambers?" Sarina asked for the third time. It had been three days since the chimney incident and she was feeling her old self. A few aches here and there, but nothing that would keep her from doing her chores. So she had asked Bernard for her new assignment.

"Yes, his private chambers," Bernard confirmed with a touch of annoyance.

"He knows you are assigning me there?" she asked incredulously. Dagon was all too aware of the damage her clumsy skills could inflict. Why would he ever want to take the chance with her in his private chambers?

Bernard smiled. "He insisted."

She nodded, though wondered over his motive. She supposed she should be grateful for the chance to be nearer to him. How was she ever going to break the spell if she kept her distance? But his bedroom? That was moving things along a little too rapidly.

"You will not be starting your duties there until tomorrow," Bernard informed her. "You have one more day of recovery."

"But I feel fine," she protested.

"Perhaps, but His Lordship specified three full days of

recovery time before you were allowed to return to partial duties.''

''Partial?'' she asked.

''He wishes you to return to your duties slowly, and since he has so instructed that is what you shall do,'' Bernard said in a tone that warned he would not argue the point. ''Now go and rest, tomorrow will be soon enough to discuss your new duties.''

Sarina wanted to scream. She had rested more than enough. She needed to be active, and she intended to do just that. There must be something that needed doing in the castle, and she intended to find it.

An hour later she walked out the kitchen door and headed toward the mermaid pond. No one would allow her to do anything. They all but chased her away, shooing at her as if she were a pesky fly.

The exquisite pond that always managed to catch her eye and give her pause did not interest her today. She walked right past it and toward the woods. She needed to be in her element, needed to feel the energy of the wood spirits surround her.

She heard the small pitiful cry before she entered the dense woods. She stopped and looked around, but heard nothing. Before she took another step, the tiny pleading cry reached her ears again.

This time she glanced up, and there on a bough huddled in the branches of the large spruce was a tiny kitten. If she hadn't been a ball of white fur, Sarina would have never seen her. She thought of Lettie, her own cat and a remarkable intelligent tabby. She had found her nestled in a rotted old stump when she was a mere baby. They had been together ever since.

She sighed, shook her head and looked with a smile to the kitten. The little ball of white fur released a moanful meow that tore at Sarina's heart.

''I guess I have no choice but to rescue you,'' she said, approaching the bottom of the tree. ''I must warn you that I am usually the one being rescued.''

The kitten meowed softly as if reassuring her.

"I'm glad you have confidence in me, because I certainly don't."

Sarina stared in awe at the towering size of the giant spruce. At least the kitten wasn't too far up, and there were enough low branches that she could use to pull herself up. She looked down at her slim skirt, hose, pumps, and the white cardigan she wore over her blouse. Not exactly clothes for tree climbing.

The kitten's meow sounded more urgent, and when Sarina looked up she could see from her position that the kitten looked about to take flight higher up into the tree. She would never be able to rescue her then.

She spoke softly to the tiny creature attempting to win its trust and keep her from moving. No time to run back to the castle and change. It was now or never, and she couldn't think of the little kitten spending the night frightened and alone high up in the tree.

She extended her arms up and jumped for a low hanging limb, missed, and fell on her backside.

She laughed at herself. "Good start, Sarina."

Her hands brushed at the pine needles stuck to her skirt, and then she dusted her hands off before attempting another jump. She missed again and stubbornly returned to her feet. Two more times and she finally made it, catching on to a low branch. Now all she needed to do was pull herself up, climb the other few branches, and grab the kitten.

She pulled on the branch and felt the tug in her sore muscles.

The moanful meow of the tiny kitten reminded her of her presence and her courageous reason for dangling from the tree branch.

Sarina smiled. "What's a little exercise after being stuck in a chimney?" With much exertion, a tear in her stocking, pine needles protruding from her disheveled hair, and her face smudged with dirt, she worked her way up toward the kitten.

Dagon sat in his study at his desk reading a report he had just received on the computer. His investments were going remarkably well, his businesses successful, and he had a major business deal pending that looked quite favorable. Not that there weren't problems to deal with, but he employed top-notch people who did exceptional work, and any problems were usually handled professionally, quickly, and accurately.

He wished he could say the same for his present problem. Sarina simply defied solving. He had contacted several witches, and while a few had heard of her, none could verify her age. One thought she was barely one hundred, another thought her closer to three hundred, and one fool thought her over eight hundred years old. One witch knew of the area in which she came from, but wasn't certain of an address. She had told him it was around the Aberdeen area, a beautiful and mystical land.

She had also remarked that Sarina was one to keep to herself and chose her friends carefully. She seemed more at home with animals and the woods than with those of her own kind, though she did have a few mortal friends.

It made him wonder why she led what seemed like a solitary existence, and how strange it was that she should leave that life to seek a servitude position. If she was young she should be in training, and that would explain her present position here in the castle, though Bernard balked at employing neophytes. He preferred that they be at least somewhat schooled in the craft.

She could be older than he thought, though if that were the case then, she should certainly possess significant powers and wisdom. Then there would be no reason for her to be here.

He turned away from the computer frustrated and stretched his arms above his head. "This is insanity."

"Sir?" Bernard queried from the doorway, holding a silver tray with tea and sandwiches on it.

Dagon dropped his arms and motioned for him to enter. "Talking to myself."

Bernard entered and walked to the table by the window. "Something I have found myself doing much too much of since Sarina's arrival."

Dagon stood and joined Bernard as he arranged the pot of tea and plate of sandwiches on the table. Dagon snatched a tuna sandwich, unable to resist Margaret's special tuna spread.

"How is Sarina?" Dagon asked before taking a bite. He had limited his contact with her in the last two days. After tending to her in his room and admitting he was more than simply attracted to her, he thought it best if he kept his distance. He didn't need an intimate involvement with a staff member, especially when he had plans of meeting with the Ancient One. It wouldn't be fair to Sarina to have a brief affair with her when he had other, more permanent plans in mind. Not that he wasn't tempted and not that he didn't dream of her naked in his arms and not that he wasn't interested in finding out more about her and not that he stopped thinking of rare love.

Bernard's voice finally intruded on Dagon's overwrought mind. "So, sir, I ordered her to rest for the day."

Dagon realized he had missed most of what Bernard had said to him, and instead of appearing the fool, he simply nodded his head.

"I will start her in your quarters tomorrow, though limit her duties until the end of the week."

Dagon understood Bernard was seeking his approval and he gave it. "Sounds fine to me, Bernard."

"Good, then—" Bernard's mouth dropped open and the teapot would have smashed down on the table if Dagon had not set it right with the quick point of his finger. "Good lord!"

Dagon followed Bernard's wide eyes and his own mouth followed suit. Both men stood staring out the window at Sarina. They watched her grab twice for the tree limb and twice land on her backside. She finally grabbed hold of the branch and hung there as if deciding on her next move. It was when, with much difficulty, she pulled herself up and disappeared into the trees that Bernard commented.

"Whatever is she up to now?"

Dagon shook his head and dropped the remainder of his

sandwich to the empty plate. "I don't know, but I intend to find out."

Dagon resembled a mighty witch approaching the woods. He wore all black from his wool trousers to his knit sweater to his flowing wool overcoat that had been left unbuttoned, the belt hanging to the sides. A chill autumn wind blew his unrestricted hair away from his face, and his blue eyes blazed with frustration as he approached the tree that Sarina had disappeared up in.

He stepped beneath the large outstretched pine branches and glanced up. "What are you doing?"

Sarina sat straddling a branch. Her skirt was bunched up to her hips, her stockings torn, and pine needles protruded from her white sweater.

"I am trying to rescue a kitten," she said, her voice sounding much calmer than she felt.

Dagon threw his hands up in frustration. "Brilliant, and who will rescue you after you rescue the kitten."

She smiled sweetly. "Well, you are here."

The dried pine needles crunched beneath his pacing feet. "I can't believe that after your last ordeal, you failed to learn your lesson."

"Lesson?" she asked, noting that the little kitten had grown curious and was making its way carefully down toward her. She encouraged its cautious approach with a soft purr of her own.

Dagon continued his agitated pacing while keeping a sharp eye on her. "Yes, lesson. You simply do not possess the power, nor the common sense," he stressed, "to handle minor chores, much less difficult situations."

Her soft purr worked, the kitten now rested on the branch where she sat, and all she had to do was reach out and scoop it up. She did just that and found herself slipping, her arms and legs immediately hugged the branch as she toppled over.

"Dagon!" she shouted as she suddenly found herself looking up at the top of the tree instead of the ground.

"Damn," he swore furiously, and floated instantly to

where she precariously hung by her arms and legs.

He grabbed for her, snatching her around the waist.

"The kitten!" she yelled when he began to descend.

He held her firmly around the waist, her back to him as he maneuvered them within reach of the kitten. Sarina snatched the little frightened ball of fur into her hands and cradled it close to her chest.

"She must be a female," Dagon said, slowly descending to the ground. "Only a female would cause such a problem."

Sarina held the kitten up to take a peek and she laughed. "Female she is." The tiny feline licked her nose most graciously and curled against Sarina's sweater when she brought her close to her chest.

Dagon deposited Sarina gently on the ground, then walked around in front of her. He intended to give her a good, sound chastising for her inappropriate actions. It was about time she became more responsible concerning her actions. She had to realize she couldn't do things other witches could and that she lacked the rudiments of mortal skills. And besides, she was worrying him half to death. He didn't know what she would get herself into next, and the thought that he might not be able to help her caused him serious concern.

She was near on top of him before he could utter a word. She kissed his cheek and smiled brightly, holding the sleepy little kitten out for his inspection.

"Adorable, isn't she?"

Dagon watched the tiny creature give a gentle yawn, close already drooping eyes, and curl contentedly asleep in Sarina's hands. He also watched the way Sarina instinctively cradled the tiny animal against her. She offered the kitten unconditional love and protection, and the kitten wisely accepted, offering the same to her.

"Is it all right if I keep her in my room?" Sarina asked.

Dagon sighed. What was he ever going to do with her? She looked a frightful mess, and her legs were scratched from the tree branches, and he wouldn't be surprised if her body was beginning to protest her climb, but here she stood worried over the kitten's welfare.

He plucked several pine needles from her hair and found it impossible to deny her request. Actually he found it impossible to deny his attraction for her. Even in this disheveled state he discovered himself lusting after her. And a lust it was, his urge so overwhelming it bordered on the insane. That word again. It haunted him of late.

He grew annoyed with himself and it showed in his response. "You rescued her, you're responsible for her."

His agitation could have annoyed her, but she refused to allow it to. Instead she teased. "Is that the way it works?"

Her smile challenged and he was in the mood for a good challenge. "I suppose it does since I am responsible for you."

"Not entirely."

A gust of cold wind swept around them, and Sarina shivered and tucked the kitten close in the crook of her arm, protecting it from the chill.

Dagon immediately slipped his black wool overcoat off and draped it over Sarina's shoulders. "You don't even have the sense to dress warm enough. And you dare to suggest I am not entirely responsible for you?"

"The wind but warns us of a change in weather which alerts me that I must be more vigilant in my choice of outdoor wear. And you need not worry about me—"

Dagon interrupted her. "Don't dare say you can take care of yourself. You've already proved you can't."

Sarina's laugh surprised him. "And you *can* take care of me?"

Dagon plucked several more pine needles from her hair. "I think the situation speaks for itself. I have taken care of you since my return."

Her smile faded. "I think it's time I took care of myself. It isn't fair that you should be stuck with a bumbling witch."

She spoke as though she was about to inform him of her departure, and he near panicked at the thought of her gone from the castle. "I am stuck with you and you are stuck with me. Until you improve your skills and show me that you are capable of looking after yourself, you will remain here at Rasmus Castle. Is that clear?"

Sarina was speechless, her eyes wide with surprise.

"Good," he said, as though her silence confirmed her acquiescence. "Now take the kitten with you to rest. From the looks of you I would venture to guess that your already sore limbs are protesting your foolish actions."

She confirmed otherwise. "I feel perfectly fine."

He laughed with a shake of his head. "Not only foolish, stubborn."

His accurate accusation got her dander up. "I am perfectly capable of looking after myself." With that said she marched along the pebbled path and proceeded to trip on the belt of his overcoat and topple face first toward the ground.

His laughter echoed in her ears, and his hands reached her before her face hit the pebbles. The tiny kitten, so exhausted from her ordeal, slumbered undisturbed in the safety of her arms. He had her firmly on her feet in seconds, swung his overcoat off her, slipped it on, and then scooped her up into his arms before she could protest.

"Do you know you're dangerous?" he said, his laughter still evident in his voice.

"I can be very dangerous," she said sternly, wishing she had just a fraction of her inherent powers.

He smirked, attempting to suppress his laughter. "I'll keep that in mind."

"See that you do or you may be sorry."

His laughter escaped yet again. "Is that a warning?"

She shook her finger in his face. "It's a promise you better not forget."

"Why? Will you turn me into a toad?"

A toad? How dare he think her capable of only childish tricks. She may not have her powers, but she certainly had her sight and she hit him exactly where she knew it would stun him. She proceeded to inform him of all the outcomes of his recent business ventures and future ones. She even told him to beware of the present business deal he thought

so favorable. His facts were not as accurate as he thought
and it could cost him dearly.

"But then with your *exceptional* powers," she said,
"I'm sure you were already aware of that."

Dagon was surprised and impressed. Her ability of sight
was remarkably accurate; not all witches possessed the
skill, and some possessed that and none other. Was that her
problem? Were all her powers focused solely on sight?

He marched into the castle, Bernard opening the door for
him. Dagon walked past several servants, who seemed not
at all surprised by the sight of him carrying Sarina. He took
her to the kitchen and deposited her on a chair. He kept his
eye on her but addressed Margaret

"Hot tea, bandages, and ointment, Margaret. She's been
at it again."

Sarina was disappointed with herself. She had allowed Dagon to disrupt her emotionally, and that was not acceptable
behavior for a witch of her capacity. She had gained her
wisdom many many years ago and prided herself in her
knowledge. And here she was allowing her own foolish
pride to dictate, not a good reaction.

And neither was the fact that Dagon could agitate, annoy,
attract. Was that what really disturbed her?

She sighed and snuggled deeper beneath the blue and
green plaid flannel quilt. The tiny white kitten lay sleeping
beside her on the pillow and a gusty wind blew outside the
window of her small room, sounding like a moanful ghost.
It was late, well past one in the morning. The castle was
asleep and so should she be, but no matter how hard she
tried sleep eluded her.

She had refused to allow Dagon to yet again tend her
wounds, and with a hardy laugh he had left the kitchen and
her care to Margaret. She had then spent the remainder of
the day finding and preparing a box for her new kitten and
seeing that she was fed.

Margaret, Janey, and Sarina debated over names for the
feline until the three had agreed upon Lady Lily. It seemed
that the tiny kitten was as demanding as any royal lady

could be, and being her fur was as white as a lily, the two names blended well.

Lady Lily had settled herself quite comfortably into her new quarters in Sarina's room, and many of the staff dropped by to make her acquaintance, giving her even more reason to believe herself to be royalty. When she had begun her pitiful wail in the box at bedtime, Sarina knew that only one place would serve the demanding lady, her bed.

The tiny kitten had curled up beside her head on the pillow and went directly to sleep. That was several hours ago, and Sarina still remained awake, her thoughts still on Dagon.

She was attracted to Dagon and he to her, but could he give her what she so desperately needed? She thought him to be the one that would help her break the spell, but she could be wrong. She couldn't see her future, though she could follow her instincts, for they had never failed her. Only now she felt confused and unsure.

What if he wasn't the one?

What then?

She had no choice, not really. She had to take a chance. There was nothing else left for her to do. It was either accept her fate and live with the results or charge full speed ahead into an uncertain future? Was she strong enough to do that?

Strong enough to face her fate?

No answer came to her, but then she didn't expect one. It was her decision to make, and she would make it. She would toss caution to the wind and take a chance. Something she had never done in her life, and while the prospect concerned her she also grew excited with anticipation.

There were no guarantees, no promises, but there were possibilities and that was all she needed to start.

She yawned and began thinking about her new assignment to Dagon's quarters—and possibilities.

Ten

"Lily, come out from under that bed this instant," Sarina said. The kitten ignored her order and remained curled in a ball sound asleep beneath Dagon's bed. Sarina had been trying to coax her out for a good ten minutes and now resorted to a raised voice.

Lady Lily was not at all intimidated, she slept on peacefully.

Sarina sighed in frustration. Here she was on her knees, her head buried beneath the bed and her backside stuck up in the air attempting to coax one stubborn feline to do her bidding.

She should have realized this morning when Lily woke with the dawn and meowed in her ear until Sarina fed her, that she expected to have her way. After she made use of the litter pan, she once again meowed at Sarina, as if ordering her to clean it. Lady Lily then deposited her chubby little ball of fur at the door, as though informing Sarina that she would go no place without her.

Sarina unwisely scooped her up and took her along with her while she saw to her newly assigned duties in Dagon's quarters. All had gone well, especially since her workday was limited to three hours, and when she was ready to leave, twenty minutes ago, she had glanced about for Lady Lily and could not find her. It took her ten minutes to locate her and another ten spent on coaxing her, and she still remained beneath the bed.

"Lily, if you make me come get you, you're going to be in serious trouble," Sarina scolded. The threat failed to work, and it was with a groan of frustration that Sarina wiggled herself farther under the bed.

Dagon hurried into his room thinking Sarina finished for the day. He had dressed in gray slacks and a turtleneck this morning, and with the cold gusty day sending a chill through the old stone walls, he had come in search of his black wool slipover sweater. He stopped abruptly, catching sight of Sarina's tempting round backside sticking up in the air and her head and shoulders shoved beneath his bed.

He stepped back and leaned against the doorjamb, providing him with a better view, and he listened with interest and watched with a smile on his face as she chastised the hiding kitten.

Damn, her backside was stunning. His eyes remained rooted to the two soft mounds that wiggled back and forth as she attempted to work her way beneath the bed, and his smile spread.

"Lily," she said firmly, and the kitten hissed and Sarina let out a yelp.

Dagon contained his laugh, knowing full well Sarina would not appreciate hearing it. He did, however, think she would appreciate his help. He could sense her agitation and her tiredness. He hadn't wanted her to return to her duties for at least another full day especially after the incident in the tree. But she had insisted, arguing with Bernard until he agreed she could work but three hours today. Even that Dagon felt was excessive, but she had been adamant, and Bernard was in agreement, so to keep the both of them happy and himself sane he had given his permission.

Her legs were now the only part of her visible, the rest being beneath the bed, and her voice was soft and cajoling. Her legs were slim, though her ankles were too thin and that small imperfection made her all the more appealing to him.

Why?

Why did everything about Sarina interest him? He was attracted to her flaws as much as her perfections. Not that he always looked for perfection. In flawlessness there was boredom; it had been the women who were different that always caught his eye. And Sarina was certainly different.

He shook his head and reluctantly took his eyes off her shapely legs, then walked around to the other side of the bed. He got down on his knees and stuck his head beneath the bed. "Need help?"

Startled, Sarina jumped and hit the back of her head on the box spring.

Lady Lily offered her sympathy with a gentle meow.

"It's all your fault," she told the kitten and rubbed at the back of her head.

"That's no way to talk to a lady," Dagon said with a grin.

Sarina glared at him and grew angry with herself. He was too handsome. No one man had the right to be that good-looking. And that long dark hair of his only added to his outrageous looks. And of course there was his charm, add to that a dash of arrogance, and the man simply was too good to be true.

Annoyed with her thoughts and the kitten she said, "I suppose you could do better?"

"Now, there's a challenge, dear heart, I can't turn down."

"Do you think yourself that irresistible?" she asked when she already knew the answer.

"Shall we find out?" he said and turned his attention on the kitten.

Sarina didn't need the gift of sight to know Lady Lily would respond willingly and graciously to Dagon's charming demands. Without delay the little white kitten strolled over to him purring and brushing up against the hand he had extended her.

He continued to speak softly to her, and she curled her

plump tiny body in the palm of his hand and waited for him to remove her from beneath the bed.

"She seems to be ready to make her exit," he said with a wink to Sarina.

Sarina simply nodded, not trusting herself to speak especially to her mutinous kitten. While Dagon slipped easily from beneath the bed with Lady Lily comfortably in his hand, Sarina proceeded to wiggle herself out. She did fine, most of her body free, her shoulders and head the only part of her that needed to follow, when suddenly she felt a tug at the back of her collar.

She stopped herself from moving any farther when she heard the gentle tear of material. She balanced herself on one hand, realizing if she didn't remain slightly alleviated whatever she was stuck on would tear her blouse to shreds. With her free hand she attempted to extract herself but found it difficult to reach the place that had her hooked solid.

"A problem?" she heard Dagon ask.

A word that once rarely entered her thought or speech and yet now it forever haunted her. She reluctantly admitted the truth. "Yes, I seem to be stuck on something."

Dagon responded by slipping under the bed beside her and glancing over the situation. "The collar of your blouse is firmly twisted in one of the frame screws."

"Can you free me?" she asked anxiously. The scent of him was making her light-headed. And it wasn't his cologne that assaulted her senses, it was him. His very own male scent, that primal odor that is natural to men and women and connect them together faster than any expensive cologne.

Dagon thought that perhaps his powers might work. After all, she simply got herself into a mortal dilemma without the help of magic; therefore, his magic should work. He learned fast enough it didn't. Once again he would need to resort to mortal ways.

"It will take a moment to work the material free," he explained, keeping his patience.

She sighed, her own patience on edge. "I don't know if I can hold myself up much longer."

He glanced to her hand and saw how it trembled with the force of her own weight. She was still recovering from her previous incident and did not possess the strength in her arms to hold her for any length of time. He therefore did the only thing possible. He turned on his back and replaced her quivering hand with his hard chest. They now rested chest to chest, her face being only one or two inches from hers.

"Better?" he asked with a playful smile.

Better was not a word she would use to describe her present situation, but she managed a nod.

"Relax, I'll have you free in no time," he said and reached his hands around to the back of her neck.

She didn't want to focus on him, she thought to close her eyes and yet they seemed to possess a mind of their own. They remained fixed on his face, studying every line and mark, and she soon became engrossed in seeing his true character. She looked past his handsome features and what she saw amazed her.

There was a bare hint of a scar just below the corner of his right eye, and she clearly saw him and a young girl play fighting with wooden swords, and she watched the corner of the sword swipe him beneath the eye. She then watched him console the distraught girl as the blood dripped from the wound. He gave freely of his love and support to her, disregarding his own well-being for the sake of hers.

She wished she could reach out and touch the thin barely visible lines that fanned out from his eyes. They told her of his concern and regard for other people. He would think long and hard on decisions and would reach the wisest ones for all concerned. He was a man who cared deeply and would love just as deeply.

His stark blue eyes always sensual and lusty now betrayed his true strength of character and depth of emotions. He was a man who would give all or nothing and do it most willingly.

And his lips? She smiled, noting the stubbornness, pride,

and determination combined with gentleness, caring, and a softness to him that could not be denied, and that was when her breath caught.

She felt the stirring deep down in her soul and attempted to convince herself it wasn't there, it was her imagination. She wasn't feeling this; it wasn't possible.

Possibilities.

They existed and her soul just introduced her to a new one. One she had never felt though heard so much about and one that frightened her more than losing her powers. This possibility could prove disastrous or a miracle. Which would it be? She would never know if she didn't pursue the issue. If she didn't take a chance.

"You want me." His statement was simple and yet so startling to her that her eyes rounded in surprise and she answered without thought.

"Yes."

She didn't realize she was free, didn't realize she rested firmly on his chest or that his arms wrapped around her, his one hand resting against the back of her neck.

"What exactly do you want from me, Sarina?" His question stunned him as much as her. Usually when he met a willing woman, he obliged her, but for some reason he wanted to hear her intentions. Why? He didn't know, didn't understand, only knew he wanted, needed to hear for himself.

"I-I'm not sure," she said with a soft shake of her head, wondering why suddenly nothing made sense. "I'm just not sure."

He felt the nervous tremble of her body ripple over and through him, and at that second he cared about nothing but the moment and her there in his arms.

"Then let's find out," he suggested and brought her head down to meet his waiting lips. His taste of her was tentative at first, as if savoring the introduction, and when their lips grew acquainted, their taste turned friendly, eager until their acknowledgment turned to wisdom and they knew what each wanted from the other.

Their kiss took on a hunger that seemed long denied.

They feasted on each other, one attempting to give more than the other until their shared passions merged and then it was as if they were one and time stood still and there was only the two of them forever joined together.

His hands moved down along her waist to her backside, and while he squeezed her firm bottom, he pulled her body over to rest fully on top of him. Their kiss then took on an urgency that heated both their bodies beyond reasoning.

He pressed her to him, and she felt the strength of him and she groaned, her own body growing wet with the need of him.

His hand raced to the back of her head, and he grasped her hair, pulling her away from him. "What do you want from me?"

"I-I-I-" She shook her head, words eluding her, reason escaping her, her own senses betraying her.

He groaned with frustration, slipped her off him, moved out from beneath the bed, and pulled her out after him. He grabbed her about the waist, lifted her, and then dropped her down on the bed, following down on top of her.

Lady Lily sent them both a glance of annoyance for disturbing her sleep on the mound of pillows at the head of the bed and then closed her eyes once again.

Sarina had no time to think or respond, he captured her mouth in a mind-blurring kiss that left her totally incapacitated and entirely vulnerable.

"Talk to me, Sarina," he urged between passion-packed kisses. "Tell me what you want from me."

Somewhere in her muddled brain a voice cautioned her to remain silent. She could say nothing. She had to believe in herself and possibilities. She was taking a chance, trusting and learning about love.

She moved her lips off his, though reluctantly and not before stealing brief pecks to assuage her tumultuous emotions. She placed a finger to his lips, preventing any protests or further attempts at distracting her. "I'm not sure what I want from you, Dagon, and until I know, it wouldn't be fair to allow our emotions to rule."

He attempted to speak and she shook her head. "Let it be, Dagon, please let it be."

She thought he would argue, but he nodded gently.

She slipped off him, her hand brushing over his body as if in farewell.

He sprang up, grabbing her wrist. "We will finish this, Sarina."

Her smile was sad. "Oh, yes, Dagon, that we will."

She left with Lady Lily tucked in her arm, and without a backward glance she shut the door behind her.

Dagon groaned and flung himself back on the bed. He was damn hard and damn annoyed. How did one bumbling witch gain so much control of his senses? He couldn't think straight around her. He couldn't function properly, and he couldn't control his desire for her.

There had been plenty of times he felt lusty in his long life, and when he had he saw to it that his lust was satisfied. But this was more than mere lust, and the trouble was he didn't know what he meant by *more*.

He barely knew Sarina, and yet he had held her in his arms naked, he had kissed her, touched her and damn well cared for her.

He sprang up off the bed, raking his fingers through his long hair. "This certainly isn't love."

He paced the floor at the foot of the bed. Why had he even voiced that thought? He had always hoped to fall in love one day especially with one of his kind. And though Sarina was a witch, she wasn't the type of witch he would consider marriage to.

Would he?

He shook his head. He would forever be taking care of her. She would never be able to do for herself. She would always need looking after in one way or another. She would forever be getting herself into trouble and he getting her out of it.

"Life certainly wouldn't be boring."

Why ever was he voicing such stupid thoughts?

He groaned and threw his hands up into the air. "No, it wouldn't be boring, it would forever be chaotic."

He wondered if that would be so bad. Since meeting Sarina life had been . . .

"Different," he said with a laugh. He had to rely more on his senses than his powers, and that was a challenge and he did so love challenges. She had brought a spark of excitement to his life and filled his days with never-ending wonder.

She was truly a remarkable woman. Though she lacked the skills of her heritage, she strived to learn and improve no matter the consequences, and there had been many. She didn't give up in the face of adversity. She possessed more strength and courage than he had first thought, and he had to admire her tenacity.

He dropped into the chair by the window and stretched his long legs out in front of him. While Sarina possessed qualities he admired, she also lacked talent he felt essential in a mate.

He sighed at his own observations. He intended to mate with a witch equal or more powerful than he but never one lacking in basic skills. It would prove to be too much of a detriment to their union. He came from a long line of powerful witches, and he wanted that bloodline to continue unblemished.

Mortal society was not accepting of witches. Mortals knew little of the heritage and thought even less of it, and while mortals could possibly one day find themselves extinct, witches would not. And he would make certain his bloodline remained strong.

So what did he do about this crazy, uncontrollable desire for her?

"Nothing," he told himself honestly.

She would decide, the choice was hers, and then she would let him know if she could accept a night of love with him.

Eleven

~

Sarina finished her chores early, and being she had the remainder of the day to herself, she decided on being herself. She returned to her room after the noon meal and placed Lady Lily on the bed for a nap. She then stripped off her working attire, black skirt, and white blouse along with her undergarments. From the bottom drawer of her dresser she took a long black knit dress and dropped it over her head, slipping her arms into the long sleeves and smoothing the knit material down over her naked body.

The soft material did not cling or hug her tightly; instead it barely kissed her skin, flowing over mounds and curves as if in respect, and the cowl neckline fell in easy folds around her neck. She brushed her hair until it shined, slipped black suede boots on her feet and swung a black velvet cloak with attached hood over her shoulders.

Feeling more herself, she pulled the cloak over her head, walked out of her room, leaving Lady Lily to nap, and so as not to be seen she made her way quietly out of the castle. She took a stone path toward the grove of trees that ran along the north end of the castle and with eager steps made her way to a place she would feel welcomed.

Once amongst the trees and surrounded by the mighty

strength of their age and wisdom she removed her cloak and shoes and planted her bare feet firmly on the ground. The dry leaves crackled beneath the soles of her feet, and the dampness of the cool earth tickled her flesh, and in seconds the earth's energy reached up to greet her. Pure and radiant the pulsating energy raced through her, filling her with its enormous powers and renewing her strength and beliefs in the cycle of continuity.

She missed the forest and all it offered her. Her journey had kept her busy, and she had failed to respect and honor her ways lately. That would not do and she could no longer neglect her heritage. She had always been proud of her unique ancestry and always paid homage to it as she had been taught and as she would teach her children to do.

She raised her hands to the Mother Sky, cast a prayer of appreciation for all her blessings, and then slowly sank down to sit with folded legs on the ground. She closed her eyes, listened to the enchanting sounds of the woods, and relished the beauty and peace of this moment.

Dagon hung the phone up feeling overjoyed. Sydney had done it. He would have an introduction to the Ancient One. A time and place was yet to be agreed upon, but that was a minor matter. She had agreed to meet with him, and that was what concerned him the most. The rest was incidental. All he needed was the introduction; he could handle the rest on his own. He had no doubt he could charm the woman. Of course he would brush up on the history that predated his birth in case there was a time or particular period she favored or wished to discuss.

If tales and legends proved to be true, she was born with the dawn of time and therefore possessed a knowledge that far surpassed his. And of course there were her tremendous abilities. While his powers were above average, they certainly could not match hers, and he would not even attempt to impress her with menial energy.

No, he would rely on his charm and grace to win her affection and sound reasoning in suggesting she accept him as a lifemate. She had yet to mate and bear children, and all witches wished for their lines to continue, prosper, and achieve. This he could give her.

He had heard tell of a tale of a lost love. A love so strong that she refused to ever love again, and though he asked Sydney and others for more information, none had been able to relate to him the truth of the tale. Many believed it true, others thought it a legend, and a few refused to speak of it at all.

Sydney warned him that the Ancient One was not easy to deal with and that he should think wisely before proceeding with his plans. She cautioned him to look with open eyes and an open heart as he may just find what he searched for right in front of him.

He was aware that she was attempting to help him, perhaps save him from disappointment or even embarrassment. But he was determined to make a wise choice when choosing his lifemate. He did not wish to make a hasty choice or rush to mate and then regret a foolish decision.

He hoped to be attracted to her, though features mattered less to him than her knowledge and skills. And surely she would see the wisdom of his own actions and fully appreciate his reason for meeting with her. He would take his time with her, come to know her, and gently pursue her.

He shook his head, catching a flash of darkness pass by his study window, and he stood, hurrying to the window to see who was about on this cloudy afternoon. He caught only the back of the woman. She was dressed in all black, a black hood making it impossible to see her identity.

What startled and annoyed him was that a rare few witches wore black. Only those schooled in the ancient arts of the craft were allowed to wear the sacred color. The misunderstanding concerning the color had started many years ago, and while there was a basis in fact for the belief it signified evil, there were even more facts signifying its true meaning.

In darkness there is born light, and so black represented the dawning of light and the wisdom it brought to the world. Those witches who wore black possessed knowledge as old as time itself. They were the wise ones who had lived through centuries of ignorance and had not only managed to survive but managed to gain wisdom and bring light to the lesser beings. They were respected, admired, and revered.

And one presently walked his land.

She was certainly welcome here, but who was she? Could it be the Ancient One satisfying her curiosity? No, she would not be so careless as to let him see her. She cherished her anonymity and would keep herself from being seen.

Then who was his visitor?

He didn't know but he intended to find out.

Foolish.

The word felt like a kick to her backside and she certainly deserved it. She was plain foolish for walking past his study. She was in a hurry to return to the castle and therefore had taken a shorter route back, yet a more dangerous one of discovery.

She rushed up the two flights of steps to her room and hurried out of her garments, then quickly folded them away. She then slipped on a long cotton lavender dress, folding the long sleeves into a double cuff and slipping on a pair of thick white cotton socks. Her hair she tied back with a white ribbon missing several strands that feel freely around her face. She then scooped up a yawning Lady Lily and rushed back out of her room and down the stairs and out the back door of the service entrance. She wanted all to believe that she had spent the afternoon abed relaxing and was just now taking Lady Lily out for a breath of fresh air.

A mistake since Lady Lily took off as soon as her tiny pink paws hit the chilled ground.

"Lily!" she yelled and took off after her.

Dagón turned the corner of the castle just as Sarina had shouted and watched her chase after the little kitten. He had never seen her dressed in anything but her servant attire and he was fascinated with the long shapeless dress she wore, especially since the straight lines alerted him to the fact that she wore not a stitch of clothing beneath it.

With a wicked smile he took off after her.

Sarina caught up with Lily in the stables. She laughed as she chased the tiny ball of fur around and finally caught her, plopping down in an empty stall on a thick mound of hay. Lily wiggled free of her grasp and snuggled on her chest as if announcing she had enough exercise for one day and it was now time to rest.

Sarina gave her no argument and patted the yawning kitten. She yawned herself, her time of solace and her recent hasty actions bringing her a combined sense of peace and tiredness.

"You're a lazy one," Sarina said to the kitten, whose attention was perked up by a noise. She looked about, saw nothing that interested her, and proceeded to stretch herself across Sarina's chest.

Dagon watched from a short distance away. They were a pair, the two. Completely unpredictable and totally lovable. Sarina looked surprisingly appealing in lavender, or maybe it was the fact that her breasts were free of any constrictions and no panty lines marred the cotton dress, and then there were those white socks.

The thick cotton hugged her ankles and he could think of nothing more than her completely naked, except for the socks. Damn but the fantasy caused his body to erupt into a lusty chaos which his loins responded to instantaneously. And gave him a good sound reason for stepping out of the shadows.

His unexpected presence surprised Sarina, though Lady Lily meowed, jumped off her chest and proceeded to investigate the hay.

"I saw you chase Lily and thought you might require help," he said, explaining his presence as he strolled over to the stall where she lay and leaned casually against the door frame.

"Strangely enough," she said with a laugh, "I don't need any help."

"You rested this afternoon?" he asked, making casual conversation and giving him a reason to remain.

Her sojourn into the woods was indeed a rest, so she felt

she spoke the truth when she said, "Yes, I had a peaceful afternoon."

He suddenly recalled his reason for being outside, and his curiosity concerning the mysterious, dark clothed stranger returned. "Did you by any chance see a woman dressed in all black?"

"All black?" she asked, hoping to divert his question.

"I know," he said, shaking his head, "a few rare witches wear the sacred color."

She nodded and sat up, folding her legs beneath her. The toes of her sock-covered feet peeked out, a tempting sight to Dagon.

He continued his search for the elusive stranger. "I thought perhaps we had an unexpected visitor."

"Do you know many wise ones?" she asked, plucking at the hay in an attempt to hide her trembling fingers.

"None wise enough to wear the sacred color and none ignorant enough to tempt the fates. Do you know any?"

Her hesitation caught his attention, and the longer she remained silent, the more he realized she was attempting to hide something. He waited patiently for an answer.

She cleared her throat, a diversionary tactic that did not succeed. Dagon simply stood quietly in his relaxed posture waiting for her response. She certainly could not lie to him, and she definitely could not tell him the truth. Somewhere between the two was an answer, but she was having difficulty finding it And the longer her silence grew, the more suspicious he became.

Finally she found words that would suffice. "Wise ones do not always like their presence to be known."

Not a direct answer but one that lead him to believe she was familiar with a wise one, and perhaps it was she who this mysterious stranger had visited with. A thought suddenly struck him and he asked, "Are you acquainted with the Ancient One?"

Her response was quick. "Who does not know of her? Her wisdom exceeds the common knowledge. She is truly remarkable and I would imagine truly lonely."

Her remark surprised him, and he ignored the fact that

she had not actually answered his question and asked, "Why do you say that?"

She shrugged and chose her words carefully. "She is said to be born with the dawn of time, therefore, she was born into darkness, a pure void of nothingness. Yet within her was the ability to gain knowledge and with that growing wisdom the power to shed light upon the darkness."

"And bring to the world knowledge, ridding it of darkness."

"No," Sarina corrected. "Controlling the darkness. The Ancient One and wise ones wear the black to signify just that. Darkness is part of every one of us, but it is only in controlling the power of darkness and light that we gain true wisdom. And think of the loneliness the Ancient One must have experienced in her pursuit of the light."

"But once obtained—"

Sarina shook her head, silencing him. "Once obtained she had to teach it, to shed the light on the darkness. Therefore, her knowledge surpasses all and she unselfishly gives of herself. Do you not think that at times she would be lonely?"

"She could love, mate, share her life with someone?"

A sad smile crossed Sarina's face. "Who would truly understand the depths of her being and who would truly be able to love her?"

Dagon walked over to where she sat in the mound of hay. He sat down beside her, a look of concern on his handsome face. "There is a tale that speaks of a lost love."

"Yes, I have heard of it myself."

"What did you hear?"

She shook her head. "Just that she loved and lost."

"No one seems to know the truth," Dagon said, disappointed.

"I hear she guards her privacy well."

Dagon reached out and plucked a piece of hay from her hair. "Can't say I blame her."

The sudden urge to kiss him grabbed hold of her and refused to let go. His lips were inviting, hinting at pleasures and promises, and she ached for the strength of his arms around her, and the feel of his gentle touch. She shivered.

"Cold?" he asked and looked at her oddly.

A quick nod and a cautious glance at his eyes told her that he was no fool and that he knew exactly why she shivered. Whatever was the matter with her? If she were honest with herself, she would admit that her reaction was not at all sudden or unexpected. He had appealed to her senses as soon as he had entered the stable. Maybe it was his walk or saunter since he swayed with sensuality when he walked. Or it could be his hands? His fingers being long and lean, and when in motion they moved with an orchestrated confidence. Then of course there was the color of his eyes, an indescribable blue, mysterious, erotic, and charged with a heated passion that betrayed the senses. But then her senses had been betraying her on a regular basis lately.

Betraying?

Or were her senses attempting to tell her the truth?

"Are you cold, Sarina?" he asked again.

She smiled and slowly shook her head. "You know I'm not cold."

"Yes, that I do," he said and leaned over to brush his lips across hers before stealing a much wanted kiss. His arm slipped around her waist, and he eased them both down together on the thick cushion of hay. Once there he kissed her senseless.

Sarina warned herself to keep her hands at her sides. Scolded herself for even considering touching him and cautioned herself that it would do little good to begin something that was yet to see fruition or may never be culminated. And yet her hands itched to explore him, come to know him, lose herself in him.

She purposely stretched her arms above her head, reaching out above her, far past him. While he in turn did exactly as he wished—he touched her. Slow and steady he explored her as if wanting to acquaint himself with every inch of her.

Having no undergarments on made his touch all the more erotic. She could feel the heat of his hand through the soft cotton material, and he made certain that the cotton teased her skin in the most intimate of places. He was persistent and insistent in his endeavors to please and excite.

And he did excite her, to the point where she was totally mindless and completely surrenderable. But still her arms remained above her head. If she dared to intimately touch him, all would be lost, and it was too soon, much too soon, to take such a daring chance. Small chances now were wise choices; major chances were better left for a more opportune time.

Now all that remained for her to do was to keep a minimum of control on her senses.

Dagon had other ideas, and Sarina was unprepared for his ability to seduce with words. "Afraid to touch me, dear heart?"

He prevented her from answering with a sensual kiss that had her curling her toes. "You know you want to."

Good lord, did she ever want to touch him. No, no, she ached to touch him. And yet she remained silent.

He laughed near her ear, and with his teeth gently nipping down along her neck, he said, "I want you, too."

She groaned and he laughed harder.

"I want those sweet, bumbling fingers of yours running all over me creating complete havoc."

Would she be clumsy at that as well? The absurd thought brought a sudden frown to her face.

Dagon quickly kissed her frown lines away and ran his hands slowly up her arms to capture her hands in his. "I think your hands hide magic, and I want you to perform your magic on me."

She shivered at the truth of his words and the sudden realization of her imminent problem. She needed to learn more about him, understand him better before she committed to a situation that could prove either lifesaving or disastrous.

And yet she wanted nothing more than to do as he asked. She wanted to touch him and make magic together.

She was grateful for Lady Lily's intrusion. The little kitten insinuated herself right under Dagon's neck and began licking him and meowing most moanfully.

"I want your tongue there, Sarina."

The man knew how to entice and excite, and she licked her lips in a slow hunger.

With a gentle hand he removed Lady Lily and with tender words and a confident stroke he assured the kitten that if she waited patiently she would receive a special treat, right after he received his. The kitten curled into a ball to wait. He then looked to Sarina. "Taste me."

She swallowed hard and her body went limp, though her tongue licked eagerly at her top lip.

"Taste me," he ordered sternly.

A taste, a simple taste, what could it hurt?

Dagon pulled back his long dark hair and offered his neck to her. "Let me feel you quench your deep hunger."

His neck was smooth, his veins thick with the heated blood that raced through him, and his scent was strictly male and all passion. She licked her lips one last time in appreciation and reached out to taste.

Her tongue touched, first skimming the surface, acquainting herself with his flavor and savoring every delicious taste. Her teeth followed, nipping his flesh, feasting on the now familiar taste of him and feeling even less satisfied than before. She wanted more, so much more from him. Now that she had tasted she was famished, and her outrageous appetite needed satisfying.

She turned on him like a ravenous creature bent on assuaging her lusty craving.

He in turn allowed her to feed her need, relishing in her unbridled passion for him. His groans filled the stable. His moans echoed deep in his throat, and his own desire soared past reasoning.

He pulled his head back away from her, and her disappointment assaulted him as strongly as the passion that raced through him. "You can feed on me as long as you like, but know there will be consequences."

Her breathing was labored, her heartbeat erratic, and her desire insanely out of control. It was obvious she had never experienced such extreme desire, and that realization quickly sobered him.

Dagon brought a swift end to this madness. He moved off her and stood but not before scooping Lady Lily up into his hand. He turned to leave, stopped, turned back around, looked down at her, and shook his head. "Don't dare wear those damn white socks again."

With that he left and Sarina broke into a fit of laughter. *Socks.*

Socks excited and upset the handsome witch. She would have to remember that.

Twelve

~~

"Are you certain you feel up to returning to full duty?"
Margaret asked Sarina, who sat at the kitchen table with
her hands cupping her mug of hot tea. "You look peaked."

"Heavy thoughts," Sarina answered with a sigh before
sipping at the mint-flavored brew. It was another hour before the household staff would rise and begin their chores.
Sarina, however, had risen before dawn, and unable to sleep
any longer, she had dressed and come to the kitchen for a
hot cup of tea. She knew she would find Margaret there,
her hands already deep in flour preparing the day's pastries.

She attempted to convince herself that it was company
she was seeking, not advice. She was wise enough to know
what must be done and yet—she longed to share her woes
with someone and hear another's opinion.

"Do these thoughts concern Dagon?" Margaret asked,
kneading a large lump of dough that hinted of cinnamon
and nutmeg.

"You are very perceptive."

Margaret laughed. "I simply have good eyesight."

"Whatever do you mean?" Sarina asked innocently.

Margaret placed the dough in a bowl and dusted the large

wooden board in front of her with a generous handful of flour. "I mean that love is hard to hide."

"Love?" Sarina seemed surprised.

Margaret placed the dough on the board and proceeded to roll it out with the flour-dusted rolling pin. "It shines in your eyes."

Sarina shook her head.

"You deny it, or are you concerned with your newfound emotions?"

"Again perceptive," Sarina said and sipped at her tea, a sense of confusion invading her along with the warm liquid.

"Your feelings trouble you."

"You read me well."

"I see clearly," Margaret insisted. "And your eyes speak of love and confusion."

"I always heard that the two go remarkably well together."

Margaret smiled. "Now you are the perceptive one."

Sarina sighed. "No, and that is my problem. I know nothing of love."

This time Margaret laughed. "No one does."

"But then how can one be sure if one loves?"

Margaret stopped rolling the dough and turned her full attention on Sarina and the impending question. "I think everyone asks that question one time or another, and I think that the question has no answer. Love is not easily definable. It is an emotion that must be trusted and firmly believed and most of all it requires faith. Faith in yourself and faith in love."

Sarina asked the question that had haunted her of late. "What if you have faith in that love but the person you love feels differently?"

Margaret picked up the biscuit cutter and dipped the edges into the bowl of flour. "That is the chance we take when we love, though I think our hearts know."

Sarina asked another troubling question. "What if it is merely lust?"

Margaret laughed robustly. "Lust is a flame that satisfies but for a moment and burns out all too quickly. Love is a flame that satisfies forever and burns continuously.''

"You're saying that love fires the soul.''

"You say it much better than I.''

"You make it understandable.''

Margaret laughed even harder and shook her head. "Understandable? Never. It has proved confusing since the beginning of time.''

"I once thought love would be easy to find and easier to capture.''

"Oh, my dear child,'' Margaret said with a bittersweet smile. "Love can never be captured, it can only be shared.''

Sarina sighed and hugged her near empty mug. "Does Dagon share?''

Margaret appeared reluctant to answer.

"Please, Margaret, I know I'm foolish—''

"No,'' Margaret said. "Foolish you are not.''

"And Dagon?'' Sarina persisted.

Margaret answered with reluctance. "He wishes true love and yet fears the search.''

"Why?'' Sarina asked curiously.

"I think he fears finding it.''

Again Sarina asked, "Why?''

Margaret smiled. "Because for once in his life he would lose total control of his emotions.''

"Something he has never done?''

"Never,'' Margaret assured her. "Which is why he attempts to make plans for finding a lifemate.''

"Plans?'' Sarina asked, a sense of distress filling her.

Margaret stopped cutting out biscuits and looked directly at Sarina. "You should know that Dagon has made arrangements to meet with the Ancient One with the purpose of proposing she accept him as a lifemate.''

Sarina was stunned speechless, and all color drained from her face. "To think I would compete with *her*.''

Margaret grasped her hand. "Love always wins out.''

"I had thought that once.''

"You sound doubtful.''

"No,'' Sarina said with a smile. "I remain hopeful and I have faith.''

• • •

Dagon sat in the small receiving parlor appreciative of the blazing fire in the hearth since outside the cold blustery wind was knocking at the windows demanding entrance. The gray skies promised that the weather conditions would soon worsen, and he wouldn't be surprised if the afternoon brought with it a chilling rain.

He had spent the early morning working in his study—at least he attempted to work. His mind refused to cooperate. His betraying thoughts constantly turned to Sarina until finally he grew so irritated with himself he left his study to come sulk in the receiving parlor.

"Tea, sir?" Bernard asked from the doorway.

"Yes, thank you, Bernard," he said and bit down on his tongue to prevent himself from asking about Sarina. It didn't work. His tongue escaped and he spoke in haste. "Sarina fairs well?"

Bernard stiffened. "She has caused no problems—*yet*."

"Perhaps she improves."

"We shall see," Bernard said without enthusiasm.

Dagon looked to the flames in the hearth and gave thought to his own frustration. He should be thrilled with the prospect of meeting the Ancient One and the possibilities it represented. Instead he thought of an inept witch who ignited a passion in him he never thought possible.

Now there was real possibilities.

Perhaps even the possibility of love.

He had thought of love quite frequently lately and recalled with pleasure the many women he had known over the years. Had he loved any? And what was love but a wild emotion that lacked rhyme or reason and therefore lacked definition? So what really was love?

Poetry often extolled the virtues of love. Great philosophers attempted to make sense of it. Psychiatrists thought to dissect it, and yet lovers simply accepted it. So perhaps one needed to be in love to know what love was.

He would soon have a headache if he continued to deeply examine the essence of love. A small four-letter word that possessed the power to break and heal hearts. Was that where the spirit of love resided, in the heart?

Dagon stood and walked to the window. Love could not be contained, and that thought suddenly brought a clearer understanding of the strange emotion. Love was like magic—belief and faith gave it life. So therefore one needed to be in love to know love.

He thought about his crazy need for Sarina and wondered if he had given love life without even realizing it.

Sarina was almost done with Dagon's room. The last thing she needed to do was shake the small hearth rug out the window. A persistent meow got her attention, and she looked to see Lady Lily sitting on the bed licking her tiny pink paw.

"Keeping yourself busy while you wait for me to finish, are you?" Sarina asked and received a meow of confirmation.

She rolled up the hearth rug and walked over to the window. "I'll be done in a minute, and then we'll go get a snack for you."

The kitten meowed her appreciation, and Sarina reached for the window latch.

A gusty wind whipped the window from her grasp, and she had second thoughts about shaking out the rug. She placed the rolled rug on the ground and reached out to grasp the latch. It rested just out of her reach, and she quickly moved a chair to the window and climbed up on it, and with her balance a bit unsteady she stretched out, reaching for the latch.

Sarina was hanging half out the window by the time her fingers finally grasped the latch, and with a smile she pulled the stubborn window toward her. The gust of wind tore around the castle and struck like a bolt of lightning. It hit the panes with a mighty force, blowing it wide open and sending a startled Sarina tumbling out the window.

Dagon sat enjoying his tea and a good mystery. Bernard, his usual attentive self, had brought a book, a favorite author of Dagon's whose work never failed to please, along

with a pot of tea and an assortment of pastries fresh from
the oven. It was obvious, though Bernard made no remark,
that he thought it a good idea for Dagon to spend a relaxing
afternoon reading.

After a sip, a taste, and the first three pages he couldn't
agree more and he settled himself in for an enjoyable afternoon.

He thought the first distant meow his imagination, but
the second sounded more like a screech and could not be
ignored. He closed his book after inserting a bookmark and
went to the staircase to find Lady Lily continuing her the-
atrics from the top step.

Dagon hurried up to console her, but when he drew near,
she gave a pitiful screech and raced away from him down
the hall. He thought to ignore her when suddenly he felt
the urge to follow her. The urge turned to alarm as he
approached his quarters, and he hurried his steps, racing
into his room.

Lady Lily sat on the chair by the open window, her anguished cries filling the room. Dagon practically flew to the
window, his heart beating madly. He was certain it stopped
beating when he caught sight of Sarina barely hanging on
to the stone ledge. His hands instantly grasped hold of her
slim wrists.

He wanted to rant with rage when his powers once again
failed in helping him. It would take mortal tactics to see to
her safety, and he wasted not another moment, especially
after feeling the first heavy spat of rain hit his arm.

"Grab hold of my wrists!" he ordered with a shout.

She nodded that she heard him, and when she released
hold of the ledge, he winced at the sight of her fingers
scraped almost raw from grasping so tightly to the rough
stone. She clasped her hands firmly to his wrists and he
used his strength to pull her to him. When she was up and
over the ledge, he reached out and grabbed her beneath the
arms pulling her completely through the window.

He held her cold, shivering and wet body close to him.
"We need to get you dry."

He tucked her safely in the corner of his arm while he

reached out to close the window against the rain and cursed his lack of powers in righting her wrongs. Whatever was the problem? A witch with limited powers could always be helped by a witch of greater powers. What prevented his intervention?

She sneezed and he hurried her over to the hearth, where the heat of a blazing fire welcomed them. She shuddered when the heat reached out and brushed over her cold, wet skin.

"You must get out of those wet clothes," he said, his fingers hastily releasing the buttons on her white blouse. "I'll go get you a warm robe."

Sarina didn't argue with him, her only thought was to chase away the deep chill and the awful fright from her body. She had feared she wouldn't be able to hold on or manage to rescue herself in any way. She had thought her fall inevitable and the consequences final, and she had never felt so helpless in her life.

Her thoughts had immediately gone to Dagon, and all she had never told him and all she had never experienced with him and she felt regret and a sadness for what they would miss sharing.

But he had rescued her once again and with mortal skill. She smiled though her teeth chattered, and she hurried to rid herself of the wet garments. Her wet skirt joined her discarded blouse on the floor, but her wet panty hose gave her a fight.

Dagon returned to the room, walking up behind her and unhooking her bra. She pulled it off as he draped the thick black velvet robe over her shoulders and ordered, "Slip your arms in."

She intended no argument and did as he directed.

He moved in front of her, his hands going to the waistband of her panty hose.

"They're stuck," she informed him with a trembling smile.

"Not for long," he said and dropped down in front of her to tug the stubborn wet panty hose along with her panties down her legs. He grasped each thin ankle firmly in his hand as he yanked off the final garments, and then he stood securing the robe closed over her naked body with a double tie of the velvet belt.

He moved the high back chair closer to the hearth and sat her down in it. He disappeared for a moment and returned with a pair of thick gray socks. He went down on bended knees in front of her and reached out to capture one of her ankles.

She assumed his intentions were to warm her feet with the socks, but instead his fingers went to work massaging her cold foot, and she sighed with pure pleasure. His lean fingers rubbed at the sole of her foot, stroked her instep, massaged her toes, and when her foot radiated warmth he slipped the thick sock on and went to work on her other foot.

She surrendered to a world of pure bliss, closing her eyes and relishing every touch and stroke. She drifted in a hazy slumber, wishing his soothing touch would never end. When he finished slipping the other sock over her foot, he scooped her up in his arms and carried her to his bed, depositing her in the middle and covering her with a plaid wool blanket.

He picked up the phone by the bed, hit a button, and ordered hot soup and a pot of tea brought to his quarters. He then stretched out beside her on the bed and gently tapped at her nose. "Tell me of your powers that be."

She sighed long and hard and was not at all in the mood to discuss her dormant powers. She snuggled deeper beneath the blanket, pulling it up and almost over her face.

Dagon would have none of her hiding and pulled the blanket down to beneath her neck. "Tell me of your powers."

"What powers?" she said with a yawn.

He kissed her then, firm and hard. "You will not fall asleep."

No, she certainly wouldn't after that breath-stealing kiss. It shocked her senses, sent her hormones surging, and her body temperature climbing.

"Your powers," he reminded.

She sighed in frustration. She was not presently capable of dealing with his probing questions, and she certainly could not relate the truth to him. How did she deal with his inquiry? She could not lie to him and she could not be entirely truthful. As usual her answer lay between the two, but she tired of avoiding the full truth.

And this time she chose to speak it. "My powers wait."

"Wait?" he repeated, not understanding her answer.

A chill raced through her and she shivered. He reached out and pulled her to him, running his hand up and down her back to warm her. She snuggled her face in the crook of his neck and eagerly sought the warmth his body offered.

Wait.

The word hung suspended and temporarily ignored as Dagon's hand became more and more familiar with Sarina's body. And in turn Sarina found his neck all too appetizing to ignore.

She licked and nipped at him until she had him moaning, and he touched and explored beneath her robe until he had her groaning. And soon their heated passion took hold and sent them tumbling completely out of control.

His hands roamed her with an urgency, her lips sought him with a hunger, and they surrendered to their unbridled desires with complete abandonment. He lay on top of her, her legs wrapped around his and her hands running up his gray sweater.

The heat of his hard flesh tingled her fingers, and she played over his naked skin like a musician testing a fine instrument and forcing it to respond to her accomplished touch.

He moaned when her fingers teased his nipples and his mouth swooped down on hers to rob a kiss that stole her breath and muddled her senses. She felt his readiness, hard and thick pressing against her, and all she needed to do was to reach down, release him, and welcome him into her.

Before sanity escaped her and with great reluctance and difficulty, she reined in her senses and moved her mouth off his to ask, "What do you want from me, Dagon?"

His hand squeezed her breast, and his tongue teased her hard nipple. "Isn't it obvious."

"Sex?" she asked candidly.

Her question startled him.

"Is that what you're looking for from me? Plain and simple sex?"

Her bluntness cooled him considerably, and he rolled off her and sat on the edge of the bed.

She closed her robe and persisted to question. "I assume it is only sex, since I have heard of your plans."

That remark shocked him. "What plans?"

"Your plans to meet with the Ancient One for the purpose of seeking a lifemate."

The idea that she was aware of his intentions disturbed him, though he would not deny the truth. "I am giving it thought."

"Which means you're only interest in me is sex."

"No," he said firmly.

"An afternoon romp?" she persisted, her own temper rising.

"No," he said even more firmly and controlled.

She sat up, rising to her knees. "A sex play toy to amuse you."

He reached out, grabbing her by her shoulders. "No!"

"Then what am I to you?" she challenged.

"Damned if I know," he said and charged at her mouth.

They could not quench the fire that raged in them. They could not understand the desire that burned inside them, and they could not break the undeniable tie that bound them.

"You're like a constant fire in my soul," he whispered harshly near her ear.

And she understood, for she felt the same familiar burning deep within herself.

"Yet you look to mate with another," she reminded him and herself.

"I don't know what I look for," he admitted.

"But you look," she said, "which tells me you have yet to find."

He raised his head and stroked his thumb over her sensitive lips. "You are wise for your young years."

"I am aware," she said. "Aware that there is more to mating than lusty cravings and heated moments."

"Magical moments," he said without thinking.

"You believe in them?" she asked hopefully.

His answer was a simple, "I do."

Her hand reached out to cup his cheek. "Then understand this, Dagon. I wish for magical moments and will settle for nothing less."

Her pale blue eyes captivated, and for a brief startling moment he thought he saw an aged wisdom in their depths that could only belong to a wise one. A witch born many centuries ago and with knowledge and powers that far surpassed his.

But that was not possible. His eyes merely played a trick, or perhaps his thoughts drifted to the Ancient One and he saw what he wished to see. Sarina possessed no such skill or wisdom. She had much to learn, and as for magical moments?

He wanted those moments as badly as Sarina did.

Thirteen

~

Sarina couldn't sleep. It was one in the morning, and she had lain awake for the last hour unable and not wanting to slip into a troubled slumber. She decided that her thoughts were much too chaotic to make sense of them, and she was simply much too exhausted to try.

Tea sounded the proper antidote for her dilemma, and so she scooped up a grumbling Lady Lily off the bed, slipped her thick white socks on her feet, but left her bathrobe behind. Her long white flannel nightgown kept her warm enough, and besides she only planned to make the tea and hurry back to her room. She didn't wish to disturb anyone, it being so late.

Lady Lily snuggled in the crook of her arm as she carefully made her way down the two flights to the kitchen. Margaret kept a small light burning in the kitchen at all times, a sure sign that anyone was welcome at anytime.

She set the kettle to boil, fixed a mug with raspberry tea, and while she waited for the water to boil, she fixed Lady Lily a small bowl of milk. She kept her thoughts silent the whole time she worked, focusing on her task at hand.

Sarina grabbed the kettle before it whistled, filled her

mug, and looked down at the kitten to see if she was finished with her milk.

Lady Lilly sat on full alert, her green eyes fixed on a spot near the kitchen door. Sarina turned to see the little mouse sitting in the doorway staring back at the kitten. Neither one moved, they both sat poised and waiting.

Sarina doubted she could scoop up Lily before she took off, and she was at least grateful the castle was quiet and all were asleep. It would make the chase after Lily that much easier.

But then she forgot how fast Lily could run.

The little kitten sprang after the tiny mouse so fast Sarina caught only a blur of white fur zipping past her. She didn't waste a minute taking off after her.

Dagon pulled his long black hair back and fastened it with a pewter clip, the design the Celtic knot. He then dressed quickly in black wool trousers and a light gray wool sweater. The phone call had come only a few moments ago informing him that Alisande, Sebastian, and Sydney would arrive shortly. He had called Bernard and informed him of their imminent arrival and requested that Margaret prepare light refreshments.

He was eager to visit with them, not having seen Ali and Sebastian since their wedding and wondering how the newlywed couple was faring. He was more than pleased that Sydney had joined them. He wished to speak with her; actually he required a touch of her wisdom and was glad for her presence.

Eager to be downstairs to greet them, he hurried from his room. Ali had explained they would arrive by car, Sebastian insisting that until he was proficient enough at travel spells, he would travel the old-fashioned, mortal way.

Which meant they would be arriving by car. He planned to be at the door himself to greet them. He quickened his step, anxious and happy over their impending visit.

Sarina chased Lily and the mouse down the hall, into and out of Dagon's study, around the dining room, through the receiving parlor back down the hall to the kitchen, sliding on the tile floor around the kitchen table to the surprise of Margaret and herself.

"Oh, dear," Margaret said, her hands steadying Sarina as she tilted to one side as she rounded the table on a fast glide.

"A mouse," Sarina said, attempting to explain as she slipped away from Margaret and continued her chase.

Margaret smiled with delight. "It's going to be an interesting night."

Dagon was descending the staircase to the foyer, Bernard was opening the front door to greet the guests who had just arrived, and Sarina was about to scoop Lady Lily up when her sock-covered feet hit the marble tile in the foyer.

Everything happened so fast Sarina didn't have time to react. She slid straight for the front door that Bernard had just opened, her arms flew out in a frantic attempt to stop her frenzied flight, but she could grasp nothing but air. She saw the crash coming and could do nothing to prevent it, and neither could the startled man she collided with.

His body was solid enough to take the unexpected impact, and they tumbled together to the floor, he landing on top of her.

Sarina blinked several times and with rounded eyes looked at the strange man who lay stretched out over her. He was a good-looking man, not near as handsome as Dagon, but a man who could turn a woman's head, and he certainly was firm in body and she imagined strength as well. She immediately sensed he was a fair and reasonable man and quite new to the craft.

He smiled at her. "Hello there."

"Hi," came another greeting and Sarina blinked twice at the woman who leaned over her head, peering down at her.

She was beautiful. Long blond hair, stunning features, intriguing green eyes, a charming smile, and she wore a white wool suit that accented her eye-catching figure. And besides all those qualities she was a witch, a witch of enormous power.

"Hello, dear," another voice said before a new face popped into view.

Her eyes rounded even wider and she found herself speechless. This woman she knew, though she remained silent, preferring to keep that knowledge between them.

"Sarina!"

For once she was grateful for Dagon's familiar voice, though when he peered down over her, his expression was anything but happy.

"A mouse" was all she could say and the strange man laughed, moved off her, and with gentle hands helped her up.

"Sebastian Wainwright," he said and took her trembling hand in his.

"Sarina," she said and held on to him for dear life.

"Alisande Wainwright." The beautiful woman introduced herself and gave Sarina's back a comforting pat.

"And I'm Sydney," the woman who needed no introduction announced with a smile.

Dagon stood with his arms crossed over his chest in a pose that demanded she explain.

"Lady Lily went after a mouse," she said to him, clinging to Sebastian's hand. It was warm, comforting, and reassuring.

"Lady Lily, what a charming name," Alisande said with a sprinkle of laughter that sounded like wind chimes.

"And a name that suits her well," Dagon said and looked down to see the little precious kitten winding her way around Sarina's sock-covered feet. He stared at her white socks, noticed the way she held tightly to Sebastian's hand, and raised an arched brow at her.

"Did she catch the mouse, my dear?" Sydney asked, reaching down to cup the little ball of fur in her hands.

Sarina shook her head and shivered.

"Cold?" Sebastian asked and slipped his arm around her, drawing her near.

Dagon did not at all care for the intimate gesture. He

stepped forward, yanked Sarina out of Sebastian's arms, and lifted her up into his own arms, shaking his head. He then walked into the receiving parlor.

Sebastian laughed and hugged his wife to him. "He's got it bad."

"How do you know?" she asked with a gentle kiss to his cheek.

"He shakes his head. It's a sure sign that you think you're losing your mind, which you are, but you don't know and when you find out it's too late."

Sydney smiled. "Your wit and wisdom amaze me."

Sebastian held his arm out to Sydney. "I learned from a very wise woman. Now let's go torment Dagon."

Dagon sat Sarina on the small sofa, retrieved the moss green chenille lap throw from a nearby chair, and covered her legs, making certain to tuck the blanket over her feet.

"Those damn socks are going to drive me insane," he mumbled.

Sarina heard him and smiled.

"So tell us about Sarina, Dagon," Sebastian said entering the parlor with Ali on one arm and Sydney on the other.

Sarina obliged him, hoping to prevent an awkward situation from turning worse. "I'm a servant at Rasmus Castle. I tend to Dagon's quarters."

Sebastian smiled so broadly he almost laughed.

Dagon sent him a lethal look, but Sebastian continued to grin.

Bernard entered with a tray of tea and scones, and conversation came to a brief halt. "Shall I serve, sir?"

"That won't be necessary," Dagon informed him.

Bernard nodded, saw to lighting the logs in the fireplace, took Sebastian's black wool overcoat from him and Sydney's white wool cloak, cast a notable glance at Sarina, and then quietly left the room.

"Margaret's scones. Blueberry and cranberry," Alisande said with excitement and proceeded to pour tea for everyone, though not before taking a bite of a scone.

Sebastian sat beside his wife, and Sarina noticed what a perfect pair they made. That they loved each other was obvious, that they were a perfect match was also obvious.

"Now about Sarina," Sebastian persisted, accepting a cup of tea from Ali.

"How are we doing with our new skills?" Dagon asked, pointing to a filled teacup on the table. The cup floated up and over to him, and he took hold of it, carefully offering it to Sarina.

She nervously accepted the delicate cup with trembling hands. Dagon wrapped his hand around hers to calm her tremors and offer his comfort. She sent him a grateful smile, and the affectionate exchange was not lost on the three people watching them.

"I'm getting better," Sebastian said proudly and pointed his finger at a sugar cube in the sugar bowl on the table. The tiny cube swiftly rose up and shot at Sebastian's cup, pinging off the side and landing in his wife's lap.

"That's all right, dear," Ali said, picking up the cube and dropping it into his cup. "Practice makes perfect."

Sebastian leaned over and deposited a tender kiss on her cheek. "So patient with my bumbling attempts."

"Darling, you never bumble," Ali said with a wickedly sinful smile that made Sarina blush.

"I can see that you're in love with this mortal as much as ever," Dagon said, sounding irritated and causing them all to stare at him with surprise, though Sebastian grinned as if he was having the time of his life.

"Is something troubling you, dear boy?" Sydney asked with concern and settled back in her chair with a cup of tea in hand, a white linen napkin spread over her lap, and a sleeping Lady Lily curled in a contented ball right in the middle of it.

Sarina felt responsible for the early morning events and voiced her own concern, pushing the blanket down and slipping her feet to the floor in an attempt to make a wise and hasty exit. "I must apologize, this is all my fault and—"

"Stay right where you are," Dagon ordered firmly and shoved her sock-covered feet back up on the couch, pulling the blanket over her.

Sebastian gently poked at his wife's arm, and she smiled knowingly.

Sydney showed no reaction at all, she simply watched.

Dagon offered a brief explanation. "Sarina has been under the weather of late."

"Have you tried a comfort spell?" Ali asked, reaching for another scone.

Sarina answered quickly. "He's been more than generous in helping me."

"Dagon is always there to help a friend," Sebastian said, stealing a piece of his wife's scone and getting a slap on the hand for his sneaky action.

"If it wasn't for Dagon's help, Sebastian and I would have never gotten together," Ali informed her and with a crook of her finger directed the teapot to refill her cup.

"Let me try that," Sebastian insisted, drawing his finger out as if it was a gun ready for action.

"That's my antique china," Dagon warned.

Ali placed her hand over her husband's trigger finger. "Another time, darling."

"Later," he said with a wink.

Ali winked right back.

Sarina smiled at their teasing antics. She had never seen two people so in love, or perhaps she had never looked before now. Their eyes often settled intimately on each other. They touched frequently, small simple gestures, they stroked with words, and then there were the pecks on the cheeks, a kiss of a hand or what looked like a whisper when really it was a whisper of a kiss.

Their affection was real and they weren't afraid to show it. Had it always been this way for them? This love that could not be denied?

"How did Dagon help bring you both together?" Sarina asked, suddenly interested.

Everyone ignored Dagon's scowl, and Ali related the story. "He was aware of my love for Sebastian and how unhappy I would be without him. And though he wouldn't admit it, he liked Sebastian and knew full well how much he loved me."

"And couldn't live without you, don't forget," Sebastian added.

Ali nodded. "He's right. His life would have been miserably boring without me."

Sebastian also nodded. "She introduced me to the delights of chaos; nothing has been the same since, and I wouldn't have it any other way."

Sarina laughed and Dagon shook his head, finally giving up his commanding stance and sat at the end of the small sofa by Sarina's feet to listen to the familiar tale.

Sarina's attention remained fixed on Ali, though she unconsciously stretched her legs out, resting her feet against Dagon's thigh, a relaxed gesture he did not object to.

Ali continued. "I unfortunately was powerless, my energy had dwindled—" She stopped abruptly. "Is your energy low?"

"Finish the story, Ali," Dagon insisted, his eyes warning her not to probe.

Her stubborn return glance informed him that she would have her answers, but for now she would concede to his wishes and proceeded with the tale. "Dagon came to my rescue."

"He's good at that," Sarina agreed with a firm nod.

Ali acknowledged the same with her own nod. "He's wonderful at rescues. He was forever saving me—"

"From yourself," Dagon finished.

"He's got you there, sweetheart," Sebastian said. "It was your own fault for casting that spell and placing our love in jeopardy."

"Excuse me," Ali said with an indignant grin. "I believed our love was strong enough to fulfill the spell. If you weren't such a stubborn mortal—"

"Stubborn?" Sebastian laughed. "Foolish I will admit to, but stubborn—never!"

"Huh, you just proved my point," Ali said with a shake of her finger in his face.

"Watch it, witch," Sebastian warned, still laughing as he drew out his own finger. "This time it's loaded."

Sarina smiled; she couldn't help it. They even fought like

two people in love. They grinned, teased, and their eyes shared an intimate glow that no witch or mortal could mistake.

They loved to the depths of their souls.

"What spell did you use?" Sarina asked, eager to hear more.

"Magical love," Ali announced with pride while Dagon and Sebastian shook their heads, and Sydney continued to watch in silence.

"Oh, my," Sarina said, stunned and with a twinge of envy. "Only the most powerful love can survive that special spell."

Ali patted her husband's leg that rested against hers. "I believed in our love and I had faith in him."

"But as usual you didn't look before leaping," Dagon said, his hand having moved to casually rest over Sarina's foot.

The intimate scene was not lost to Sebastian and Ali. Sydney simply smiled.

"I looked," Ali insisted and turned to look at her husband. "Right into his eyes and knew then and there he was all I ever wanted, and I intended to have him."

"Was he hard to capture?" Sarina asked innocently.

That caused a burst of laughter from Dagon and Sebastian.

"Ignore them," Ali instructed. "Men, especially mortals"—she paused, glanced briefly to Dagon, and continued—"and a few arrogant male witches are the last to realize and admit that they are in love."

"Really?" Sarina asked with interest. "I would think that at least a male witch would be attuned to his emotions and better understand."

"You would think," Ali agreed, "but males, whether mortal or witch, are a stubborn lot."

"That I most certainly agree with," Sarina said and reached out to place her teacup on the table. The delicate china tumbled out of her hand and fell to the floor.

Ali and Sebastian immediately attempted to right the falling cup with a point of their fingers. Dagon simply reached out and caught it in his hand before it hit the carpet. He returned it safely to the table.

Sydney saved Sarina from further embarrassment by saying, "It has been a long journey and I think it's time for me to rest." She surprised all but one with her next words. "Sarina, why don't you show me to my room."

"I would love to," she agreed and hurried off the couch and over to Sydney. "It has been a pleasure meeting you," she said to Sebastian and Ali, feeling awkward standing there in her flannel nightgown, vulnerable and all too powerless.

"We'll talk again," Ali assured her.

"A pleasure running into you," Sebastian said with a teasing smile.

Sarina blushed with the reminder of their unusual meeting.

Sydney stood, lifting Lady Lily along with her, bringing Dagon and Sebastian to their feet, and she bid everyone good night. She reached out and took Sarina's arm and leaned close, whispering softly near her ear. The two left the room with whispers trailing them.

Dagon looked directly to Sebastian. "There will be no plotting against me."

"Like the way you did against me?"

"My plotting worked well."

"And you think mine wouldn't?"

"Boys, boys," Ali said sweetly, "if there's any plotting to be done, I will see to it."

"Good lord, you're in trouble now, Dagon," Sebastian said with a hardy laugh.

"Sit down," Ali ordered the two men. "Tell me about Sarina. She is quite lovely, utterly charming, and she appears young to the craft. Have you mated with her?"

The two men shook their heads and dropped back into their seats.

"That is none of your business," Dagon said.

"I don't know about that," Sebastian said. "Since you interfered in our relationship, I think it is only fair we interfere in yours."

Dagon found the situation amusing and smiled. "And do you think I would allow your interference?"

"Darling," Ali said on a dramatic sigh, "you have no choice."

Sebastian reached for another cup of tea and poured it the mortal way. "Now tell us about Sarina."

Sarina sat with her legs crossed in the middle of Sydney's bed while Sydney proceeded to change behind the painted wooden dressing screen that depicted the beauty of the highlands.

"Dagon knows nothing?" Sydney asked.

"Nothing," Sarina confirmed.

"Do you plan on telling him?"

Sarina rubbed the back of her aching neck. "Admitting my identity would do little good and perhaps would even hinder my chance at breaking the spell."

Sydney walked from around the screen, tying the royal purple velvet robe she wore securely at her waist. "You feel keeping yourself a mystery would better serve your purpose?"

"What good would the truth do me or him? It would only make a difficult situation more difficult. And besides, I look for—"

Sydney finished, "A love that is rare."

"Is there such a love?" Sarina asked as if her life depended on the answer.

"You ask me for advice?" Sydney seemed surprised.

"I feel lost," Sarina said candidly. "All that was familiar to me is gone. All I depended on is no longer. I feel like a babe just born with no place to turn."

"But you have loved before."

"Simple love yes, but then most of us are capable of that basic emotion. A love that is rare is almost impossible to find. It is said to exist, but yet I have never met anyone who claims to have experienced it."

"And do you think Dagon is capable of this love?"

Sarina laughed softly. "Strangely enough I sense that he himself searches for it."

"And you?" Sydney asked, sitting down at the bottom of the bed.

"My feelings for him frighten me."

"How so?"

"That's the problem," she said looking to Sydney with concerned eyes. "I don't know. My emotions are completely out of control when it comes to Dagon. I cannot understand my actions or reactions toward him, they make no sense. And then there are these feelings of safety and comfort when he is near, but the most disturbing emotion of all is the unrelenting need for intimacy with him."

Sarina shook her head at herself and continued. "Not just mating, but more." She sighed in frustration. "Does that make sense? This need to touch not only his naked body but deep within him, to reach out to his soul and touch on a level a rare few are ever able to do."

Sydney remained silent, sensing she wasn't finished.

"I ache for him more times than I care to admit or is even possible to act upon. It is an endless feeling of desire that haunts my body and soul." She cast Sydney a gentle pleading look. "With all my wisdom I don't know what to do?"

Sydney reached out and patted her hand. "I suggest you do nothing."

"That does not seem a wise choice."

"You once told me that not all choices are wise, some are necessary, though necessary choices often turn out to be the wisest ones of all."

"So nothing then is necessary?" Sarina asked.

"What other choice is there?"

Sarina grew silent in thought. Sydney pointed out the obvious. She could do nothing about Dagon, only herself. She had to trust her own emotions and not fear them, but let them take flight, let them soar, let them free. Only then would she truly discover what she searched for.

Fourteen

~

Dagon and Sebastian intended to roam the castle grounds. They were prepared for the brisk November weather dressed adequately and casually in heavy wool sweaters, turtlenecks, jeans, and boots.

They both decided early that morning, after very little sleep, that exercise would do their bodies and minds good, and besides Sebastian made it known that he would love to explore the castle grounds. The extensive gardens were too magnificent to ignore, and the surrounding woods held a hint of mystery and myth.

"We'll be back for lunch," Sebastian informed his wife, who stood at the front door hugging her arms against the chill that crept through her tan knit sweater and ankle-length skirt. He reached out and hugged her to him, running his hands up and down her back to chase away the chills.

She sighed her disappointment. "You could have slept a little longer."

Sebastian kissed her pouting lips. "We weren't sleeping."

"We would have"—she paused and returned his kiss with a little more fervor before adding—"eventually."

Dagon grinned. "Leave him be, Ali, the man needs his rest."

"Then he should be in bed," she insisted.

"He'll get no rest there." Dagon laughed and yanked Sebastian away from her. "Besides I have decided that your visit calls for a small dinner party. Be a dear and take care of the arrangements for me."

"A dinner party, how delightful," Ali said. "I'll take care of everything."

The two men were almost out the door when they both turned around and in unison said, "Stay out of the kitchen."

Ali did not take orders well; she went directly to the kitchen.

She was surprised to find Sydney there sitting at the table with Margaret, having tea.

"Good morning, dear," Sydney greeted her. "Do join us."

Ali sat and Margaret filled another cup with Earl Grey tea for her. Banana bread and apple spice loaf tempted Ali, and she decided on trying a small slice of each.

"Margaret is going to the market, and I have decided to join her. There are a few items I cannot get in the States, and besides it has been too many years since I've enjoyed the chaos of market shopping."

"Sounds delightful," Ali said. "Dagon just informed me that he intends to have a small dinner party while we are here, and he asked me to see to the arrangements."

"Oh, do invite the MacTavishes and the McEwans," Sydney said. "It has been too long since I've seen them, and Teresa McEwan and I share much history together."

"Bridie and William Douglas as well," Ali said, making mental notes of the names. "She and I tormented Dagon mercilessly when we were very young, not that we succeeded, though we had fun trying."

"Shall I see to the menu?" Margaret asked.

"Of course," Ali said. "Sebastian and Dagon have already warned me to stay out of the kitchen."

Sydney agreed. "Good advice."

"You can't be that bad," Margaret argued.

Sydney shook her head. "Even with her magical skills she cannot produce a decent meal."

"All right, so I am inept in the kitchen," Ali said and smiled. "I make up for it in other ways."

Both women laughed.

"Well, I think anyone can learn to cook," Margaret said. "And I have a favor to ask of you, Ali."

Ali beamed with pleasure. "Does it entail cooking?"

"A step toward learning to cook," Margaret corrected and stood. She retrieved a large ceramic bowl from the counter nearest the wall oven and returned to the table with it. "This is bread dough and in an hours' time it will need to be punched, reshaped, and set to rise again. Do you think you can do that for me?"

Ali peered at the lump of dough. "It doesn't sound like a difficult task. I just punch it once, shape it nicely into a ball, cover it, and that's it?"

"That's it, really quite a simple procedure," Margaret assured her.

Ali looked to Sydney. "I can do that."

"Are you sure? The preparation of food has never been your forte."

"If you have any problems, you can ask Sarina for help," Margaret said. "She has been helping me with the kitchen duties and has been doing quite well."

"A helping hand," Ali said with a smile. "How can I go wrong?"

Sydney grinned. "I don't know, my dear, but somehow you'll manage to."

The castle was quiet, the servants off busy with their chores, and Ali busy making her list for the dinner party when she recalled her task in the kitchen. With a squeal of delight she hurried into the kitchen and yanked the towel off the bowl filled with the ball of dough.

She pushed up her long sleeves and with a gleeful smile sent a stunning punch into the soft dough.

•   •   •

Sarina finished dusting. She had changed the sheets, made the bed, seen to the bathroom, and decided to dust, though the chore wasn't necessary. She actually looked for things to do in Dagon's quarters that would extend her daily chores. The man simply did not make a mess; he was neat and clean and there was hardly a thing for her to do.

And try as she might to be assigned other duties, Bernard absolutely refused her repeated requests. She was accustomed to keeping herself busy whether it was seeing to her own place, tending her expensive garden, having friends visit or visiting with friends, or simply enjoying the silence. She had always kept herself comfortably occupied.

Activity always helped her with her thoughts. While her hands were busy, her mind was focused, and she could reach many understandings in the process. Like now with her thoughts settled on what she had learned from Sydney the previous evening.

The brief conversation had helped her to realize that she could not control the situation, she had to allow the situation to proceed without interference. She had to trust herself and her beliefs even if some appeared foreign to her sensibilities.

The spell was quite specific, and if she had focused more on the casting of the spell, she would have been more prepared to deal with the consequences, but it was never too late. She would look with much wiser eyes now and see with much wider eyes, and she would allow the universe to work its magic.

"All finished, Lily," Sarina said to the kitten, who was as usual in the middle of the bed sleeping. She turned around to gather her cleaning bucket before reaching for Lily and stopped abruptly, her eyes stunned by the sight in the doorway.

"I have a problem I thought you could help me with," Ali said calmly. Gobs of dough were stuck to her face, hair, neck, and shoulders.

Sarina smiled, feeling she had finally met a kindred spirit. "Whatever happened to you?"

Ali held up a fist. "A small punch."

Sarina understood. "A delicate punch."

"Margaret never mentioned *delicate*, and I'm afraid I have simply ruined her bread dough, and try as I might my powers refuse to re-create the ball of dough."

Sarina completely understood. Margaret had requested her help this morning with baking the bread. It was her dough that Ali worked with, therefore rendering her powers useless. "Let's see what I can do to help."

"Oh, thank you," Ali said relieved. "I was so worried Margaret would return to a disaster, or heaven forbid, my husband and Dagon would return and see the mess I made. And after they ordered me to stay out of the kitchen." She shook her head.

"We'll have another batch of dough made in no time," Sarina reassured her and left a slumbering Lady Lily on the bed while she and Ali took off for the kitchen.

Dagon and Sebastian sat on a felled tree sipping hot cider from the thermos they had brought along with them.

"This is beautiful country," Sebastian said, relishing the breath-catching view of the mist-capped hills rising up behind Rasmus Castle. They had explored a good portion of the castle grounds when Dagon invited him to view his home in all its splendor. He had then brought him to a small rise that wound its way through the woods to a clearing. It was here the castle could be viewed in its entirety, and it was a magical sight to behold.

"It has been in your family for many years?" Sebastian asked.

"My family laid the first stone and a Rasmus has seen to its care ever since, but it has been no burden, rather a pleasure."

"You have modernized it over the years."

"A necessity, I assure you," Dagon said with a laugh.

"Modern amenities do come in handy, and I imagine a full staff is one of them," Sebastian said and poured Dagon more cider before refilling his own plastic mug.

"The castle's upkeep requires full attention."

"You only employ those of your kind?"

"A safety measure," Dagon confirmed, "and of course it serves well for those young witches who require extra training and or life experience."

"How did Sarina happen your way?"

Dagon admired, respected, and trusted Sebastian and felt comfortable discussing Sarina with him. "It's the damndest thing. Bernard said she appeared at the door looking for a position and one had just become available. Her references were excellent, her skills adequate, so he hired her."

"I take it her skills are less than adequate?"

Dagon rubbed at the back of his neck. "The incident last night made that obvious."

"You didn't even attempt to use your powers to save that teacup; you reacted as a mortal would."

Dagon cringed. "Please don't remind me."

"I thought your actions rather telling."

"How so?"

"You obviously understand Sarina well and reacted accordingly. You appear remarkably attuned to her."

Dagon glared at him as if he had just sprouted two heads. "Attuned?"

His obvious surprise brought a grin to Sebastian's face. "You react to each other as if you are intimate mates. She thinks nothing of resting her feet against you. You think nothing of rubbing her feet. She drops her cup, you retrieve it without thought. And most of all," he said with a gleeful rub of his hands against his mug, "you're jealous."

Dagon took exception to that remark. "I most certainly am not."

"You most certainly are. You looked about to kill me when I hugged her shivering body to me," Sebastian said with a nod. "Damn but it feels good to nod. It's your turn to shake your head, and might I add you are doing a good job at it."

"You're crazy," Dagon declared and held his head firm as he grabbed for the thermos of cider from Sebastian, wishing it was whiskey.

"I thought I was, though Ali does continue to drive me

insane at times. But you'll see for yourself that it's a wonderful kind of insanity.''

"Are you suggesting that I love Sarina?" Dagon asked incredulously.

"I am suggesting you open your eyes and discover for yourself whether you do or not.''

"She possesses none of the qualities I would look for in a mate,'' Dagon argued.

"Well, I certainly wouldn't have chosen a witch for a wife, but when love finds you, it contains no rhyme or reason. It arrives without fanfare or notice, creates chaos in your life, and then delivers a punch that knocks you senseless and from which you never recover.''

"I have received no such punch,'' Dagon insisted and downed the last of his cider.

Sebastian leaned over to him. "Then a word of warning, pal, be prepared, it's on its way.''

Dagon grew indignant. "I'm always prepared.''

"Not for love,'' Sebastian warned.

"I handled you and Ali quite nicely,'' Dagon reminded.

"Of which I am forever grateful to you, but we're talking about *you* and love.''

Dagon stood. "Of which I am entirely prepared. I am making plans to meet with a woman called the Ancient One.''

"Sydney mentioned something about her being very old.''

"And wise,'' Dagon said. "She is one who would suit me well. She possesses all the qualities and more that I want in a lifemate.''

Sebastian laughed.

"What's so funny?''

"Don't bother making a list of what you want in a wife, it doesn't work that way. We're sent the one we're supposed to join with, flaws and all.''

"Ali has flaws,'' Dagon challenged.

Sebastian stood and faced him head-on. "She most certainly does. Her biggest one being her abilities—or lack of—in the kitchen.''

They both took a moment to think that over.

"I think it's Margaret's day to go to market," Dagon said.

"I think we better get back," Sebastian suggested.

Dagon reached for the thermos. "We ordered her to stay out of the kitchen."

Sebastian shook his head. "Which means that's exactly where she is."

"Are you sure we can replicate the dough?" Ali asked.

"I have no doubt we can," Sarina assured her. "I helped Margaret blend the dough this morning and recall exactly what she did. With your help we can have another batch made in no time."

"About my help," Ali said as they entered the kitchen. "I am not very skilled in the preparation of food."

"I'm not very skilled at all," Sarina said, "but I think we're capable of making bread."

Ali sounded skeptical. "I don't know about that."

"I'm sure you'll be fine," Sarina encouraged. "Now help me gather the necessary items."

Flour soon covered the wooden tabletop, dusted the chairs, and was sprinkled over a good portion of the kitchen floor, not to mention the fine coat of flour that covered both Ali and Sarina.

"Recipes should be followed," Sarina attempted to explain for the umpteenth time.

"But it's all stuck together, it needs more flour," Ali insisted and tossed a handful of flour into the bowl.

Sarina held her patience. "It's suppose to be that way."

"Oh," Ali said and waved her finger over the bowl to undo what she had just done. "Has Margaret cast a protective spell over her kitchen? My powers refuse to work here."

"Let's do the best we can on our own."

"That could prove disastrous," Ali said.

Her lack of a smile and the last thirty minutes of working with Ali warned Sarina of that distinct possibility.

"I'll add more water," Ali offered and before Sarina

could stop her, she spilled a half a cup into the bowl on top of the flour, sending gobs of wet flour spraying all over them.

Sarina shook her head and sighed.

"My goodness," Ali said. "Cooking certainly can be dangerous."

"I never realized just how dangerous it could be," Sarina said, regretting her words when Ali's plentiful smile turned sorrowful.

"I'm no good in the kitchen. I try, but I never manage to succeed."

Sarina slipped her arm around her. "I'm even worse in everything I do. The only reason I know how to do this is because Margaret had the patience to show me. It took me weeks to learn how to peel a potato or carrot without scraping giant chunks out of them."

"Really?" Ali asked with renewed hope.

"Really," Sarina assured her with a gentle squeeze. "Now let's take another shot at this."

"You know what I was thinking?" Ali said, hurrying over to the large refrigerator, opening the door, and grabbing a jar to hold it up. "Cherries. I love cherries. Why don't we make it cherry bread?"

Sarina nodded, not believing she agreed. But then the kitchen was already a mess, the dough a disaster—what else could possibly happen?

Dagon and Sebastian heard the startled cries as they neared the back of the castle and took off on a dead run.

"Turn it off, turn it off!" Sarina screamed.

"How? How?" Ali yelled back, the motor on the electric mixer sounding like a motorboat and drowning out their words.

Flour, milk, and gobs of dough were shooting out everywhere, hitting Sarina and Ali, the cabinets, the walls, and even spatting against Margaret's cow clock.

Sarina attempted to approach the table and the angry machine. It spit out a wad of dough that stuck to her cheek, not to mention the gobs of the mess that already stuck to her hair and to her clothes.

She supposed she looked just as bad as Ali, who was covered from head to toe with the flying dough, was dusted with a film of flour, and looked completely at a loss of what to do next.

That's when the foolishness of their situation hit her, and she began to laugh.

Ali stared at her strange reaction, and as if finally understanding the absurdity of it all, she burst into a fit of laughter.

Dagon burst through the door first and wisely ducked as a lump of dough flew toward him, leaving it to hit Sebastian square in the forehead. Dagon laughed, though his humor was short-lived when he stood and was pelted in the face and chest with several gobs of gooey dough.

"Sarina!" he yelled and headed straight for her.

Sebastian wisely headed for the table using his arm as a shield. He grabbed for the projectile machine and rendered it helpless with the snap of a switch.

Ali held her hands up in surrender. "I thought my powers could right my wrongs, but Margaret must have a protective spell cast over her kitchen."

"I don't think it worked," Sebastian said, taking slow steps toward his wife as he wiped the gobs of dough from his face.

"It's all my fault," Sarina said, close to tears.

"Nonsense," Ali said. "I am absolutely clumsy in the kitchen. Sebastian knows that for a fact, and Dagon is also well aware of my lack of cooking skills."

Sarina's concern rushed over Dagon almost causing him to shudder. He felt her vulnerability and her isolation, and he ached to take her in his arms and chase her fears away. Instead he reached out and gently wiped a gob of dough from her cheek. "Ali made the worst mud pies as a child and has yet to improve."

Her smile, though faint, filled him with pleasure.

"Making a mess of my kitchen is one thing, Ali; making a mess of Margaret's kitchen is another," Sebastian warned and wiped a spot of dough from the corner of her mouth.

Ali's chin went up defiantly. "Sarina and I are not finished. The kitchen will look spotless by the time we're done."

Sarina came to her defense. "Ali's right. The kitchen will be returned to its usual spotless condition."

"And the bread will be rising—cherry bread," Ali said adamantly.

Sebastian laughed. "This I've got to see."

Dagon caught Sarina's sigh, empathizing with her momentary doubt, though she agreed with Ali. "Yes, there will be cherry bread for supper this evening."

He was impressed by her fortitude and courage to help a friend even when she thought the task impossible. She did not retreat or surrender; she remained strong and he was pleased by her unselfish actions.

"I suppose we should leave them to their task at hand," Dagon said to Sebastian. "We can clean ourselves up and drive over to Stirling for lunch, since the kitchen is presently out of service."

Sebastian kissed his wife. "Have fun, sweetheart." And he strolled out of the kitchen.

Dagon whispered near Sarina's ear, "You are quite beautiful, dear heart."

Both women stared at the retreating men. One making plans to bake cherry bread if it killed her, and one stunned by Dagon's remark and the sincerity in which it was delivered.

Fifteen

~

"More cherry bread?" Ali asked with a self-satisfied grin as she extended the basket across the table to her husband.

He accepted a piece with a suspicious sniff.

"It's absolutely delicious, dear," Sydney said, having broken off a small piece from the slice on her bread place and reaching to take another more generous one.

"It is," Dagon said with surprise after finishing a sample and deciding on a bigger slice.

Sebastian popped a piece into his mouth, and his taste buds raised a ruckus, demanding more of the deliciously flavored bread. "This is really good."

Ali beamed proudly. "I told you we would have cherry bread for supper."

"Margaret didn't help you?" Dagon asked, certain someone had lent an experienced hand somewhere.

"No," Ali assured him, "though I could have never baked such a marvelous-tasting bread without Sarina's help and firm kindness."

"Firm kindness," Sebastian repeated.

Ali thanked the server, who placed a bowl of steaming leek soup in front of her, and then continued with her explanation. "After you both left us in the kitchen, Sarina took charge. She told me that we were going to clean up the kitchen, and then I was going to make cherry bread under her strict supervision. I was to follow her every word and ask for her advice before I decided to alter the recipe. And you know it works quite well following a recipe.''

"You actually followed her instructions?'' Dagon asked, surprised.

"She can be quite persuasive, and in a strange way she seemed more knowledgeable when she took control of the messy situation. It was almost as if she were a wise teacher confronting an irate pupil that she was adequately equipped to handle.''

"You should have invited her to share supper with us,'' Sydney said and looked to Dagon sitting at the opposite end of the table. "I don't think Dagon would have minded.''

"Not at all, Sydney, she would be more than welcome to join us,'' he said and wished for her presence beside him.

"I asked her,'' Ali informed them, "but she said she had other plans.''

"What plans?'' Dagon asked, sitting straighter in his chair and intent on Ali's answer.

Ali shrugged. "Don't know, it wasn't my place to inquiry as to her personal business.''

Dagon wondered over her plans. Had she remained in the castle or had she gone out? And if so, where would she go? He was suddenly very curious.

Ali purposely changed the subject. "I am finalizing the dinner party plans. You will have ten guests here the night after tomorrow; all eagerly accepted and are looking forward to the evening. Margaret is seeing to the menu and no doubt will outdo herself as usual. Your staff is excellent in their duties. The silver is polished, the crystal and china shines, and the table linen is all ready for use. I requested that the gardener make certain there were fresh flowers for the dining table—''

Dagon interrupted. "Did Sarina say she was going out?''

Sydney, Sebastian, and Ali smiled, though Ali answered

him. "I really couldn't say, Dagon. She didn't mention what her plans were, and as I said I didn't feel I should snoop."

Dagon nodded but made no other reply.

"Is there anything else you feel that is needed for the party?" Ali asked, though she didn't wait for a reply. "I had thought to ask Sarina to join us, but I didn't think it was my place to invite her without your permission."

Dagon stood abruptly, nodding his head. "With all the help she gave you today, I think it would be only fitting to invite her."

Ali smiled sweetly at him. "Perhaps you should ask her now before she makes plans."

"A good idea," Dagon said, continuing his nod. "Please excuse me."

Sebastian laughed at his quick exit. "Poor guy, he's nodding and shaking his head. He's got it bad and doesn't even realize it. At least I knew I was crazy about you."

"But you took your sweet time in admitting it," Ali informed him, raising the bread basket across the table to him again.

"You're going to make me eat the whole loaf, aren't you?" he asked and snatched up another piece.

"Just think of it as if you were eating your own words," she advised him pleasantly.

Sebastian's smile was pure wicked. "No problem, sweetheart, I love cherries, especially yours."

Dagon entered the kitchen in a rush.

"Something I can do for you, sir?" Margaret asked, busy slicing the roasted lamb for the main course.

"Do you know where Sarina is? Ali said she mentioned something about having plans this evening."

"Those would be the same plans she has every Thursday evening, sir."

Dagon waited, concerned by her weekly rendezvous.

"She's in the laundry room doing her laundry," Margaret said and continued slicing the lamb.

Dagon breathed a sigh of relief. "That looks and smells delicious, Margaret."

"Thank you, sir, shall I wait to serve it?"

"No, continue to serve and advise my guests I will return momentarily."

Margaret nodded and smiled when he left the room. "An interesting day."

Sarina sat in one of the three wooden rockers provided for the staff that chose to wait until their clothes finished washing and drying instead of running up and down the many flights of steps. Lady Lily slept peacefully in the wicker laundry basket on top of Sarina's freshly laundered flannel nightgown.

She had changed into comfortable clothes, a long brick-red knit jumper with an ivory cotton tee beneath and thick ivory socks on her feet. She disliked confining her feet to shoes and went barefoot whenever possible or wore socks, which kept her shoe selection extremely limited. She pinned her hair up with a clip and as usual stubborn strands fell loose to tease her neck. She brought a book to occupy her time, though her jumbled thoughts did not allow for concentration.

The rocking motion soothed her, and she gave free rein to her disturbing thoughts and the words that haunted her mind.

You are quite beautiful, dear heart.

Why had he told her that? When he leaned down to whisper in her ear, she had been prepared for a scolding, and his words took her completely by surprise. And it wasn't only his words that had startled her but the sincerity in which he delivered them. He had meant every word. Truly and honestly he thought her beautiful.

She sighed, drawing her legs up to rest on the seat edge of the rocker, wrapping her arms around them and resting her head on her knees. She had to remain patient and yet she wanted so badly for him to take her in his arms and love her.

Love.

When had it become so important in her life? Her long life had always been busy, active, and happy. She had many friends and had a few relationships along the way. And *love* had simply been a word. Now love was an emotion that tore at her heart, touched her soul, and made her act foolishly.

Foolishness was not something she was accustomed to and yet—she smiled. She enjoyed those unexpected moments with Dagon. Magical moments. When he lost his senses as badly as she did and they surrendered to their unbridled desires. *Almost* surrendered.

She wondered what it would be like to completely surrender to him. To release her fear, her doubt, and her vulnerability. An unconditional love that held no promise or commitment only love in its purest form.

Was that what she truly wanted? To disregard the spell and love him whether he could help her or not? And if he couldn't, would she be able to walk away from him in the end?

The sad thought brought a tear to her eye.

"Sarina."

His gentle familiar voice startled her, and her feet slipped off the rocker so swiftly that the sudden movement caused the rocker to jerk forward, smacking her in the back of the head.

"Damn," she heard him say and he rushed toward her.

He went down on bended knees in front of her, his hand going to the back of her head to tenderly survey the damage. But it was the tear that fell from her eye that brought another "damn" to his lips.

He wiped the lone tear off her cheek with his finger. "Are you all right?"

How did she tell him that now that he was here she was fine? That his presence was a necessity in her life? That she wanted nothing more than to be with him here and now and if possible forever?

So this was love?

Another tear slipped from her eye. No one had ever warned her that it would hurt so much.

"I'm fine," she said quickly, not trusting her voice.

"I'm sorry," Dagon said. "It's all my fault."

She stared at him. Why did she sense that he wasn't talking about the bump on her head?

"I should have been more careful, more attentive, more—"

She stopped him with a finger to his lips. "It's all right."

He kissed her finger and moved her hand away. "No, it's not."

He kissed her then, a gentle, soft, and achingly tender kiss as though he were afraid she would break or fade away from him. His hands reached up and cupped her face, and after a lingering brush of his lips over hers, he rested his forehead to hers.

"Whatever am I going to do with you, Sarina?"

"Whatever you'd like?" she invited freely.

He pulled back to look into her eyes, his hands still cupping her face. "Don't tempt me."

"Why? You forever tempt me."

"And what if I invited you to do whatever you liked?"

"Then we tempt fate," she said softly. "Do you have the courage?"

"Now you issue me a challenge," he said with a brief laugh and a smile that melted her insides.

"Do you accept?" she asked hopefully.

He gave her a quick kiss and said, "I never turn down a challenge."

Her smile was teasing. "I rather thought you didn't."

He looked about to kiss her and grew hesitant, his hands falling away from her face to rest in her lap.

"You think of your plans," she said, knowing his troubled thoughts and also knowing that he questioned them.

"You brought chaos to my orderly world."

She wanted to kiss him badly but instead ran her finger over his tempting lips. "Perhaps it was your orderly world that brought the chaos."

He looked at her oddly, losing himself in the depths of her amazing soft blue eyes. They imprisoned him and yet freed him, and they made him feel alive with every bit of his senses and every breath he took.

Kiss me, Dagon, please kiss me.

He heard her soft plea in his mind, and it echoed down to his soul. Without thought or reason he stood, grabbed her around the waist, and lifted her up, his mouth meeting hers.

The kiss shocked them senseless, rationale thought escaped them, blind passion devoured them. He carried her to the washing machine and sat her down hard on top of it. His hands rushed down her legs and up her jumper all the while his mouth continued to feed with hers. Two hungry souls aching for the nourishment of love.

His fingers squeezed along her thighs and slipped between her legs with an eager roughness that excited them both. He worked one finger beneath the edge of her panties, finding her already swollen nub of passion and tormenting it beyond reason.

She moaned and tore her mouth away from his, her head falling back and her sensual moans resonating around him, fueling his own feverish emotions. His fingers moved to swiftly enter her, and she cried out at the sheer pleasure of his determined entrance.

She moaned, his fingers working their magic so fast and furiously that she was sure to climax, and she cried out to him, "Dagon, please, I'll—"

"Come," he urged, "I want you to."

His fingers turned frantic and his whispered urgings pushed her over the edge. She climaxed fast and furiously, her satisfied cries filling the room. When she thought it over and a final shudder drifted away, he ran his thumb intimately over her one more time causing a small yet powerful climax to shudder her entire body.

He pulled her to him, her head dropping to rest on his shoulder, her legs draped limply at his sides and her arms barely able to hold on to him.

He brushed a kiss over her lips. "I like the feel of you when you come."

She breathed a heavy sigh and shivered in his arms.

He held her close and whispered in her ear, "You did say whatever I liked."

She nodded against his shoulder, her breath laborious, her heart pounding, and her body pleasured beyond reason.

"You drive me to the brink of insanity, Sarina," he said, nibbling at her neck.

She sighed, her skin still tingling from the aftermath of her climax, and her reply was barely audible. "Then join me in this madness, for I want no one else."

He looked into her eyes and saw the sweet gratification he had given her, and he shook his head. "You were not part of my plans."

"Nor you mine." She kissed him gently and urged, "Come tempt fate with me."

He shook his head again, and she knew he attempted to shake sense into himself. She would not push, nor grow impatient. She had made her choice, and now he must make his. And she must accept the consequences.

She offered him time. "Think on this, Dagon, for the next time we come together, it will be a complete joining or none at all. And the decision will ultimately be yours."

Dagon sat alone in the small receiving parlor, brandy in hand and his eyes intent on the low flame burning in the hearth. He had not fared well at all after leaving Sarina in the laundry room.

He returned to his guests after freshening himself and found his mind constantly wandering to Sarina and his conversation with his dinner guests sorely limited. She tormented his thoughts and his heart, not to mention his emotions. He did not know what to do about this unexpected situation. He had thought his plans were set, his future basically secured, and now?

He wanted to throw his hands up in surrender to a blue-eyed, powerless witch.

He was crazy.

"Troubled thoughts?"

Dagon looked to the doorway with a smile, and he held an inviting hand out to Ali. She hurried to the sofa to join him, her bare feet peeking out from beneath her long white silk robe. She cuddled beside him on the couch, stealing his glass to sip at his brandy.

"You torment yourself, you know," she said, handing the glass back to him.

"I don't recall asking for advice."

"You need it."

He laughed. "From you?"

Her expression softened to one of concern. "I owe you, Dagon, for all the scrapes and troubles you got me out of, for all the times you have protected me even against myself, and for always being there like a big brother and loving me no matter how irrational or how foolish I act. You're like a brother to me and I love you and I want you to find a love as rare and magical as the one I share with Sebastian."

Her words touched him, and he hugged her to him. "I love you, too, and you are a sister to me in heart and soul. The first day we met when your parents visited here with mine and left us to play by the mermaid pond, I knew I would spend the rest of my life looking out for you."

"It was your fault I fell into that pond," she said with a playful poke to his ribs.

Dagon smiled. "I wasn't the one looking for a toad you insisted you could make fly."

"You told me there were toads in there."

"No, I told you there *might* be, but as usual you leaped before you looked."

Ali laughed. "And you got all wet saving me."

"And scolded for not watching you properly."

"Your own fault for telling me there were toads in the pond," she said and snatched his brandy glass to take another sip.

Dagon shook his head and snatched his brandy glass back when she finished sipping. "I envy the love you share with Sebastian."

Ali remained quiet, knowing he needed to talk.

"I think that's why I wanted so badly to help the both of you. After watching your heart almost break and Sebastian hurt with the pain of loving you yet feeling himself helpless, I realized you both shared a love worth saving. It also gave me reason to pause and examine my own life.''

"You want love," she said, understanding his need.

"So badly that it frightens me," he admitted. "And I had thought to secure it for myself and yet now I wonder if I do the right thing.''

"If you question it, then perhaps you have your answer.''

He tapped her nose with his finger. "How did you become so wise?''

She smiled with appreciation and love. "My big brother taught me.''

"If he's so bright, why does he feel so stupid?''

"Love can rob you of your senses.''

"How did you know you loved Sebastian and wanted him for a lifemate?'' he asked seriously.

Ali answered just as earnestly. "I knew the moment I looked into his eyes. I could see and feel the love. Oh, how I felt it, Dagon. It wrapped around me and invaded my heart and soul.''

"You were that certain?''

"Love doesn't come with a guarantee or a refundable receipt.''

"Then how—''

"Could I be certain that I loved Sebastian?'' she finished and answered quickly, "I made a choice and took a chance.''

"On love," Dagon confirmed.

"Yes, that's all any of us can do, whether witch or mortal.''

"I thought I knew of love, but . . .'' He shook his head.

"Don't look to know love, Dagon, free yourself to feel it.'' She kissed him on the cheek. "I'd better get back to Sebastian.''

"You mean you *want* to get back to Sebastian,'' Dagon said with a grin.

"That's love, darling,'' she said with a smile and a pat to his cheek. "Try it.''

She hurried out of the room and up the stairs. Her robe fell to the carpet after shutting the door to their room, her nightgown followed, and she slipped naked into the bed.

Sebastian's eager arms greeted her. "Is he feeling any better?"

She cuddled against him, running her leg up and down his, the tiny bell on her toe ring chiming. "I don't know, I hope so, but it wouldn't hurt for you to speak with him."

"Not now," he said firmly.

Ali laughed softly and ran her hand over his body until she cupped him intimately. "No, darling, not now."

Sixteen

"Has anyone seen Sarina?" Dagon asked of anyone who could provide an answer when he entered the formal dining room.

Several servants shook their heads and returned to their tasks.

Ali, who was seeing to the seating arrangements for the dinner party that evening, said, "You've lost her?"

"Something needs to be found before it can be lost," Dagon informed her, attempting to keep the irritation out of his voice. He had searched for Sarina for a better part of an hour and had not been able to locate her. He had wanted to invite her to the dinner party this evening. He felt it only right she attend after having been of so much help to Ali—at least that was the excuse he gave himself. If he were honest with himself, which he was trying to avoid, he would admit that he wanted her with him tonight.

Ali cleared her throat to revive his attention.

He shook his head, shaking himself from his mental stupor.

Her charming smile warned him that her words intended to impact. "We often don't realize we've found something until it hits us square in the face."

Dagon looked about to retaliate when he suddenly shook his head, thinking better of it, and walked out of the room. He met up with Sebastian in the foyer. He looked relaxed and refreshed, his cheeks full of color from the crisp fresh air and his jeans stained with the rich soil of Mother Earth. He held an armful of freshly cut white mums.

"Sarina?" he asked, as if Sebastian was his last hope.

Sebastian told him what he knew. "Last I saw of her was this morning with Margaret in the kitchen."

"I have already looked there," Dagon said, sounding extremely disappointed.

"Is something wrong that you're looking for her?"

Dagon glanced around the large foyer, making certain no one lurked about, and then spoke low to Sebastian. "I want to invite her to the dinner party tonight."

"You mean you have yet to extend her an invitation?" Sydney asked from the top of the steps.

"Now you're in for it," Sebastian said with a laugh and left Dagon on his own.

Dagon knew better than to disregard Sydney's question, and he walked to the bottom of the staircase and politely waited for her to descend before he answered. And besides it gave him time to formulate an answer.

"I will have the truth," she said to him and held out her hand as she reached the last step.

"You're intruding," Dagon said as politely as possible and took her hand, slipping her arm through his and walking with her to the receiving parlor, where he wasn't surprised to see tea and biscuits waiting.

"No, dear boy, you are not concentrating, you have left yourself open."

He sighed and rubbed at the back of his aching neck after assisting Sydney to sit on the small sofa and then sitting down beside her. "I can't seem to think straight of late. My thoughts go here, there, and everywhere."

"Without focus and awareness we see and hear nothing," Sydney said like a schoolteacher reminding a student of an important lesson. She went on as if continuing the lesson. "I am sure if you focus, you will realize Sarina's whereabouts, instead of acting like a witless witch."

"You are scolding me," he said, accepting the direct reprimand as a loving gesture.

Sydney shook her finger at him but once. "I remind, never scold—even when scolding is necessary."

Dagon smiled and reached his hand out to take hers, so slim and delicate and yet possessed of a power and a wisdom that he hoped to attain one day. "I once told Sebastian to be foolish, for in his foolishness he would find the answer. Should I now be foolish?"

Sydney gave his hand a comforting pat. "What does your heart tell you, dear boy?"

"I'm not sure."

Sydney spoke softly. "Then you aren't listening."

Dagon grew annoyed and slipped his hand from Sydney to once again rub at his neck.

"Your mind and heart war," she said soothingly.

"Constantly," he confirmed in a heavy sigh. "One minute I convince myself that I am doing the right thing, making the right decision, and then the next moment I'm confused and concerned that my decision is wrong. I have never been this indecisive in my entire life. I always knew what I wanted and went after it. I never questioned myself, my actions, my decisions. I was always firm in my beliefs and abilities, and now . . ." His words drifted off with a shake of his head.

"Now suddenly you are mindless," Sydney said, and Dagon's shaking head turned to a nod. "Then what you are telling me is that you simply cannot listen."

"That's it," Dagon said in relief. "I can't listen, I can't hear, and I feel as if I am blind to the obvious. Presently everything fails me."

"The heart and soul never fail us," Sydney advised. "And it is at those times when we feel the most vulnerable, alone, or lost that they work their magic, but only if we believe."

"So what you're saying is that the answers are there."

"Waiting for you to discover," she said with a smile.

"And drive me crazy."

Sydney's smile remained, as did her patience. "Discovering is half the fun."

"It's frustrating."

"It's fascinating."

"It's senseless," he insisted

"It's significant," she assured.

He smiled this time. "It's laughable."

Sydney's steady smile widened. "It's love."

Dagon stood abruptly. "I know where Sarina is."

"Then go, dear boy."

He did, but not before apologizing for his hasty departure and giving her a grateful kiss on the cheek.

Dagon watched Sarina chase the little ball of fur around the mermaid pond. They romped and played like two children. She wore the brick-red knit jumper she had on the other day in the laundry room, only this time she wore a tan turtleneck beneath it and a heavy tan wool sweater over it. And though the day was chilled by a touch of winter wind, she was barefoot.

His eyes caught on the gentle curve of her slender ankles, and he got the sudden urge to kiss her right there on that curve, to rest his eager lips against her pale skin, to stroke the curve with his tongue, and to slowly work his way up her leg until he could finally taste all of her.

He sensed that she saw him, that her movement had stilled, and that she watched him with the same sensual intensity that he watched her. His glance drifted slowly up her body, and he walked toward her with an arrogant gait that all but announced that he wanted her.

The wind swept at his black overcoat, fanning it out; it wiped through his hair, sweeping several silky strands across his cheek; and it whooshed against the dark gray sweater he wore, flattening it against his hard midsection.

He was a sight to behold, and Sarina's heart skipped several beats, her breath threatened to lock in her throat, and her hormones decided to surge and soar completely out of control. Her only choice of defense against herself was firm action, so she scooped up a startled and protesting Lady Lily and walked directly toward him.

"You wanted me," she said almost breathless.

Want could not near describe his desire for her, and he wasn't even certain if *desire* was an accurate word. He couldn't quite explain his emotions to himself. They raged, roared, and reared near out of control every time he was in close proximity to her. And close proximity was where he wanted her. He worried about her, grew anxious when he could not locate her, and then grew mindless when he did.

And the more he pondered his dilemma, the more he wondered if love had anything to do with his insanity.

"I was looking for you," he finally answered, stopping only a few feet from her.

"You needed something?"

Why did her simple questions sound sensual? He ignored his *need* and answered her. "I wish to invite you to the dinner party this evening. You were more than helpful to Alisande the other day, and I think it would be only fitting that you join us for the evening festivities."

Sarina began walking toward the castle, Lady Lily quiet in her arms. If he had invited her, simply invited her, because he wished her to be there with him, she would have accepted his invitation immediately. However, his invitation sounded like a gesture of appreciation for a job well done, and she had helped Ali out of basic kindness and because she liked her. It had turned into an enjoyable afternoon, not to mention a memorable one, and she wanted to remember it as such.

"I don't think it would be proper," she said as she continued to walk.

He easily matched her hurried strides. "Why not?"

"I am a servant here at Rasmus Castle, and a servant does not attend an employer's dinner party."

Dagon could not believe that she refused his invitation, and his voice turned firm. "If I wish one of my servants to attend a function in the castle, that is my decision."

"It is unseemingly," Sarina persisted.

"Regardless, you'll come anyway," he ordered.

"I don't think so."

Her refusal stopped him dead in his tracks.

She kept walking.

His groan was one of agitation as he hurried to catch up with her. "I know so. Be in the large parlor by eight this evening dressed and ready for the dinner party."

This time she stopped walking, and he halted right alongside her. "And if I refuse?"

"You do not have the option," he informed her bluntly. "And I will not hear another word on the matter."

She stamped her foot like an irate child and immediately regretted her rash actions. She winced, cried out, and stumbled, and he instantly reached out to grab her arm.

"What's wrong?" he demanded, his arm going around her waist to support her tilting body.

"My foot," she said, and before she could explain further, she was swiftly scooped up into his arms.

Bernard shook his head when they entered the kitchen. Margaret smiled with a nod and continued her baking, and two servant girls giggled near the sink where they prepared the fresh vegetables.

"A footbath, antiseptic, and bandages, Bernard," Dagon ordered and proceeded straight through the kitchen without another word.

He took her to his study. She loved it there, the musty smell of the old books, the antiques so familiar to her, his scent so rich and potent in every corner, in every piece of furniture, in every part of the room. His essence resided here, and it was warm, welcoming, and loving.

He placed her on the chair nearest the fire that had dwindled to mere embers. He took a sleeping Lady Lily from her arms and placed her on the soft cushioned stool directly next to the hearth. She meowed once at him and promptly settled back to sleep. He then added a large log to the hearth, and the dying embers quickly caught hold of the dried wood and burst into a bright blazing flame that reached out to heat the drafty room to a toasty warmth.

He removed his overcoat, flinging it across a chair, and

relieved her of her bulky wool sweater. He then balanced himself on bended knees to examine her foot.

With a tender touch and a close eye he surveyed the sole of her foot, brushing away debris that had lodged itself to her skin. Her sole was remarkably soft for a woman who did not care for footwear, and her toes were long and slender like her ankle. She actually had beautiful feet.

His eyes spied the culprit, and he wiped the area around the tender spot, announcing, "Splinter."

He placed her foot on the floor, retrieved the wide mahogany leather ottoman that matched the high-back chair near the window, setting it in front of her and lifting both legs to rest upon it. He then went to the desk, browsed through a couple of drawers, and returned with tweezers in hand.

He sat on the wide ottoman and rested her foot in his lap. "I'll try not to hurt you."

"I trust you," she said and she did explicitly. He would never intentionally inflict pain on her or cause her to suffer in any way, of that she was certain.

He probed the inflicted area with the greatest of care, and she felt only the slightest of pressure and a few brief pinpoints of pain, but nothing that was not bearable. And besides, his hand wrapped securely around her ankle got more of her attention than the splinter removal.

His hand was firm, his intentions clear, he would not let her go. He grasped her ankle as if she belonged to him, and no amount of debating, arguing, or discussion would change his intentions. She sighed with the pleasure of his stubbornness.

"I hurt you?" he asked, concerned.

"No," she said, "your touch is tender and painless."

He unconsciously stroked the curve of her ankle. "Relax, I'll have the stubborn sliver out in no time."

She rested her head back and kept a steady eye on him. She recalled the many times she thought of a lifemate, recording list after extensive list of qualities she desired in such a man. Features were not at the top of her list. Handsome was not a quality she searched for in a mate. Trust was important. She wanted to be able to trust her mate with her deepest darkest thoughts. She wanted to share her dreams and nightmares with him, and she wanted the same from him.

Wisdom was another important quality. Life wisdom. She had hoped he would have gained knowledge throughout his many years, enhancing his heritage and powers.

And she hoped, prayed, her mate would want many children. She loved children and wanted a castle full.

Bernard entered the study after a brief knock and just as Dagon yanked the sliver of wood from the sole of her foot. She bit on her lower lip to prevent herself from crying out, the wood having been embedded more deeply than she had thought and the extraction a bit more painful than she expected.

He gently stroked the top of her foot. "Are you all right?"

She nodded and attempted a smile.

"Liar," he accused softly.

Bernard placed the requested items beside Dagon on the floor. "Will there be anything else, sir?"

"No, Bernard, thank you," he answered, and with a stiff posture Bernard left the room.

"Why do you go barefoot or shoeless so often?" Dagon asked, moving the ottoman and arranging the footbath so that Sarina could soak her injured foot.

"I like the feel of Mother Earth; her energy refreshes and revives."

He placed her foot in the square plastic tub, holding firmly to her ankle. "You must have played often in the woods when you were young."

"I still do," she said with pride.

"You are young, the young favor the woods," he said and reluctantly released her ankle and retrieved the other items off the floor.

"The woods know no age difference."

"You're right," he agreed, "but the young love to romp and play in the woods. They are forever entertaining the fairies with their antics. The wiser witches seek solace in the woods. It is there in the silence that they learn and further develop the craft.''

She sounded disappointed. ''You don't play in the woods anymore?''

''I seek the woods when necessary for growth and direction, for casting particular spells, for ceremonies—''

She interrupted him, ''But not to play?''

''I'm all grown up, if you haven't noticed,'' he teased.

She leaned forward in her seat. ''You are never too grown up to play in the woods.''

He grinned and brushed his lips over hers. ''You're right, and I know a delightful game we could play in the woods.''

To his surprise she returned his teasing. ''Will you teach me?''

''Any time,'' he offered and reached down to remove her foot from the tub, returning it to his lap, which was now covered with a thick terry towel. ''When I'm finished here with you, you are to go directly to your room and get ready for this evening.''

She was about to protest when he raised a hand. ''Don't bother, you're attending the dinner party, and that is my final word on the matter.''

She attempted to argue. ''I still think it would be best if—''

''—you obeyed me in this matter,'' he finished and placed a bandage across the sole of her foot.

She again attempted to protest. ''The other servants—''

''—obey me as they should and as will you.'' He stood and extended his hand out to her. She took it cautiously. ''I appreciate what you did for Ali, and I wish to thank you.'' He paused and grinned. ''Besides, it is safer to have you eating at the table than serving at it.''

She couldn't help but laugh, his remark being truthful. ''Though I object, I will do as you say.''

''A wise choice,'' he commended with a wink and walked her to the door. ''I look forward to this evening with you.''

''I will attempt not to disappoint,'' she said, not certain whether she meant to reassure him or herself.

He leaned his head down, his lips not far from hers. "You never disappoint me, Sarina, you excite, enliven, and enchant me."

His kiss was as unexpected as were his words, and she remained speechless long after the kiss ended. He turned her around, gave a squeeze to her waist, and whispered in her ear, "Hurry and get ready so you can join me for a drink before everyone arrives."

She was out the door and down the hall when she realized she had forgotten Lily. She turned to see Dagon standing in the doorway.

"I will see to Lady Lily and you will see to getting dressed."

She smiled, nodded, and walked off without a limp to a light step.

His calling out her name stopped her once again. "Sarina."

She turned her head.

"Wear shoes."

She laughed and said, "I'll think about it." And then she took off before he could call out to her again.

Excitement quickened her steps. She was thrilled with the prospect of attending the party this evening, but more thrilled to be spending the evening with Dagon.

His company was fast becoming a habit that she discovered was worth the risk. How this whole dilemma would turn out, she didn't know, and at the moment she didn't care. A strange thought, since her journey had a specific goal. That goal presently was not important to her; Dagon was. If the two should merge, then that would be wonderful. If not? She would face that answer when necessary.

She entered the kitchen and was immediately struck with an overwhelming sense of guilt. Margaret was busy preparing the food as she always did, the mortal way. Two young servant girls helped, but there was so much to do.

She did the only thing she could do. "Can I help?" she asked.

"I could use the extra hands," Margaret answered gratefully.

Sarina pitched in, doing whatever Margaret asked of her. When the two girls were ordered to help with the final preparations in the dining room, Sarina shared her excitement about the evening ahead with Margaret.

"Do you have something to wear?" Margaret asked, seeming pleased by the news and eager to help her.

"I've been debating over two dresses, and I think the plain winter white one would be my best choice," Sarina said, certain her black dress would not suit the occasion and might give Dagon ideas.

"White would look lovely on you, though I think black would go remarkably well with your coloring."

Sarina thought her remark strange. Margaret knew black was a sacred color and worn only by a chosen few and the wise ones. Why would she suggest black and why comment that it would look well on her?

Did she suspect something?

Bernard entered the kitchen looking perturbed. "Sarina, you will help serve dinner this evening."

"But I—"

"Don't bother to offer any excuses, none are acceptable. And while you would be my last choice for this assignment, I have no choice in the matter. Two of the servers have taken ill, and you are the only one available, the other staff members already having left for their evening off."

Sarina sent a silent plea of help to Margaret. She shook her head as if informing her that she had no choice but to do as directed.

"Wear your hair up," Bernard ordered. "There are extra serving uniforms in the garment room, and for heaven's sake handle every dish with extra care this evening. Now hurry and get ready, much needs tending."

Sarina did as she was told. A quick shower, a hasty twist and pin of her hair, and only a minute or two to slip on gray stockings, a slim gray skirt, a gray blouse with a plain white collar, and a tailored white apron tied securely around her waist, and she was almost ready. The last item, gray low-heeled pumps, did not at all appeal to her, and with the bottom of her foot tender they held even less appeal.

She cast her comfort aside and slipped the shoes on,

With a wince and a groan she hurried from her room.

Dagon looked at the clock on the mantel for the third time. She was fifteen minutes late, and he was annoyed.

Stolen moments alone with her was what he was hoping for, and with the sounds of Sydney, Ali, and Sebastian approaching the parlor, it looked as though his plans were about to falter.

He walked to the door and held his hand out to Sydney. "You look as beautiful as ever."

"And you, dear boy, are as charming as ever, even though annoyed," she said softly and took his arm to walk to the sofa.

"Can I keep nothing from you," he said in a whisper near her ear.

"Nothing," she whispered back and smoothed the blue silk of her long skirt and matching jacket. A strand of diamonds and sapphires hugged her neck and sparkled at her ears, her hair being swept back and up in an intricate braid so as to show off the eye-catching gems.

Ali took a chair by the hearth, her ankle-length, pure white wool dress caressing every curve of her slender body. Long strands of tiny pearls hung from each ear almost to her shoulders and her blond hair was a creation of utter confusion that looked remarkably stunning on her.

"You look extra special tonight, Dagon," Ali said with a teasing smile and accepted the glass of white wine her husband offered her.

He had taken extra time and care with his appearance this evening. He always made certain to look his best, but tonight he wanted to look his best for Sarina. He wore a white wool suit with a matching vest. His white collarless shirt was embroiled down the front in a Celtic design and his long dark hair fell over his shoulders in stark contrast to the white.

Sebastian came to his rescue, announcing, "I think we all look terrific." And raised his glass of wine in a toast.

"That we do, darling," Ali agreed and swept an appreciative glance over him before joining in the toast. "And

I'm so happy you chose to wear light gray instead of your usual dark colors.''

"I agree," Dagon said, "you look good." And Sebastian did, the light gray wool suit fitting him handsomely, and the darker gray shirt and silver tie made for an excellent combination and highlighted his darker features.

"Now all we need is for Sarina to join us and complete our perfectly delightful ensemble," Ali said jokingly.

As if cue Sarina entered the parlor, silver tray in hand.

Seventeen

~

"Wrong attire for a dinner party, dear heart," Dagon said with an edge of annoyance.

Sarina entered the room ignoring all but Dagon. She went directly to him, and he stood as she approached, reaching out and snatching the serving tray from her hand. He held it out to Sebastian, who took it with a smile and played servant, offering the delectable choice of appetizers to his wife and Sydney.

"Two of the servers took ill and the other staff members have left for the evening, I had no choice," Sarina explained, sounding as disappointed as Dagon did annoyed. "Bernard instructed me to follow his orders and would hear no excuses."

Dagon softened his tone. "Did you make Bernard aware of the fact that you were to attend tonight's gathering?"

"I tried," she said, "but he was upset and—"

Dagon finished for her. "—you felt guilty about not helping."

"Yes, I did," she admitted.

The doorbell prevented any further discussion, though Ali did offer a solution. "Perhaps we can all share a night-cap later this evening."

"Sounds great to me," Sebastian said, helping himself to another cheese puff.

Dagon scowled at him, and Sebastian popped another puff into his mouth.

"Me, too," Sarina agreed, though looked to Dagon for confirmation.

The offer appeased though no way satisfied Dagon, but there was little he could do. He acquiesced with a nod.

Sarina smiled her thanks to Ali and Sebastian and acknowledged Sydney with a gentle nod. She then hurried to see to her duties.

"Sarina," Dagon said as she reached the door.

She turned and knew immediately his thoughts.

"Be *very* careful this evening."

Her smile faded and she said softly, "Yes, sir."

Three pairs of eyes fell on him accusingly when he turned around, and he shook his head and reached for his wineglass.

Sarina was grateful that all was going well. Granted, the appetizers had only been served and the remainder of the full course meal had yet to be delivered, but making it through the beginning without any incidents gave her hope that all would proceed smoothly.

Margaret filled the soup tureen with the tasty leek and carrot soup, and Sarina sniffed the scented air appreciatively. "You make the best soups, Margaret."

"I made extra, and as soon as the guests set to enjoying the main course, you and Janey can help yourself to whatever your taste buds favor," Margaret said, placing the silver ladle in the flowered china tureen and securing the top on it. "Are you certain you feel comfortable serving this?"

Where Bernard could be critical of her work, Margaret was concerned; even Janey had offered to do more than her share of the serving. They were obviously concerned that she might falter and make a scene that would embarrass Dagon and make matters worse for herself.

But she was determined that nothing should go wrong. She was extra careful and cautious of her every move, and so far her precautions had paid off, and she would continue to see that the evening proceeded without incident.

"I can serve the soup without a problem," she said confidently.

"I'll help," Janey offered, entering the kitchen with the empty appetizer plates. "Four hands are better than two."

Sarina was not about to lose her newly gained confidence. "I'll serve, you can hold the tureen."

Janey nodded, grabbed the serving pot holders, and lifted the china tureen, and together they left the kitchen.

Dagon sat at one end of the table and Sydney at the other, Sebastian and Ali sat on either side of Sydney with Teresa McEwan beside Sebastian and her husband Eden beside Ali. Bridie and William Douglas followed and John and Catherine MacTavish sat on either side of Dagon.

Conversation drifted around the table sprinkled with laughter and highlighted with contented smiles. Dagon loved to entertain especially good company, and the people gathered around his impressive table were old and dear friends.

There was, however, one person missing whom he had wanted to share the evening with, Sarina. He wanted her at his table, not serving his guests, and yet she was a servant in his castle and not a very good one at that.

He had wondered over her inadequate abilities and her sudden appearance at his doorstep, and the longer he debated the issue the more he thought that there was more to her than she revealed. He thought her a young witch in need of guidance and practice, and yet there were times she possessed the wise ways of an older more experienced witch.

And then there was the problem of her wrongs not being able to be made right. He had researched the problem, looking for various reasons for such an occurrence, and there were several ranging from an insignificant problem that could be overcome with time and proper training to the most severe, that being a powerful spell.

He was never one to dismiss anything without further

investigation, and he planned to do just that until he found the answer.

Conversation turned to the coming holiday, the Winter Solstice, and the many activities planned. All recalled past holidays of fun and pleasure and hopes of future ones to come. Everyone was so engrossed with talk that no one paid attention to Sarina and Janey when they entered the room, none that was, except Dagon.

He was relieved to see that she did not carry the soup tureen, though when he realized she would be the one to serve, he almost cringed. He silently berated himself for not having any confidence in her, especially since she appeared confident.

Her obvious self-confidence filled him with pleasure, and he relaxed, watching her approach Sydney. The gray slim skirt hugged her round backside, and the white apron accented her narrow waist. The gray blouse was a bit too large for her and hid the swell of her handful-size breasts, and the idea that they were concealed, hidden away from him, enticed him all the more.

His eyes followed her graceful movements, and he was suddenly anxious for the evening to pass and for them to be alone. Alone to talk, alone to touch, alone to tempt fate.

He smiled and decided exactly how he wanted the evening to end.

Sarina caught Dagon's sinful smile, sensed his heated desires, and did all she could to ignore them. Now was not the time for her thoughts to turn lusty. She needed her wits and senses about her. She would not embarrass herself nor Dagon with less than skillful hands this evening.

She chased all thoughts from her mind and focused on her chore at hand, pouring the soup into each guest's bowl. She began with Sydney.

"It smells delicious, dear," Sydney commented after Sarina filled her bowl.

A simple nod and thank you was all the response expected of her, and she turned to Ali and filled her bowl without incident. She, too, commented on the delicious aroma.

All was going perfectly and she glowed with the satisfaction of a job well done as she approached Sebastian.

Everything happened so fast Sarina was at a loss to react. She lifted the full ladle from the tureen and was about to pour it into Sebastian's bowl when out of the corner of her eye she caught Lady Lily scooting into the room.

She looked briefly to Sydney, who acknowledged the little dilemma and attempted with a casual point of her finger to send Lily in the opposite direction. It didn't work; instead the little kitten twirled around like a top and sped straight into Janey's feet.

Janey lost her balance, Sarina reached out to help her, the ladle went flying out of her hand—how she couldn't imagine, since she thought she had a firm grasp on it—and Janey and she collided. Sarina grabbed for the full tureen that wobbled in Janey's hands, the two fighting to prevent it from falling but having no such luck.

It toppled over, Janey grabbing the rim but not before it dumped a good portion of the soup in Sebastian's lap. The hot soup caused him to jump up, knocking into Teresa, who sat next to him, who knocked her water glass into William Douglas's lap; he in turn, startled by the cold drenching, jumped up, sending Catherine MacTavish's wineglass flying across the table, spilling over her husband's white shirt; John MacTavish's surprised reaction caused his elbow to hit Bridie Douglas in the arm, sending the water from the glass she held to spill all over her chest; her stunned response caused her to bring her glass down on the table catching the edge of her spoon accidentally, sending the utensil flying in the air to land in Ali's soup bowl, splashing leek and carrot soup all over Eden McEwan, who sat between Bridie and Ali.

The chaos did not stop there. The ladle that had gone flying through the air toward the end of the table deposited its contents over Dagon's head, the soup dripping slowly down along his face.

Sarina and Janey's uniforms were partially drenched with the soup. Sydney was the only one who had miraculously escaped the deluge.

Complete silence filled the air. Not a breath or sigh was heard, not a word was murmured. And all eyes turned toward Dagon.

He took his white linen napkin from his lap and slowly wiped the dripping soup from his face. "My apologies," he said calmly and turned heated eyes on Sarina.

Sarina's emotions soared to the surface, and with a burst of tears she rushed out of the room.

Sebastian sent his wife a knowing nod and excused himself, following after Sarina.

Ali took charge of the delicate situation. "Dear," she said, addressing Janey. "I think we have had enough soup, and it's a good time to serve the salad, and do bring extra napkins."

Eden McEwan burst into a fit of laughter after wiping the soup from his face with his finger and tasting it. "Damn good soup, Dagon."

William Douglas joined in the merriment. "Yes, we can always count on you for entertainment."

Teresa McEwan smiled and pointed her finger. "Allow me to freshen everyone up."

Dagon was about to stop her useless gesture when Sydney interrupted. "Please, allow me, since I went unscathed." Without waiting Sydney cast her hands out, sending a ripple of energy rushing over the guests and table and instantly returning everything and everyone to their previous condition. Everyone, that was, but Dagon.

"You missed Dagon," Catherine MacTavish informed Sydney, lifting her glass of merlot.

Sydney smiled. "So I did." She pointed a finger at him "Shall I?" she asked.

He knew her finger was accusing, letting him know he had not behaved properly. But at the moment he was too furious to care what Sydney thought. He had wanted Sarina attending the dinner party, not serving at it, and for a good reason. He wanted her beside him, not a damn servant in his castle. And now look at the mess she had made, creating pure chaos, drawing attention to herself, and then running out of the room in tears. And who followed her, Sebastian.

And who handled the aftermath, Ali, and who accused him of wrongful reaction, Sydney. The night was not going as he had planned.

"By all means, Sydney," he said and suddenly realized that Sydney had righted Sarina's wrongs. How?

Sarina sat in the garden crying. She had fled without thought, making her way to the wildflower garden that was now barren, the numerous beds covered with a heavy protective mulch. She sat on the stone bench, her face buried in her hands, finding it hard to calm her rushing tears.

The night air was chilled though not uncomfortably so, and besides Sarina was too lost in her own misery to care that she needed a sweater.

Sebastian on the other hand was practical and had grabbed Margaret's sweater from the hook by the kitchen door as he ran out. He placed the heavy beige cardigan over Sarina's shoulders.

His unexpected presence startled her.

"I thought you might need a friend," he said and sat down beside her.

His generous offer caused a stirring of tears that she fought to control, especially when the light from the near full moon slipped across him and she saw what damage her unskilled hands had done to his suit.

She offered the only words she could. "I'm sorry."

"It wasn't your fault."

"Yes, it was," she insisted. "I should have paid closer attention. I should have been more careful."

"You were doing excellent. There's no reason to blame yourself."

She shook her head in disagreement. "No, it's all my fault. I'm such a powerless witch. If I were skilled I could have prevented the whole terrible incident, but with less than adequate abilities, I could do nothing but stand there and watch the small accident turn disastrous."

"You'll learn," he assured her.

She wanted to laugh, scream, and cry until no tears remained. Her plight was useless. She was doomed, completely doomed.

"Don't get discouraged," Sebastian said. "My first few attempts at developing my newly acquired powers turned out less than favorable."

Sarina sighed, wishing for all the world that her powers were restored and she was her natural, vibrant, powerful self.

"Practice makes perfect," he said with a pat to her hand. "At least my wife tells me that."

Sarina liked Sebastian. He possessed a strong sense of himself and had the courage and strength to deal with a castle full of witches. He allowed no one to intimidate him, not his beautiful wife or Dagon, whose arrogant pride could disarm any mortal or witch.

"I don't think that saying applies to me," she said with disappointment. "I'm a hopeless witch." And she surely felt like one, having been unsuccessful in any attempt to make right her awkward situation.

"I think you worry overly much on doing wrong."

He was a wise mortal and her opinion of him blossomed.

He continued giving her advice. "You need to take small steps and one at a time. If you attempt giant-size steps, you'll miss one and have to go back."

"How did you begin?" she asked, curious.

"I began as soon as I found out I was capable of magic." He smiled. "It was our wedding night."

Sarina looked at him with wide eyes. "You practiced your first magic feat on your wedding night?"

He nodded with pride. "Of course, Ali helped me and warned that one was enough for the night, and being I had more important matters on my mind, I didn't argue."

Sarina couldn't help but giggle.

"After that I practiced every chance I could and constantly pestered my wife for lessons."

"Was Ali patient with you?"

Sebastian grinned. "Her patience wore thin after I deposited her on her bottom one too many times and of course there was that time I accidentally dropped her in the pool."

"The pool?"

He offered an explanation. "You see, I didn't believe in witches when I first met Ali, and the night she attempted to convince me with a few small tricks, I still refused to believe her. So she resorted to a harsher demonstration and with a crook of her finger, she had me suspended over her indoor pool."

Sarina enjoyed another giggle. "You wanted to get even."

He put his finger to his mouth. "Shhh, she mustn't know that or I'll suffer a dunking myself."

"But your other lessons went well?" she asked anxiously.

"Not quite," he admitted. "One day Ali cast her hand over a rosebush, gently separating a beautifully bloomed rose from the bush, and she presented it to me. Wishing to reciprocate, I attempted likewise."

"What happened?"

Sebastian shook his head and laughed. "I uprooted the whole bush from the ground."

Sarina joined in his laughter.

"Then there was the fairy dust incident."

"Fairy dust? You tried working with fairy dust while a novice?" she asked in surprise.

He nodded. "What did I know? A sprinkle here, a sprinkle there."

"What happened?" she asked, anxious to know the results.

"I became invisible for almost an hour."

"Good heavens, how much dust did you use?"

"Evidently too much. Ali banned me from using it until further notice."

Sarina laughed, finding it difficult to stop.

"See, you're not the only one that gets herself into difficult situations."

Sarina's laughter slowed and she smiled gratefully at him. "Thank you for being my friend when I needed one the most."

He took both her hands and held them tight. "Friends

are always there for each other. Whenever you need a shoulder to cry on or to bubble with laughter, I guarantee I can promise you both.''

Sarina leaned forward and kissed his cheek. "Again, Sebastian, thank you. You are a true friend, and I am grateful for our newly found friendship.''

"The feeling is mutual,'' he assured her. "Now let's get back and enjoy Margaret's magical cooking.''

Sarina stood along with him. "Margaret uses no magic to enhance her cooking skills. She cooks as a mortal.''

"Then she is truly a magician,'' Sebastian said, and they strolled back toward the castle discussing the various dishes Margaret had waiting.

Sebastian returned to the table, and before he sat, Sydney quickly had him looking refreshed.

He leaned over by her and said, "I tried that but I guess I couldn't quite get it right.''

"Practice, dear boy,'' Sydney said and patted his hand in reassurance.

Dagon finished his conversation with Catherine Mac-Tavish and looked down the table to Sebastian. He simply smiled and acknowledged Dagon's attention with a nod, then turned to speak with his wife.

Dagon wanted to throttle him. He expected at least a word on Sarina, and what did Sebastian do? Smile, nod, and completely ignore him. It wouldn't be proper for him to leave his guests. Sydney herself would reprimand him for his rude behavior, so he had little choice but to see the meal through. Then he could seek out Sarina, but first he would have a word with Sebastian.

The meal proceeded without incident, though Sarina did not return to serve the meal. Janey assisted Bernard in finishing the serving, and Bernard took over the serving of dessert and after-dinner drinks in the parlor.

It was after eleven when the guests left, and it was Sebastian who said to Dagon, "I wish to speak with you.'' He then turned to Sydney, gave her a good night kiss on the cheek, and then kissed his wife gently on the lips, whispering how it would be worth her while to wait up for him.

With that he marched toward Dagon's study.

Dagon's annoyance had grown throughout the evening, though he kept his temper concealed. All evening he wondered over Sarina, his mood alternating from concern to anger before blending a little of both to form a strong annoyance.

And the thought that Sebastian was the one to console Sarina angered him all the more A peck on Sydney's cheek, a mumbled good night to Ali, and he was directly behind Sebastian, his strides just as determined.

Sydney hooked her arm in Ali's. "What say you to a cup of Earl Grey and a little chat? I have a feeling your husband will be awhile."

"I was thinking the same myself," Ali said, "though I thought we would invite Sarina to join us."

"You stole my thought," Sydney accused with a laugh.

"You planted it," Ali challenged, and they walked toward the kitchen in search of Sarina and tea.

Dagon slammed the door behind him.

"Don't go getting your temper up with me, Dagon," Sebastian warned. "This evening was your own fault."

"My fault?" Dagon repeated, slipping out of his jacket and tossing it on the back of a nearby chair.

"Right, your fault. You had more than enough time to invite Sarina to the dinner party, but you waited until the last minute, and when she was put on the spot, you knowing she had limited abilities, what did you do?"

Dagon went to answer, but Sebastian did it for him. "Nothing. You did nothing. You placed her in a precarious situation, and she courageously faced the challenge."

"She was doing well," Dagon defended himself and her. "And besides, she's stubborn and would do as she pleased anyway."

"Yes, I'm familiar with tenacious women."

Dagon ran his hand through his hair. "I have always handled them well, but Sarina is . . ." He shook his head as his words drifted off.

"Different?" Sebastian suggested.

Dagon dropped down in the chair next to the burning hearth. Sebastian took the chair opposite him. "She's like no other woman I've encountered."

"She has a refreshing, simplistic quality about her," Sebastian said. "She appears young and innocent yet worldly and wise as if she has lived for so many years she understands the true mysteries of life."

"I know what you mean. I sometimes think she has much to learn, and other times I think she knows much. She is an enigma and it drives me crazy."

Sebastian laughed. "You mean you're not totally crazy yet?"

Dagon didn't find the situation amusing. "I am in full control of my faculties."

"Are you?" Sebastian questioned with amusement. "Tell me your first thought after the chaos subsided in the dining room this evening."

He answered immediately. "I was angry, but"—Dagon paused and ran his hand through his hair again—"the anger was with myself while my concern was for Sarina."

"You wanted to shield her from the hurt and embarrassment of the unfortunate incident."

"I wanted to scoop her up into my arms and rescue her from the disastrous scene."

"Do you always want to rescue her?"

He nodded. "She always needs rescuing."

"Perhaps she's rescuing you."

Dagon raised a brow. "From what?"

"Only you can answer that question."

"Playing with words, mortal?"

Sebastian grinned. "Witch to you."

Dagon smiled. "I forget how much I helped you."

"Helped me?" Sebastian laughed good-naturedly. "When you didn't bother to advise me of how to seal the spell once cast?"

Dagon leaned forward. "I had confidence in you, mortal. I knew you'd figure it out for yourself."

Sebastian sighed with the sheer pleasure his memories

brought and nodded slowly. "I had no problem, no problem at all."

"Some things are better left to be discovered by one-self," Dagon said.

"Have you discovered for yourself?" Sebastian asked in a serious and concerned tone.

Dagon gave thought to his words. "I've discovered that a clumsy witch has robbed me of my senses."

"Did she rob you or did you freely give them to her?"

"You begin to irritate me."

"Because I make you question?"

Dagon shook his head. "I do nothing but question myself lately."

"Then what have you discovered?"

"That I am going crazy. That I can't get the bumbling witch out of my mind. That I think about her day and night and in between. That my emotions are completely out of control around her. That I worry over her. That I ache for her. That I—"

He paused abruptly and stared at Sebastian.

"That you love her," Sebastian finished.

Dagon stood rubbing at the ache in the back of his neck.

"That pain won't go away until you come to terms with this issue. You refuse to face and accept the truth, or is it that you have and you don't know what to do about it?"

"I am not as stubborn and foolish as you when it comes to love."

Sebastian agreed. "That you aren't; if you were, this would be a whole lot easier."

Dagon scowled.

"Hey, pal, I didn't know the answer to that question when it came to me and Ali. I was also dealing with the fact that she was a witch. You clearly know Sarina is a witch, perhaps not one that meets your rigid standards, but a witch. You also clearly know the answer to the question. You simply refuse to act on it."

Sebastian paused, grinned, stood, and walked over to him, slapping him on the back. "I guess that does make you stubborn and foolish when it comes to love."

Dagon rolled his eyes. "Advice from a mortal, what is this world coming to?"

"Witch, witch," Sebastian corrected. "Want me to prove it?"

"No," Dagon said, but too late. The crystal decanter filled with brandy floated in the air . . . upside down.

Eighteen

Sarina sat with Sydney, Ali, and Margaret at the kitchen table enjoying a pot of chamomile tea and light chatter. Ali had mentioned upon entering the kitchen that Dagon and Sebastian were deep in discussion in the study. Sarina needed no magical skill to tell her that she was the topic of conversation, or that Sebastian was probably presently defending her actions to Dagon. A friend would do that.

A confrontation with Dagon would come soon enough, and she actually hoped to delay it at least until tomorrow. She was completely worn out and tired from head to toe, body to soul, and that depth of tiredness left one vulnerable. Not a good place to be for an unskilled witch, especially when confronting a powerful witch.

"Deep thoughts?" Sydney asked of Sarina.

"Too many thoughts of late," she admitted freely.

"Love does that to you," Ali said, drawing all attention to her. Ali sighed dramatically and shook her head. "It's obvious Sarina is in love with Dagon, why should we all deny it?"

It was Sarina's turn to be the center of attention with three questioning glances falling on her. She was about to dispute it when she realized there was no point in denying the truth any longer. She simply shrugged and said, "I'm a fool."

The three women laughed.

"Love does that," Ali assured her. "Love makes you feel and act foolish. You do and say things you never imagined you would. Love robs you of your sensibilities. You don't even know who you are."

Sydney continued from there. "And that's the best part, you get to discover a knew part of yourself. You don't look with the same eyes, hear with the same ears, feel with the same senses. Your awareness takes on a new more deeper awareness. That is why passion usually rules early in a budding relationship. The senses are aware much sooner than the people themselves."

"And still we doubt," Sarina said.

Ali spoke. "You must remember that love tampers with all the emotions because it is the highest of emotions. Love cannot flourish if it does not integrate with all that is part of you."

"Which is why love drives you crazy," Margaret offered with a smile.

Sydney and Ali nodded their agreement.

"I foolishly thought it would be easy to love," Sarina said.

"Love is easy," Ali said. "It's the falling part that's hard."

"Love is part of all of us," Sydney explained. "It is when we reach out to share that love on a deeper, more meaningful, and intimate level that it becomes difficult, but yet remains simple."

"We make it difficult," Sarina said with a smile.

"A wise witch once advised me on love," Sydney said. "Her words were not profound, yet they were meaningful. She told me that love is simply love. If we demand or expect too much from it, we lose the very essence and purity of its being. Love is and always will be, it is up to us to simply love."

"And yet love remains elusive to many," Margaret said with a sad shake of her head.

Sydney responded. "Because they expect too much, demand too much of themselves and others. They never simply love for the sake of loving. They always want more when they already have an abundance, but then greed always leaves one feeling dissatisfied."

"What do you plan to do about your love for Dagon?" Ali asked.

Sarina thought of her dilemma and how Dagon could possibly be the one to help her. She had searched far and wide, and every time she had met someone, she had thought of her problem but never of love. Only since meeting Dagon did she begin to think differently and now her only desire was to love Dagon whether he could fulfill the spell or not.

She answered Ali with a generous smile. "I plan to simply love."

Ali clapped her hands. "The poor man doesn't stand a chance."

They all agreed with a hearty laugh.

"I thought I'd find you here," Sebastian said to his wife upon entering the kitchen and walked over to give her a kiss.

"A late cup of tea, small talk, and good company," Sydney explained.

Sebastian stood behind his wife with his hand on her shoulder. "Sounds like fun and mischief in the making."

Ali dramatically pressed her hand to her chest. "Are you implying that we're up to something?"

He leaned down, placing his cheek to hers. "Sweetheart, you're always up to something."

She squatted playfully at him as he backed away from her.

Sarina yawned, the long day catching up with her. "Excuse me, but I think it's time I said good night." She had thought perhaps that Dagon would request to see her, but Sebastian made no mention of him, and she did not intend to pry into their meeting.

"I agree," Ali said and stood, bidding all a good evening and latching on to her husband's arm to stroll out of the kitchen like two lovers intent on a pleasurable night.

Sarina attempted to clean up the table, but Margaret stopped her. "You've done enough work for one night. I'll see to this."

Margaret shooed her from the room, ordering her to get a good night's sleep. Sarina did so gratefully, yawning as she waved good night to both women.

"Did it turn out as you had hoped?" Margaret asked in a whisper.

Sydney produced a smile of pure satisfaction. "Better than I expected."

"Then Lady Lily made her entrance at a good time?"

"Couldn't have been better."

"And I suppose Dagon is presently wondering how you can right Sarina's wrongs."

Sydney filled her teacup once again. "I imagine he does, poor dear. He doesn't realize Sarina had nothing to do with tonight's fiasco, therefore, it was simple to right my own misdeeds. The spell cast on Sarina is much too powerful for my meager skills to correct."

"Yet you interfere."

"I think a little interference is necessary at times."

Margaret once again whispered, as if fearing to be over-heard. "You don't fear retribution?"

Surprisingly, Sydney lowered her own voice. "I think this spell on Sarina was cast in haste, not intentionally."

"I must admit and with regret that while Dagon is pow-erful, I fear he is not powerful enough to handle a spell of this magnitude."

"I've given that thought myself," Sydney said with con-cern. "But Dagon possesses an arrogance of pride and de-termination that is rare. And if anyone is capable of confronting this power, he is, and of course a little help goes a long way."

"Little and limited," Margaret reminded.

"A little can go a long way."

"Soon, I hope."

"My sentiments exactly," Sydney agreed. "Time is of the essence here."

"You thought tonight would see them united, didn't you?"

Sydney raised her teacup. "The night isn't over yet."

Sarina expected sleep to claim her as soon as her head hit the pillow. That was over an hour ago, and she remained wide awake. Lady Lily slept comfortably on the pillow beside her as if she had not a care in the world.

A strong wind whistled outside her window, and a chilly draft filled her room. She snuggled more deeply beneath the blanket, glad for her white flannel nightgown and thick cotton socks.

She assumed it was the night's unexpected chaos that kept her mind fertile. She had played the scene over and over and over again and still could not understand the sequence of events. Two things continued to trouble her about the evening. One was the way she remembered Lady Lily twirling like a top toward Janey's feet. At first she thought it was her imagination, but she recalled it too clearly to doubt her own eyes. The other was the fact that her wrong was made right. There was simply no one present who was powerful enough to right her wrong, which led her to believe only one thing. The unfortunate incident was not her fault to begin with.

But if not her, who? And why?

She had been so embarrassed she could barely look at Dagon, and while he appeared furious with her, she was momentarily stunned by his desire to once again protect her, to rescue her from herself, to ease her hurt, her pain, her disappointment. But then she would do no less for him.

She turned over on her stomach, burying her head beneath the pillow, attempting to shut out her thoughts. Her defensive action did little good. Her incessant musings continued to plague her; actually Dagon plagued her. She could not chase him from her thoughts. He was always there in some shape or form, and admitting his constant presence in her life made her realize just how much she liked him there.

Perhaps that was why it was easier to admit her love for him. When Ali had questioned her, her first instinct was to dispute her claim. But how did one deny the truth? It was not possible and denying it to others when it was so obvious was just as wrong.

She was glad she had talked with the women. They had helped her to understand herself and to remember what love was all about. Now she only needed to confront Dagon, not with demands, for she wanted nothing from him that he did not choose to give. She simply wanted to love him.

In her attempts to solve her problem she had lost her way, misunderstood and misguided herself. She flopped over on her back, staring at the ceiling and the faint light of the bright moon shining through the window. She had forgotten her own teachings, her own lessons, her own wisdom. In essence she had lost herself, but the beauty of the whole experience was that she was free to once again discover herself, and that was a unique opportunity.

Tomorrow *she* would seek out Dagon and talk with him. She would not wait any longer—she would once again take charge. She suddenly felt like her old powerful self, and she smiled with a wisdom she had lately ignored.

Tomorrow was a new day, but then, it already was tomorrow. Why wait any longer?

She laughed softly and hopped out of bed, causing Lady Lily to protest with a gentle meow at being disturbed. She thought to dress, but then thought better of it. Dressed in her white flannel nightgown, her dark hair tousled, and her feet covered with slouching white socks, she headed for Dagon's bedroom.

Dagon tossed and turned until he thought he'd go mad with the want of sleep. He didn't want to think. He wanted nothing but pure, uninterrupted, dreamless sleep. And he was getting none of it. Instead his thoughts were driving him insane. He could not get Sarina out of his mind. She haunted his every thought whether waking, resting, or sleeping. She was there, a permanent thought in his mind.

He hadn't even given consideration to the Ancient One. He was actually losing interest in his well-formulated life plans. What he once thought important—a powerful mating and an exceptionally skilled wife—seemed dull and unattractive to him. Chaos had entered his life in the form of a bumbling witch named Sarina, and he wondered if he could ever live without her.

He had once considered his life to be full, yet he didn't know the true meaning of abundance until Sarina.

He grabbed for the pillow beside him and placed it on top of the other pillow beneath his head. If sleep was to elude him, he might as well be comfortable.

His intentions had been to speak with Sarina this evening before he retired, but after his conversation with Sebastian he thought better of it. He needed time to think this through, to better understand what he felt. Besides, he didn't think Sarina would welcome him.

He smiled, recalling how Sydney once told him he had never known true love, and he now could agree with her. Love was a crazy emotion that could not be understood or ever fully grasped. Too often people chased after love when love never ran from them in the first place.

He had chased after it in an attempt to capture its essence when all the while it was right there in front of his eyes, and yet he was too blind to see its beauty. He foolishly thought he could manipulate, plan, and produce love the exact way he wanted it.

Love had other ideas.

He now understood why love was considered the highest of emotions. Love set no limits, asked for no guarantees, love simply was.

And he simply was in love with Sarina. And it felt good, right, perfect. He wanted her in his life permanently. He wondered when it had happened. When had he fallen in love with an unskilled witch who dangled from a chandelier and a window, got stuck in a chimney and a tree, flooded the laundry room with suds, and walked barefoot through the woods?

He laughed softly at the many memories and wondered what other adventures awaited him and wondered if perhaps he had not fallen in love with her the very moment he saw her dangling from his chandelier. Had he failed to pay attention to the obvious? Had he not listened to his own heart, his own emotions when dealing with her?

Last night was a prime example of his disregarding his emotions. He instinctively knew he should not have waited to invite Sarina to participate in the dinner party. It was his own fault that she was forced to serve, and that could have been avoided as well. One word from him to Bernard, and she would have been released from her duties for the evening. But he foolishly did not pay attention to his instincts. He had allowed her to serve, and naturally chaos prevailed.

Though it still disturbed him that Sydney had been able to right her wrongs. Her powers did exceed his, and perhaps they were substantial enough to deal with Sarina's inadequate skills. He would have to remember to discuss the matter with her.

Right now he was thinking that he needed to talk with Sarina. There was much for them to discuss. And there was much for him to learn and understand about her. He should have summoned her to his study after speaking with Sebastian. Instead he retired to his room to sulk like a spoiled child. When what was necessary was for him to understand and admit how much he loved her.

Admitting his stubborn foolishness was not easy for him to do. He always prided himself on his intelligence, especially his ability to deal with any given situation. He would sense what was necessary and proceed accordingly, but then those situations had never involved him being truly in love.

True love did not play fair.

He drew his hand slowly down his face. He had never felt more frustrated in his whole three hundred years. He was not reacting at all like himself. If he were himself, he would have this whole dilemma settled by now. He would take charge and charge in, and fate be damned, he would succeed.

He sprang up in bed. What was he waiting for? Did he expect fate to intervene and determine the outcome? Or did he intend to be himself and determine his own outcome?

He would do what he did best, take charge. If he could

straighten out the mess Ali had gotten herself into over Sebastian, he could certainly handle his own dilemma. And besides, there was no spell involved in this situation. He did not have to concern himself with a time frame or worry about words that could break or seal a spell. He was free to pursue Sarina at his leisure or in haste.

She was young, perhaps barely a hundred years old. There was much he could teach her, and he would be patient with her lessons. Of course, she did possess the gift of sight and a remarkably accurate sight. A worthy skill to pass on to children.

Children!

He hoped she wanted many for he had always planned on a castle full. He laughed thinking of a daughter with less than adequate skills chasing after Lady Lily, whom she would probably have flying upside down through the air.

He threw the covers off himself and walked naked to the chair where his silver silk robe lay and reached for it. He was tired of waiting. Waiting to talk with Sarina about last night's events, waiting to tell her how much he loved her, waiting to tell her he wanted to spend the rest of his life with her, and waiting to tell her he wanted to make a baby with her as soon as possible. The ultimate act of sealing their love.

With determined strides he marched toward the door and flung it open.

Sarina jumped back startled.

Dagon smiled, stepped back, and waved her in.

Nineteen

~

Before her courage could fail her, Sarina rushed into the room, tripping over the hem of her white flannel nightgown, and landing safely in Dagon's arms.

"At least I have you where I want you," he teased and was about to steal a kiss when she nudged him away from her.

"We must talk."

"Funny, I was thinking the same thing myself—that's why I was on my way to get you."

His admission startled her. "You were coming to my room?"

"Yes," he confirmed and shut the door. "It is my castle and I am permitted to go where I please, and it pleased me to talk with you."

"About this evening?" she asked.

"That among other things."

Sarina looked to the rumpled bed. It seemed to invite and beckon, she could almost smell the scent of him on the warm sheets, and she very much wanted to slip beneath his covers and lose herself to him. Instead she walked over to the hearth, extending her chilled hands out to the warmth of the welcoming fire.

Dagon followed, though took a seat in the chair not far from where Sarina stood. He sensed her desire. It was palpable but along with it came apprehension, and he wanted her doubt vanquished before they joined together in his bed.

"Where shall we begin, Sarina?" he asked softly and extended his hand out for her to take a seat.

She shook her head. "No, thank you, I'll stand."

This time he shook his head. "Not a good idea. Your nightgown may be flannel, but it is a light flannel, and with the light of the blazing fire shining on you—" He once again shook his head. "My imagination only needs to wonder how many ways I will enjoy you. And lets not forget those socks I've warned you about. They will definitely remain on you, the *only* thing that will remain on you."

Sarina immediately took a seat in the chair opposite the other end of the hearth from where he sat and crossed her legs and arms.

He laughed. "It will do you little good to lock yourself away from me. But first things first. What is it you wish to speak to me about?"

She wondered where her jitters came from. Her decision to come here had been easy, so why now was she apprehensive? She was aware of the consequences of her actions, had counted on them in helping her to settle this problem. Why think of retreat now?

She shook her head without thinking.

"You don't know what you want to speak with me about?"

She kept shaking her head slowly, her glance settling over him as if she were seeing him for the first time. He was much too handsome especially sitting there like a king on a throne, arrogant, proudful, and much too appealing. His long dark hair was tousled from his restless slumber. His silver robe fell open down to his waist, and his bare chest rippled with defined muscles. His bare feet were crossed at his ankles, and though his robe covered his legs, she was aware that he was completely naked beneath.

The thought that all she had to do was simply untie the

belt at his waist and he would be free of all restrictions sent
her passion soaring and her hands itching.

He leaned forward in his chair. "Dear heart, we are definitely going to have a problem if you give your thoughts
rein in that direction—unless of course that's why you
came here?"

"No, yes, no, ohhh," she said in frustration.

He smiled. "Calm down, Sarina, and tell me your
thoughts—well, maybe not your present thoughts, but the
ones that brought you to my door."

"I couldn't sleep," she began.

"I suffer from the same infliction," he admitted.

She relaxed, though her body's alert posture told him she
remained on guard. "I thought about this evening and how
I must have disappointed you."

"I was not disappointed with you this evening."

His voice was firm, almost angry, and she looked at him
with wide curious eyes.

"The evening was my fault and I take full responsibility
for it."

She protested, "But I created the mess."

"No," he insisted, "you did your job and most adequately."

"By dumping soup on Sebastian and creating a chain of
events that left no one untouched?"

"Sydney managed to escape the chaos," Dagon said,
thinking that somehow that was an important piece of information for him to remember. "Regardless, Sarina, the
incident was not your fault, and I am not angry nor disappointed with you. I am, however, disappointed that we
did not get to spend the evening together."

"I didn't think you wanted to see or speak with me after
what happened."

"And I thought perhaps you didn't care to see me."

A soft smile stole over Sarina's face. "I don't think
we've been honest with each other."

"Then perhaps now would be a good time for us to
start."

"You're right," she said. "Let's start with why you were coming to my room."

Her wit was sharp and he admired that quality. "One reason was to apologize for placing you in an awkward position this evening."

She attempted to disagree.

He held his hand up. "I apologize and I will hear no more about it. Now tell me what else is on your mind."

"Too much," she admitted, hugging her arms.

"I know the feeling; it overwhelms at times."

His honesty amazed her. "Then you feel it, too?"

"All the time. There isn't a moment that it doesn't intrude on me day or night."

"Do you mind this intrusion?"

"I welcome it," he said on a whisper.

"So do I," she admitted just as softly.

"Now the question is what do we do about it?"

"Explore it?" she asked innocently.

His smile was wicked. "Aren't you afraid of where it will take you?"

"No," she said without hesitation. "It will take me exactly where I'm supposed to go."

"Where do you want to go?"

She stood and walked over to him. "Anywhere you want to take me."

He thought of all the things he wanted to say to her, all the things he wanted her to say to him, and yet at that moment in time he felt the only way either of them could be truthful with each other was through their actions.

He stood.

"Are you ready to tempt fate?" she asked softly and untied his belt, letting it fall away, and running her finger down the lapel of his robe to spread it open.

"Are you ready for the consequences?" he asked, grabbing hold of her hand.

Consequences born of love, how bad could they be? She no longer doubted herself or him, they loved plain and simple. She felt it in his heartbeat that kept steady rhythm with hers, in his desire that heated and raced his blood righ along with hers, and much deeper, where only true love dares to go, she felt it in their souls.

"I'm ready," she said and waited for him to surrender her hand and himself.

His hand slipped off hers, and she continued to spread his robe open.

"There'll be no turning back, Sarina," he said, her finger sliding down his chest to his waist as she moved the silk material out of her way.

"No turning back," she repeated confidently.

She was deliberately slow in her perusal of him, her finger trailing along the silk material, dipping beneath to tease his bare chest and then returning to further push the material aside.

Her emotions ran opposite of her actions. Ripping his robe off and tossing him on the bed to land on top of him ran more in accordance with her raging desires, and yet she found the need to proceed slowly, to take her time and explore him to her satisfaction. It wasn't that she didn't want to please him as well, it was that she wanted this time with him to be a magical moment for them to remember always.

Of course dragging her feet would serve no purpose, and she was eager to view him in all his male splendor. With that pleasing thought in mind she ran her hands along his chest, moving up and over his shoulders to slowly slip his robe off.

She watched its graceful descent, her eyes following down along his body until the robe landed in a silver pool at his bare feet, handsome feet they were, slender and long.

The rest of him did not disappoint. His body reminded her of a majestic beast, strongly defined, taut and solid, yet lean and slender. His slim waist narrowed to slight hips and long muscled legs. And of course how could she ignore—

She sighed and almost purred in appreciation.

"I please you?" he asked with not a trace of a smile but a look that was so titillatingly wicked she felt herself moisten with desire and her response sounded as sinful as she felt.

"I've yet to find out."

His laugh was low and rough. "Let me introduce myself properly."

He wrapped his arm around her waist and pulled her body to rest against him, leaning into her and slipping his hands down over her bottom to gently urge her closer. He then kissed first along her neck, taking his time to work his way up near her ear, then over and around it, the tip of his tongue teasing every sensitive spot until gooseflesh covered near her entire body.

He seduced her mouth next, tormenting her moist, needy lips until her lips chased his teasing ones, and they joined together in a flourish of maddening kisses that left them both breathless and wanting.

With his breathing labored he said in a whisper against her ear, "You feel how much I want you; now it's my turn to feel how much you want me."

His hands took hold of her nightgown, his fingers drawing the white flannel up and up until it was bunched in his hands at her hips. Then in one deliberate motion he pulled the nightgown up and over her head, leaving her naked, except for her white socks.

His smile was smug. "I'm going to buy you dozens of socks."

She laughed with delight and threw her arms around his neck. "Good! I detest shoes."

He lifted her up into his arms and carried her to the bed. "Good, then wear them no more, you actually need wear nothing anymore. Naked is just the way I like you."

He fell with her on the bed, his body taking partial possession of hers as he lay half over her, his hand instantly moving to intimately explore her. "Your skin is soft and smells so sweet."

He kissed her breasts gently. "I want to touch and taste you forever."

His fingers traced a lazy path down along her slender midriff and over the slight rise of her stomach to drift into the tangle of soft black hair and crawl maddeningly slow inside her.

"My, my, dear heart," he said with a teasing grin. "You do want me."

She moved on bended knee to rub at his hardness. "As much as you want me."

He kissed her soundly and his laugh was a low rumble. "Tonight we share a magical moment. . . ."

Her breath caught at his words.

"The first of many," he finished and his mouth claimed hers once again, and he didn't stop there. When he ended the kiss, to her reluctance he moved down along her neck to taste her breasts with a tongue that charmed and titillated with every deliberate stroke.

Her nipples ached in their hardness and suffered the delicious torment all the more when first his tongue teased the sensitive buds with quick darting strokes before capturing each one in his mouth.

Pleasure took on a new side of madness, and she squirmed beneath him, but he only laughed before moving farther down her body, his charmed tongue creating his own indolent path.

She gasped and cried out when she felt his fingers spread her in readiness for his tasty entrance, and her cries soon turned to moans of exquisite torment as his tongue pleasured her with a sensual wickedness she did not think possible.

Her hands reached out to tug at him, stop him, warn him that she could not go on like this. She could not control her raging emotions and very soon she would burst, explode, erupt in sheer pleasure.

He pushed her hands away. "Come," he urged. "I dare you to."

"No," she cried softly between labored breaths. "This time with you."

"Oh, dear heart, tonight you will come over and over again with me."

She groaned and arched her back after his tongue entered her with a quick jab that was meant to send her to the edge and it did. She teetered there briefly, and when he followed with strong solid thrusts she fell, crying out his name in her maddening descent.

Her climax was a fiery explosion that she thought could not be duplicated, but Dagon had other ideas. After one last intimate taste of her he moved over her with the grace of a powerful beast staking his territory; slow and predatory his body claimed hers.

"Now another magical moment," he whispered and brushed her lips with his tongue to excite her senses with the taste of herself.

She groaned and reached out for his mouth, the mingled scent of them too intoxicating to deny. She fed off him like a hungry cub aching for his familiar scent and for his love that she felt in every taste, touch, and kiss.

Dagon felt his restraint slipping. He chose to bring her pleasure first and selfishly wanted to taste her sweet surrender. But now he wanted to surrender fully and completely himself, and he wasn't at all surprised though extremely pleased when she reached down to take him in her hand and stroke him full and hard.

"When do I get to taste you?" she asked in an excited whisper.

He almost erupted in her hand, and his hand moved quickly and gently to free himself from her firm grasp. "Later," he promised with a kiss. "It's time for us to join."

She looked with wise and loving eyes at him. "I give myself freely to you."

He was aware her surrender was without conditions, his however was not, but that would be better left to discuss with her at another date. He simply said. "And I to you, dear heart."

He entered her slowly, wanting to create an everlasting memory of their first joining, one they would remember forever and never fail to relive over and over and over again. And he himself wanted to remember the feel of every inch of her, recall her every moan of pleasure, her every cry of passion, and he wanted to erupt in total surrender along with her.

"Dagon," she released his name on a long sigh.

He slipped farther into her.

Her sigh turned heavy. "Dagon."

His thrust turned strong and determined.

She drew out his name on a breathless sigh. "Daaagon."

He went deep and established a rhythm she immediately responded to.

This time his name sounded like a plea. "Da—gon."

He enjoyed hearing her call out to him over and over, and he changed his rhythm to a demand, and she responded, wrapping her legs around his.

His name was urgent on her lips. "Dagon."

"Wrap your legs around my waist," he ordered. "I want to go deeper. I want to touch your soul."

She did as he asked, for she wanted to touch his as well.

His thrusts turned rapid, his rhythm furious, and she matched both, their bodies moving in unison.

Rational thought escaped him, he could think of nothing, absolutely nothing but the exquisite sensation he felt being inside her, deep inside her. He wanted this to go on forever, he never wanted it to end, he never wanted them to part. And when he thought he reached the pinnacle of passion, he felt her explode around him, heard her cry out his name, and felt himself erupt in a fury that stunned and shattered him to his very soul.

They convulsed in a breath-stealing climax, clinging tenaciously to each other as their bodies continued to surrender all of themselves to each other, deep down to the cores of their beings.

They shuddered together, their bodies draining themselves of the last vestige of mindless surrender. And it felt good, gloriously wonderful and they clung to each other enjoying every memorable minute.

She tightened herself around him, and he moaned with the pleasure she brought him, though thinking she might have hurt him, she eased the pressure of her embrace.

"Don't," he said on a hasty breath. "That feels good."

She smiled and closed herself intimately around him, and he moaned again and kissed her.

"I like the feel of you inside me," she said honestly.

He raised his head and grinned. "That's good, dear heart, because that's where I intend to spend most of this night—inside you."

"Promise," she giggled.

"You may not be able to walk tomorrow by the time I get done," he teased.

She teased back. "And you may have a permanent grin on your face by the time I finish with you."

"That is a promise you better keep," he warned with a laugh and moved gently off her to gather her against him in his arms.

With their breathing calmed and their bodies replete they shared the simple pleasure of laying quietly in each other's arms, both favoring the soothing melody of their satisfied hearts.

Sarina never realized how delicious love could feel, a love made of no demands and given from the heart and soul. Why had she not been wise enough to see this from the start? Why had she wasted so much precious time?

Her answer came easily.

Dagon.

She had not found that rare love until she had found Dagon. And now? Her smile was for herself alone. She had tempted fate and would wait for the outcome, but in the meantime she would enjoy.

She stroked Dagon's leg with her sock-covered foot and with her finger traced circle after circle on his chest.

He grabbed her hand and stilled it. "You want to give me time to recover?"

She looked with wide innocent eyes at him. "Must I?"

He kissed the tip of her small nose. "Yes, you must."

"Can I at least continue to touch you?" she asked, sounding like a spoiled child denied her favorite treat.

He released her hand. "You can touch me whenever and wherever you like."

"Carte blanche, I like that," she said and continued to trace circles, her hand drifting lower and lower.

"You're headed for trouble," he warned with a grin.

"No," she assured him with a shake of her head. "You are."

It was near dawn when her breathing calmed for the fifth time that night. She lay on her side, Dagon wrapped around her after pulling the covers over them and making certain she was comfortable.

She had been comfortable all evening with him. Their last joining had been fast and furious. They had been laughing and teasing each other beneath the covers when they both suddenly lost control of their emotions. Dagon wasted no time in entering her, nor did she waste time in accepting him. They coupled like two primal beasts, scratching, clawing, and biting their way to a unified climax.

She sighed with the pleasure of the recent memory.

"Are you all right?" he asked anxiously. "I was far from gentle."

"Neither was I," she admitted freely. "But I did enjoy it."

"I didn't hurt you?"

His anxiousness disturbed her until she realized the reason for his apprehension. No spells would cure her ills, she would suffer as a mortal would until her hurt healed naturally. He could do nothing to prevent her discomfort or to heal her. And that concerned him greatly.

His tender regard touched her heart. "I'm all right."

"Really?" he asked and his hand moved to gently touch between her legs.

She flinched and cried out from the unexpected soreness.

"I think not," he said in an angry tone.

"It's my own fault," she insisted, taking responsibility for her actions.

He turned her on her back to look directly at her. "The responsibility is mine as well."

She was not upset that he read her thoughts so clearly. Their joining had brought them closer together, much closer than she had expected or dared to hope. But now she would have to be much more careful.

She reached her hand out to touch his face. "I chose to

join with you and you with me. A little soreness matters
not after such a memorable night.''

He took her hand and kissed her palm. ''I don't wish to
see you suffer.''

She grinned. ''You certainly didn't mind me suffering
earlier this evening.''

He grinned himself. ''You inflicted suffering of your
own on me.''

''I did, didn't I?'' She giggled foolishly yet with delight.

''That you did, dear heart. And I must admit I thoroughly
enjoyed every minute of the tormenting pleasure you
caused me.''

''And I enjoyed all you gave me.''

''But I, unlike you,'' he said with a playful tap to her
nose, ''am not physically suffering.''

''A small discomfort,'' she insisted.

His hand moved between her legs to once again prove
his point, but this time her hand grabbed for his. ''I'm all
right and by tomorrow I'll be fine.''

''You will tell me if you're not?''

''I will complain to you immediately,'' she said, ''so you
may suffer along with me.''

He kissed her then gently. ''If you suffer, I suffer.''

She was startled by his admission. ''I don't wish you to
suffer.''

They stared in silence at each other as if both of them
at that very moment understood the essence of their remarks and knew without a word being spoken that they
loved each other.

Sarina gently cuddled up against him and just as tenderly
Dagon wrapped her protectively in his arms, and they
drifted off into a contented slumber.

Twenty

~

The weather was cold and gray outside, but it mattered not to Sarina—she was bursting with sunshine. She felt radiant and wonderfully warm. She had quietly slipped out of Dagon's bed early this morning, leaving him to sleep soundly. She on the other hand was much too excited and feeling much too grand to spend another moment in bed. She had hurried to her room and taken a hasty shower, dressing in her usual uniform of black skirt and white blouse, and planned to join Margaret in the kitchen for early tea.

She chose to ignore the tenderness that had remained and continued to cause her some discomfort. It was a small price to pay for a loving evening and would heal with time and care. She had applied an herbal cream that helped ease the soreness and refused to allow the minor discomfort to spoil her day.

She entered the kitchen with a huge smile and a warm greeting. "A wonderful morning to you, Margaret."

Sarina's happy smile was contagious, and Margaret's face broke out in a large grin. "And a good morning to you, Sarina."

"It's a wonderful morning, Margaret," she said, eagerly hugging the woman before proceeding to the stove to pour a cup of tea from the hot kettle. "Simply wonderful."

Margaret had to ask. "A good night?"

Sarina giggled like a young girl revealing secrets. "A great night."

"I am pleased for you."

Sarina disregarded the tea and rushed over to Margaret, who welcomed her with open arms. They hugged and shared tears until Sarina finally returned to the kettle.

"I have no regrets. I am happy in my decision."

"Then it was a wise decision," Margaret said with a nod.

"The best one I've made in a long, long time."

"What is?"

Both women looked up to see Ali standing in the kitchen doorway dressed in white knit pants and a white soft cable-knit sweater that fell past her hips. Her long blond hair was pinned up in a messy mass that as usual looked stunning on her. She yawned, her hand going to her mouth as she entered the kitchen.

"I barely got any sleep, though I did enjoy the night," she said with a smile. "And of course my husband sleeps while I ache for a cup of hot tea." She pointed to the kettle as she headed to the table. "Now tell me, what is this best one you made in a long, long time?"

Sarina laughed; she simply adored Ali. The woman was positively outrageous and unpredictable. She filled a teapot with hot water and added Earl Grey teabags, then took three mugs from the hanging rack and carried them to where Margaret sliced warm apple spiced bread at the table.

Sarina spoke while pouring the tea. "I made a wise decision last night."

Ali squealed with delight, jumped up from her seat, and rushed around the table to hug Sarina. "I'm so happy and pleased for you. It is what you and Dagon needed."

"I couldn't agree with you more," Sydney said from the doorway. She looked elegant as usual dressed in a soft gray knit dress, her slim waist accented with a silver belt and her long hair twisted artfully and pinned to the top of her head.

Sarina collected another mug, and Margaret cut extra slices of bread.

Sydney gave Sarina a gentle yet loving hug before sitting at the head of the table. "Tell us everything." She quickly amended her remark to "Almost everything."

The women laughed and incessant chatter soon filled the air.

"Love makes intimacy all the more natural and so perfectly right," Sarina said. "It was as if we were meant to be."

Ali shared her own feelings. "I know what you mean. I never once doubted that I wanted to be intimate with Sebastian."

"You were downright eager, dear," Sydney teased.

Ali agreed wholeheartedly. "Eager and impatient. I thought the man would never get around to surrendering himself to me."

"Bernard was putty in my hands," Margaret said with a satisfied grin.

Sarina looked surprised.

"He's not as staunch and stubborn as he seems, my dear," Margaret said and laughed. "He's actually quite romantic. Often after a busy day I'll return to our quarters to find he's run a steaming bath for me filled with glorious bubbles, and the bathroom itself is glowing with numerous scented candles. He'll massage my back and . . . well, the rest I'll leave to your imaginations."

"Sebastian is romantic," Ali said, reaching for another slice of apple spice bread. "He prepares candlelight dinners for me and takes me to small, quiet restaurants."

"That's because he wants to keep you out of the kitchen, dear," Sydney said.

Ali sighed. "It's so wonderful not being able to cook."

The women laughed.

"The important point," Sydney said, "is that all three of you love your mates and would do for them as they would do for you. You share love, not demand it or expect it, but share it and that is important to remember."

Doubt nudged at Sarina, but she chose not to acknowledge it. She promised herself that the choice was hers and she would accept the consequences of her actions no matter the outcome. And while she felt Dagon's love as strongly as her love for him, he had yet to admit his feelings. That choice was his.

Margaret looked to Sarina. "Did Dagon say you were to continue your duties?"

Sarina shrugged. "We never discussed my duties. I merely assumed I would continue working here."

Sydney shook her head. "I don't think he will allow you to continue on in your current position."

Sarina grew worried. "But it's my job and he has made no mention of other arrangements, nor do I know if I'll agree to them."

Ali clapped her hands. "Oh, this is simply wonderful. Dagon has finally met his match."

"His powers far surpass mine," Sarina reminded.

Ali laughed slowly. "No, no, dear, you have more power than you think. You just must use it wisely."

Sydney patted Ali's hand. "I don't think you should give Sarina advice on using powers wisely."

"I'm not talking about magical powers, I'm talking about womanly powers."

Sydney nodded. "Then by all means, dear, give her advice, and, Sarina, by all means, listen to Ali. She's exceptionally talented at using her womanly wiles to her advantage."

Ali smiled, pleased by the compliment.

Sarina caught the time on the cow clock and hurried out of her seat, the quick movement causing her to wince.

"Are you all right?" all three women asked with concern.

"I'm fine," she said, embarrassed to admit anything more. "I promised Janey I would tend to her duties in the small receiving parlor today so that she could meet with the young man she has been seeing."

"Dagon doesn't know you're gone from his bed, does he?" Ali asked.

Sarina shook her head. "No, he doesn't."

"Let me help you," Ali said to Sarina's surprise and stood.

"A good idea," Sydney said, pouring herself another cup of Earl Grey. "Margaret and I are going to discuss recipes for the coming holiday."

Ali hooked her arm in Sarina's before any objections could be made, and together they left the room.

Ali sat on the small couch while the feather duster she instructed with her finger saw to dusting the furniture. Sarina, however, was busy manually polishing all the glass pieces in the room.

"Let me tell you something about Dagon," Ali said, and Sarina listened, anxious to learn all she could about him. "He can be demanding, irritatingly so at times, but he means well and he cares deeply. He would never intentionally hurt anyone. He respects our ways and lives by our code, never harming a soul, though he does threaten when he feels it necessary. But it is his intelligence he resorts to when a problem needs dealing with."

"I've learned that," Sarina admitted, remembering all the times he dealt with her dilemmas.

"He growls and stomps around like a beast at times, but regains control quickly, of course," she said with a huge grin. "He's never been truly in love."

Sarina stopped polishing and joined Ali on the sofa. "You believe he truly loves me?"

Ali took her hand. "You do yourself or you would have never surrendered yourself to him or him to you."

"We haven't spoken of love."

"Love announces itself in many strange ways."

Sarina smiled. "Yes, that it does and I suppose when love is ready, it spills willingly from lovers' lips."

"Very willingly," Ali assured her and reached for her hand, squeezing it gently. "Trust Dagon with your heart, he will never hurt you."

Sarina already knew that and was about to tell Ali when they both jumped at the shout of her name echoing down the staircase and through the hall.

Ali patted her hand. "Stay right here and let him find you."

"But—"

Ali would hear no protest. "Right here. He has no business shouting for you."

"He's upset," Sarina said, sensing his concern.

"Upset because you weren't there when he turned over in bed ready to make love again."

The two women jumped again when this time Ali's name echoed through the castle.

"Oh, he's in for it now," Ali said with a smirk, and Sarina laughed.

"We both remain here?" Sarina asked.

"You're damned right we do. Those two beasts better turn into *gentle*men before they reach this room or else."

Sarina was encouraged by Ali's courage and stayed put.

Dagon flew into the room first, and he actually looked as if he flew, he entered the room so suddenly and stopped just as abruptly. He wore his silver robe and nothing else, Sarina was sure of it when she caught sight of his bare feet, though his hair did appear combed, although he probably raked his fingers through it a dozen times or more in aggravation before leaving his room.

Sebastian entered next with equal speed and almost crashed into Dagon if it was not for the sharp wit of his wife, who with the crook of her finger altered their near physical altercation.

He, too, wore a robe, though it was dark blue and his feet were bare, which meant—

Sarina and Ali grinned at each other.

"Something we can help you with, *gentlemen*," Ali said calmly.

"Oh, no, no," Sebastian said, coming to stand in front of the sofa with his hands on his hips. "No, you're not going to make this look like it's my fault."

"What's your fault?" Ali asked sweetly.

Dagon walked around the sofa to stand in front of Sarina while Sebastian answered, "Nothing is my fault."

"Of course it's not," Ali assured him.

Sebastian shook his head and looked to Dagon.

"She's your wife, mortal, not mine."

"True enough," Sebastian admitted, "but since you're also standing here in your robe, I'd say you're having the same problem, wife or not."

"Not for long," Dagon said and reached down, grabbing Sarina's wrist and yanking her to her feet.

She cried out from the discomfort the sudden jolting caused.

All eyes turned to her misty ones.

"You're in pain," Dagon said with concern.

Ali tugged at her husband's hand, and he quietly helped her up, and with soft silent steps they left the room.

"A little discomfort," she admitted, knowing it was senseless to hide the truth from him.

He glanced around the room. "You're working?"

Before she could respond, he shook his head and with a growling mumble scooped her up into his arms. Unfortunately he was not as gentle as he should have been, and his quick actions brought a sting of pain and a rush of tears. She simply buried her face against his chest where his robe had fallen open.

He felt her tears tickle his chest and swore beneath his breath. "I'm sorry."

"It's all right," she said. "It's not your fault."

"Damned if it isn't. In my unrelenting hunger for you I did not consider the consequences," he said and walked slowly out of the room and up the stairs. "My intentions were to love you, not hurt you."

She slipped her arm around his neck. "And you did love me and I loved you with just as much eagerness."

"Still, it was my responsibility to see to your care."

She sighed with the pleasurable memories. "You certainly did that."

"About your absence from my bed, you left my bed to see to your duties?" he asked, seeking confirmation of what he already knew.

"Yes, I made a promise to Janey to help her out today. I could not go back on my word."

"I'll see that her duties are seen to, but you will cease all duties until I say otherwise. Is that clear?"

Her protest died on her lips. There was no point in arguing with him now, he would have his way regardless of how much she objected. She would wait and speak to him when he was in a more reasonable mood.

He entered his bedroom, the bedcovering rumpled from their last night's activities. He kicked the door shut and gently sat her down on the bed. He walked to the phone and picked it up, pressing a button.

"Bernard," he said, "Sarina is relieved of her duties until further notice from me, and please see to it that Janey's chores are seen to by someone else today." He remained silent listening to Bernard's response. "Yes, have breakfast for two sent to my room, but not for at least an hour."

After hanging up the phone he returned to stand in front of her. "Get undressed, I'm going to run a tepid bath for you."

She attempted what she knew would be a useless protest. "It isn't necessary."

"It is very necessary," he insisted and reached down to unbutton her blouse.

She covered his hand with hers. "I'll do it."

He nodded. "Join me in the bathroom when you're done."

The sky outside had turned a darker gray and rain began to patter on the windowpanes as Sarina removed the last traces of her garments. A chill rushed over her even though fresh logs had been added to the blazing fire that spread its warmth throughout the room.

She couldn't be nervous. She had been intimate in so many ways with Dagon last night that there was no reason to feel nervous around him and yet she did. Why?

Perhaps she felt vulnerable, perhaps she was more uncertain of their future than she cared to admit, or perhaps she loved him so much that the thought of a future without him upset her terribly.

She walked with cautious steps to the bathroom. The

water ran in a steady flow into the tub, the lights were dim, and the pattering of rain had turned incessant against the windowpane. Dagon stood with his back to her, his naked back. He had discarded his robe and was busy lighting candles along the vanity. She admired his firm round backside and long sturdy legs, and then there was the width of his shoulders. She sighed, enjoying the view.

He turned and smiled. "You do like looking at me naked, don't you?"

She answered honestly. "Very much."

"Then I shall not deny you your pleasure, look to your heart's content."

She did, hugging her chilled body as she explored him with her eyes slow and steady. She retreated a step when her glance connected with the affects of her lingering perusal.

He was hard, magnificently hard.

And she was tender, not a good combination.

His voice was gentle. "It's obvious that I want you— actually you might as well get used to seeing me aroused, since in your presence I'm in a constant state of arousal."

"Really?" She wanted to laugh with the joy of that knowledge.

"Really," he confirmed and walked to the tub, extending his hand out to her. "While I would love at this moment to be intimate with you, your present needs prohibit our joining, so instead I will see to your care. I added an herbal mixture that should help soothe your discomfort."

She didn't hesitate in walking to his side and taking his hand. He reached down and turned off the faucet and then helped her into the tub, following behind her. They eased down into the tepid water together, Dagon stretching out full length and spreading his legs for Sarina to nestle between them.

She relaxed back against him, his hard body remarkably comfortable as she stretched out along it, and the warm water was soothing as it rose up to settle just beneath her breasts.

Dagon wrapped his arms protectively around her, and she

settled contentedly in his embrace, sighing with the pure pleasure of a perfect moment.

"Comfortable?" he asked.

"Extremely," she admitted, another satisfied sigh confirming the truth of her response.

"I missed you this morning when I woke."

"I was much too excited to sleep."

He kissed her temple. "Then you should have awakened me."

She lovingly stroked his forearm where it rested beneath her breasts. "You were sleeping so soundly, I didn't wish to disturb you."

"Never think you disturb me, Sarina. I will always be there for you, whenever you need me"—he paused and laughed softly—"and even when you don't. You actually may find me a pest."

"Never," she said adamantly. "I like being with you and will stay—"

"—as long as I say," he finished, deciding now was not the moment to tell her they would be spending a lifetime together. If he was truthful with himself, he would admit that he was concerned that she may have other plans for her life and that he was but a mere interlude. He chose to share more with her, and while he was almost certain she felt the same as he, there still remained that margin of doubt that could distress a budding relationship. He would not have it torment theirs.

He realized that she gave no response. Was her silence on purpose, and if so what did it mean? Would she willingly remain or did she have other plans she did not wish to share with him?

He sought a more definitive answer. "Have you made life plans, Sarina?"

She kept her mind clear and her answer brief. "No."

He pursued his query. "You must have at least given it thought."

"Now and again."

"What then did you think?"

Again she chose brevity. "Not much."

He sensed her unwillingness to talk on the subject, and her reluctance made him all the more curious. He decided to skirt the issue and see what he could discover. "Perhaps you wish to seek the knowledge that will help develop your skills."

She smiled to herself. "My skills will come with time."

"At least you know the value of patience."

"I learned it many years ago."

"Who taught you?"

She laughed. "Patience cannot be taught. It must be learned on one's own, or one never benefits from its magic."

"Wise words for one so young," he said as if questioning her age.

She immediately sought to change the subject. "Young witches sometimes are remarkably insightful, and the youngest witches are the most delightful, that's why I want many children."

Her words pleased him. "I feel the same way about children myself. I'd like to fill the castle with the laughter and joy they bring."

"Children would grow and flourish here, and you would make a wonderful father."

His hand moved down over her stomach. "And you a wonderful mother."

Without thought she placed her hand over his. "I've thought often how magical it would be to create a child and feel it grow inside me."

"Then you do have certain life plans," he said, returning to the subject she preferred to ignore.

When she went to move her hand off his, he quickly slipped his hand over hers and kept it pressed against her stomach. "You wish for a baby inside you, so therefore you must wish for a lifemate."

"Don't we all wish to be part of another, to share a love so strong that it bonds two together as if they are one? And once that love is established, wouldn't the two wish to create another from the depths of their love? Isn't that what the life cycle is all about? Love that continues on forever through every one of us, a love so rare yet so simple it unites the souls.''

He moved his hand off hers and gently grasped her chin to turn her face toward his. ''You wish for a love that is rare.''

Her heart skipped several beats and her eyes fluttered closed and then drifted open. ''Yes, I do.''

He kissed her lips softly and sweetly. ''So do I.''

She settled once again into his firm embrace, and once again no words of their love passed their lips, yet they sensed without saying that they loved, and soon, very soon it would be time for them to openly admit their emotions.

Time once again to tempt fate.

Dagon ate his breakfast and read the paper while Sarina slept peacefully in his bed. She had grown sleepy in the tub, and he had wrapped her in a huge terry-cloth towel, dried her, and carried her to his bed, tucking her beneath the covers. Her eyes had drifted closed as soon as her head rested on the pillow. He then dressed in dark gray trousers and a white knit sweater, leaving his long hair free to dry as he slowly enjoyed his morning meal.

He liked this scene—Sarina asleep content in his bed, and he content watching her. In his search for a lifemate he had foolishly ignored the simple things that made life more pleasing. He had not given enough serious thought to how he would feel about sleeping and waking with a woman every day. He was more intent on skills and power and failed to realize that love was a serious commitment that required serious consideration.

Did he wish to spend the remainder of his years with a powerful witch for the sake of creating powerful children, or did he wish to spend his years with an inept witch who smiled at the joy their joining brought her and who longed to create a child from their love?

The answer was not difficult, though he was grateful that he had asked the question. He had searched so hard for love that he had forgotten love's true qualities and he had forgotten that love could never be found because it is never lost.

He looked to Sarina cuddled beneath the covers and whispered, "I love you, and soon, very soon, I will hear you admit the same."

A soft knock at the door caught his attention, and he stood and walked over to open the door quietly.

Bernard stood on the other side. "Sorry to disturb you, sir, but Lady Lily is completely uncontrollable in the kitchen and will allow no one near her. I assume she is concerned to her master's whereabouts, and while I attempted to capture her and bring her here, she clawed and spit and refused any offer of help or comfort. And poor Margaret cannot get her work done."

"I'll come along and see to her," Dagon said, and before he took a step out of the room, he glanced back to Sarina, smiled, and stepped out the door closing it behind him.

Twenty-one

~

Lady Lily sat purring contentedly in Dagon's arms as he walked toward the staircase. The little ball of fur who was rounding in size quite nicely had created havoc in the kitchen. She had jumped from countertop, to countertop, to the table, and right onto Margaret's floured board. She repeated the process, her stained white paws leaving her tiny tracks all over the kitchen.

Fortunately for all she had calmed down at the sight of Dagon, and with a heartfelt meow wandered over to him most willingly, cuddling against him when he picked her up.

He made apologies to Margaret and quickly exited the kitchen. He was about to take her upstairs to Sarina when Sydney intercepted him as he passed the receiving parlor.

"Just the man I wanted to speak with," she said and hooked her arm in his, turning him around and heading straight for his study.

Dagon knew better than to protest. Obviously this was a command, not a request, and he went along most willingly.

Sydney shut the door and ordered, "Sit down, we need to talk."

Dagon walked to his desk, leaning his backside against the front of it while he continued to appease Lady Lily with gentle strokes of his hand. "If it's about Sarina—"

"It is about the Ancient One."

Dagon immediately grew attentive, and Lady Lily grew quiet.

Sydney walked behind his desk and sat, forcing him to turn and take the seat in front of the desk.

"Sebastian and Ali have chosen to leave before her arrival. Ali doesn't think Sebastian is ready to meet someone of her status just yet. I intend to remain to make the introductions."

Dagon hesitated to respond, not certain of how to inform Sydney of his change in plans.

"Something troubles you?" she asked, and he realized she sensed his apprehension.

He spoke truthfully. "I don't think the meeting with the Ancient One is necessary after all."

Sydney rose slowly, placing her hands flat upon the desk. "You don't think it necessary?"

He wisely remained silent, knowing she didn't actually expect a response.

"You insist that I arrange a meeting with a witch, who with the snap of her fingers, could bring this castle crumbling down around you, and when I make those arrangements, you decide it is no longer necessary? Are you a fool?"

He nodded; disagreeing was futile.

"Well, at least we agree on something," she said with annoyance and stood straight, folding her arms over her chest—a sure sign that she was angry. "You have no choice but to meet with her."

"But if you explain—"

"Explain!" she said in a near shout. "Explain what? That a foolish male witch demanded an introduction with her and has now changed his mind? She will want to know why—"

She held up her hand to prevent his response. "And she will accept no explanation."

"You're saying she is not a reasonable witch?"

Sydney laughed at him as if he were an ignorant child. "She was born with the dawn of time. Do you understand the magnitude of her powers?"

"She is wise, therefore she must be reasonable," Dagon insisted, growing agitated that he may have gotten himself into a situation that he may have difficulty extracting himself from.

Sydney nodded slowly. "Yes, reasonable enough to think that if someone wished to meet with her that he had given that meeting careful consideration, which meant it was important to him and therefore he would not waste her time and would never consider canceling it."

"You're telling me I'm stuck with this meeting."

"Precisely," Sydney informed him and sat down.

Dagon gave his predicament thought while petting Lady Lily. "I suppose my only recourse is to formulate another reason for meeting with her since I am in love with Sarina and wish her to become my lifemate."

Sydney smiled and allowed Dagon to feel her pleasure over his words.

"You're happy for me," he confirmed with a smile of his own.

"Happy, pleased, and delighted that you have finally found love."

"True love, a fantastic love, a rare love," he admitted freely.

"You deserve the love you have found with Sarina and you both deserve happiness, but remember your words, dear boy, they will serve you well."

Dagon looked at her oddly. There was an important message behind her reminder, but how to decipher it he wasn't sure.

"You must be truthful with the Ancient One when she arrives."

"Has a time been set?"

"No, we are still negotiating an equitable time frame."

"Then I have time yet to give this matter thought, though I think I know how to appease her."

Sydney grinned. "Then you will be the first—" Sydney paused and shook her head before she continued. "The second who has learned the secret."

"You make her sound ominous."

"She has her moments, but you must remember the vastness of her knowledge, the scope of her existence, the demand for her powers, and the loneliness she must have endured over the centuries."

Dagon suddenly realized of what Sydney spoke. "She looks for love."

Sydney shook her head. "She knows the true meaning of love and has suffered for it. Be gentle and wise in your opinion of her. She does what is best, and she does it for love. Understand this and you will understand the magnitude of her magic."

"You guide wisely, Sydney."

"I had an exceptional teacher."

"The Ancient One."

"Yes," Sydney said with pride. "She teaches without teaching and guides without guiding. She knows the way of the soul and understands the heart. She does nothing without knowing it is the wise way."

"And wise choices can bring pain."

Sydney smiled her pride in her own student. "Very good, dear boy. You have learned well."

"I had an exceptional teacher."

"Then the cycle continues as it should," she said, pleased.

"You will teach my children?" he asked.

"Planning children already?"

"I'm already three hundred years old! I think I've waited long enough."

Sydney laughed at his teasing. "I would be honored to teach your children."

"It is I who would be honored, Sydney."

Her laughter erupted softly yet again. "Perhaps not."

"Why?" he asked curiously and answered his own question. "Don't tell me. Ali and Sebastian's child will grow along with mine and Sarina's and no doubt will create havoc as only a mixture of mortal and witch could."

"Sebastian is now a witch."

"A bumbling witch." As soon as his words escaped his mouth, he winced.

"Think wisely before you speak."

He thought about Sarina and how hurt she would have been if she had heard him speak those words. "I am a fool."

"A fool in love," Sydney corrected.

"A fool nonetheless. Those words were unkind of me."

"Yes, they were, but since you realized you erred, the words hurt no one but you."

"Always the teacher," Dagon said proudly. "Of which I am forever grateful."

Sydney's expression turned serious. "Wise witches look and see, listen and hear. While many witches understand this concept, they never truly practice it. Look and see, listen and hear, Dagon, and you will learn more than you ever thought possible."

"You're telling me I have more to learn."

"We all have more to learn. I for one would never want to stop learning, and heaven forbid Ali should. I'm still hoping she'll master the art of cooking."

Dagon laughed. "I plan to teach Sarina much."

"And she you."

Dagon raised a brow. "She teach me?"

Sydney sent him a look that warned he was a pupil disappointing a teacher.

He thought better of his remark. "Let me amend that to 'I look forward to whatever Sarina may teach me.' "

"Now you are being a wise witch."

Dagon felt honored by her words. It took many centuries and many life experiences to acquire the title of a wise witch. He hoped to one day earn that title, and with Sydney's praise and encouragement he was well on his way. "Thank you."

"You receive what you earn," she said, though pride in her student remained evident in her smiling face. "Now to return to the problem of the Ancient One. You must be certain you will be able to appease her, or you will suffer her wrath.''

''What could she do to me?''

Sydney spoke low, as if wanting no one to hear her response. ''She could take Sarina from you.''

''Why?'' Dagon demanded in an angry shout.

''Shhh,'' Sydney ordered with a finger to her lips. ''I can say no more.''

It was then at that very moment that Dagon realized the startling truth. ''You know Sarina.''

Again Sydney pressed a finger to her lips in caution. ''I can speak of this no more.''

''I want to know,'' Dagon demanded with concern.

Sydney answered softly and with patience. ''Would I tell you if I could?''

Dagon bent his head back and sighed to the heavens. ''There is more going on here than I realize.''

''Much, but you are wise enough to unravel the mystery if you put your mind to it.''

''You can give me no help?''

''Little.''

He attempted another question, but she raised her hand. ''Fate has already been tempted. The remaining answers are within, look and you will see, listen and you will hear. That is all I can tell you.''

''This has something to do with the lack of Sarina's powers?''

''You look and see already,'' Sydney said, standing. A signal that their meeting was at an end.

''You said you will remain,'' he said, standing with a sleeping Lady Lily nestled in the crook of his arm.

''Yes,'' she confirmed. ''I will not desert you.''

''Again, thank you.''

''Always remember your greatest source of strength and you will never fail,'' she advised with a kiss to his cheek and left the room.

It was barely noon and he felt as if the day had already been spent, it had been such a busy morning. And he had yet to conduct any business. His first thought was to return to his bedroom and check on Sarina, but there were business matters that needed his attention, especially that one business deal Sarina had warned him about. It wasn't going as smoothly as he had anticipated, and a successful outcome was extremely doubtful.

He looked to his computer and then down at Lady Lily. He would return to his room and deposit the kitten with Sarina, giving him a chance to look in on her, and then return to his study to work.

"Busy?" Sebastian asked, sticking his head around the open doorway.

"Business," Dagon said, "but it can wait."

"Good," Sebastian said with a smile. "I was hoping you would help me with some magic."

Dagon almost cringed and then recalled Sarina and all her failed and frustrated attempts to sharpen her skills and how Sebastian did not hesitate that disastrous night to help her, so he smiled. "Sure, I'll help you, though," he warned with a pointed finger, "no levitation."

"Damn," Sebastian grumbled, "no one lets me practice that."

And both their glances immediately fell on Lady Lily, and they smiled in unison.

Sarina woke to the spit and crackle of logs and rubbed sleepy eyes to see Sydney poking at the logs in the hearth. She yawned loudly to let Sydney know her noisy endeavors worked, she was awake.

"Oh, did I wake you, dear?" Sydney asked innocently.

Sarina was wise to her ways and let her know it. "You wished to speak with me?"

"Never could fool you."

"You tried often enough."

Sydney laughed, walking toward the bed with Sarina's lavender dress in her hand. "Many of us did and failed."

Sarina sat up, the covers dropping off her, and reached for the dress to slip over her head. She climbed out of bed, and the dress slid down her body to rest at her ankles. Sydney handed her lavender socks. She pulled them on, folding over the thick tops, and walked to Dagon's bureau in search of a comb.

"You've spoken to Dagon."

"Your sight is as powerful as ever."

"One skill that could not be damaged," Sarina said and ran the silver-handled comb through her tangled hair.

"But cannot help you, yourself."

"Still, there are advantages to retaining it, but my sight is not in question." She stopped combing her hair and looked directly at Sydney. "You have interfered."

"Marginally."

"I appreciate the thought, truly I do, but you know I must do this alone."

"A little help can go a long way."

"Like last night when you made Lady Lily spin like a top into Janey's and my feet causing complete chaos?"

Sydney looked contrite. "I knew you would realize the truth."

"I didn't at first, but then I was too upset to see clearly. It was when I had time to think about it that I realized the incident couldn't have been my fault, otherwise the guests would have remained as they were, a mess."

"A little push in the right direction."

"But it was Sebastian who came to my rescue, not Dagon."

"But it was Dagon you sought out," Sydney corrected.

Sarina nodded. "This is true and look at the results."

"As they should be."

"I am wise enough to realize the results are of my own doing. You had no hand in that, though you gave a *little* push." She walked over to Sydney after returning the comb to the bureau and gave her a hug. "I am grateful for your *little* interference, your *little* push. Your actions helped me to realize what I had failed to see."

Sydney waited in silence.

"I searched for a man. A man to rescue me from this crazy spell, and it wasn't until I arrived here at Rasmus Castle and met Dagon that I understood that the spell was not about a man. It was about love. A rare love that demands nothing but gives all and in giving it receives everything. But you knew this, didn't you, Sydney?"

"I had my suspicions," she admitted. "And now what do you do?"

"Nothing," she said, walking to sit on the edge of the bed.

Sydney sat down beside her.

"There is nothing I can do. It is now out of my hands and in the hands of another."

"You can continue to love."

"I will never stop loving Dagon," Sarina said, hugging herself as if she hugged his love to her and would never let it go. "And I know his love is strong and everlasting, but there is a tempest to face, and our fate remains there."

"You worry he will not be able to fulfill the spell?"

"I have confidence in our love, but there still remains a part that I am not sure can be fulfilled, and that worries me."

Sydney took her hand and offered a comforting squeeze. "You now know the main source of the spell—love. Simply let it work its magic."

"There is no stronger power," Sarina admitted.

"No, there isn't," Sydney agreed.

"And it is what started this whole mess."

"And it is what will settle it."

A terrible screeching pierced the castle walls, causing Sarina and Sydney to jump off the bed and race for the door. Once the door was open, Sarina's fear was confirmed upon hearing another pitiful wail.

"That's Lady Lily!"

The two women raced down the steps and were joined by Ali running out of her room.

"What's happening?" she asked.

Sarina explained as they quickly descended the stairs. "It's Lady Lily! Something dreadful must have happened to her."

They all followed the pitiful cries.

The three women came to a sudden stop and near collision in Dagon's study, their wide eyes fixed on Lady Lily.

who floated high in the air, on her back, around the room.

"Sebastian!" Ali shouted his name, and startled, he turned around.

Lady Lily descended rapidly, but Dagon immediately came to the rescue, slowing her fall and drifting her in his direction so she landed safely in his arms. She in turn wasted no time in jumping out of his arms and heading straight for Sarina.

Sarina's welcoming hands scooped her up and hugged her tight while the annoyed kitten protested with several screeching meows and a few hisses for her own satisfaction.

"You have explaining to do and an apology to make, Sebastian Wainwright," Ali said, walking over to her smiling husband.

"I was doing good," he protested.

"Need I remind you Lady Lily was screeching," his wife said, wagging her finger in his face.

"Watch that finger, witch," he warned with a laugh. "The only reason Lily grew annoyed was that I kept turning her in circles while attempting to float her on her back. She grew dizzy, and besides, I promised her fresh fish for supper tonight as a reward for helping me."

That brought a generous meow from Lady Lily.

"See," Sebastian said as if the cat had confirmed their agreement.

Ali looked to Dagon.

"He's your husband, and you won't help him learn to levitate people."

"He's landed me on my backside too many times, and I didn't see you volunteering," Ali said with an accusing glance.

"You can levitate me," Sarina offered to everyone's surprise.

Sebastian smiled his appreciation. "Thanks, Sarina, that's sporting of you."

Dagon was about to object when he realized she herself needed to learn as much as Sebastian, and how would she learn anything if someone did not trust in her? He felt he had just learned a large lesson. And was about to offer himself as a guinea pig to Sebastian when Ali spoke up.

"All right, you can levitate me."

Sebastian grinned from ear to ear. "Really?"

"Yes, really," she said and slipped her arms around his neck to kiss him. "But we go slow, and we don't levitate over any hard surfaces."

"You got a deal," he said and hugged his wife to him. He looked to Sarina. "Sorry about upsetting Lady Lily."

"I'm sure she'll forget the ordeal after she eats that promised fish."

Lily meowed her agreement.

Sebastian laughed. "I'd better go talk to Margaret about a special meal."

Lily jumped out of Sarina's arms and walked over to Sebastian, purring as she wound her way around his legs.

"Come on, sweetheart," Sebastian said, scooping her up. "Compensation time."

Sydney followed Sebastian and Ali out of the study, closing the door behind them.

Dagon walked over to Sarina, his arms going around her waist. "Feeling better?"

"Much."

"You have nothing on underneath this dress," he said, surprised as his hands roamed over her.

Her smile was inviting. "Not a stitch."

Twenty-two

Dagon moved to step away from her, but she grabbed him around the waist. "I like you where you are, here beside me."

He grasped her chin with a slight roughness. "If I stay right here, it won't be beside you."

Her response was a mere whisper. "Inside me is where I want you."

He groaned, his fingers remaining firm on her chin as his lips descended down on hers. His kiss was full of agitation and impatience and quickly sent her hormones tumbling. She leaned into him, felt his own desirous need, and slipped her hand down over the hard length of him.

His reaction was swift. He pulled away and distanced himself from her, standing behind the high-back chair near the fireplace. "Enough," he said, his stern tone a clear command for her to obey.

She had other ideas, and besides she was enjoying the chase. She advanced on him. "I've just started."

"You've just ended," he said firmly.

She stopped her purposeful steps and sent him a deliberate pout. "You don't want me?"

"You know damn well I want you, and quit that pouting,

it makes your lips look much too appealing.''

She continued her slow approach. ''Good, because I want to taste you.''

''Sarina,'' he warned in a low moan and reminded. ''Your tenderness—''

''Has turned to an ache.''

Her words inflamed his own need, turning him rock hard and most uncomfortable.

She continued softly and suggestively. ''And besides, tasting you would in no way affect my discomfort, though it might alleviate yours.''

She was almost on top of him, near enough to reach out and touch, near enough to hear his rapid breathing, and she smiled as she raised her hand.

Dagon smiled back and floated up and out of her reach.

''That's not fair,'' she said with a petulant stamp of her foot.

''No, it is not,'' he assured her, continuing to float out of her reach each time she attempted to move closer to him. ''It is not fair that I receive pleasure and you don't.''

She licked her lips deliberately slow. ''The taste of you will pleasure me.''

''Sarina,'' he warned, again his own resolve melting away at the sight of her tongue playing so sinfully with her own lips.

She stopped and extended welcoming arms out to him. ''Please, don't disappointment me, Dagon. I ache to taste you.''

His resolve hung by a thin thread, another word, a mere whisper, and he was finished. He did not expect her next move, and it simply did him in completely.

In one fluid motion she stripped herself of her dress and stood naked in front of him, except for her socks, and extended her arms out in an invitation any sane or insane man would not refuse.

And he didn't. He went to her without hesitation.

She pressed her finger to his lips when he attempted to speak. ''Shhh, listen to the silence and feel, feel it all.''

And he did, closing his eyes as her hands went to his zipper and slowly pulled it down.

Dagon sat staring at the fire in the hearth, perplexed yet content. Sarina had left his study over an hour ago, happy and hungry. He laughed softly to himself. This time it was a different kind of hunger. She had well satisfied him and was now looking for a more viable kind of sustenance. With her lavender dress in place and her face flushed she had deposited a quick kiss on his lips and fled the room.

He gave a brief thought to joining her, but his need for solitude overwhelmed him, and he allowed her to flee, for now. His mind was in turmoil, and issues needed to be addressed before this situation slipped from his grasp.

But then, hadn't it already?

He had surrendered completely to her will, and the thought disturbed him. She had driven him mindless with her touch, tongue, and taunting. He had never imagined feeling the way he had felt or surrendering so completely to another.

When she had told him to listen to the silence and feel, he had no idea of the depth or strength that her suggestion evoked. Her touch was pure magic, it tingled, it stroked, it aroused in him a sensation he had never experienced before. He had learned what it felt to feel truly alive, to feel the core of your being, to sense all and more, to know without knowing, and to surrender absolutely to love.

His mind played over the physical intimacy they had shared, the way her hands had cupped and stroked him with infinite and precise care and how her tongue had explored him with a brief hesitancy at first and then with a mindless relish. Her mouth taunted, her words excited, and the combination proved lethal. But it was the emotional intimacy that remained strong and constant, forever a part of them both, and that was a rare and treasured gift he refused to lose.

He stretched himself out of the chair and walked casually to his desk. Sarina was a part of him now, an intricate part of him. He supposed he could compare the necessity of her in his life to his breathing. Without breath there was no life. Without Sarina life did not exist.

He shuddered at the intensity of his realization. He had hoped to love but never dared to think he would find a love so strong that his life would seem empty without her. He had found a rare love, and that was a rare occurrence.

Now he needed to take certain steps to secure their relationship and deal with the impending problem of the Ancient One's visit.

A steady rap at the door sounded before Sebastian stuck his head in. "The women are having their usual chat session, thought you might want some company."

Solitary time to make some decisions was more on his mind, but then a good talk with a friend might be just what he needed. "Let's go to the tower room. I think you'll find it interesting."

"Tower room?" Sebastian asked suspiciously.

Dagon laughed. "It's not a dungeon."

"It does sound ominous," Sebastian said, falling into step with Dagon as he left the study.

"I suppose it does, but I call it the tower room because it's located at the top of the tower."

"Makes sense," Sebastian said, climbing the stairs behind Dagon. "Funny thing, I always thought everything needed to make sense until I met Ali. She taught me otherwise."

"Women have a way of making men see things differently."

"You can say that again. I had my life all planned quite nicely, thank you."

Dagon agreed. "As did I. No bumps, detours, or major hurdles to leap, just a nice solid straight road."

On the third floor they walked to the end of the hallway and mounted a curving staircase.

"Solid can be boring," Sebastian said, his fine-tuned physical condition not even causing him to break a sweat or breathe heavily from the steep climb.

"I've discovered that myself," Dagon said, opening the door at the top of the stairs.

Sebastian gave a low appreciative whistle when he entered. "This I like."

Dagon smiled and walked to the brass and glass wine rack where it sat between two long narrow windows. "It's actually my collector's room, or I suppose you could refer to it as my memory."

Sebastian eyed the various weapons mounted on wood, protected by glass, or simply suspended by wire. Then there were the period costumes all protected by glass cases. Old maps framed in dark solid wood circled the brick wall, and expert lighting reflected on each object at just the precise angle, highlighting the beauty and workmanship of the piece right down to the minute hand stitches of the clothing.

Sebastian stared with respect and awe at each and every piece, fearing he would not have enough time to study every one of them. "These all belonged to you through the centuries?"

Dagon poured them each a glass of merlot. "Me, family, and friends."

"This collection is priceless."

"In more ways than one," Dagon said, handing Sebastian the glass of merlot.

He took it. "I can understand. A piece of your history is contained in every object."

Dagon walked over to a glass table in the center of the room that sat in the center of a group of soft cushioned beige tweed chairs. "You'll be interested in this collection."

Sebastian joined him, taking a seat beside Dagon and looking curiously at the odd collection beneath the glass top. "These look like plain ordinary stones."

Dagon relaxed back in his chair. "They are, though their history is fascinating."

His curiosity caught, Sebastian sat back and waited.

Dagon didn't wait, he plunged right ahead. "Ali is responsible for this collection."

Sebastian held up his hand. "Don't tell me—she threw these at you one time or another."

Dagon laughed. "You are perceptive."

"I understand my wife. Actually I wouldn't be surprised if you had a recent one in there."

Dagon pointed to a smooth white stone about the size of a quarter. "Last year."

Sebastian laughed. "Did she hit you?"

"Never," he said with pride.

Sebastian raised his glass in tribute. "To continued victory."

"With Ali that's easy," Dagon said, his glass clinking with Sebastian's.

"With Sarina?"

"I'll have my victory, of that you can be assured, but answers elude me."

"What are the questions?"

"I forget your business is security"—Dagon shrugged—"but then maybe you can help."

"I always find the answer," Sebastian insisted, "with a little help," he added, recalling the help Dagon had given him.

"This pertains to magic."

"I'm learning, and in my ignorance I may see the truth others don't."

"Wise words only a witch could speak."

Sebastian basked in the praise. "Thanks, I appreciate the compliment."

"You deserve it. Now tell me your professional opinion of Sarina."

Sebastian obliged him. "She's not who she seems to be."

"Elaborate on that, would you?"

"She hides her real self. She is much too intelligent to be an inept witch, something that is so obvious I just don' understand why anyone hasn't realized it."

Dagon sounded disappointed in himself. "I'm just beginning to."

"Don't berate yourself, it wasn't your fault."

"How wasn't it?"

"You fell in love, and love, as everyone knows, i blind."

"I don't like to group myself with the common denominator."

"None of us do, but we all fit the mold. When love hits we've had it, we all become idiots."

Dagon attempted to rationalize the situation. "So in my blind love I failed to see her true nature."

Sebastian shook his head. "Not too good at this, are you?"

"Explain," Dagon said impatiently.

Once again Sebastian obliged him. "Sarina does not hide her true nature, she simply hides her identity."

"Who she really is?"

"Exactly, and she is no inept witch. I'd say she's a wise witch."

"That would make her old."

"Have you bothered to ask her age? A question I would suggest you don't wait until your wedding night to ask, and take that bit of advice from experience."

"No, I've never asked her age. I always assumed—"

"Never assume, assuming leads to trouble. Know, it's important to know."

Dagon paused in thought before proposing his next question. "If she is older, then she is wiser, so why the lack of powers?"

"Could she need a recharge like Ali did when we first met?"

"If that were the case, believe me she'd be running on overload."

Sebastian laughed. "Had yourself a good night, did you?"

"Night and morning," Dagon said with a smug smile.

"How about a spell?"

"Possible, but if she was a wise witch, she could probably block or prevent most any spell attempted on her, plus a wise witch would not work as a servant. She would have too many friends and admirers who would offer her help."

"And what would be the reason for none helping her?" Sebastian asked.

Dagon thought over his question, and his eyes narrowed

and darkened. "A witch of great power and magic could frighten others away."

"That would explain why she would choose to hide as a servant in a castle. Who would think to look for one of knowledge in such a place?"

"But who does she hide from?"

Sebastian pondered the question with a sip of his wine. "Think of why a spell would be cast, and the answer may come more easily."

Dagon looked at him with doubtful eyes. "There is a ton of reasons to cast a spell, though the only requisite is that it never causes harm to a person."

"Come on, let's be honest here. You're telling me that one witch never got mad enough at another witch to cast a grudge spell?"

"It's been known to happen," Dagon admitted, "though not frequently, and usually a wise witch steps in to settle the dispute."

"What if it's the wise witch that the spell was cast on?"

"It would take a wiser witch to remove a powerful spell or help correct it."

"Sydney is a wise witch," Sebastian said. "Is there something she could do?"

Dagon stood and walked over to retrieve the bottle of merlot and bring it back to the table. He sat down and refilled both glasses. "I think she's been up to something."

"Up to something like in helping you out or up to something like in playing with magic?"

"A good question," Dagon said. "I realized that Sydney knows, actually knows Sarina, and yet she will not confirm or deny that fact. And while I feel she is offering her assistance, I cannot determine if it is me or Sarina she helps."

"But the question is why would both of you need help?"

"A logical answer would be that we are dealing with something far beyond our capabilities."

"You're relying on logic?" Sebastian asked, his smile near to a laugh. "A witch resorting to mortal reasoning?"

"When necessary."

"Or when you know of nothing else to do."

"That, too" Dagon admitted, hiding his grin with a sip of his wine.

"Then let me teach you the finer points of reason," Sebastian offered and leaned forward in his chair.

Dagon didn't argue, he listened intently.

"Reasoning is like an intricate puzzle. You need to find all the pieces and then attempt to make them fit."

"Did you do that when involved with Ali?"

"I tried," he admitted with a shake of his head. "But I was missing one very important piece of the puzzle."

"Which was?"

"I didn't believe in witches and definitely not magic. By not even allowing for a slim chance of their existence, I made my search all the more difficult. You on the other hand are a witch and are aware of all the probable pieces. Look at all the pieces and then start to make them fit, to make sense, and that is when you will discover the answers."

"What if I don't have all the pieces?"

"Start with the pieces you do have," Sebastian said. "One will link to another and then another, and there will be ones missing in between, but it is the linking pieces that will provide you with the clues you will need to find the missing ones."

"You make it sound easy," Dagon said, sounding doubtful.

"It is," Sebastian assured him. "Let's use these stones as if they were pieces of the puzzle. The white one, quarter size, is where we'll start. That piece is Sarina, a clumsy witch who appears out of nowhere."

"The MacDougals recommended her."

"Good, another piece, so we move to the small gray stone. Now we ask the MacDougals about her."

"Can't—they're on an extended vacation."

"An unexpected extended vacation?" Sebastian asked suspiciously.

Dagon was about to answer when he realized, "Now that you mention it, they usually never travel around the holidays. They love being home this time of the year, and they throw many lavish parties. It is unusual for them to be away."

"Then perhaps they know more than they wish to share."

"And escaped an inquisition."

"Now we return to something you mentioned earlier about a witch having friends and admirers who would help," Sebastian said, "and you see how a puzzle begins to take shape."

Dagon rubbed his chin. "This puzzle begins to intrigue me."

"Then hunt for more pieces," Sebastian suggested re-filling their empty wineglasses. "And be careful not to disregard any as trivial; all pieces are important no matter how small they may seem to appear."

"Thanks for the advice," Dagon said with a raise of his glass.

Sebastian raised his own. "My pleasure, though you must consider the most important piece of putting the puzzle together."

"Which is?"

"You may not like what you find."

Twenty-three

Dagon slammed doors and stamped though the castle, his determined footsteps sounding more like an advancing legion of troops than one solitary man on a mission.

And he was on a mission.

He had stretched to wakefulness, to reach out and wrap himself around Sarina, who had fallen asleep in his arms last night, only to find her gone yet again. And this time he was furious. He had intended to wake with her beside him this morning and take his time making love with her.

He had thought to make love with her last night, but when she had crawled with a yawn into his bed and he watched the droop of her tired eyes and the way she had settled into a comfortable cuddle against him, he understood she was exhausted from her eventful day and previous night and that sleep would soon claim her. With a promise to himself of an early morning romp, he slipped into a contented slumber, waking to find himself ready to fulfill his promise, only to find his desires once again quelled by her disappearance.

Dagon slammed several more doors, and when Ali popped out of her room, looking as though she had just dragged herself from bed, he yelled at her.

"Go back to your husband, this doesn't concern you."

She was about to protest his tyrannical attitude when she was yanked back into the room and the door slammed shut.

Dagon smiled, getting a small sense of satisfaction from Sebastian's commanding action. He continued his search, grateful the early morning saw many still in their beds. The servants would have glowered with fright if they had seen him advancing through the halls and down the stairs, his dark hair looking wild and unkempt, his black silk robe hanging lose and near to open at his waist and him stark naked beneath.

Dawn had barely broken on the horizon, shadows and darkness played like haunting ghosts along the walls and filled the rooms, and Dagon moved with the grace and speed of a man who was friendly with both.

He found her in the kitchen, alone, wearing his white terry robe, her hands hugging a mug of hot tea, her head bent and her eyes shadowed with concern. His anger immediately cooled and his heart warmed.

"Sarina," he called out to her softly, and she turned a gentle smile on him.

"I couldn't sleep and I didn't want to disturb you."

He joined her at the table. "I don't like waking and finding you gone."

She spoke honestly. "I planned on returning after finishing my tea. I didn't intend on you waking alone."

"I'm glad to hear that, though I would have much preferred it worked out that way."

"I'm sorry," she said in a whisper and leaned over to place a tender kiss on his cheek.

He felt as if he should be apologizing, she appeared so forlorn and lonely. "What troubles your sleep?"

"Dreams that haunt."

His hand went to rest on her arm. "Tell me of them."

She shook her head slowly. "They are gone now and better left unspoken."

"Are they gone or do you hide them?" he asked, her dark eyes filled with more truth than her words.

"I don't wish to speak of them."

"Too real, are they?"

She spoke with the confidence of one who knows. "Dreams are a gateway, and until a person is ready to enter that gateway, it is better that it is left closed."

"So you will let these dreams haunt you?"

She laughed softly, almost teasingly. "I let you haunt me."

He leaned close. "My haunts are pleasurable."

She titled her head to the side and laughed with glee. "Confident, are we?"

"Always," he said and brushed a faint kiss across her laughing lips.

Her laugh slowly faded, and the sudden concern in her dark eyes alarmed him.

"Tell me what troubles you."

"The Ancient One."

He had not expected such a direct and honest answer, and he did not expect her thoughts to be concerned with the Ancient One, but then the whole castle was aware of her impending visit and the reason behind it.

"You know her arrival is pending?" he asked, though the question itself was foolish.

"Who here doesn't?"

"Many think her a mere legend."

"They are foolish."

"Perhaps more afraid," he said. "Her powers are said to be unequaled, and I hear she has a temper."

Sarina was unable to hide her smile. "I guess at her age she is entitled to throw a fit on occasion."

"Do you think she was born with the dawn of time?"

Sarina seemed hesitant to answer. "I think it isn't nice to refer to a woman's age. Advice you might want to consider taking when you meet with her."

So this was the reason for mentioning the Ancient One; she was attempting to determine if he still intended to meet with her. Sebastian was right, Sarina was a wise witch. But he was no dummy himself, and he had his own agenda concerning this matter, and supreme confidence all would work in his favor.

"I'll heed your advice, though age has little bearing on a relationship," he said candidly.

"So age matters not to you?"

"No, it doesn't, the essence of the person is what is most important, especially if a relationship is to last, mature, evolve."

"Then you don't want your relationship standing still."

"Heavens, no," he said with a laugh. "That would be utterly boring. I want a relationship that challenges, expands, and evolves with the years. If we both were to remain the same or have so many similarities, we would grow bored with each other in no time. I would prefer to teach my lifemate and learn from her; this way our relationship would forever be evolving and strengthening in character and love."

Sarina's fascination was held firm. "What could you teach someone as old as the Ancient One?"

He answered quickly. "That there was much yet to learn."

"She might take offense."

He shook his head. "Not if she was wise; she would realize the truth of my words."

"She would be lucky to have a mate like you."

He heard the disappointment, almost sorrow, in her voice, and while he held the power to dispel her fears, he also held the power to strengthen her convictions.

"What do you want in a mate?"

She shrugged as if she hadn't given it thought, and yet he sensed she had given it considerable thought, and with his own curiosity rampant he intended to find out. He pursued answers.

"Does age matter to you?" he asked casually, his hand going to her face to tuck several strands of her dark hair behind her ear.

"No," she answered quickly. "Age is not a consideration."

His easy touch soothed her. He could see it in the way she relaxed her body toward his. "Skills?" he asked in continued pursuit.

She pondered that question for a moment. "At one time I would have thought of them as important, but I must admit after meeting Sebastian he has changed my opinion on the matter."

"Like him, do you?"

"Oh, yes," she said with a generous smile. "He is so caring and charming, and he loves Ali so very much. And he possesses an uncommon strength of character."

He was beginning to feel jealous and for no good reason, simply because she praised the qualities of another man. Still it annoyed him. "You think of him as uncommonly strong?"

"Yes," she admitted with a firm nod. "How else would he deal with Ali?"

Dagon erupted into laughter, enjoying every minute of the hearty laughs that racked his body. When his laughter finally subsided, he agreed with her. "You are so right, it requires extreme, even outstanding, strength to cope with Ali."

Her hand went to gently press at his chest, her fingers falling unintentionally between his robe to land on his warm flesh. Her unexpected simple touch caused a natural reaction; he grew hard.

"And love," she insisted. "You mustn't forget love. His strength is derived from his love for her."

"You want that strong of a love." It was not a question, simply a statement of fact.

"It is uncommon," she said, as if suggesting it would be hard if not impossible to find.

"Rare," he confirmed, aware that he already possessed the impossible and had no intentions of losing it. Not now, not ever, not to anyone, and that included the Ancient One.

Silence fell between them, and while no words were spoken, much was understood. They both were keenly aware of the other, of the strong passionate emotions surging through each of them, of the sense of connectedness, of the desire to join and be one.

"I think we should go upstairs," he said in a whisper, moving his mouth closer to hers.

She reached out her lips to him. "Yes, upstairs, your bed."

"You read my thoughts." His lips swept across hers in two faint strokes.

"You know my desires," she said, before catching his mouth with a gentle nip of her teeth.

Their lips joined then in a soft, teasing play. A prelude to a deeper passion that simmered impatiently much too near the surface.

"Upstairs now," he nearly growled, "or I will take you on this table."

She laughed deep and low and nipped more demandingly at his lower lip. "That sounds inviting."

"Another time," he promised, yanking her out of her chair and up into his arms. "Margaret is due here any minute, and I want more than a minute with you."

She rested her head on his shoulder as he walked out of the kitchen, and she taunted him with nibbles and whispers to his ear. "Two minutes then?"

His voice was a low warning. "You're asking for it, you know that, don't you?"

She sighed like a petulant child and tormented his ear with her tongue before whispering, "Promises, promises."

Shivers racked his body and a groan rumbled low in his throat as he headed up the stairs. "Be careful, Sarina."

She gave his earlobe a rough yet playful bite, then tormented his neck with a tickle of her tongue. "I don't want to be careful, I want to be wicked."

"Sarina, I'm—"

"Wet for you," she finished for him, though they were not his words.

He groaned again, a primal, urgent groan.

"And you're hard and aching for me, aren't you?" Her question was but a murmur in his ear.

"Sarina." Her name was a harsh, needy caution on his lips as he approached his bedroom.

A sensual whimper ran across his mouth before she stole anxious kisses from him. "I don't want to wait. I want you now, right now."

He almost laughed. In her attempt to seduce him, she also seduced herself, and now they both were hot, ready, and impatient. He walked through his open bedroom door and slammed it shut with a kick of his foot.

He dumped her on the bed, opened his robe, spread her robe wide, and entered her all in one sweeping motion.

She cried out with pleasure at the feel of his swift entrance, and together they forgot the world existed. They were aware only of this moment and the magic they created.

An hour later Sarina lay stretching on the bed like a pleased cat while Dagon admired her naked body.

"That felt so good," she said, giving her feet an extra stretch.

"Which one, the stretch or the climax that had you almost screaming the castle walls down?"

She playfully swatted at his chest. "I was not that loud."

He laughed. "Oh, yes, you were, dear heart."

She chose to defend her actions. "Well, it was an exceptional climax."

"I'm glad to hear that," he said with a smug smile.

She turned on her side and tenderly ran her finger over his swollen lips, where her nips had been less than gentle. "I've never failed in having a generous climax with you. You satisfy me most completely."

Her sincere praise stroked in all the right places, and he chose to return the compliment with the same sincerity. "The feeling is mutual."

"I did not hurt you with my overzealous kisses?" she asked, her fingers faintly stroking his lips.

He kissed her fingers. "No, I quite enjoyed your frantic kisses and cherish the reminder of them."

Her smile was slow in forming when suddenly her eyes caught sight of the clock on his nightstand and widened considerably. With a rush and tumble of blankets she hurried off the bed before Dagon could stop her.

"Where are you going?" he demanded, watching her rush to dress.

"I promised Margaret I would help her with the morning

meal," she said, slipping an oatmeal-colored, ankle-length jumper over a brown knit turtleneck. Brown socks and brown ankle boots finished her outfit, and leaving her dark hair to fall naturally after a quick stroke of the brush, she headed for the door.

"Stop," Dagon said much too demandingly to be ignored.

She looked with questioning eyes at him. "I promised."

He got out of bed, slipping on his black robe. "And I specifically ordered you to refrain from doing any work in the castle without my permission."

"Margaret needs help," she insisted.

"Margaret got along quite nicely on her own before your arrival. Now, do you want to tell me the truth of the matter?" He remained by the bed, his arms folded across his chest, and waited for an answer.

She knew she had to be truthful, and besides, the situation had caused her some discomfort. "I don't feel it is right that I am not carrying out my duties."

He understood her concern. "Does the staff gossip?"

She frowned. "I think most are relieved that I am no longer working."

He felt her disappointment in how others perceived her and how she perceived herself. "You enjoy helping Margaret in the kitchen?"

"Yes, she has taught me much, and I am becoming a good cook," she said proudly.

"Then you may help Margaret, but"—his eyes cautioned, though his lips warmed with a smile—"not in the early morning."

Sarina smiled with delight, ran up to him, deposited a hasty and kindly kiss on his lips, and dashed out of the room.

Sebastian was seated in the dining room enjoying scones and coffee when Dagon entered. "I wish I could steal Margaret from you. She is pure magic."

"And yet uses none," Dagon said, joining him at the

table and pouring himself a cup of steaming coffee from the silver coffeepot.

"Well, she certainly has a magical touch when it comes to food." Sebastian helped himself to another scone, a blueberry one. He was about to spread a generous portion of honey butter on the warm scone when he looked to Dagon. "Maybe you can explain something that has bothered me."

"If I can, I'd be happy to."

"I keep wondering why, with Ali's powers, she just can't whip up a decent meal. She is simply useless in the kitchen."

Dagon reached for a cranberry scone. "Have you ever watched Ali attempt to *whip* something up?"

"No, but I've seen the battlefield when she's done."

Dagon laughed. "The kitchen does look like a war zone when she gets finished."

"She's battle scarred herself," Sebastian said with a laugh and a shake of his head.

Dagon spread a liberal amount of honey butter on his scone. "Watch her in the kitchen when she is about to prepare a dish."

"Only if I get to wear full protective armor," Sebastian joked.

"You'll need it. Ali has a tendency to change recipes as she goes along, adding this, taking out that. When we were young, she even changed the recipe for mud pies."

"Mud pies? But mud pies are nothing but mud and water, what could she change?"

"She decided that the pies needed crunch so she added sand, and then she thought the pies too dark, so she added grass for color, then she felt they needed a topping, so she placed a ring of pebbles around her pie."

"What did the finished pie look like?"

"You don't want to know, and besides, it didn't matter. She claimed my mud pie as hers and won the acclaim of the forest fairies for the best structured and prepared mud pie of the class."

"And you?" Sebastian asked, attempting to hide a laugh.

"While the fairies praised my creative nature, they explained that the ingredients and consistency of a mud pie is what gives the pie its character, therefore, I was given extra lessons in mud-pie making.''

"So what you're basically telling me is that Ali marches to the beat of a different drummer.''

"She doesn't even hear the same tune as anybody else.''

Both men laughed.

With his laughter subsiding and his smile still warm, Dagon said, "But Ali is a gem you are lucky to have.''

"I couldn't agree with you more. I'm a very lucky man.''

"That you are,'' Ali said, entering the room. She wore a pale gray knit dress that wrapped and curved with precise precision around her body, down to her ankles, where it met with black suede boots. Her hair was pinned haphazardly here and there. Several free blond strands tickled her face and neck and made her look utterly appealing.

Sebastian held his hand out to her. She took it and kissed him softly on the lips. "Hmmm, blueberry,'' she said with a lick of her lips after tasting him. "I must get the recipe.''

Dagon mouthed *good luck* to Sebastian. Sebastian simply shook his head.

Conversation turned to old friends and the approaching holiday.

"Will you be home for the Winter Solstice and Christmas?'' Dagon asked of them.

Ali answered. "Yes, the Wyrrd Foundation has several holiday events planned, and with this, our first holiday season together, we hoped to spend it at home.''

"What about you?'' Sebastian asked Dagon.

"There are usually a number of parties to attend; invitations have already come in for several.''

"You don't sound enthusiastic about them,'' Ali said.

"I was thinking that perhaps this year I would spend a quiet holiday at home.''

"Doing what?'' Ali asked, staring directly at him as she waited for an answer.

He tapped her nose. "Decorating the castle, stringing popcorn for the tree, greeting the dawn of a new tomorrow after the passing away of the longest day of the year.''

Ali reached her hand out to Sebastian. "You should share the joy of the Winter Solstice with someone."

"I love the Winter Solstice," Sarina said, entering the room with a platter of steaming scrambled eggs. Her face was flushed red from the rising steam, and she wore a broad smile that was too contagious to ignore and brought a round of smiles from the table.

Janey followed her in placing a platter of sausages and bacon on the table and then taking her leave.

"Join us," Dagon said, though it was more of a demand that was not meant to be ignored.

Sarina gladly took the seat to his right across the table from Sebastian and Ali. It took no coercing for everyone to help themselves. Everyone immediately dug in, and the conversation continued around the flourish of passing plates.

"I love gathering the pine to make swags and wreaths and then decorating them with berries and pinecones," Sarina said with excitement. "Oh, and picking a Yule log, that's so important because it must last and burn steadily. And of course there are the special candles that must be made and empowered with the birth of a new dawn. Margaret and I were just discussing how we should get started on the preparations."

Sebastian listened with interest to Sarina.

Ali and Dagon listened with curiosity.

"Candles empowered with the birth of a new dawn?" Sebastian asked.

Sarina realized then she had said too much.

Dagon answered his question. "It is a very old custom known and practiced by wise witches. The Winter Solstice is considered a time of death and rebirth. The day is dark for the longest time of the year, the sun dies, the harvest cycle ends, and with the dawn of a new day comes a birth, an awakening of a new cycle and life begins again. The wise witches would cast candles on the solstice imbibing them with their powers. Legend has it that the candles cast by a witch on the Winter Solstice will last all year long."

"Wow," Sebastian said, impressed, and asked his wife. "Can you do that?"

Ali slowly shook her head. "No, my powers aren't that old or strong."

"You're not a wise witch yet," Sebastian said, beginning to understand the nature of the craft.

"Not in the true sense of the word," Ali confirmed and looked to Sarina. "How do you know of the legend?"

"You mean it's not true?" Sebastian asked disappointed.

"It's true," Sarina assured him with a forced smile. She was on shaky ground here, and while she could not deny the truth of her heritage, neither could she admit the whole truth of her existence.

Curiosity had Dagon on edge, but Sebastian's need for solid reason had him beating Dagon to the question. "How do you know this?"

How did she avoid telling them that she was a wise witch who cast candles on the Winter Solstice? How did she avoid admitting her secret?

Sydney solved her problem by strolling into the room and calmly announcing, "The Ancient One arrives in two weeks' time."

Twenty-four

All in the room remained silent and looked to Dagon.

He spoke with a confidence that startled everyone. "It will be an honor to have her here, and I look forward to her arrival."

Sarina stood and offered Sydney her seat. "Please sit, I'll bring fresh coffee and hot eggs for you." She gathered her dishes in her arm and carefully moved a clean place setting in front of the seat. With a soft, "Excuse me," she left the room.

Sydney took the vacated seat and directed her remark to Dagon. "She will arrive how and when she pleases, as is her way."

"She cannot give a precise time?" he asked, annoyed.

Ali answered abruptly, "You requested her presence."

"That doesn't mean she can't be civil," Dagon snapped back.

"With her powers she can do as she likes."

Dagon was about to argue when Sydney interrupted their tirade. "Enough, she will arrive in her own good time, and she will certainly be civil unless circumstances prove vexing, then you may find her demeanor changing."

Ali interpreted for him. "She is attempting to warn you to be on your best behavior."

"Which is why you won't be staying around for her visit," Dagon said bluntly.

Sebastian entered the debate. "I don't know. She sounds like a witch worth knowing."

Ali turned wide eyes on her husband. "We are leaving tomorrow." She stood, dropping her napkin to the table. "I am going to pack now."

Sebastian protested. "But I'd like to meet this Ancient One. I bet she'd let me levitate her."

Ali paled, shook her head, and hurried out of the room.

"That wasn't nice," Sydney scolded.

"But most effective," Sebastian informed her and stood. "I better go help her and soothe her ruffled feathers."

Dagon held his hand out to him.

Sebastian took it. "You owe me for that one, pal. Otherwise we would have spent the next week here with Ali instructing you on your behavior with the Ancient One."

"Thank you, I won't forget."

Sarina returned with hot eggs and fresh coffee surprised to see only Sydney and Dagon remaining. She silently placed the platter on the table and filled Sydney's cup with steaming coffee. She then scooped up the remaining dirty dishes.

Dagon was about to protest her domestic flourish when he felt Sydney's hand to his arm. He remained silent until Sarina had vacated the room.

"You wish to talk with me alone?" he asked.

"No, I sensed Sarina's unease with the situation. It would be best for you to speak with her alone concerning this matter."

Dagon's irritation returned. "There is nothing to discuss with her, I have the matter well in hand."

Sydney sighed and added a drop of cream to her coffee. "Do you, now?"

"I know what I'm doing," he insisted.

"If you say so."

"If you have advice to offer, then offer it and be done with it."

Sydney tossed a defiant chin at him. "You obviously don't believe you require any assistance; therefore, it is pointless to offer any."

Remarks flew back and forth, and Sarina listened quietly on the other side of the doorway. She shook her head with a sad smile and walked to the kitchen, grabbing the heavy navy blue cardigan from the peg by the door.

"You need more than that sweater if you're going outside. The air has a winter bite to it today," Margaret warned.

Sarina seemed not to hear or chose not to pay attention; she simply slipped out the back door and walked down the nearest path, needing and wanting to be away from the castle if only for a while.

She was at a loss as to how to proceed from here, and giving it serious thought, she realized that her hands were tied. She had made choices, taken a chance, and now what was needed was faith.

Faith in love and faith in Dagon.

But how would he react when he learned the truth? The answer came easy. If he loved her, truly loved her, it wouldn't matter.

She sighed away her frustration and hugged herself.

"Cold?"

Sarina turned to smile at Sebastian.

He wore a brown, worn leather bomber-style jacket with a heavy navy knit sweater beneath and chinos. His casual attire fit his casual mood, and she felt relaxed with his easygoing yet strong nature.

"Not really, the bite in the air feels good."

He walked up beside her and strolled along the pebbled path with her. "I know what you mean. I enjoy the sting of a good cold day."

"It refreshes."

"It is also the place to be when your wife chases you out of your room," he confided with a smile.

Sarina nodded. "I understand. I felt my own need to escape the castle."

Sebastian didn't pry, he seemed to understand and continued the conversation. "I was wondering about those candles."

"Candles?"

"The ones cast during the Winter Solstice? You never did get a chance to explain how you knew about them."

Sarina stopped by the mermaid pond and decided honesty was her only sensible choice, and besides, she sensed Sebastian was only seeking confirmation of what he already suspected. "I've cast the candles."

He nodded slowly. "I thought so, and if I'm correct, that makes you a wise witch and an old one."

She smiled. "It's not polite to ask a woman her age, whether mortal or witch."

"Can't help it, prying is in my blood, and my instincts tell me that you're older than Sydney." He waited for confirmation.

"Your search-and-find skill is not only remarkable, but natural as well. It is no wonder why you do so well in the security business."

"I feel my business is more like a hobby—that's how much pleasure I derive from it. But diverting my attention away from my question will not work. I'm still waiting for an answer. "How old are you?"

Sarina was as honest as possible. "Older than you think or want to know."

"And your powers?"

"Waiting."

"Don't understand that one," he admitted.

"It's best you don't."

Sebastian accepted her answer and didn't pressure her to explain, though he did add his own opinion. "It will all work out well."

"Do you think?" she asked hopefully.

"Dagon won't have it any other way."

Sarina hugged herself tighter. "He may not have a choice."

Sebastian shivered at the helplessness in her voice and was stunned by her sudden change when she turned to him and asked, "Let's practice levitation."

Sebastian rubbed his hands together and grinned. "At last—a viable volunteer."

Dagon retained his controlled demeanor while Sydney and Ali lectured him. Ali had returned looking for her husband, and when she didn't find him in the dining room, she proceeded to join Sydney in berating Dagon for his foolish actions where the Ancient One and Sarina were concerned.

"You think me dim-witted?" he asked, looking from Sydney to Ali.

Ali considered his comment. "Dim-witted, never. Stubborn, definitely."

"We do have something in common, don't we," he said with a teasing laugh.

"At least I'm not foolish," she said.

"That's a debatable issue."

Sydney allowed the two free rein, sitting back and savoring a second cup of coffee.

"Why don't you admit you love Sarina?" Ali asked, standing face to face with him near the tall narrow window.

"That's for me to decide."

"I admitted my love of Sebastian to you."

"You practically shouted it from the rooftops."

Ali narrowed her eyes. "You're impossible."

"First I'm stubborn, now I'm impossible, make up your mind."

"You're impossibly stubborn."

"Like brother, like sister."

"So help me, Dagon, I—" Ali stopped abruptly, her eyes widening. "Oh, no!"

Dagon followed the path of her shocked glance and his own eyes widened.

Sarina lay flat on her back floating in thin air over the mermaid pond, and she was smiling most delightfully.

Dagon and Ali raced out of the room not hearing Sydney's warning.

"Don't disturb Sebastian's magic." Sydney shook her head and went to the window to watch what she was certain would be a predictable and entertaining scene.

Sarina laughed with pleasure. "I had forgotten how delightful this was."

"I'm doing good, then?" Sebastian asked anxiously.

"Excellent," she assured him. "You have moved from novice to pro."

"You're not nervous? After all, I am really nothing more than an amateur witch."

Sarina scolded softly. "Never refer to yourself as such. You must believe in yourself, or you will never possess the full power of your skills. Belief and faith in yourself make you who you really are. And to prove how much I believe in your abilities, I want you to turn me slowly around so that I am looking down at the pond. I would love to view the water from an aerial angle."

Sebastian sounded reluctant. "I don't know if I should attempt that feat. What if I accidentally make you spin?"

"I'll grow dizzy and it will pass."

"What if you drop in the pond?"

"I'll get wet and I'll dry off."

He laughed. "You have an answer for everything."

"I wish."

They both laughed.

"Give it a try," she urged. "I don't mind, and when next do you think you'll get someone to practice on who is as willing as I am and enjoys it as much as I do?"

"You've got a point."

"Then go for it."

Her encouragement convinced him, and he used his finger to execute a perfect turn that had her looking facedown at the pond.

She shouted her excitement. "Hurrah, you did it!"

Unfortunately her gleeful shouts sounded like screeching pleas to Dagon and Ali, and they broke into a run, Ali shouting out Sebastian's name.

Sebastian thought his wife's anguished shout a cry for

help, and he turned suddenly, forgetting about Sarina. She descended rapidly toward the water. Dagon and Ali immediately pointed in her direction to guide her out of harm's way. Unfortunately Sebastian got in the way and went tumbling into the pond from the force of their magic, bumping into Sarina and falling with her into the water.

Ali and Dagon stood speechless at the pond's edge watching the two attempt to stand. They were laughing much too hard and slipping with every step they took, and they looked to be having the time of their lives.

After several failed attempts, Sebastian and Sarina emerged dripping wet from the pond. They hung on to each other as they stood confronting Dagon and Ali.

Sebastian immediately took charge. "We were doing fine until you two interfered."

"He's right," Sarina agreed, hugging his arm, to Dagon's annoyance.

Sarina's wet hair dripped water in her face, and water dripped from the hem of her jumper to pool at her feet. Her clothes stuck to her, and she shivered when a gust of wind wrapped around her. Dagon wanted nothing more than to wrap her in his arms and carry her to the warmth and safety of his castle.

Ali had different ideas for her husband. "Interfered? You dropped her."

"Because of your shout," Sebastian accused with a shake of his finger.

"He's right," Sarina agreed again and irritated Dagon all the more.

"You had no business being outside the castle," Ali said with a firm stamp of her foot.

"You told me to get lost," Sebastian said with a laugh. "And while I didn't take you literally, I thought it best to vacate the premises for a time."

Ali pointed to Sarina. "So you convince this poor girl to let you practice your magic."

Sarina laughed at her remark. "I volunteered."

"To allow a novice to levitate you over a pond?" Dagon asked incredulously.

Sarina was quick to defend. "Sebastian is no novice and he was doing excellent with his lesson until you two, who I should point out should know better than to interfere with a person's magic, did just that—interfered!"

"So it's our faults?" Dagon asked in disbelief.

"Exactly," Sarina and Sebastian said in unison.

"Two inept witches practicing magic, and yet it is the fault of two skilled witches," Dagon confirmed, though he shook his head at the absurdity of the notion.

"Now you understand the problem," Sarina said with a tilt of her chin and another shiver that was obvious to all.

"You're cold," Dagon said, concerned.

"Chilly," she corrected defiantly.

Dagon turned to Ali. "This is all your fault."

"Mine?" she said, shocked.

"Yes, if you would allow your husband to practice his magic on you, he wouldn't seek out anyone else's help."

Ali placed her hands on her hips ready for battle.

"He's in for it now," Sebastian whispered with a smile to Sarina.

Sarina agreed with a nod and her own grin.

"This is your fault," Ali accused back.

Dagon laughed at her remark. "How is that?"

"You should teach Sarina how to countercommand a spell."

"And how do you suppose I do that when she doesn't have a lick of powers."

"Sebastian barely possessed the ability to cast a decent spell, but I've trained him," Ali said defensively.

Sebastian raised a brow and looked to Sarina. No words needed exchanging, they both understood each other completely.

"So what you're saying is that I have lacked in training Sarina properly?"

"You haven't given her the time and patience she requires to develop her skills, therefore, this is your fault."

Sarina spoke. "I think you both need cooling off." With that Sebastian pointed his finger at them, and with a croo and a whirl of his finger he sent the startled couple flying into the pond.

"That was fantastic," Sarina said, praising his magical feat. "Perfectly executed and completed."

"Wow, I even impressed myself," Sebastian said, staring for a moment at his fingertip. "I guess I'm getting the hang of this after all."

Ali and Dagon swatted at each other like irate children until finally they both burst into a fit of laughter and fell into each other's arms. They then made their way easily out of the pond and hurried to catch up with Sebastian and Sarina, who were strolling back to the castle.

It was two laughing couples who burst into the kitchen with Dagon demanding, "Send hot tea and brandy to mine and Sebastian's quarters."

And with peals of laughter following them through the hallway, not to mention trails of puddles, the couples made their way to their rooms.

Margaret looked at Sydney, who had been sitting at the table, a hot cup of raspberry tea in hand. "Love is good."

"At any age," Sydney said with a raise of her teacup.

Dagon and Sarina fell laughing into his room, their hands hurriedly undressing each other, their chilled bodies seeking warmth. Dagon retrieved a beige, soft knit blanket from the closet and wrapped it around the both of their shivering bodies as they sat down on the thick carpet before the blazing fire.

A knock on the door announced the tea and brandy had arrived, and Bernard entered at Dagon's command. He arranged the silver serving tray on the floor beside them and brought two towels from the bathroom to place alongside Dagon.

With a thank you from Dagon, Bernard left the room as quietly as he had entered it.

Sarina saw to pouring the hot tea and adding a liberal amount of brandy while Dagon reached for the towels, quickly drying his hair as best as possible and then seeing to hers. When he finished she handed him a teacup, and they both relaxed against each other and allowed the heat of the tea and the strength of the brandy to warm their insides.

"In all my years here, I have never fallen into that pond." His free hand wrapped around her waist, drawing her closer to him.

She went willingly, content in the safety of his arms. "I thought it a delightful dunking and a good time amongst friends."

Dagon thought it best to tell her of their planned departure. "Ali and Sebastian are leaving tomorrow."

He felt her disappointment in the slight tensing of her body against his.

She sighed. "I will miss them."

"Sydney will remain."

Sarina said nothing, but understood everything. The time was drawing near, the spell would be tested. What would be the outcome? Would she disturb or hurt the spells cast if she admitted to Dagon her love for him now? Could she take the chance?

"You grow quiet. Is something wrong?" he asked with a hug to her midsection.

"Deep thoughts."

"Share them with me," he urged. "I would like to know more about you."

The tea and brandy were beginning to relax her, and she sighed contentedly, nestling back against him. And while she would have loved to tell him of her life, she wisely chose to avoid the issue. "There's nothing to tell."

He placed his empty teacup aside and wrapped his other arm around her, resting his cheek against her temple after kissing there lightly. "There's always something to tell. Tell me what you enjoyed most as a child."

She smiled and ran her hands along his arms, favoring the feel of their strength wrapped so protectively around her, and chose a safe answer. "Wandering in the forest."

"You favor the outdoors."

"The Mother Earth holds the essence of life; what bett

place to learn?'' She moved the questioning to him. ''And you? What did you enjoy most as a child?''

His answer came easily. ''The freedom to explore who I am.''

''And did you find your answer?'' She held her teacup up for him to take a sip.

He did, then answered. ''I feel I did and yet I still question at times.''

''A natural reaction and one shared by many. We think we know who we are, but we fail to understand that we change, grow, evolve with the years. So, therefore, who we once were we no longer are, and the search continues, an exciting journey for sure.''

She sounded much wiser than a mere one hundred years, and he felt it was time to confront the issue of age.

''Don't ask me, Dagon,'' she said, sensing his question and hoping to prevent it.

His arm tightened slightly around her waist. ''Why?''

''You may not like the answer.''

He recalled Sebastian speaking those very words to him, but then he wanted to solve the whole puzzle, and he persisted. ''Tell me your age.''

She attempted tact. ''It isn't nice to ask a woman her age.''

He was firm in his resolve to learn the truth. ''I think that at this point in our relationship it is necessary—not that it will change anything.''

''Are you so sure?''

''Age matters not to me, I told you this.''

''Then why ask?''

''Let's say it's a piece to a puzzle I am trying to solve.''

''Am I the puzzle?'' she asked, moving out of his arms and walking to the closet to retrieve his black silk robe and slip into it.

He admired the trim, firm set of her body and the way she moved with grace and ease, comfortable with herself and with him. His arousal was quick and expected, though he chose to ignore it. This talk was necessary, and he would have his answers.

"You must admit, you are like a puzzle, so many pieces yet nothing fits, nothing makes sense." He eased himself off the floor, wrapping the blanket around his waist to conceal his desire from her as he walked to his closet.

Sarina reached in the closet and grabbed his silver robe, handing it to him. "And I must make sense to you?"

"It would help," he said, putting his robe on, letting the blanket fall to his feet and stepping over it he walked back to the fireplace. He picked up the silver serving tray and placed it on the table by the window, pouring them each another cup of tea and brandy.

"Now will you tell me your age?" he asked, handing the cup to her.

She walked over to him and accepted the tea, wishing the cup held only the brandy. She hoped her answer would appease him, though she doubted it would. "I am older than you think."

He realized she intended to skirt the truth and attempted to at least pinpoint her age. "Are you older than I?"

She nodded and sipped her tea.

"Listening to your wise words of late, I had the feeling you might be."

He did not seem upset, and she hoped he would stop there. He didn't.

"Are you older than Sydney?"

"Dagon, please don't pursue this," she urged, her voice filled with concern.

"You are, aren't you?" he persisted, placing his cup on the table and approaching her. "Why do you fear telling me your age?"

She reached past him and placed her cup beside his, then she ran trembling fingers through her damp hair. "The answer will only bring more questions."

He took her by the arms and held her firm. "Questions you don't wish to answer?"

Her dark eyes turned soft, and he once again caught a glimpse of her wisdom and it startled him as did her response. "Questions I have no answers for."

He felt the need to offer her solace. "Perhaps I can help."

She eased out of his arms and stepped in closer to him, her hands going to cup his face. "You don't know what you ask and I fear—"

She grew silent and with a shake of her head she stepped away from him. How did she tell him she feared losing him? How did she tell him she could not bear to live life without him? How did she tell him that she loved him from the deepest depths of her heart and soul, and still that might not be enough?

He refused to let her go, and he reached out, pulling her back into the circle of his arms. "Let me help you with your fear."

"You don't know what you ask, Dagon."

He pursued regardless of her warnings. "The wise witch dressed in black that haunted my grounds recently was you, wasn't it?" He attempted a guess at her age. "Eight hundred years old?"

Her lips remained locked.

He slowly released her and stepped back away from her. "You're over a thousand years old, aren't you?"

She confirmed his suspicion with a simple nod.

He was stunned by her admission. And asked the next logical question. "A spell stole your powers?"

She answered with another nod.

He closed his eyes, shook his head, and rubbed at his temples. Her powers far surpassed his, and that meant that it took a witch of equal or greater powers to have cast a spell on her. His meager skills could not hope to compare to her opponent's, and yet there had to be a way of helping her. He loved her much too much to lose her.

An idea hit him. "I will speak to the Ancient One on this matter when she arrives, perhaps she can offer help."

Pleased with his decision, he opened his eyes.

Sarina was gone.

Twenty-five

Dagon left the castle without a word to anyone. Dressed all in black, his long overcoat left open, his long dark hair free and blowing in the gusty wind, he walked with a determined gait into the woods that surrounded his property.

He had first thought to go after Sarina when he saw that she had hastily vacated his room, but after only a few steps he realized that she required time alone as did he. Their relationship had begun on a chaotic note with twists and turns he had never expected, and even now he still did not know the truth about the woman he loved.

He had gathered a number of new pieces to the puzzle, but he was having difficulty linking them together and making them fit. The one positive about the whole troublesome situation was that he loved Sarina.

That was not in question. How he could help her was.

Cold, brisk air stung his face, and he cursed himself for not bringing along his gloves, for his hands were beginning to feel the cold. He stuck them deep into the pockets of his wool overcoat and continued his trek along the narrow path that wound deeper into the woods.

He didn't know why he chose to lose himself in the woods. Perhaps it was the silence he sought, perhaps the closeness of Mother Earth, or perhaps it was because Sarina had mentioned her love of the forest and being here he felt close to her.

He stopped abruptly, threw his head back, and roared at the heavens, releasing what he could of his pent-up anguish and confusion.

With that done his thoughts turned to Sarina, and he felt the urge to go to her, be with her, hold her to him, and convince her that all would go well. He turned, intending to return to the castle, when a gentle voice stopped him.

"She's needs time. Let her come to you."

Dagon smiled and looked to his right shoulder. There stood a plump little fairy with a beautiful face and one crooked wing. A wreath of wildflowers sprinkled with gold dust sat lopsided on her head, and she wore a soft white wool dress with a hooded cloak that was trimmed in gold braid. "Beatrice, I'm pleased to see you."

"Thought you might be," she said, walking along his shoulder to kiss his cheek. She then flew off to flitter in front of his face, her crooked wing tilting her to the right. "What's troubling you?"

Dagon offered his hand as a seat, and Beatrice accepted, plopping down into his cupped hand and fluttering off it just as fast. "You never did remember your gloves even as a child," she scolded gently, and with a soft yet hardy blow of her breath over his chilled hand she warmed it. She then comfortably nestled in his palm. "Now talk with me."

"I'm in love," he said, walking to sit on a large smooth rock.

Beatrice clapped her hands. "How delightful. I am so happy for you."

Dagon's expression grew grime. "There's a problem."

"There's always a problem where love is concerned."

"But can problems always be solved, especially when love is involved?"

"That depends," she said.

"On what?"

"On the strength of the couple's love."

"Love solves all problems, is that it?"

She shook a tiny finger at him. "Don't go doubting what you know is the truth. You know the power of love, its potential to heal, to create, to join."

"But what if something more powerful stands in the way?"

"What could be more powerful than love?"

He answered quickly. "A spell."

She shook her finger and her head at him. "Do you forget your lessons?"

"Remind me," he said with a smile, feeling warm and loved in her tiny yet immense presence.

"Why do witches cast spells?"

His answer was the same as it was when he was a young boy and she first had asked it of him. "To help."

The lesson continued. "Why would a witch want to help?"

"Because she or he cares and wishes no harm to befall anyone."

"And why would she or he care?"

He gave her question thought, though he answered quickly. "Because witches know the strongest power is that of love."

"Think on this wisely, Dagon, and you will have your answer to your problem."

He was about to speak when Beatrice held her small hand up. "More questions will do you no good. You have all the pieces you need to solve this puzzle."

Dagon looked surprised. "You've spoken to Sebastian."

"We visited recently. He is a good friend to you."

"He asked you to help me, didn't he?"

"He is returning the favor. You requested I help him and he was grateful. Now he requests that I help you."

"And I am grateful. I miss talking with you."

Her usual brilliant smile faded. "I have been very busy. There is one who soon will need my help, and I fear I may not be strong enough to help her. She will come up against great magic, and no one knows the outcome."

"I will cast a spell to the heavens for her safety."

"This is kind of you and I thank you for your thought-

fulness." She stood, her tiny feet resting in his warm hand.
"You must remember of what we spoke. It is vital to your
situation."

"One more question," he said as she floated slowly up
to flitter lopsidedly in front of his face.

She shook her head. "There is only one answer, Dagon."

"To all my questions?"

"To all your questions," she confirmed.

"Will you be close by if I should need help?" he asked
anxiously.

"Yes, it is imperative this situation is resolved."

"Why?"

"You will understand," she said and gave his cheek a
gentle pat. "And remember, always remember what I've
told you. One day you will need to know the answer."

"The answer to all my questions?"

She nodded. "Yes, know it and know the secret." She
waved to him as she flew up and away, disappearing in a
shaft of sparkling light.

He had much to think about as he walked back slowly
to the castle.

Sarina sat alone in the kitchen. The castle was quiet when
she finally made her way downstairs from her room. She
had sat for over an hour in thought and could come to no
easy solution. Silence was her only option at the moment,
and while she had always learned from the silence, she
presently felt trapped by it.

Tired of sulking in her room, she had slipped on an off-
white free-flowing knit dress and white knit socks. She
wore white bikini panties beneath and nothing else. She
needed to feel free of any restrictions and this garment provided her with that sense of freedom. She had felt confined
much too long, and she wished for her own home, the small
cottage that opened onto woods and meadows where she
could run free whenever she chose.

She sighed, tired of this constant worry, and stood
abruptly. Action was better than inaction. She needed to

divert her thoughts and what better way than to bake something, keeping her hands and mind busy.

Margaret, Sydney, and Bernard had gone off to the market and would not return for several hours. Sebastian was busy with business in Dagon's study, and Ali was busy packing. She did not know Dagon's whereabouts, but if he wished to speak with her, he would certainly have no problem finding her.

This time was hers, and she intended to bake away her troubled thoughts. She took a cookbook from the pantry where Margaret kept a stack of them and decided on baking a batch of sugar cookies. She covered her dress with a large white apron and began gathering all the ingredients.

"What are you doing?" Ali asked, entering the kitchen.

"Baking cookies," she said, measuring the flour into the large mixing bowl.

"Can I help?" Ali asked, excited at the prospect.

Ali's lack of skill in the kitchen did not disturb Sarina, and besides, she was a patient teacher. "Only if you promise to do as I tell you."

Ali nodded enthusiastically. "I promise."

"Get an apron from the pantry for yourself."

"I don't need one," she said, but changed her mind fast enough when she saw Sarina raise a brow at her. "I'll get one."

They were soon mixing, rolling, and cutting out stars, moons, and angel-shaped cookies, chattering and laughing the whole time.

They were decorating the last batch of cookies with Ali carefully spreading a creamy white icing on the angels and adding a touch of gold sprinkles.

"Sebastian is never going to believe I baked these cookies," she said with excitement. "I'm so pleased with myself, and you are such a patient teacher, Sarina."

Sarina smiled and dusted a star with silver sprinkles.

"You're very old, aren't you?" Ali asked in a whisper, almost in reverence.

"Yes, I am," Sarina admitted with pride.

"I know there is much more to your magic problem than

we all realize, and I am concerned for you and Dagon. He is wise but he cannot match your wisdom, and I worry for him.''

''I do as well, but I also believe in him and have faith in our love.''

''He's told you he loves you?'' Ali asked with surprise.

Sarina shook her head, though she smiled. ''He has not spoken the words, but I feel his love every time he holds me, touches me, kisses me, makes love to me. It is there for me to see if only I look.''

''I understand,'' Ali said on a sigh. ''I see Sebastian's love all the time and it thrills me, especially when he gets that sensual sparkle in his eyes. There's just no hiding the fact that he wants to make love with me. Of course I tease him on occasion, but it makes our joining all the more fun and satisfying.''

''You have found a magical love.''

''Yes, and I am grateful every day for having him in my life.'' Ali grinned, a purely wicked grin, and scooped up several cookies to place on a plate. ''I think I'll go offer my husband some fresh-baked cookies.''

For a brief second Sarina was envious of Ali being so safe and secure in her love and commitment with Sebastian and that she felt naughty enough to seduce her husband with cookies.

Ali seemed to read her thoughts. ''Take cookies to Dagon.''

Sarina laughed softly. ''I don't think I'm as naughty as you.''

Ali shook her head slowly. ''I bet you can be real naughty when you want to be. You just have to want to, you have to believe.''

''Who's the teacher now?'' Sarina asked, giving her suggestion serious thought.

''Whoever needs to be the teacher,'' Ali said and placed several cookies on another plate, then discarded her apron over the chair. ''Now let's stop being teachers and cooks and turn ourselves into vamps.'' She held a plate out to Sarina.

"I don't think Dagon's in the castle."

Ali untied Sarina's apron and pulled it off, tossing it to join hers on the chair, then forced the plate of cookies on her. "Wait in his room." She pushed Sarina toward the door.

"What about milk?" Sarina asked. "You can't eat cookies without milk."

"Sweety," Ali said exasperated. "They'll be lucky if they get to eat the cookies."

Ali gave her another shove and they were out the kitchen door and into the hall. "Now go," Ali ordered, pointing to the staircase, and with a sinful sway of her hips Ali headed to the study.

Sarina climbed the stairs slowly. She couldn't understand her reluctance to seduce Dagon. After all, she had done it before, and she did feel comfortable being intimate with him. So why suddenly a case of nerves?

Perhaps it was what was left unspoken between them that caused her to tremble. What yet they had to say, what yet was to be. And of course the outcome.

She approached his closed door with apprehension, grabbing hold of the knob. He could be elsewhere in the castle or not in the castle at all, in which case it would not matter. She would leave the plate of cookies and make a hasty departure.

She turned the knob and with her breath paused she entered.

His room was empty, the remnants of their morning indulgence gone, his bed made. Trepidation was instantly replaced by disappointment, and she walked over to the table near the window and set the plate of cookies down.

With a sigh of regret she turned to see Dagon standing in the doorway.

Her breath caught, her heart raced, and her blood heated in a mere second of looking at him. He was a compelling sight all in black, his long hair windswept, his handsome face stern, and his deep blue eyes focused intently on her.

"Cookies," she said, though she sounded more like she croaked the word.

He regarded her strangely as he entered and shut the door behind him.

She stepped aside and pointed to the plate, repeating more clearly, "Cookies."

He slipped off his overcoat, tossing it on the back of a chair as he approached her. "You baked them?"

She nodded and held the plate up to him.

He noticed her tremble but made no comment. He chose a star cookie. "Sugar cookies, my favorite." He took a bite and chewed slowly, all the while keeping his eyes on her.

She returned the plate to the table, her hand trembling too much to hold on to it.

"Very good," he said and broke off a piece to place near her lips. "Taste."

She took the small piece, his fingertips brushing her lips as he offered it to her.

The fresh earthy and pine scent of his chilled fingers sparked her senses, and she never felt quite so alive. Her eyes drifted closed as she savored the intensity of her emotions. The buttery richness of the sugar cookie melted in her mouth and tingled her taste buds, making her want more. Sounds flowed like a rich melody around her, the soft murmur of his steady breath, the potent beat of his heart. And then there was the urge to touch.

She forced herself to open her eyes and stop the madness, and when she did she saw the same madness in his eyes.

He dropped the partially eaten cookie to the plate and took her face in his hands with an urgent roughness. "Taste."

The simple word suggested so much, and once again her eyes drifted closed and she lost herself to her heightened senses.

They had kissed many times, gentle, rough, slow, hungry, but never had she tasted the essence of him. This was magic pure and simple.

It didn't take long for their hands to pull and tug at each other's clothes, to fall naked on the bed, to join with an urgency that had their hands locked together as tightly as their bodies. And to ride as one on a wave of pleasure that had them both crying out as they burst in a sudden climax that shuddered and trembled their bodies over and over and over again.

Dagon moved slowly off her and collapsed on his back beside her, his breathing still labored.

Sarina sighed with the pleasure only a good climax can bring and lay contented, her body much too relaxed to move a muscle. "I should bring you cookies more often," she said teasingly.

His breathing having calmed, he said, "Dear heart, you can bring me cookies any time."

She laughed and turned on her side, her hand reaching out to rub his stomach. "You may get fat."

He shook his head with a laugh. "I'll make certain to get plenty of exercise."

They continued to tease and taunt each other until their playful antics once again aroused them, and once again they joined together forgetting the world existed, forgetting everything but the magical moment they shared.

Ali was teary-eyed when she hugged Sarina good-bye the next day, and it was with reluctance that she quit hugging Dagon. She had said a quick good-bye to Sydney at breakfast, knowing she would be home before her.

Sebastian gave Sarina a kiss on the cheek and with a whisper reminded her that if she was ever in need of a friend he was close by. And for all to hear he said, "I can't thank you enough for helping my wife combat the kitchen."

"Just make certain she follows the recipes I gave her."

Ali smiled sweetly and said, "I think the cherry pie recipe may need extra cherries."

Dagon slapped Sebastian on the back. "At least she'll be testing that recipe at home."

Sebastian gave Dagon's hand a hardy shake. "Under strict supervision."

Ali ran her hand slowly down her husband's arm. "I like when you help me in the kitchen."

"In the car, witch," he ordered playfully, grabbing her stroking hand.

Ali shook her head. "You think he would pick a more civilized mode of travel."

Sebastian nibbled at her neck. "I don't feel civil."

Ali's eyes sparkled as she issued orders to the driver to take his time.

With promises that Dagon would visit with them soon and waves and kisses thrown, Sebastian and Ali finally departed.

"I'm going to miss them," Sarina said, climbing the stone stairs to the castle.

"Ali has a way of staying on your mind and in your heart, and I must admit I find Sebastian a closer friend than I had expected."

He took her hand as they climbed the last few remaining steps to the front door, and she accepted it gratefully. She was uncertain of how much time they would have together, and she wanted to make certain she enjoyed every minute with him.

"What would you like to do today?" he asked her as they entered the castle.

Bernard closed the door behind them, and she held her tongue until they walked into the small receiving parlor.

"What of my work?"

He answered with patience and not a bit of annoyance. "We need time together, Sarina. Time to know each other and time to know what we want from each other. Will you share that time with me?"

"With pleasure," she said without hesitancy.

"Good, then I repeat, what would you like to do today?"

She didn't need to give his question thought—she knew. "Gather the pine and cones to make the wreaths and swags for the Winter Solstice."

"And a tree for Christmas," he added with excitement.

She grew just as excited. "A big one?"

"As big as you want."

She laughed and threw her arms around his neck, giving

him a big sloppy kiss, which he eagerly accepted. ''This will be a wonderful holiday season.''

''The best,'' he agreed. *And the first of many.* He kept his thoughts to himself, though they were more of a promise to himself. He knew of only one way to make her understand how much he loved her, how he ached to spend the rest of his life with her, how he wanted her and her alone as a lifemate. And he would help her rid herself of whatever spell was cast upon her, and if that were not possible he would love her for who she was forever and always. But for now they would laugh and love and live and not worry about the future.

''Go change into something warm and suitable for the woods while I do the same.''

She deposited a hasty kiss on his lips and warned, ''Don't be long. I'll meet you out by the mermaid pond.''

''I'll be waiting,'' he said and rushed past her.

''No fair,'' she called out and hurried after him.

Dagon turned the corner of the castle and rushed to the pond, seeing Sarina approach. She laughed as she tried to outrace him, and he grinned at the enticing picture she presented.

Ribbed black tights hugged her slim legs, and black boots rode up to her knees. A knit gray turtleneck sweater fell over her slender hips. A dark gray wool jacket dotted with silver stars topped the sweater, the two star buttons being left undone. She had tucked her dark hair beneath a silver knit hat, a wisp of bangs falling over her forehead and along her temples.

He in turn had chosen black jeans, black turtleneck, and a heavy gray wool slipover sweater that served him as well as a jacket. They seemed almost a matching pair, and he liked the thought.

He caught her up in his arms as she rushed at him, and they laughed like a young couple in love and hurried off down the path to the woods, hand in hand, their gaiety a delightful tinkle in the air.

Sydney watched from the window in her room with concern. Time was drawing near, and she could do nothing more to prevent the collision that was certain to take place.

Nothing except offer a cast of protection.

She raised her hands up, drawing a circle with her fingers around the couple in the distance. "Love surround them with your faith; keep their hearts forever safe; unite their souls to form one; and let no one prevent what I have begun."

Twenty-six

Dagon bundled together the batch of pine branches they had gathered while Sarina scouted the nearby trees for just the right size pinecones. She glanced up at the tall pine trees. She had explained that different sizes were needed in the decorating of wreaths and swags. The proper size pinecones and the plump red berries are what gave the wreath character.

Sarina stared at the tall pine with graduating branches that bore a plethora of pinecones and announced, "This tree has what we need."

Dagon looked up, noticing the sky had darkened considerably since they had left the castle almost two hours ago, and the brisk wind had grown tempestuous. "We best hurry. The weather is about to turn dreadful."

She quickly hurried to his side and draped her arms around his neck. "All ready."

"For what?" he asked, though he understood what she expected.

"For you to take me up to those high branches so I may pick the pinecones."

His arms went around her waist to hug her snugly to him. "You think I should take you with me?"

She delivered a whispered kiss to his lips. "I know you should take me."

His teasing persisted as he slowly floated them up in the air. "You will only get yourself in trouble."

She felt them leave the ground, felt the strength of his arms tightly around her, felt the power of his magic circle them, and smiled. "And you will rescue me."

He rubbed her slim nose with his. "Always."

"Promise?" she asked anxiously.

He settled them on a sturdy branch and ran a tender kiss across her lips. "You are worried about something." It wasn't a question, he knew the answer. Her tense body made him keenly aware of her concern.

"A senseless worry," she said, attempting to reassure him—or perhaps herself.

He accepted no resistance. He intended an answer. "Not senseless if you gave it thought. Tell me."

She answered with reluctance and apprehension. "What if one day you cannot rescue me?"

He kissed her lips softly and whispered. "Always, always I will rescue you, never doubt it."

"But—" she attempted to protest.

"No, *buts*," he warned her with a kiss that silenced her. "There is nothing, absolutely nothing in this world that will prevent me from rescuing you."

"There are magical powers greater than you," she challenged.

"Great magical power brings great wisdom and can be reasoned with."

She laughed gently as if she knew something he didn't. "I wouldn't count on that."

He claimed a kiss that left her breathless. "Count on that and count on me, I will never fail you."

Joy filled her to the brim, and she felt hopeful that all would turn out well. She was about to voice her confidence in him when a sudden gust of wind whipped through the tree branches and swirled in a whirlwind around them.

Dagon instantly tightened his grip around her waist and shielded her with his body. The wind died as instantly as it had surfaced, and Sarina looked about in surprise.

"Expecting someone?" he asked, watching her searching eyes grow wide.

She sounded as if she asked herself the question as well as him. "Rain?"

"Soon," he confirmed, "which means we'd better hurry."

Sarina kept an arm around Dagon's neck as they floated from branch to branch plucking pinecones. They laughed, teased, and kissed often, and Dagon used his magical skills to bring the basket up off the ground to float alongside them, making collecting the cones that much easier.

The basket full and raindrops beginning to fall, the laughing couple floated with haste to the ground and hurried off with their finds to the castle. They entered the kitchen just as the rain turned to a torrential downpour. Margaret had lunch waiting—vegetable soup and beef sandwiches on thick crusty bread.

Unfortunately, Dagon had received several frantic business calls and reluctantly could not join her. Sarina tried to hide her disappointment, assuring him she would be fine on her own. After all, there was so much to do to prepare the pine and cones for assembling.

He took her hand, kissed her palm, and drew her into his embrace whispering, "I will make this up to you this evening."

His promise appeased her, and she relaxed against him. "Then I look forward to this evening."

A kiss to her lips and he was gone.

She ate her soup and chatted with Margaret about the holiday decorations, proudly showing off her collection of pinecones. Soon the table was cleared off and paper spread over it and the pine branches placed on top along with the basket of pinecones.

The scent of fresh pine permeated the kitchen, and as soon as the two women began to twist, bend, and shape the branches, the aroma grew even stronger. With a strong sense of friendship the women worked side by side, their hands working their magic though no magic was needed.

Both had done this enjoyable chore for many years, and it never failed to excite and please.

Sydney burst into the kitchen. "Why did you not tell me of the severity of the spell?"

Margaret remained quiet, her hands continuing to twist and bend the branches into a beautifully crafted wreath.

"How do you know of the spell?" Sarina asked calmly, her hands stopping their work.

Sydney softened her response in respect of a wise one. "I am not at liberty to say."

Sarina nodded in understanding and smiled. "If I were to venture a guess, I would say that a little fairy told you."

Sydney conceded. "I forget about your remarkable sight."

"If the fairies have begun to talk, then they are worried," Sarina said with concern.

"Very much so, they fear your prediction."

Sarina sighed her frustration. "I meant no harm, I only wished to help."

"They know this," Sydney reassured her, "and they are frantic to help you."

"They cannot."

"Which has them all the more worried."

Sarina spoke softly, her dark eyes filling with age-old wisdom. "Tell them that all will be well. There is one who will rescue me."

A bittersweet smile crossed Sydney's face. "And once he does, the rest remains up to you."

"I have given it much thought," Sarina said, "and I realize the answer will not come to me if I chase after it."

"Then what will you do?"

"Wait and know that the answer is already mine."

Dagon returned several calls, handled a business problem, conducted a meeting over the computer, and managed to eat his lunch in between. He had several more E-mails to answer and a contract to download and read later. When all he wanted to do was spend the remainder of the day with Sarina.

When had she become so essential to his life? He had thought his life full, and once he chose a lifemate, it would be complete. But complete was an ending, not a beginning, and with Sarina life had just begun. When they were together, he experienced a joy of life so potent, so desirous, that the sensations astounded him. He sometimes wondered if she were real or merely a fantasy of his own making. Then he would touch her and have his answer.

Life plans had once been essential to him; now he realized life had plans of its own, and when two were meant to be one, there was no stopping the magic.

The phone rang and he reached for it with a smile.

"Dagon, it's Sebastian."

"You're in Ireland already?" he asked, glancing at the clock and noticing it was already late afternoon.

Sebastian gave a quick laugh. "Lost track of time, did you?"

"You know that old saying, time flies when you're having fun."

"You can say that again, and I'm about to have some fun of my own when I get off the phone. But first the reason I called."

"Which is?"

"I discovered some information about the Ancient One that might prove helpful to you."

Dagon sat forward in his chair. "I'm listening."

Sebastian wasted no time. "Did you know that she was once deeply in love?"

"I heard something about one love in her life."

"He was a powerful warlock."

"Warlock?" he repeated with surprise.

"My exact response. I remember Sydney saying something about warlocks being evil."

"They practice the darker side of magic. Which makes me wonder why a witch of her immense wisdom and power would associate herself with a warlock."

"That I couldn't find out, I could only piece together what I discovered and make assumptions from those facts. So the facts are that we know she loved a warlock, that

love was somehow lost, perhaps never returned, and she
has never loved since, leaving her—"

Dagon finished. "A wiser woman where love is concerned."

"Which might just work to your advantage."

"This information definitely has helped me, thank you,
Sebastian."

A brief pause proceeded Sebastian's response. "A word
of caution."

Dagon listened in silence.

"Keep your patience. Her powers are tremendous, and I
hear her temper is legendary."

"I'll keep that in mind, and thanks for the help, Sebastian. I truly appreciate it and your concern."

"No problem, take care and good luck."

Dagon returned the phone to the receiver and gave
thought to his helpful and cautionary words. He never
lacked confidence in his powers, he was a potent witch and
intelligent, and it was his intelligence that he would need
when dealing with the Ancient One. His powers were of
little consequence where she was concerned for her powers
far exceeded his.

Reason, patience, and wisdom would serve him well. But
in the end he knew the most powerful weapon at his disposal would be that of love. If she loved once and lost that
love, then she would understand his feelings, her wisdom
would not allow for anything else, and in the end love
would be his saving grace.

He looked out on the rain that pelted the windows, vicious and intent, demanding entrance, yet he was safe as
was Sarina and that was how he would keep her—safe. He
would allow no harm to befall her. He would be there for
her always rescuing her, caring for her, loving her. She was
part of him and he part of her. They were joined as one
forever and always.

He loved her plain and simple.

And while love wasn't simple, it also wasn't perfect. And
he accepted that and looked forward to the challenge love
would offer them. Life was suddenly wonderfully delirious,

and he chose to experience every fruitful moment to its fullest.

He stood, switching his computer to sleep mode. He had conducted enough business for one day. It was time to find Sarina.

Dagon watched from the kitchen doorway. The three women—Sydney, Margaret, and Sarina—were laughing and chattering while their fingers were busy twisting the pine branches. Several wreaths sat piled waiting for decorations, and half a dozen swags sat to the side glittering with a generous sprinkle of gold dust.

Mugs of hot chocolate sat amongst the branches, and a plate of shortbread cookies sat aside from the pine and looked to have been steadily enjoyed. The rain that pounded the windows mattered not to them. They were engrossed in the moment they shared together, and he envied their easy camaraderie. They appeared lifelong friends.

Dagon thought a moment and realized that they could very well have known each other for many years, and he suddenly felt the need to learn more about the woman he loved, much more.

"The castle will look magnificent," he said, strolling casually into the kitchen.

Sarina smiled with delight. "Yes, it will look simply stunning. We're working on swags for all the fireplaces and a special one for over the door, though I think we may need more pine branches."

"No problem. When the weather clears, I will collect more for you," he said and looked longing at her hot chocolate.

"Want some?" she asked and raised her mug to him.

He took it like a greedy child along with a shortbread cookie.

In no time the women had him helping, dusting the pinecones with gold and stringing the berries in bunches. The tasks were simple, the company delightful, and the momen a memory maker. This time he would remember forever.

He blessed Sydney when she sighed in his direction an

told him she was simply too tired to join him for supper and preferred her meal sent to her room. Before he could suggest that Margaret send a simple fare to his room for supper, she suggested that it was a good evening for hot soup before the hearth and informed him that she would have a meal for him and Sarina sent to his room.

He was much too intelligent to think this a coincidence. The two women had planned this little maneuver, and he smiled in appreciation of their deviousness.

Margaret and Sydney shooed Sarina out of the kitchen along with Dagon, insisting that they would clean up, and that tomorrow was time enough to resume the task at hand. By week's end the wreaths and swags would be ready for hanging, and the thought excited Sarina.

Her childish thrill was contagious, and Dagon hurried along hand in hand with her as she detailed where the wreaths and swags would hang. She talked of the trees that would grace the foyer and the living room and insisted that they be uprooted carefully and replanted in an area of their choosing.

She chatted about the fairy dust that would light the trees, and the cones and berries that would decorate them, and it was during her endless chatter that he realized the extent of her knowledge. She spoke with the wisdom of the wise ones who were familiar with the Mother Earth and who would do all in their power to protect her children.

His silence silenced her and she looked at him with age-old eyes that knew.

He brought her to the sofa in the small receiving parlor and sat, easing her with a gentle tug down beside him. "Tell me about your youth."

Her willingness to share her past appeared in a generous smile, and she eagerly slipped off her boots with some help from Dagon, and casually draped her legs across his. He in turn ran a tender hand along her leg as she spoke.

"Much of my youth was spent in the forest. It was where the most knowledge could be acquired. There is where the meaning of life is most prevalent. The continuous cycle, never-ending, a constant renewal, and that is where my lessons began.''

"You sound as if you enjoyed every moment."

"Enjoyed and cherished. It was an experience I will fondly remember. And when I need reassuring or consoling, I return to the woods and am once again renewed by its energy."

"Who taught you?"

"My sight, my touch, my senses were my teachers and I listened. The silence taught me well."

Dagon wondered if all her time was spent alone and asked, "This was a solitary classroom?"

Her laugh was joyous. "How could life in the woods be solitary? There is so much to see and learn and so many friends to share it with."

He understood. "You are attuned with the animals."

She looked at him oddly. "I am aware of life."

"I guess I just learned a lesson."

"Perhaps relearned," she suggested. "Often we forget the simple knowledge and at times require a nudge of reminding."

His stroke of her leg turned slow and lazy. "If I had a teacher like you I would have remembered my lessons well."

"A pity," she said on a sigh. "Then you would never have required extra help."

"You think there is more you can teach me?"

"There is always more to learn."

"Show me," he challenged, his hand creeping up her thigh beneath her long sweater.

She swatted his hand away, and with a smile that promised magic she slid across his legs, coming to nest with an intentional wiggle of her bottom in his lap. Her arms she draped casually around his neck.

His hands slipped around her waist and down over her hips to cup her backside firmly. "I'm all ready, teacher."

"That you are," she said with a slow stroke of her bottom intimately against him.

"You're playing with fire," he said on a groan.

She gave a low throaty laugh before her teeth descended with playful intent on his lower lip. "Let me teach you more about fire."

And she did, her lips in no hurry in their deliberate torment, her tongue a weapon of sensuality, and her rocking hips an instrument of erotic rhythm. His blood raced like hot lava through his veins, igniting his loins hard and fast.

Now.

His desire for her rang loudly in his head, and he attempted to vocalize his passion, but only a groan escaped his lips that were busy being bruised with her own endless need for him.

Now.

He wanted her and him naked right now, this very moment and then—then she could continue to teach him about fire.

The hot urgency that raced through his blood had him grabbing her around the waist and standing with a sudden swiftness that startled her but not for long. Her own urgent need had her wrapping her legs securely around his waist.

With their blood running hot Dagon mounted the stairs quickly, and after a hurried slam of his door he proceeded to learn just how wicked fire could be.

Twenty-seven

The week passed in a flurry of activities. The castle blazed with decorations for the approaching holidays. Pine swags decorated with an array of pinecones and berries and dusted with gold fairy dust graced the door tops. A large wreath dressed with pinecones and bunches of red berries greeted all who arrived at the front door while smaller wreaths dressed the numerous windows. A drapery of pine sprinkled heavily with gold dust dipped along the mantels. Fat white candles wrapped with small pine wreaths graced tabletops and mantels throughout the castle, and berry wreaths hung above doorways.

A large tree trimmed with the precious gifts of Mother Earth sat in splendor in the foyer. Sarina had painstakingly strung red berries, collected empty bird nests and swigs of dried heather, and made snowflakes from tissue paper to hang on the tall tree that reached to the ceiling. The top of the tree was bare as was the old way, for on the eve of the Winter Solstice she would call on the night sky to send her a special star that would shine its brilliant light on the new dawn.

The tree in the living room was tall and plump and was adorned with stars, angels, moons, and suns; many made from cookies, others made from paper and some fashioned from pines and berries. As was the mortal way a sparkle of white lights and a string of popcorn circled the tree. The top was once again bare, for Sarina intended to request two stars to help guide their way for the new dawn, the new cycle that would greet the new day.

Dagon found her on her hands and knees tending to the fat tree in the living room. She was arranging a thatch of pine needles around its base to keep the balled roots moist and fresh. Her derrière moved invitingly in his face as he entered the room, and he stopped to enjoy the show.

Thoughts of their joinings filled his head. They simply could not get enough of each other. They made magic often and shared magical moments at every opportunity. He never tired of kissing her, of reaching out to touch her, of stripping her bare and sharing the most intimate of unions with her. They fell asleep in each others arms and woke up wrapped in each others arms with Lady Lily usually snuggled contentedly between them.

He rescued her from tilting and swaying ladders. She baked him cookies and cakes. They laughed, they teased, they loved, and the week drew fast to an end.

More pieces of the puzzle seemed to fall into place, and he began to speculate over her lack of powers, and he wondered and considered and hoped he was wrong but he had the strong sense that somehow, some way she was connected to the Ancient One.

And if his assumptions proved correct, he wondered in the end if he was powerful enough to rescue her when it mattered the most.

He pushed his concerns aside and tilted his head along with her swaying backside. She wore the lavender dress that gave her no shape or form, and he knew she rarely wore any other clothing beneath it except socks. Lord, how he loved her in socks and nothing else. And she had socks on, lavender ones that matched the dress.

Damn, but if he didn't want to find out what else lay beneath that dress.

He walked over to her.

"First I'll tend to the tree and then I'll tend to you," Sarina told him, her head remaining buried beneath the low hanging branches of the tree.

"Promise," he asked and ran a teasingly slow hand over her backside.

She shivered at his languid touch. "I'm like a child in a candy store with you. I am simply not satisfied with one taste. I constantly want more."

His exploring hand told him what he already knew, she was naked beneath. "That's because I taste so sweet."

Her laugh was brief and hardy. "Your taste is far from sweet, though it is addictive."

"Good, come out from under there and sample me."

She wiggled her way out from beneath the low hanging branches, his hand extended to help her up. She was in his arms in no time, their lips nearly touching when Sydney all but flew into the room.

"*She* arrives within the hour."

Sarina went rigid in his arms. He himself stiffened briefly and then he kissed her soft and tender, reassuring her of his love, though they had yet to voice their feelings aloud.

"I should change," she said and slipped out of his arms to quietly leave the room.

"You look fine," Sydney told him, casting an approving glance over his dark gray attire, from trousers to sweater to sport jacket. His ensemble bore a striking resemblance to the sky outside, an ominous gray, a portent of the storm that was yet to break. His dark hair, so long and lustrous, spilled over his shoulders, and his handsome face was a mask of strength and determination. It was obvious he intended to have his way, and Sydney shivered at the possible cost.

"I will make sure that she sees reason," Dagon said and began to pace in front of the large tree that twinkled with a plethora of white lights.

"You called her here for an introduction," she reminded.

Dagon stopped pacing, his look intent and his bearing regal. "A simple introduction."

Sydney glared at him. "When one requests an introduction with the Ancient One it is with intent.''

''My intention could be for anything!'' he nearly shouted, his nerves dangerously close to the edge.

''Fine,'' Sydney acknowledged with a wave of her hand. ''But I warn you, make certain your intentions are clear from the start.''

Dagon turned silent with Bernard's entrance. ''Excuse me, sir, I heard the news and wondered if you had any specific instructions.''

Dagon looked to Sydney. ''Does she have any preferences?''

''A good wine and a light fare would be appropriate.''

A sudden gust of window and torrential rain pounded the windows, startling the three.

Bernard shook his head before regaining his composure and quickly excused himself.

''She arrives on the wind of a storm,'' Sydney informed him with a shiver and then rushed to Dagon's side, taking his hand in hers. ''Your powers will do you little good. Your strongest weapon is your heart.''

Dagon had no chance to respond. The room suddenly filled with a gust of wind, though nothing in the room was disturbed, a swirl of blinding light followed, and then in a flash it disappeared, and there before him stood the most stunningly beautiful woman he had ever seen.

Her long blond hair fell to her waist in reckless waves and was streaked with a red so bright that the startling combination gave the silky strands the appearance of raging flames. And her features were so outstanding that not even an accomplished artist could capture her true beauty. Her skin was a peachy cream color, smooth and, he suspected, silky soft. Her pale green eyes remained steady on him, and he was mesmerized by the depth of aged wisdom they possessed.

Her dress was a unique creation. It was as white as newly fallen snow and looked to be of the softest wool and it draped, wrapped, and hugged every curve and mound of her luscious body. She wore white slippers, really just the barest of covering and her feet were rather small for her height, which he thought to be at least six to seven inches over five feet.

Not even the hint of a smile passed across her full, plump lips the color of ripe apricots and she held her head at a high enough angle to announce to all that she was waiting and not patiently.

Sydney stepped forward and with a respectful bow of her head made the introduction. "Tempest, may I introduce Dagon Rasmus."

Dagon stepped forward. He was secure in his ability to charm witch or woman, and while this witch definitely robbed a man of sense and reason, he worried not, his heart would always belong to Sarina.

He gave a brief, old-fashioned bow from the waist down before reaching out to take her hand.

She shocked him and, he hated to admit it, insulted him by intentionally stepping away out of his reach. Her tone was curt and impatient. "Why did you request an introduction?"

He watched her float a few inches above the floor toward the large tree and noticed that her slippers were not soiled. Did she never walk?

Her wide eyes warned, her stern voice cautioned. "It is not for you to question where my feet touch."

Granted she deserved respect for age alone, but rudeness in his own home he would not tolerate. "My thoughts are private."

"Not when they concern me."

Sydney moved forward to interfere, but Dagon prevented her intervention with an outstretched hand. "I repeat, my thoughts are private, and I will not have them invaded. You are aware of our rules, and I ask that you respect them in my home."

He thought he caught a glimpse of admiration in her glowing eyes, though he couldn't be certain, it was so brief, but regardless he intended to stand his ground with this witch who was aptly named.

She did not acknowledge his request, but then again she

did not mention his thought of her name suiting her, so he assumed she would oblige him.

She drifted around the tree, her touch delicate as she examined the decorations and skimmed fingertips over the pine branches. Her fingers were long and graceful in their tender movements, and he could have sworn the tree responded to her every stroke, the branches seeming to stretch out so that the pine needles could whisper gently across her skin.

"A beautifully prepared tree for the Winter Solstice," she commented, taking a bird nest off a branch to rest in the palm of her hand. "You have been generous with your gifts to her and she is pleased." She carefully replaced the nest and ran a light touch over a bunch of berries. "I see you wait to call down a star for the top of the tree." She turned and sent him a direct look. "Is this why you called me here to top your tree for the Winter Solstice?"

She certainly had a sharp tongue, but he had sharp wit. "While I would be honored for you to perform this special feat, I would not dare trouble you to do so."

Bernard quietly entered the room and stood with a silver serving tray in hand waiting for further instructions. A brief nod from Dagon informed him to proceed. He did so with direct and firm strides toward Tempest, honoring her by offering her the first glass of wine from the tray.

After she accepted a glass, he bowed his head and said, "It is an honor."

Remarkably, her reply was pleasant. "As is your gracious hospitality."

He then served Sydney and Dagon, placing the tray with its lone glass of wine on the glass-top coffee table.

"Someone is joining us?" Tempest asked, her eyes on the single glass.

"Someone I wish you to meet," Dagon said, determined to keep the conversation flowing until Sarina made her appearance. What he had to say concerned her, and it was she who he wanted most to hear what he had to say.

Astute to his energy Tempest redirected the chatter to Sydney. "How have you been, dear friend?"

Dagon examined her more closely. Where had that soft melodious voice come from? Gone was her curt, sharp tone and demanding manner. It was almost as if she were two people in one. And there was something familiar about her eyes, but he couldn't quite recall what it was.

"I am well and so very pleased to see you once again," Sydney answered with a generous smile. "It has been too long."

Tempest sipped her wine. "Much too long. That is why I responded so willingly to your request; I was assured that you would not disturb me unless it was important."

Damn, but her name suited her to perfection. If she once loved and lost, he could very well understand why. And spending only a few minutes with her made him realize how lucky he was to have found Sarina and how fortunate he was not being involved with her. Actually he felt sorry for any man who would even attempt a relationship with such a tempest.

Sydney looked with worried eyes to Dagon, and he sought to ease the tension and appease the temperamental witch. "Have you known love, Tempest?"

Her green eyes blazed with contained fury. "A foolish question, but perhaps you require a lesson. In understanding love, you understand the universal answer."

Dagon surprisingly retained his patience. "Understanding it and knowing it are two different experiences. I wish to know if you yourself have *known* love."

For a brief startling second Dagon sensed a long buried pain, a hurt so deep no mere mortal or skilled witch could bear to experience it. And he empathized with her loss and understood her need to ignore it.

"Love simply is. It is a daily part of my existence, it is who I am and what I give, it is all of me and more. It is the never-ending cycle of life. There can be no growth, no evolving, no wisdom without love."

"And you give this love to all," he said.

"It is who I am, I can do nothing else."

Dagon tried again. "Then let me rephrase my question Has a love as strong as you been returned to you?"

Sydney stifled a gasp, and Tempest with an icy calm directed her near empty wineglass to the tray and was about to turn her full attention and wrath on Dagon when her glance shifted and with wide stunned eyes settled on the doorway.

Dagon's eyes followed Tempest's startled ones, and it was with shock he stared at the woman he loved. She looked absolutely magnificent. She wore the sacred color of a wise witch, black, dark, and powerful like the endless night sky. The soft wool hugged her body, the cowl neck falling in gentle folds and the long sleeves coming to rest in points on her hands. And he smiled seeing the hem sweep teasingly across her bare feet.

Her hair was twisted and pinned high on her head and her bangs fell in wisps along her forehead and temples. Her dark eyes shined with the power of her wisdom, and her skin glowed with ageless beauty. It was at that very moment that he fell in love with her for the second time and knew he would forever fall in love with her over and over and over again through the ages.

He stepped forward and offered his hand to her. She took it, and together they approached the Ancient One.

The storm outside suddenly hushed its fury. The silence hung heavy in the room, the fire blazed more brightly in the hearth, and the pine tree appeared alert and waiting.

Sydney cast a silent prayer and stepped back out of the way.

It was time.

Dagon spoke, his hand tightly woven with Sarina's. "I am grateful for your patience with me this evening, and I express my gratitude for your presence in my home. I ask that you bless a forthcoming union, for a union blessed by the Ancient One is known to last for eternity, and I wish for that with Sarina."

Sarina blinked back tears as she stared speechless at him. She had waited to hear those words, had thought to first hear them in privacy, and yet here he stood proclaiming his love for her in front of the Ancient One. He truly did rescue her. He was her hero.

Dagon continued. "I had thought I had known all about love, but when I met Sarina I realized I never knew love, truly knew love, until she entered my life. We have shared magical moments, and I possess a love so rare for her that I even wonder at times if such a love is possible, but then I touch her"—he paused and ran a single finger gently down her cheek and continued—"and I know, I know with all my heart and soul, that our love is real."

Sarina took his hand and placed it over her heart. "I give you my heart, for it overflows with love for you."

Dagon brought his lips to hers and before kissing her, said, "I will forever cherish you, my bumbling witch."

The castle began to quake around them, and Dagon grabbed Sarina tightly to him. The walls trembled, the flames in the hearth shot outward, thunder roared, the large tree swayed, and a rush of wind swept in and swirled in fury around Tempest.

She floated up in the swirl of wind, her hair flying out around her head resembling shooting flames, and her eyes shined like polished emeralds. She pointed a finger at Sarina, her voice potent and powerful. "So, *my dear sister,* the rest is now up to you. You have a full moon's time before my return and before the spell must be completed."

With her warning issued, the swirling rush of wind swallowed her up and swept her away.

The room returned to normal, the storm outside quieted, and Sydney discreetly vanished.

Sarina attempted to step away from Dagon, but he would only allow her an arm's length, his hand catching hold of her wrist.

"Your eyes," he said.

"Eyes?" she repeated not understanding his strange remark.

"Your eyes are like your sister's. That is why they were so familiar to me when I looked at them, but it was the difference in color, yours light blue, hers dark green, that prevented me from realizing the similarity."

"Yes," she acknowledged with a nod. "Anyone who

knows the both of us always comments on the likeness of our eyes. Strange''—she paused, her nod turning to a brief shake—''I did not expect you to respond so calmly to my sister's antics.''

He laughed with a softness that tingled her skin and drew her near. ''Give me time, I'm still in shock. No one ever mentioned that the Ancient One had a sister.''

''Few know, and I need to explain—''

He silenced her with his lips and then urged. ''First, tell me you love me again.''

''With pleasure,'' she said and rubbed her cheek softly against his. ''I love you, Dagon. And I will love you for always.''

His question was whisper soft. ''Why?''

Her smile came slow and hinted at a tease. ''Because you rescue me—''

He attempted to interrupt her, but a quick hard kiss stopped him.

She placed a finger to his lips to keep him silent. ''You rescue me from me. You have shown me love in its rarest form and in so doing taught me the true magic of love.''

His arms went around her waist, and he nipped at her finger to chase it from his lips. ''I knew you loved me.''

''Did you now?''

He laughed as he nibbled playfully at her bottom lip. ''And you damn well knew I loved you.''

She giggled. ''It was obvious.''

He pinched her bottom which produced a small squeal. ''I demonstrated my love in more than just physical ways.''

Her expression grew serious. ''Yes, you certainly did, and that was why I had confidence in your ability to face my sister.''

Dagon sighed. ''A subject we better discuss.'' He took her hand and together they sat on the couch.

She waited for the inevitable question.

''Why didn't you tell me that the Ancient One''—he paused, shook his head and continued—''Tempest, was your sister?''

"Tempest and I keep our relationship quiet for many reasons, which I am sure you can understand. And when I discovered that you requested an introduction to the Ancient One in regards as a possible lifemate, I thought it best not to mention I was her sister."

Dagon brought her hand to his lips, kissing her palm, and was pleased when he watched a shudder run through her. "You do realize you will be my lifemate. I want no other."

She didn't respond as quickly as he would have liked and her continued silence began to worry him.

"You don't wish to mate with me for life?"

"Of course I do," she said on a frustrated sigh. "But there is much you need to know before we can commit to such a potent union."

His voice betrayed his annoyance. "I need to know nothing. I love you, you love me, and that is all that is necessary. We will mate for life and that is final."

"I would be honored to mate for life with you, but we have a problem."

"Your powers," he said with a shrug. "I assume your sister robbed you of them, but it matters not to me. I love you whether you are a powerful witch or not."

She slipped her hand out of his and sat with a stiffness to her posture that worried him. "It is a little more involved than that."

"I'm listening."

Where did she start? She supposed the beginning was the best place. "Tempest is far older than I, and she always felt responsible for me. She taught me much of what I know, though I could never hope to achieve her degree of knowledge and powers, but—" She paused almost reluctant to continue. "I possess one power that surpasses her."

"The power of sight."

Sarina confirmed with a brief nod. "I can see many things, the past, the present, and the future. I can do nothing to change these events I see, but I can caution those who come to me seeking advice and help direct them wisely

One important rule that I have always lived by is to never read a person without their request. It would be an intrusion, an invasion of privacy, so therefore it was a rule I strictly adhered to—'' She paused again.

Dagon grew impatient by her lengthy silence. ''And?'' he asked anxiously.

''And one I broke.''

''Your sister?''

She nodded, her eyes betraying her sorrow. ''I saw an event that would befall her and wanted to warn her, to help ready her, to protect her.''

''She did not realize you warned with love?''

''I don't know what she thought. She immediately grew furious with me. I am sure you have noticed she possesses a temper.''

He laughed then, strong and hard. ''Someone certainly aptly named her.''

''She is really sweet and kind and wonderfully wise, but she is highly emotional.''

''Can you tell me of this event in her life that you saw and caused you worry enough to warn her?''

''I suppose it does not matter now. You should know all of it, and then perhaps you will better understand why she cast the spell on me.''

''The spell that robbed you of your powers?''

''Yes, it all started when I saw *his* return.''

''His?''

Sarina spoke low, almost fearfully. ''I will not speak his name, no one will. He was a warlock of immense powers. He lived many, many years ago. And strange as it may seem, they fell in love. She thought to help him, to teach him wisdom, but in the end she was forced to use her skill and banish him.''

''The lost love that everyone speaks of,'' Dagon said.

''Yes and her only love. He was more handsome than you, if that is possible.''

Dagon smiled at the compliment.

''He was feared and respected and he could charm the purest of souls.''

"He charmed your sister?"

"No, Tempest saw a spark of light within him and hoped to—"

"Change him?"

Sarina shook her head. "No, she is too wise to think one person can change another. She hoped that by knowing her, loving her, he would discover his true self and that light would grow and he would evolve out of the darkness into the light."

"I assume this did not happen."

"No, it didn't. No one is certain what exactly happened. All I know for sure is that she banished him from Mother Earth until a time he could return and have a chance to right his wrongs."

"She allowed him another chance," he said with admiration for her wisdom and courage, but most of all for her unselfishness.

"Tempest believes that where there is light there is hope, and with hope grows love and the wisdom it brings. So she gave him another chance."

"Am I to understand she didn't know when he would return?"

"Nothing of it, not where or when, not even if he would resemble his old self. His memories would be buried along with his powers until such a time that he himself would recall them. It is hoped that by the time he recalls his past, he would have stepped out of the darkness and into the light."

"And is it believed that he will seek out your sister?"

"Many believe he will; I know he will."

"You saw his return?" Dagon asked.

"Clearly and he is not far away."

"He has already returned to Mother Earth?"

"He has been here for some time and grows restless," she said with a concern to her voice that worried Dagon.

"Has he learned anything?"

She sadly shook her head. "Nothing, but he continues to search, and that is a good sign."

"What did you tell your sister of his return?"

Her sigh was heavy, her burden obvious. "I told her that he had incarnated and the two of them would soon be forced to face their fates."

"And she did not take well to your prediction?"

"I was foolish to tell her."

Dagon slipped an arm around her and drew her close. "You wanted to protect her."

"But perhaps it would have been wiser to remain silent."

"She is better off knowing," he insisted.

"Tempest thinks not and released her fury on me."

"Exactly what did she do?"

Sarina moved out of his arms and stood, needing to pace, which she did in front of him as she explained. "She flew into a rage, similar to the one tonight. Wind and fire are her friends, forever by her side, and when her temper flares, so do the elements. Her spell was fast and furious, the wind wrapping tightly around me as she issued forth the cast."

"Tell me the spell," Dagon urged, needing to hear it so that he could determine what they would face.

Sarina recited it clearly and with the melodious voice of a skilled caster. "You dare to predict my fate; for this I cast a spell of wait; your witch's powers will dwindle with time; until you are loved by one of our kind; magical moments you must share; and he must proclaim a love that is rare; when all this is complete, you—my dear sister—must perform your best feat!"

Concentrating on the spell, he slowly stood, preventing her from pacing by coming to stand in front of her. "Until this spell is completely satisfied, you lack your powers?"

She nodded with a worried smiled.

He worried but kept his concerns to himself, chasing them from his thoughts so she would not sense them. They needed a break from this chaotic madness, and he would see that they had it. He scooped her up into his arms and centered his thoughts on her naked in his bed. "I have a spell of my own I wish to cast."

Her worried smile eased and she nuzzled his neck. "And what is it?"

He murmured in her ear. "It's a spell without words."

She moved her lips to meet his and whispered, "Show me."

Twenty-eight

It was a long and lazy joining, a coming together of souls uniting in love. Dagon undressed himself first, refusing to allow her to remove her clothes. Undressing her, he insisted, was part of the pleasure. And he did it with deliberate slowness.

He first removed the pins from her hair. He wanted it free and flowing around her face, framing her beauty. He then worked her wool dress up and over the curves and mounds it tenaciously clung to. A black lace bra and bikini panties greeted him, and he smiled with eager anticipation as his hands reached out to caress the black lace that cupped her breasts so intimately.

He ran an anxious finger over the swirl of lace, teasing the nipple to a hard inviting pebble that he could slip between his lips into his mouth for his teeth to nip and torment. And she responded as he knew she would, melting against him and moaning her desire.

His hands stroked the narrow curve of her waist, moving over her hips to snuggle between her legs, which she eagerly parted for him. His fingers trailed over the veil of black lace that prevented further intimacy, and he smiled as his mouth continued to feed on her pert nipples and his fingers proceeded to invade the lace.

With deliberate laziness he slipped a finger beneath the thin material and teased the already sensitive flesh to chaotic senselessness. Her warm liquid spilled into his hand, and he shivered at the invitation she presented. Her skin was warm, her scent alluring, and he, hard and ready to take the plunge. But he wanted more this time. Where before they had shared magical moments, he wanted this to be a magical loving that they both would remember in the years to come.

With one snap he released her bra, and with anxious hands he picked her up and lowered her to the bed, divesting her of the black panties that invited him with the scent of her.

She reached out for him, but he pushed her hands away. He needed to taste her, to drink deep of her flavor and satisfy the lusty quench that ached inside him.

Sarina gripped the bedposts and arched her body when his tongue invaded her with a sharpness that shocked and pleasured her. He had tasted her many times before, and he had always pleased her but never, never with the intensity he now displayed.

He went deep, making her shudder with each forceful thrust, and his fingers followed suit teasing the small budding flesh that was certain to bring her to a furious climax.

But he refused to allow her release. Each time she teetered near the edge, he snapped her back, extending her pleasure, intensifying her need, and whispering his intentions.

She begged and pleaded and he promised, he swore he would let her climax, insisted she do so, and then he would torment her again and again, until again her pleas softly echoed in the room.

Finally he kept his promise and with a scream of pleasure and her body surging in an arc on the bed, her hands gripping frantically to the sheets, he made her come in a burst of startlingly light and shuddering climax. His name resounded repeatedly on her lips and when she thought it over, he moved over her, his body claiming hers in a soft intimacy that had her melting against him.

How could she want more when he had so thoroughly satisfied her, and yet she ached for him to fill her with the strength of him, and she moved her naked, damp body against his in invitation.

Dagon worried his need was too great, his desire too strong, and he didn't wish to hurt her, and yet his overwhelming need had him locking his fingers tightly with hers as he slipped comfortably over her body, licking his way up and over her highly sensitive skin, to circle her swelling breasts with a teasing tongue and claim her hard nipples with a rough bite that had her wincing with pleasure.

His own need had been held in check far too long, and sliding a leg down hers he parted her for himself. He penetrated her with a sudden sharpness that had her calling out his name.

He was frantic in his need for her, his rhythm was forceful, his thrusts deep, and his love potent. He felt the heat of her wrap around him and tighten with every plunge, and he sank more deeply within her.

Reason vanished, time stood still, and only they existed, only their driving love and their need to unite and become one forever and always. This was magic in its purest form, this was the light of life, the continuing cycle, and together they rode to breathtaking heights and shattered, spiraling to earth in a maddening descent.

"Dagon," Sarina said on a satisfied sigh and wrapped her arms and legs around him, holding her tightly to him, never wanting him to leave her.

He in turn relished the snug heat of her intimately cradling him and never wanted to part from her. They remained wrapped around each other, kissing lightly, whispering softly, and repeatedly declaring their love for each other until finally their damp bodies protested with the shivers.

Dagon immediately secured them beneath the covers, tucking her in his arms. "Warm enough."

"Your arms never fail to warm or protect me. And," she

said with a playful nip to his chin, "I like your wordless spell."

"Then we will practice it often."

"I am at your mercy," she volunteered.

Her words caused his worry to surface. "Speaking of mercy, your sister seemed to lack it when casting the spell on you. I realize that I, actually my love for you, has fulfilled part of the spell, but it has yet to be completed, and she did set a time limit."

"The last of the spell calls for me to perform my best feat, which means I must outshine my sister's magic or all is lost."

He hoisted her over him so that she could stretch out full upon him, and he rested his arms around her waist and asked the one question that troubled him. "If your own skills remain dormant how could you possibly succeed?"

He felt her sigh against his chest. "I have asked myself the same question time and time again."

"Do you think she never intended for you to break the spell?"

Sarina raised her head to look at him and to his surprise she wore a smile. "Though it may not seem it, Tempest has a big heart and would never cause hurt or harm to anyone."

"Then answer me this," he said with obvious worry. "What are the consequences if you fail to fulfill this spell?"

Her smile faded, his concern grew, and her answer came reluctantly. "I must forfeit my love and return with her."

He swiftly lifted her off him and onto her back, leaning over her with a look so terribly lethal that it frightened her.

His voice was sharp, his tone adamant. "You think I will allow this?"

Sadly she admitted, "You have no choice."

"No choice?" he all but screamed.

Sarina raised a tender hand to his face. "Her powers far surpass yours."

"You expect me to accept this?"

"I expect you to understand."

His laugh was more of a sneer. "Understand that I am to relinquish the woman I love because her sister cast a selfish spell?"

Her hand fell away. "Tempest is not selfish."

"Perhaps you should take a better look at your sister."

"She does nothing without reason."

"And she had good reason to cast a vindictive spell," he insisted.

"I don't believe that."

He looked at her incredulously and shook his head. "Perhaps then you have an explanation."

"She was upset and gave no thought to her actions."

"Then she can damn well erase the spell."

"I don't think she will do that."

Her soft blue eyes damp with tears prevented any further outburst from him, and he leaned his forehead to hers. "I love you, Sarina, and I don't intend to lose you. Somehow we will find a way out of this."

She found his lips and kissed him softly. "But promise me that you will not grow upset if you cannot rescue me from this dilemma."

A low rumbling laugh followed his smile. "Heroes always rescue maidens in distress."

She giggled. "I think you have the wrong time period."

"A hero is a hero no matter the place or time."

She draped her arms around his neck. "Then there is nothing to fear. You will save me."

"Always, Sarina," he said on a whisper. "I will always save you, on that you have nothing to fear."

Her hands slipped down along his back, and her smile was sly and suggestive. "Then let me reward you now for your gallantry."

Dagon left Sarina sleeping contentedly the next morning. It was early, dawn had barely risen, and though he had slept barely four hours, he was wide awake and eager to greet the day. There was much to do and much to consider, and his first consideration was that he needed advice from people who possessed more powerful skills than his.

He had always thought his energy superior to many witches and on many occasions that proved to be true, but now—now he felt inadequate to help Sarina. And he did not like the feeling.

A hero never failed in his duties to protect, and he had not failed her to this point, but then the rescues had been simple. This rescue was not, and he would seek whatever assistance necessary to make certain the spell was fulfilled.

The castle was quiet as he descended the steps to the dining room, and he thought of the many years he had spent here. There were some troublesome years, times when he had to hide his abilities and be careful whom he called friend. And times when he watched the innocent suffer because of ignorance. Through those dark times he had always remained true to his heritage, and it had hurt him and so many other witches to watch their heritage be defiled and labeled evil.

To avoid persecution they had to remain silent and endure the degradation of their beliefs. But in their silence they grew strong, and in the ensuing years mortals began to discover the light, slowly, one by one, and things continued to change for the better. And it would be here in this promising new world were his children would grow and flourish, if he could rescue Sarina.

He simply could not understand why her sister would cast such a damaging spell. If what Sarina said of Tempest was true, that she would hurt or harm no one, which actually was the way of the witch, why then cast this spell?

Dagon entered the dining room with a shake of his head.

"Tempest has that effect on people," Sydney said with a smile from where she sat at the table. "Come, have coffee and talk with me, for I depart soon."

A hefty sigh followed Dagon to the table. He leaned over and kissed Sydney's cheek before taking his seat at the head of the table. "Just when I need you the most, you leave me."

She patted his hand in reassurance. "Confidence in your self was something you never lacked."

"I never went up against the Ancient One."

"But it is not you who will face her."

"You're wrong," he said firmly. "Sarina and I are one. What one faces, so does the other."

Sydney smiled, pleased by his response. "Then between the both of you failure is impossible."

"You saw her powers," Dagon reminded. "And you also know her better than most. What can you tell me about her that might help us?"

Sydney sipped her coffee before answering. "She is an excellent teacher."

"You could have fooled me," he said with a laugh. "For a minute there the other night I thought the castle was about to lay at my feet in ruins."

"At least you have retained your humor."

"I do not wish to upset Sarina with my own concerns, though the situation troubles me more than I care to admit." He looked to Sydney and produced a charming smile that never failed to please a woman. "And, my dear, you know how much I hate to lose."

"Turn that smile on Tempest and she may just melt."

"Melt? I would say she is too icy to melt easily."

Sydney scolded with a shake of her finger. "You lack full awareness because of your love for Sarina."

"Are you referring to the old mortal saying that love is blind?"

"Mortals do not understand that it is awareness they are blind to. So much sits right in front of their eyes, and yet they fail to see because they fail to look."

"Okay, I get it. You're telling me that I'm not looking clearly."

"You were always my prize student," Sydney said with a pleased smile.

"Who needs reminding of his lessons."

"Who knows his lessons but has not called on them for assistance."

"My worry over losing the woman I love is preeminent on my mind."

"Which negates necessary action on your part," Sydney reminded.

"I sought your help," he insisted, feeling like a foolish schoolboy who failed to learn his lessons well. "At least I took a step."

"I am glad you sought my help, but remember, it is your actions and Sarina's that will prove to be your best defense."

"How about love? Can it not conquer all?"

"It depends on the truth of the love."

"Our love is true," he argued.

She laid a gentle hand over his where it rested on the table. "Do you truly know love, Dagon?"

He was about to shout his love for Sarina at the top of his lungs when he suddenly calmed himself and spoke gently. "Now I do."

"Then rely on it to help you."

He wasn't quite sure he understood her message, but he would think on her words. Presently, he wished more information on Tempest. Sebastian once told him that you could never gather enough information on someone. That after a while you see a pattern that offers you more exact information than you thought possible. He was looking for that pattern. "Tell me more of what you know of the Ancient One."

"She is wise."

"She is a good teacher and she is wise. Why did I see a different person?" He raised a hand to prevent her response. "Don't tell me, I failed to look."

"Very good, I taught you well."

"Evidently not well enough. I did not see."

"You did not look. Tell me what you saw when you met Tempest."

His response was quick. "A beautiful witch with an attitude."

Sydney laughed. "She can be temperamental."

"Why?" he asked, suddenly realizing that it was a small bit of information that might prove invaluable.

"Even the wisest witch can grow upset."

Curiosity grabbed hold and Dagon leaned forward to rest his arms on the table. "But why would she be upset by request for a simple introduction? I am sure requests to meet with her are common, and she has the option to refuse any or all of them. So why be upset over one she had agreed to?''

''That I cannot answer,'' Sydney said honestly. ''I can only tell you that she becomes most upset when—''

Her pause and tightened brow had him waiting anxiously for her to finish.

''When she thinks she has failed in helping another.''

''Helping?'' he asked confused. ''She certainly didn't appear to be helping her sister last night or by casting the spell over her.''

''Perhaps the answer is in the spell.''

''The spell seems obvious.''

''Sometimes the most obvious are the ones we fail to fully comprehend.''

''I will keep that in mind,'' he said. ''Do you think the love she lost could have anything to do with the reason she cast the spell? She was angry at Sarina for predicting her fate.''

''But Sarina did not actually predict her fate, she merely warned her of his arrival, not of the consequences.''

Dagon nodded slowly. ''You're right. I didn't think of it that way. She never did tell her the outcome of the reunion, only that they would once again meet. So her fate will be of her own making.''

''Which upsets most people when they realize their fate is actually in their own hands.''

''But a wise witch should know better.''

''Perhaps she does, perhaps she realized more than you think.''

''Now that remark puzzles me. Want to explain it?'' he asked hopefully.

Sydney smiled sweetly. ''How will you learn if I give you all the answers?''

''How did I know you were going to say that?''

''Because you are aware?'' she asked teasingly.

''Awareness,'' he said with a shake of his head. ''What am I not aware of?''

"What is right in front of you."

"I suppose you think that is a sufficient answer."

"An accurate one," she corrected. "And one that you would be wise to understand. Now, if you have no more questions, it is time for me to take my leave."

"One more question," he said anxiously.

Sydney remained patient.

"Can you tell me what would make a wise old witch like Tempest fall in love with a warlock? I cannot understand the attraction or the sane reasoning behind such a strange relationship. Or is it the fact that love is blind rings true?"

"I can only tell you what I know of Tempest. I have never known her to be blind in any situation. I have seen her face adversity that would make most witches crumble in fright, and I have watched her defend and protect the weakest of creatures with great danger to herself. She is a woman strong in her convictions and powerful in her energy."

"Then could it possibly have been the power of the warlock's energy that drew them together?"

"His power was dark; hers is light."

"But wouldn't she wish to cast light on the darkness? And strangely enough, doesn't the darkness attract?"

Sydney was honest in her response. "I must agree with you on both. Where darkness exists Tempest would attempt to bring light and yes, the darkness does attract many and many are captivated by its intoxicating essence. It is the wise ones who see the truth in the darkness and attempt to cast light."

"The Tempest you speak of doesn't fit the Tempest I met."

Sydney folded her white linen napkin on the table. "You did not look with open eyes. You saw what you wanted to see. You were prepared to battle, to defend your love before she arrived, and yet it was you who invited her into your home."

"I was not rude to her."

"In a manner you were—" She raised a hand to silence

his protest. "You were not truthful with her when she arrived, and she understood that and became defensive."

"I did not lie."

"You did not speak the truth. You did not tell her the real reason why you wished an introduction."

"That would have been rude to tell her that I thought I might be interested in her as a lifemate but changed my mind when a bumbling witch entered my life."

"It would have been the truth, and the Ancient One respects the truth."

Dagon felt thoroughly chastised. "My manners disappointed you."

"You can only disappoint yourself, and I suspect if you gave it thought, you would realize your error and find a way to correct it."

"I don't think Tempest would be interested in an apology from me."

Sydney stood and tapped a finger to his temple. "You don't think, dear boy, at least not clearly in this matter. Now you have asked enough questions, and it is time for me to take my leave."

Dagon stood, suddenly feeling sad over her departure.

Sydney pressed a warm, loving kiss to his cheek. "You take care and enjoy the holidays with Sarina. And do not worry, all will turn out well."

"You have confidence in me," he said with a charming smile and a generous hug.

Sydney gave his shoulder a playful slap. "I have confidence in Tempest."

Twenty-nine

The Winter Solstice appropriately dawned bright. A new cycle had begun, new life would flourish, grow, and produce. It was a wonderful time.

What was even more wonderful was that Sarina and Dagon had the castle all to themselves for the next week. Dagon had generously and selfishly given the week off to the entire staff to the surprise of everyone, especially Bernard.

Dagon had wanted time alone with Sarina, time to love and time to prepare and the holiday was the perfect excuse to send everyone away. And they left with haste and glee before the lord of the castle changed his mind. That was, all except Bernard.

He had argued most vehemently with Dagon, insisting someone had to stay and see to the castle and to preparing meals. When Dagon informed him that Sarina and he would see to their own meals, he gasped out loud and shuddered at the suggestion.

It was Margaret who made her husband have a change of heart. She told him if he didn't leave with her, she would leave without him. In a matter of days she had arranged for a trip to the Greek Isles and nothing, not even a stubborn husband, would spoil her plans. She had heard of this little restaurant whose chef had yet to gain national recognition, yet whose cooking was gaining fame, and she hoped to learn about his much-talked-of olive sauce that was said to have a magical taste.

Bernard realized quick enough that where food was concerned, his wife would go with or without him and he decided, he didn't want his wife alone in the Greek Isles.

Of course, now that the two were alone and the holiday was upon them, not to mention Christmas but four days away, Dagon suddenly had second thoughts. His mind quickly changed when he walked toward the kitchen and a delicious aroma stung his nostrils.

He entered the kitchen with anxious anticipation and smiled when he caught sight of Sarina. She wore white knit leggings, thick white socks and a white V-neck sweater that skimmed her slim hips. Her long sleeves were pushed up, her hair was twisted up and clipped with a large white hair clip, and she wore a red bib apron that depicted a winter snow scene with various animals cuddled together around a fire. She looked absolutely charming.

Her hands were buried deep in dough while filled pots bubbled softly on the stove and luscious smells drifted from the oven. A tray of cookies sat wrapped with ribbons of white and gold, an apple pie sat cooling on a wire rack, and yams sat dripping in a colander ready to be wrapped and baked. It was definitely going to be a tasty holiday.

"Need help?" he asked and eyed the cookie tray with intent before giving her a kiss.

"How about you make us some hot chocolate and we have some cookies. I could use a break right after I finish shaping this dough."

"And to think Bernard thought we would starve," Dagon said, taking the milk carton from the refrigerator.

"Margaret left me precise instructions and told me if I did most of the cooking at once we would only need to reheat the rest of the week. And since I wanted time with you . . ." Her words drifted off though her intentions were clear.

Dagon turned the flame on under the pot of milk and then walked over to Sarina, slipping his arms around her waist and burying his face in the back of her hair. "You may grow tired of me. After all, it is a lifetime we will be spending together."

Her body tensed at his words. "I want so very much to spend a lifetime with you."

"And so you shall."

"I want to believe—"

"Then believe—it is that simple, believe."

She molded the bread in the pan and placed it aside, covering it with a clean dishcloth. With a quick brush of her hands she touched them to Dagon's arms, which remained secure around her waist. "We have only a couple more weeks left before her return."

"We will solve this puzzle," he insisted.

"Even if we don't have all the pieces?"

"We will find them," he assured her and with his cheek pushed her hair aside to nuzzle her neck with his lips.

She shivered to the tips of her toes. "You start that and we may just wind up ruining the meal."

"The milk!" he shouted and turned to see it near to bubbling over. He hurried over to shut off the flame and gather mugs and the powdered chocolate. "First the milk and cookies, then—" He sent her a wink.

Sarina cleared the table, placing the two loaves of bread to rise on the counter. It was a quick cleanup since she had grown accustomed and relaxed around the kitchen. Dagon sat at the head of the table and she to his side, the plate of cookies sat between them, and they both enjoyed the assortment he had chosen, though their favorites remained the star sugar cookies with vanilla icing. Hot mugs of chocolate steaming with heat and clouds of whipped cream floating on top sat cooling beside each of them.

"Tell me of some feats that might impress your sister," he asked, hoping this day of new beginnings would be a good day to discuss the spell. Later they would give thanks and cast prayers for a generous year for all, but for now he wished to discuss their most urgent dilemma and hope that the power of this special day would somehow help in solving it.

Sarina nibbled at the end of a star. "I am uncertain of what would impress my sister. She is so very powerful, any feat I perform would appear meager next to hers."

"She didn't speak of her own best feat, she spoke of yours," he reminded. "Her words in effect were that you were to perform *your* best feat."

"That is true, so then she doesn't expect me to outshine her, though she does intend that I impress. But without my powers, it's useless," she said with a dejected shrug.

Dagon held the jam thumbprint cookie that he was about to take a bite of up in her face. "Did you use magical powers to bake these?"

"You know I didn't."

"And they turned out delicious, didn't they?" he asked and took a bite. "Damn, they are delicious," he mumbled between eager bites.

She smiled and wiped at a crumb in the corner of his mouth. "Cooking is not an impressive feat."

"I think Sebastian would disagree with you."

That brought a hardy laughter to Sarina. "I suppose you're right."

He took her hand. "What I'm saying is that maybe magic isn't important in performing your best feat. Look how much you have accomplished over the last few months without the help of magic."

She gave his words thought and realized the possibility. Could she possibly have learned enough to perform a feat that would require no magic and that would impress her sister? Yes, there was possibility. She would have to think on it.

To Dagon she said, "You could be right."

He squeezed her hand. "I will not lose you."

He had repeated those words so often to her of late that she was beginning to believe them. How they would remain together she did not know, but she was beginning to believe that they would, and with faith in her belief she knew it was possible.

Her fingers wrapped around his. "I am glad we have this time alone together."

"So am I," he said and leaned over to steal a kiss.

"I was going to ask a favor of you," she said in whisper.

"Anything," he said, his body temperature on the rise.

She ran a teasing finger across his lips. "Promise you'll do what I ask?"

"Whatever you want, dear heart," he insisted, ready, willing, and most definitely able.

"I want you . . ." she said with a nip to his bottom lip.

He inched closer to her, his hand slipping under her breast, and damned if she wasn't wearing a bra.

". . . to go outside and collect a few fresh pine branches for the lighting of the candles tonight."

Her breast rested in his stilled hand, and his look was that of a stricken young boy who had just been denied a treat. "Outside?"

She nodded. "I prepared the sacred candles for the solstice, and I require fresh boughs of pine to help with the cast."

He shook his head, looking heartbreakingly sad. "I thought—" He couldn't finish, he simply sighed.

She laughed softly as his hand drifted away from her breast, and she hastily cupped his face in her hands, giving him a quick kiss. "I will not deny you what you want, and I know you want to make love now. I thought to wait until this evening, at high solstice when we could cast the candles together and make love at that special time that will seal our love forever."

He could not believe her words. He knew she loved him but this, this sharing of the ancient ritual on the Winter Solstice, was rare. Wise witches only cast the candles, and to cast them with another was forging an enduring commitment, one that never would be denied or challenged but would be forever. A rare love.

"I never expected you to ask this of me," he said in disbelief.

"I will understand if you do not wish to—"

He silenced her with a kiss and leaned his cheek to hers.

"Not wish? Dear heart, I am honored that you asked and accept your generous and loving offer with all my heart and soul."

"Does that mean you'll gather the pine boughs?"

They both started laughing and kissed and hugged and laughed some more before Dagon slipped into his dark gray overcoat and headed out to gather the branches.

Naturally the sun disappeared, as was its way this time of year, and clouds drifted overhead, but to Dagon the sky was aglow with sunshine, he felt so elated. Nothing could damper his spirits, and he hurried to accomplish the chore at hand.

He had picked a few as she had asked him, insisting he take no more than they needed. Their scent was strong as he leaned over, tying the ends together for easier carrying.

"Casting the candles with her, are you?"

Dagon was not disturbed by the unexpected voice. He was too familiar with the forest fairies to ever be startled by their presence. He lifted his head to see Beatrice descending slowly with fluttering wings to land on the pine branches.

"Such a lovely batch for casting, and proud they are that you have chosen them for such a sacred occasion."

"Sarina will be happy to hear that."

"She will know without you saying," Beatrice said and began pacing along the pine needles.

Dagon had never seen Beatrice upset, but her pacing alerted him to her distress. "Something troubles you?"

Beatrice stopped pacing and placed her hands behind her back as she looked up at him with serious eyes. "Have you the answer to your questions?"

"The one answer you told me would answer all my questions?"

"Yes, that's the one and an important one it is."

"I think I only learned it a short while ago."

"It matters not when you learned it as long as you learned it," Beatrice assured him. "Now tell me the answer."

He didn't hesitate. "Love. Love is the answer to all the

questions I had. Love makes you look at things differently, makes you feel differently, makes you respond differently. Love is awareness in its highest form.''

Beatrice smiled, pleased by his response. ''This is good. You know and you will need this answer to help others. Remember that when the time comes.''

''Why do I still feel you are worried about something?''

''Sometimes it is hard to be friends with someone you dislike, but necessity dictates that you must; it is at that time your love must be the strongest.''

''I don't understand, Beatrice.''

''This spell that Tempest cast means more than you know. Remember the answer and use it wisely when you are faced with an adversary you think yourself unable to beat.''

He shook his head. ''You confuse me. Are you speaking of Tempest?''

''She is not your adversary. She is friend and defender of all, and it is in her strength that you and Sarina will find victory.''

Beatrice flew up to flutter next to his face and kiss his cheek. ''Love is a powerful weapon, Dagon, use it wisely and it will never fail you. And remember, I will always be there when you need me.''

She disappeared in a flash, leaving a twinkle of bright light in the tiny space she had occupied. She had not only confused him, she worried him. If there was more to this spell, what was he missing—and what harm could it bring Sarina and him?

Puzzles and pieces, he was beginning to hate them. Why couldn't he just once receive a straight answer, something simple and direct?

But he had, hadn't he? Love was a simple answer, and yet complicated when he stopped to think about it. There were many levels and facets to love. He loved Alisande like a sister and he loved Sebastian as he would a brother. There was Sydney who was like a mother to him, and then there were his parents whom he loved with all his heart.

And there was a love of humanity that he supposed Tempest understood far better than he. Then if that was the case, why the spell on her sister?

He finished tying the branches and stood when suddenly he was struck by the unlikely yet plausible notion that, "Tempest cast the spell out of love?"

He shook his head. "A ridiculous notion."

But his mind was already piecing the puzzle together. A witch never cast a spell that would cause any one hurt or harm. Not that revenge spells weren't cast, they just weren't cast by wise, knowledgeable witches. They knew better and they knew the consequences.

Sydney had remarked that Tempest was a wise teacher. Was she attempting to teach her sister a lesson? And if so, what was it?

"Damn," he mumbled. "Just when I think I have the answers, I get more questions."

You have the answer.

The soft voice in his head reminded him, and he wondered how love fit into this equation. The spell spoke of magical moments and a rare love—were these things she wanted for her sister? But what of the feat? What did she expect from her sister if love was the answer?

He gathered his branches with a shake of his head and headed back to the castle. He was tired of spells. First Ali got herself into a mess because of one and now the woman he loved. What could possibly be next?

He didn't want to know. He hurried his steps, aching for the warmth of the castle and Sarina's welcoming arms.

She was at the kitchen door to greet him, a sprinkle of rain turning his hasty steps into a run. She reached out for him and he dropped the bundle of pine, snatching her up into his arms. He buried his face in her dark hair that had fallen loose from the clip. She smelled so good, like fresh-baked bread and hot chocolate, and she felt incredibly warm and soft against him.

He wanted her there and then. He wanted to feel her warm naked skin against his, he wanted to join with her and forget the world existed. He wanted this moment for them and them alone.

His urgent kiss plumped her moist lips, and her familiar groans resonated in his ears. If he didn't stop kissing, if his hands didn't stop roving, if he didn't stop thinking of her, he would not stop at all.

"Sarina." Was he requesting permission from her or himself?

His name slipped slow and soft from her lips as he rained love-starved kisses over her face, and he knew she would not deny him. She would never deny him. She loved him.

"Tonight?" he asked, not wanting to spoil her plans.

"Will be ours as is this moment," she said and reached down to open his zipper.

They loved like two reckless adolescents, quick and fast and with lots of laughs and awkward movements. After all, the kitchen wasn't conducive to a romantic interlude, but for a hot joining it proved to be passion packed.

The countertop turned into a playful platform, a chair was shared, the table used for bracing, and the hard floor the final stage for a joining that had both of them on their knees and panting like animals in the throes of a heated mating. Together they exploded in a primordial climax that had them roaring out their passion.

Dagon held her close to him, her head resting back on his chest, their breathing ragged and their bodies satiated.

"My bread!" she suddenly yelled and freed herself from him to run to the oven, snatching a cow pot holder off a peg near the sink along the way.

Dagon stood and stretched like a well-satisfied male lion as he watched her tend the oven without a stitch of clothes. "Remind me to give the staff a holiday more often."

She laughed after looking down at herself. "I didn't know cooking could be so much fun." She pulled the two bread pans from the oven and set them to cool on a wire rack on the countertop. She flicked the oven off and tossed the cow mitt on the table. "All done baking. What do you say we share a shower?"

He walked slowly toward her, his strides powerful, his long mane wild from their recent untamed activities, and his male scent alluring. She was already hungry for him, and when he reached her side, he scooped her up into his arms and attacked her neck with ravenous kisses that soon had them clawing at each other yet again.

They dressed in pure white robes in honor of the new sun, the new cycle, a new life. The pine boughs covered a long narrow table in the living room that sat beneath a tall window. The candles Sarina had made, all white and all various sizes, sat comfortably amongst the pine needles waiting to spark to life.

Each of them held a small lit candle in their hands, and it was Sarina who cast the ancient prayer in the ancient language that Dagon did not know but did not fail to understand. She blessed the Mother Earth and gave thanks for her generosity, then she asked for the new year to be filled with love, hope, and peace for all. And she asked that all would come to know the beauty of magic and allow its essence to touch their hearts and souls.

At opposite ends of the table they stood, and in unison they reached out their lighted candles to spark one candle, and then with a soft whisper of a breath from Sarina over the unlighted candles the magic of the cast took hold and she cried out in delight as candle by candle sparked to brilliant life until the twenty-one candles that covered the tabletop flickered with light.

She clapped her hands like an excited child, and her smile displayed her wonder and joy. She had feared that her meager power would fail her, but a small surge of energy still lingered, and it was all that was necessary for the cast to work.

"Bless you all," she whispered to the candles, and their flames rose up and dipped as if in respect to her magic before settling to a normal flicker.

Dagon stared at her in awe. "I have never seen anything like that."

"It's beautiful, isn't it?" she said with pride.

"Will these candles really burn all year now?"

"Yes, they will. They are blessed with the magic of the solstice. Place them wisely throughout the castle, and they will offer light and protection."

He walked over to her and she took the candle from his hand to blow out along with the one she held. "Thank you for this special night. It will linger long in my memory."

She discarded the unlit candles to a nearby tray, and with a slow spreading smile she wrapped her arms around his neck. "We have more memories to make."

An hour later with laughter on their lips and their bodies still damp from their enthusiastic lovemaking, they slipped back into their robes and attacked the table spread with a bounty of food.

"I'm starved," Sarina said, piling her plate with sliced ham, turkey, oyster stuffing, and a fat yam. She frowned when she realized there was no more room on her plate and she would have to make a return trip for the vegetables.

Dagon opened a bottle of chilled chardonney and filled two glasses for them. They picnicked in front of the large stone fireplace on the warmth of the hearth rug, sitting opposite each other so that they could share their plates of food.

Lady Lily enjoyed her own special treat, fresh milk and a fillet of fish broiled to her liking, and of course there was her new bed pillow scented with pine and on which she curled up to sleep after satisfying her stomach.

It was a joyous time for them, and they took advantage of every precious moment. They did not think of the past or the future, only the moment, and when they thought themselves stuffed, unable to eat any more, they both spied the tray of cookies on the table and tripped over each other in an attempt to beat the other to the tray first.

Sarina made them Earl Grey tea, and the teapot soon emptied and the cookies vanished, and they slumped together on the couch both proclaiming they would never eat another bite.

And wrapped in each others arms they fell asleep to the

crackle of the fire and the contentment of their full stomachs, knowing tomorrow's new sun would bring new promise and new hope and with a little magic a solution to their dilemma.

Thirty

Sarina slipped quietly from the bed, adjusting the covers over Dagon's naked shoulders. Lady Lily swatted at her from her contented perch on the top of Dagon's head. She did not like to be disturbed when she was cuddled by Dagon, and she let Sarina know it. With a soft meow she curled back into a ball and closed her sleepy eyes. Sarina hurried into the white terry robe that had carelessly been tossed over the chair the evening before in their haste to make love.

They simply could not get enough of each other. They had behaved like two young lovers who had only recently discovered the joys of sex. She shivered, grateful for the warmth of the robe around her chilled body as she rushed over to the hearth and proceeded to add logs to the dying embers. The dry wood caught instantly and flamed to life. She sat cross-legged on the hearth rug and held her hands out in front of the roaring fire for it to toast them warm.

Tomorrow was Christmas and they would share the holiday together, though many phone calls would be made to family and friends. And then . . .

Then right after the new year her sister would return.

She had thought that perhaps their crazed lovemaking

was due to the fact that this might be their only time together. And the thought so upset her that tears pooled in
her eyes and teetered dangerously close to spilling. Tears
would not solve her problem and would only serve to make
her more despondent.

Wisdom was her best weapon.

Love.

The word was a bare whisper in her head, and she smiled
knowing who sent the single-word message. She rose
quickly, gave Dagon's cheek a soft kiss, and fled the room
in a rush.

She hurried to her own room to dress, the clothes she
needed being there. It was with haste and excitement she
dressed in her black dress with the cowl neck. She slipped
black suede ankle boots over black silk stockings and
swung her black-hooded cloak around her shoulders, pulling up the hood to cover her tousled hair that she barely
ran her fingers through this morning.

Dawn had peeked on the horizon barely an hour ago, and
peeked was all it could do since dark gray clouds hurried
in overhead and blanketed the sky with a promise of foul
weather. A good storm was brewing and the temperatures
had dropped considerably overnight. Perhaps a few snow
flurries would grace the ground for Christmas, though it
was probably more of a downpour they would see.

Sarina hurried her steps along the pebble path, around
the mermaid pond, smiling at the delightful memories, and
with a quick step entered the woods. She looked as if she
flew around trees, over fallen logs, around low hanging
branches, and whirled to a stop in a small clearing where
pine needles cushioned the earth and an old worn tree
stump provided a seat.

With the absence of the sun and the thick covering of
the plethora of tall trees and fat branches, light was near to
nonexistent. But that did not matter to Sarina; she simply
took her seat and waited patiently.

A twinkle of light suddenly flitted overhead, followed by
another twinkle and then another and another and . . .

Sarina smiled with pleasure as she watched the fairies descend down around her.

It was a beautiful sight to behold, their small wings sparkling, the merry tinkle of their voices, and the soft flutter of their wings, it was a melody that never failed to touch her heart.

They were all dressed in white and gold in honor of the Winter Solstice. Gold fairy dust sparkled in their hair and glittered on the soft wool of their garments. Their head wreaths were pine and donned with tiny gold berries and pinecones.

When they all finished descending, the small clearing stood aglow with a soft glittering light that would leave mortals breathless, but Sarina was familiar with the fairies' glow, and she basked in its magic.

"Wise one, it is a pleasure," Beatrice said and executed a respectful bow while continuing to flutter in the air in front of Sarina.

"It is always a pleasure to see you, Beatrice," Sarina said with an acknowledging nod. "As it is to see all of my friends." She extended her hands out over all the fairies and they murmured their own joyful greetings.

Sarina had grown up with most of the fairies that surrounded her. Some had taught her and some she had taught, but all were friends since fairies knew no other way.

"I heard your message," Sarina said to Beatrice.

"We wanted you to know our love and thoughts are with you in your time of need," Beatrice explained. "And we wished to extend our blessings for a joyous new cycle."

Sarina spread her hands out once again and sent a hushed warm breath to whisper across the fairies. "My blessings to you all."

A flutter of excitement rippled through the small creatures and murmurs of delight were heard as were whispers of reassurance that she the wise one would protect them.

Sarina looked to Beatrice. "They worry about something."

"Your prediction of *his* return has spread throughout the lands, and they grow concerned. They fear this time he wil win, and if he does . . .'' Beatrice shook her head sadly.

"Trust my sister's strength and courage; she will allow no harm to befall you."

"Your sister possesses a love few come to know or understand, and she uses that love wisely. We have faith in her, in you—and in Dagon."

Sarina had the strangest feeling that Beatrice understood more about future events than her message was relaying.

"He is my hero."

Beatrice smiled. "It is the one whom no one suspects who will be the true hero."

"He will save me?"

"He will save you all."

Sarina smiled. "Is this why you summoned me here—to tell me riddles?"

"To remind you," Beatrice said, adjusting her lopsided head wreath for the third time.

"Of love?"

"You understand?" Beatrice appeared startled.

"Your gentle reminder sparked a memory, and I feel foolish for not having discovered the missing piece to this amazing puzzle sooner."

Beatrice fluttered her wings, the crooked one tipping her to the right as she flew to place a kiss on Sarina's cheek. "We all have faith in you."

"And my sister."

Beatrice bowed her head in reverence. "She is the Ancient One. She knows all and protects all. She would never hurt nor harm a soul."

"I said those words to someone recently, though I failed to completely understand them. Tempest truly is wise."

"You will help her?" Beatrice asked anxiously.

Tiny heads bobbed in agreement with Beatrice, all looking for reassurance from her.

Sarina did not hesitate. "I will always help my sister."

Tiny cheers joined each other until a small echo of delight filled the air, and as each fairy ascended they blew kisses that rushed across Sarina's chilled cheeks and heated them to a toasty pink warmth.

"You know now what must be done?" Beatrice asked, waiting to be the last to bid her farewell.

Sarina held her finger out for Beatrice to perch on. "I think I knew all along. That is why I made such wise choices."

"Then all is well," Beatrice said with a satisfied grin.

"Not all," Sarina said with a look to her crooked wing. "Shall I fix it again for you?"

Beatrice pushed her head wreath up yet again away from her eye. "It would be nice to fly straight again, though I will probably manage to fly into another tree soon enough."

"Then I will repair it again for you," Sarina said and with a soothing touch of her finger over the crooked wing straightened it completely.

Beatrice tried out the repaired wing, fluttering up in a straight line and grinning with sheer delight. "Thank you, oh, thank you, wise one."

"Thank you," Sarina said on a soft whisper and sent the words up on a gentle breath as Beatrice flew away to join the others.

She sat in silence, the wisdom of the ages pouring through her, and she admonished her own foolishness time and time again. Part of her knew the truth, understood it, and yet failed to see it and apply it.

Her chance was here and now, and she would wisely embrace it and then . . .

She would have a long talk with her sister.

Lady Lily paced the kitchen floor right alongside a nervous Dagon. He was simply beside himself. He had thrown on his black jeans, and bare-chested and barefooted, he had searched the entire castle, and that was no easy chore to accomplish, though being a witch helped, and yet he still was unable to locate Sarina.

He detested waking up and finding her gone. He much preferred waking to her warm, naked body next to his. He would stroke her to wakefulness, and she would respond most eagerly, and their morning would begin with a slow and gentle loving.

It was a great way to start the day.

But this day, this morning, he woke alone.

A loud meow caught his attention, and he looked down to see the white furry kitten winding her way around his ankles. "Okay, I wasn't alone, you were with me."

She purred contentedly.

He shook his head, certain the kitten could read minds. "You take after your master. And if she doesn't—"

He spotted her out the kitchen window racing across the lawn, her black cloak fanning out behind her as she rushed toward the castle. He understood her haste when the first spat of rain hit the windowpane, and he smiled as he watched the skies open up and drop buckets full over the land and over Sarina.

He greeted her at the back door with a large towel. "A morning stroll?" He couldn't keep the annoyance out of his voice.

She patted his cheek. "Miss me?"

"Damn it, Sarina, you know how I hate waking up without you beside me."

"No," she corrected with a sweet grin. "You hate not having me there to make love with."

"That, too," he confirmed curtly.

She laughed as she slipped out of her black dress and discarded it to the peg next to where her wet cloak hung. She stood before him in nothing but black silk stockings that hugged her thighs with a band of black lace and black ankle boots.

His body responded with lightning speed, though he stood shocked senseless, unable to make a move.

Her hips swayed with the inviting gait of a female in hot pursuit as she approached him. And when she reached out to unbutton his jeans, he grabbed her hand.

With a smile he said, "Promise me this isn't the only morning I'll find you so seductively attired."

She tickled his ear with her tongue. "Wait until you see what you get to unwrap Christmas morning."

He laughed with pleasure and proceeded to seduce the siren he held in his arms.

Early that evening with the rain turning gentle and the air turning colder, they sat before the hearth in the living room toasting marshmallows. He could tell something disturbed her; she was more quiet than usual and her dark eyes more distant, as if she were elsewhere.

"It's burning," he said to her, gently watching the fat marshmallow on her stick engulfed by flames.

"What?" she asked and looked at him absentmindedly.

He pointed to her burning marshmallow.

She gasped and yanked the stick back, blowing wildly at the flames that ensconced the sweet, fat piece of confection. "Ohhh," she bemoaned.

Dagon took it from her and surrendered his perfectly toasted marshmallow to her.

She smiled at him gratefully and with small bites enjoyed the treat.

Dagon skewered a fresh marshmallow to another stick and began to roast it. "What troubles you?"

"Troubles?" she asked with a pretend smile.

He raised a brow. "You've prepared a feast for us for the holidays and yet you burn a simple marshmallow? Something is definitely on your mind."

She sighed. "I was thinking of my sister."

"Now, there's a depressing thought."

"Dagon," she snapped.

"Sorry," he apologized and could almost feel the sting of condemnation from Sydney and Beatrice for his thoughtless response.

"She spends much time alone, and when she is with others they always want something from her. Some bit of wisdom, a piece of advice, the gentleness of her love."

He pulled the stick from the flames, his marshmallow perfectly roasted, and his tongue salivating for a taste. "She must have *some* friends."

Before the plump treat could reach his mouth, Sarina grabbed the stick and handed him her empty one. He licked his empty lips and proceeded to place another marshmallow on it. This one was his, he assured himself, and stuck it in the flames.

Sarina blew at the hot confection. "Friends?" She shook her head. "None like Ali and Sebastian."

"How about Sydney?" he asked, his eye on the marshmallow that was browning nicely.

"Sydney was her student and as such respects her as a teacher would, and while I am sure Tempest regards her as a friend, it is not the type of friendship of which you share close thoughts and secrets."

"Do you share that with your sister?" He eyed her marshmallow suspiciously. She had almost finished it, and he feared his treat might just be in danger of disappearing again.

"The past few years have been difficult," she admitted reluctantly, but her eyes brightened as he took his marshmallow from the flames. She reached for it enthusiastically, and he couldn't deny her. He surrendered his treat to her yet again.

He was not one to give up, and so he skewered another marshmallow to the stick. "Why the difficulty?"

She nibbled at the sweet plump treat, licking her lips and making him envious. "She insisted that it was time I searched for a lifemate. She told me that I spent much too much time alone."

That caught his curiosity. "Did you?"

"I have friends."

"That's not what I asked."

"I went out," she said defensively.

"To the woods?"

She plopped the last of the marshmallow into her mouth and eyed the one roasting in the flames.

"Don't even think about it," he warned her.

She crossed her arms over her chest and pouted.

"So your sister was right then, you did spend too much time alone."

Sarina intended to argue and suddenly thought better of it. Her sister had been concerned for her for some time. It had started off with a suggestion that she go here or there, or Tempest would tell her of a male witch that she had met whom Sarina might find interesting, but her response was always the same. She always claimed she was far too busy.

"I suppose I did," she admitted with reluctance.

He yanked the marshmallow from the flames and waved the stick gently to cool it down. "Then perhaps you could present that as your best feat, finding a lifemate."

She watched him bring the gooey roasted fluff to his lips, and she turned sad eyes on him.

The marshmallow sat barely an inch from his mouth, he could smell its sweetness and almost taste the brown roasted parts, but then there were her eyes, pale blue and longing, and he melted as badly as the marshmallow.

"Here," he said and shoved the stick at her.

"Oh, thank you," she said with glee and greedily took the treat.

He had no intentions of roasting another, she'd only steal it away from him. "So what do you think?"

"I think you roast the best marshmallows in the world."

He smiled and shook his head. Damn but he loved her, really honest to goodness loved her. It surprised him sometimes just how strong his love was and how much it had enriched his life. Was that what her sister wanted for her?

"Your sister loves you."

"Very much," Sarina agreed.

He grew excited. "Then the spell wasn't cast to hurt you but to help."

She nodded, finishing the last of the marshmallow. "I realize that now. I thought her angry, and while she probably was to some degree, she would have never taken her anger out on me, it just isn't her way."

"So then this might just work."

"What might work?"

"Your best feat being that you found a lifemate. After all, she knew you would possess no powers, so, therefore, your feat would have to be more of your own making, and what better feat than finding a lifemate."

"Perhaps?"

"What do you mean, perhaps?" he asked, perturbed.

"Well, witches find lifemates all the time—there's no great feat to it."

"Really?" he asked curtly. "And how long did it take you to find someone with whom you could share magical moments and who would proclaim a love that is rare?"

She refused to answer, she just stared at him.

He refused to be denied. "How long?"

She relented with a snappish reply. "A year."

"So it wasn't easy, then?"

"No, it wasn't. It was hard. I couldn't find anyone that suited me."

"Or would tolerate your clumsiness," he said with a laugh.

"Well, you didn't exactly find it simple to choose a lifemate," she retaliated. "Actually you set your standards so high you would have never been satisfied."

"I did not!" he defended with a huff.

"You didn't?" she asked incredulously. "Choosing the Ancient One as a lifemate without meeting her first or even bothering to determine if she would be interested in you is normal?"

"Why wouldn't she be interested in me?"

"Because my sister would never hurt me that way," she said, before thinking.

Dagon looked shocked. "What do you mean?"

Sarina dropped her chin and stared at her hands in her lap.

"Sarina," he said softly and reached out to lift her face. "Tell me."

His blue eyes embraced her with a love that swelled her heart and made her confession all the more easier. "I fell in love with you shortly after you rescued me from the chandelier. I knew my feelings for you were foolish and warned myself of the resulting consequences until finally I could no longer deny it, and I realized that if I only shared a short time with you, the memories we made together would be worth it. So I loved you freely with no expectations or demands."

"And you had no intentions of telling your sister of your love for me the night of her arrival?"

"It would have served no purpose. Your love for me was the one in question, and I wanted you to give of it as freely as I gave of my love to you."

He laughed and brushed his lips over hers. "You stole my love."

"How?" she asked eagerly and slipped her arms around his neck.

"You slipped into my heart when I was too busy looking elsewhere and stole all my love, and when I finally realized that my own foolishness had almost lost me a rare love, I vowed to let no one now or ever stand in the way of our love."

She kissed him then, hot and urgent like the need that pulsated through her, and as always in their joining she felt his need and it equaled her own. Their hands grabbed for each other, their mouths fed on each other, and soon their bodies would join with each other to celebrate their love.

Unfortunately the phone rang.

"We won't answer it," Dagon demanded, his mouth working on Sarina's neck.

"It could be important."

"Damn, why do women always say that?" he asked, his head leaving her neck reluctantly. "What could be more important than—"

"Sex?" she asked with a teasing twinkle.

"Making love," he corrected and cursed the relentless caller. "Damn, but I'm going to—"

Sarina slipped away from him and rushed for the phone, afraid his phone manner might prove inappropriate.

"Ali, Sebastian, Merry Christmas," she said with delight.

Dagon muttered beneath his breath all the way to the phone. "Good hour to call," he said after an initial holiday greeting.

"Disturb you, did we?" Sebastian asked with an obvious laugh.

"I'll be sure to return the favor," Dagon said. "Home for the holidays?"

"Yes and it's snowing here in Virginia," Ali said with excitement.

"We have rain here," Sarina told her. "But Dagon roasted the best marshmallows."

"I taught him," Ali said, which brought a chorus of laughter from the other three. "I did," she insisted vehemently.

Dagon finally agreed between laughs. "Actually, she did, though I could never figure out how she learned herself."

"A secret no one will ever know," Ali said. "But forget the marshmallows, we have wonderful news."

"You're going to have a baby!" Sarina nearly screeched into the phone.

"Yes, yes!" Ali shouted back. "Isn't it wonderful?"

"Oh, I'm so happy for you," Sarina said, her eyes brimming with tears.

"Congratulations, dear heart," Dagon said, "and congrats to you daddy."

Before Sebastian could respond, Ali piped in with, "He's nervous the baby will possess more powers than he and he'll have his hands full."

"Will he, Dagon?" Sebastian asked. "She keeps telling me I have time."

Dagon was honest. "You have a couple of years before the baby demonstrates his abilities, and by then you should be possessed of enough power to counter any unfortunate mishaps."

"What do you mean?" Sebastian asked anxiously.

"He doesn't mean anything," Ali said.

"Oh, yes, I do," Dagon disagreed. "Be prepared, Sebastian, if you have a little girl and she takes after her mother. Ali was forever casting spells and creating complete havoc when she was little."

"Sarina, are we having a girl?" Sebastian asked.

"Don't answer him," Ali said. "I want him to be surprised."

"I have had more than my share of surprises this past

year! Now I want some cold hard facts,'' Sebastian insisted firmly.

"Give the poor guy a break, Ali,'' Dagon said in defense of his friend.

Sarina remained silent, aware that she could supply no information about a person without their permission, but feeling upset for Sebastian. He was a good friend to her, and she wished she could ease his worries. Though she could do that.

"You will make an excellent daddy,'' Sarina said with a quiet softness to her voice that caught everyone's attention. "Your child will be very close with you, the child and you will share many similar interests and''—she paused and chuckled softly before continuing—"you will be grateful that the child inherited some of your sensibility.''

"It's a girl! I knew it!'' Sebastian shouted.

"Sarina said nothing about the child's gender,'' Ali argued.

"She didn't have to. It's a girl, I know it, I know it and you're not telling me any differently,'' Sebastian insisted adamantly.

Sarina laughed and Dagon joined her.

"Watch that finger, witch,'' they heard Sebastian say. "I've got one of my own that's proving mighty powerful.''

Sarina could only imagine the scene so many miles across the ocean. Two witches facing off with pointed fingers.

"I've created a monster,'' Ali said on a giggle.

They heard kissing and laughter, and then Sebastian and Ali chimed together, "Happy holidays, talk with you soon, and our love and prayers are with you.''

Sarina returned the phone to the hook and looked up at Dagon with teary eyes. "They are so much in love and so very happy.''

"Then it is only natural that a child should follow, completing the cycle of life,'' he said, his finger reaching out to wipe a trail of tears from her cheek.

A gentle smile spread across Sarina's face, and though

her eyes glistened with tears, they also sparkled with delight as if she was seeing something no one else did. "A little girl."

Dagon caught her up in a hug and laughed. "Poor Sebastian, how I envy him."

They stared at each other, silence surrounding them, and their thoughts colliding.

"Make magic with me?" Sarina asked softly.

"Funny, I was about to ask the same of you."

They smiled, kissed, and descended to the carpet to make magic in front of the large tree aglow with white lights and gold fairy dust.

Thirty-one

"Four days," Dagon said to Sarina as they strolled the castle grounds hand in hand.

The holidays had past, the staff had returned, and so would Tempest. Sarina knew all this, accepted it, and would deal with it, but Dagon was counting the days now, and she could see the worry on his handsome face.

She voiced her sudden thought with a smile. "When we have a son, I hope he looks like you."

Dagon stopped and cast her a reproachful glance. "You're attempting to change the subject."

With a tinkle of laughter she shook her head. "Not really, though I wouldn't mind if we did, and I really, really wouldn't mind having a son that looked like you."

Her smile was much too contagious, and he found his own mouth turning to a generous grin. "And what if I give you three, four, maybe five sons that look like me?"

She bubbled with laughter. "We certainly would have our hands full with the women who chased after them."

"Then I will teach them about bumbling witches and the power of rare love."

She kissed him soft and long and released his mouth on a sigh. "I don't wish to think of my sister's return today

It is much too beautiful a day to waste, the sun is bright, the air is chilled, and I wish to spend a magical, memorable day with you.''

"Then let's spend the day in Edinburgh."

Her eyes widened in surprise.

"We can be there in an hour, walk around the old town, browse the shops, and have supper out before we return."

"It has been some time since I have been there," she said.

"Some time?"

"A hundred years," she admitted with reluctance.

"It's changed." And with a shake of his head added, "Your sister was right, you didn't get out much. But that's about to change."

He took her hand and tugged her along behind him since she found it hard to keep up with his purposeful strides. Orders were issued to her along with the staff. She was to get dressed, comfortable shoes he insisted she wear, and he shouted for Alastair to ready the Rolls.

They were in the car within the hour, he dressed in black with the exception of the white silk scarf that was draped around his neck and tucked in his black overcoat. It highlighted his good looks and would no doubt draw women's eyes to him.

She had chosen a long gray wool skirt and sweater that draped and curved along with her body lines. Comfortable ankle boots and a matching wool gray swing coat finished her ensemble, and it was with much excitement that she accepted a glass of champagne from him as they headed toward Edinburgh.

Their talk was conversational, as if they were on a date, and she realized that this actually was their first date, and the thought thrilled her.

They talked, they laughed, and her eyes turned wide when she caught sight of Edinburgh Castle high on the hill. The hill was ravaged by time, but the castle itself sat with bold pride looking down upon the town. It stunned her as did the city itself, so vastly different from when she had last seen it.

The gray, almost black buildings were in the process of being cleaned of the soot that had penetrated the stone from years of mining. It was as if a bleakness were being washed away slowly but surely and the hardiness of its people was once again shining through.

Alastair dropped them off in the old town, where history thrived and where she had once walked its cobblestone streets. They climbed the steep road hand in hand, her eyes darting to the many tourist shops and quaint restaurants.

"It's called the Royal Mile," Dagon explained. "From the castle down to the bottom here at Holyrood, it actually links four streets."

"Castlehill, Lawnmarket, High Street, and Canongate, the heart of the ancient city," Sarina said without thinking.

He grew concerned over her frown. "Do the memories upset you?"

"Some do," she said and forced a smile. "But all this chaotic splendor excites as well. I always loved the narrow lanes that ran between the tall buildings and that Robert Louis Stevenson explained so vividly in his book *The Strange Case of Dr. Jekyll and Mr. Hyde*. He captured the essence of that time period perfectly."

"One of my favorite reads," Dagon agreed, and they walked, stopping every now and then for Sarina to peek down the narrow lanes with wide eyes.

"The smells are more delicious than when I was here last."

"Yes, a great improvement. I know a perfect place to eat later, but if you would like we could stop now for tea and something light."

She shook her head vigorously. "No, I'm not hungry yet, though I imagine these titillating smells will eventually do me in. Right now I'd like to see everything."

"We could start up at the castle and work our way down."

Her smile was impish. "Could we stop in some of the shops along the way?"

His delight in reintroducing her to the city shined a

brightly in his eyes as did the excitement in hers. "Whatever you want, dear heart."

He was toting a small shopping bag by the time they entered Edinburgh Castle. He had indulged her every whim, buying her sliver and onyx earrings in an antique shop, a stuffed bear dressed in a fashionable kilt, a book on Scottish landscapes, and a video of *Braveheart* after having listened to her explain that Mel Gibson looked nothing like William Wallace. He could only imagine how she would critique the popular movie.

They both opted not to use the guided tours or the headphone tours. They knew the history well, probably better than the written history itself. They walked in quiet reverence, Sarina placing her hand on the gray stones and wiping a tear or two away as memories assaulted her.

"You know most of the kings and queens were advised by witches," she said as they neared the end of their tour. "Many sought my sister's favor."

He had not thought she would mention her sister today, but then perhaps memories had a way of stirring things. "And did she give it?"

"She chose wisely as to who she would advise. She trusted few and those she kept at arm's length. She complained that in their ignorance and greed they failed to learn the truth and in so doing chose their own demise."

"I can only imagine what Tempest must have experienced in her long life."

"She has watched, helped, and prayed for the growth of humanity, and never has she faltered in her hope and love for mankind."

Dagon was beginning to gain a new respect for Tempest. He only hoped she would prove true to her character. He felt Sarina's distress and sought to change it. "Hungry?"

"I thought you would never ask," she said, hooking her arm in his. "I'm starving."

"Good, I know a perfect restaurant, with the perfect atmosphere, and the most delicious menu."

He hurried her along, their laughter ringing in the chilled air, his arm tucked snugly around her until they came to a

narrow lane between two tall buildings with a sign that read
THE WITCHERY.

She smiled with delight. "How perfect."

Hanging plants and potted plants greeted their entrance
as did a slim woman with a pleasant smile. They were led
down steps to a table tucked in a corner with plants whose
vines grew up the walls. Chamber music played its somber
and repetitive melody, and tapestries depicting historical
events graced the wall. The atmosphere was wonderful, the
waitress cheerful and helpful with selections, and Sarina
relaxed with a glass of chilled chardonnay in hand.

"They chose a good name for this place."

He was about to tell her the reason for the name when
he thought better of it and remained silent.

They were much too attuned for her not to sense his
silence was on purpose. "The name has significance?"

Dagon was reluctant to repeat the tale, realizing it would
probably upset her.

She reached out her hand to cover his. "They named it
after the supposed witches that were burned nearby here."

"Many think it a mere tale."

She shook her head sadly. "It was no tale and not what
most thought."

"We don't need to speak about it; I don't wish to upset
you."

She cast bright eyes around the lovely dining room. "At
least this delightful place stands in remembrance of those
who were so wrongly accused. At least they will never be
forgotten."

"You knew of the burnings?"

"I didn't witness them, my sister did. When she heard
of the conflict, she knew there would be a problem, and
she attempted to stop the senseless slaughter of mortals. But
she wasn't successful."

"They say three hundred burned."

"I don't think there was that many, and it was not far
from here were the chaos took place. Fear and ignorance
drove righteous men to do evil deeds, and yet they thought
themselves God-fearing men. Do you know not one true

witch has ever been executed throughout all of history?''

''I have been taught that, but I have wondered over its validity. I have thought maybe one or two might have succumbed by mere accident.''

She smiled. ''You don't remember your lessons. There are no accidents where magic is concerned.''

''I stand corrected,'' he said with a raise of his wineglass.

Their conversation continued as dinner was served.

''What help did your sister offer those unfortunates?'' he asked.

''First she saw to securing the safety of the witches in the area. All were immediately dispensed elsewhere. Then she attempted to reason with the unreasonable.''

''I'm surprised they didn't accuse her of being a witch; she is certainly beautiful enough to be termed a seductress.'' He bit his tongue as soon as the words left his mouth.

Sarina hid her smile with a frown.

''I didn't mean it the way it sounded,'' Dagon attempted to explain. ''It's just that beautiful women, though she's not as beautiful as you, have often, through the ages, been accused of being witches.'' He stopped and shook his head. ''I'm just putting my foot farther in my mouth.''

She laughed then and leaned over to kiss him. He didn't relinquish her lips, he tasted them and savored them until Sarina pulled away nervous that they might draw attention.

''No one pays attention to witches, or lovers today, dear heart,'' he said and kissed the tip of her nose. ''Now let me correct my blunder.''

''You didn't blunder, you were correct in your assumption,'' she informed him. ''Tempest was accused of witchcraft, and it was her beauty that caused the accusation, that and a man denied.''

''How did she escape?''

''She could have simply vanished in thin air, but there was one whom she could not leave behind.''

Dagon remained silent, eager to hear the tale.

Sarina continued. ''A young girl, barely twelve and possessed with the power of sight—''

"But not one of us?" he asked.

"No, though I am sure somewhere in her bloodline was a witch, needing saving. Tempest simply would not leave her behind to suffer a vicious and senseless death. She cast a spell over the guards and went in search of the girl. The man who had propositioned my sister had the girl. He was telling her that he and he alone could save her."

Dagon shook his head in disgust. "And by submitting to him, evil itself, she would save her soul."

Sarina nodded. "Fortunately, Tempest had other plans.

"She materialized in his home, and he all but fainted at her feet. She then cast a spell over him that would only allow him to make love with a woman if there was love in his heart."

"Damn, your sister's good. Didn't hurt or harm him, but taught him a much deserved lesson."

"Yes, my sister is wise," Sarina said with pride.

"What happened to the young girl?"

"Since she wasn't a witch, Tempest couldn't transport her to safety as fast and easily as she wished. She had to journey with her for several weeks until they finally reached a safe place. She then talked with the young girl, and I suppose you could say they became good friends. She died in Tempest's arms when she was ninety-two, never having betrayed Tempest to anyone, not even her husband or children."

The story tugged at Dagon's heart. "Damn, I'm getting to like your sister."

"She really is likable."

"You could have fooled me."

Dagon ordered tea and dessert.

"I would like you to get along with my sister," Sarina said after the waitress had left.

"As long as she does nothing to hinder our relationship we'll get along fine."

"She is accustomed to having her way."

"So am I," he said firmly.

"You two will forever clash," she said with a shake of her head.

"I disagree," Dagon said with confidence. "All she needs to realize is that you will be my lifemate, and she is not to interfere."

Sarina threw up her hands. "That's all? How simple. And did you follow your own dictates when dealing with Sebastian and Ali?"

"That was different," he protested.

"How?"

"Ali needed protecting and help."

"And what if my sister thinks the same of me?"

"She doesn't need to, I'm here to protect and care for you now."

"And Tempest should just accept this after looking after me for over a thousand years?"

"You're over a thousand years old?" he asked with surprise.

"Damn," she muttered.

"You told me—"

"No, you assumed."

He shook his head. "I better get some mighty good life insurance on you."

They both laughed and it eased the mounting tension.

She took his hand, turning it over to trace circles on his palm. "You do realize that when my powers are restored, they will far surpass yours."

"Warning me, are you?" he asked, her playful finger causing heat to rise within him—and that wasn't all that was rising.

"Will it disturb you? My powers being greater than yours?"

"I'll worry about it when the time comes."

Her finger ceased its gentle play. "You don't think my powers will be restored?"

"Let's just say that your powers are not significant to our relationship."

The thought should have delighted her, but it didn't. She missed her powers and yearned for their return. "If the spell is fulfilled, then I return with my sister and it matters not about my powers."

"You're not going anywhere," he said firmly and with a grasp of her wrist. "We are going to be lifemates, and nothing, not even the Ancient One, is going to prevent that feat."

"You certainly are tenacious."

He leaned close to whisper in her ear. "And aroused, dear heart. Your playful finger worked its magic."

"Should we go back to the castle?" she asked with her own anxiousness.

He brushed his lips across hers. "I was thinking more of a hotel room."

She turned wide, teasing eyes on him. "Sir, are you attempting to seduce me?"

His smile charmed and his blue eyes invited. "I can only seduce if there is love in my heart."

Her smile warmed, her hand slipped into his. "I love you, Dagon."

"That's all I needed to hear."

She didn't know the name of the hotel and didn't care, though she realized it was expensive. The lobby had been grand, the staff gracious, and the room they were showed to was simply stunning. Large and expensively decorated in blue and gold, and the bed a king-size that openly invited lovers.

Their clothes were discarded in haste, their hands reaching out to roam as they collapsed on the bed together. He teased her nipples with his tongue and his teeth, she moved in an exotic rhythm against his hardness, and they both moaned in pleasure.

This would not be a fast joining, they would take their time, pleasing and teasing each other, driving themselves to madness and enjoying every crazy, passion-filled moment.

His fingers penetrated, hers cupped, his teased, hers stroked, and they both sparked and flamed their raging desires.

Their bodies grew damp, though they felt no chill, they rode on a fever pitch that had them aching for all they could give and more.

And when he entered her with a methodical slowness, she cursed him and arched beneath him, but he merely laughed, pulled back, and leaned over her to nip at her breasts and lips, and instructed her to be patient.

She cursed him again and he laughed again, though he reached out and grabbed her wrists tightly in his hands. "It's patience I'll teach you, witch."

He yanked her up along with him as he moved to bended knees, forcing himself deeply into her, and she yelled out with the pleasurable penetration of his full hardness. But then he released her wrists and slipped his hands down to her waist, grabbing hold of her slender curves, and ordered her to wrap her legs around his waist.

When she did he set a rhythm with his body and his hands on her waist, that was tormentingly slow, but erotically aware, and together they rode on a crest that swelled and peeked and collided like a crashing wave on shore.

That was only the beginning. The night was spent in a frenzy of lovemaking. Tender and slow, fast and furious, quick and urgent, patient and gentle, they shared it all. And Sarina fell in love all over again, but then she had the distinct impression that she would do that time and time again throughout their lifetime together.

Dagon felt the same. When he thought he knew everything about her, understood her every move and feeling, she surprised him and he discovered her all over again. He would never grow bored with her, never tire of making love to her, never stop telling her how very much he loved her.

They fell asleep wrapped around each other at the foot of the large bed, the sheets twisted around their damp bodies and their breathing finally returned to normal.

Sarina was embarrassed the next morning when she looked about the room. The bedcovers were torn from the bed and lay in a heap on the floor—only a crumpled sheet remained on the mattress. The couch cushion lay clear across the room, and the chair cushions were strewn beneath the windows along with the throw pillows. Empty champagne bottles lay discarded on the table and floor, and all that was left of a bowl of plump strawberries were the stubby stems.

She immediately began to straighten the room, rushing around naked, picking up pillows and tripping over sheets.

Dagon simply laughed at her antics, scooped her up, and demanded she shower with him. The bathroom looked no better, and she blushed when she recalled their time together in the tub and out of it.

He merely laughed and dragged a protesting Sarina under the warm pulsating shower spray.

She slept in his arms all the way home, and he held her tightly, protectively.

"Three days," he said to himself, and they still had not come to a rational decision of how to handle her sister. Tonight, they would talk this out and make definite plans. He would not lose her. She belonged to him and he to her, and they would join as lifemates. Her sister would simply have to understand. He would make her understand.

Thirty-two

Dagon paced the floor in his study. Tempest was due to return today, and Sarina and he had yet to reach any sort of understanding about how to handle this delicate and awkward situation. Actually Sarina did not even seem the least bit upset, and he had tried repeatedly to convince himself that she had matters well in hand.

She was after all a wise old witch who knew far more than he. And though she was powerless, she did not lack wisdom, she would know how to cope with her sister. But on that slim chance that things didn't work out, he wanted to be prepared—and yet how?

He just couldn't find an answer. How did a three-hundred-year-old witch match wits with an ancient witch? There was simply no answer.

Love.

Dagon stopped his pacing. One answer to all his questions Beatrice had told him. Could it be that simple? Could love combat the spell? It seemed worth a chance, and a chance was all he needed. Somehow, some way, Sarina would be his. He refused to accept otherwise.

He gave a curt nod of his head as if confirming his decision to himself and walked out of the study in search of Sarina.

He found her in the kitchen talking and laughing with Margaret as her hands were busy stirring a batter. "You're baking."

She smiled broadly at him. "Apple cinnamon bread. Tempest adores it, and I thought I would bake her a loaf."

"This is your great feat, bread?"

Margaret gave Sarina's arm a supportive squeeze before quietly leaving the room.

"My sister is wise enough to enjoy life's simple pleasures, and she would appreciate the fact that I took the time to bake her a loaf of her favorite bread. No great feat but a gift given with love."

Dagon felt contrite. "I'm sorry."

Her smile remained. "I understand, but please don't worry yourself. All will go well."

He approached her with enthusiasm in his voice. "You have decided on a feat that will appease your sister?"

She extended her lips for a kiss, her hands remaining busy.

He obliged her with a fast peck, and she stopped her stirring and glared at him in disappointment. "You call that a kiss?"

"You call that an answer?"

"You are going to worry yourself senseless."

"Until this day passes and I find you in my arms permanently, I will worry."

"And there is nothing I can say that will change that?" she asked.

"Tell me you have settled on a feat that will prove successful," he said with hope.

Her laughter surprised him. "I can guarantee nothing and you know it."

She returned to stirring her batter; he sat at the table in a chair opposite her.

"I am being foolish, I know it, and yet I cannot stop myself."

Her voice was comforting. "You are not accustomed to not being in control."

"You're right," he admitted. "I have controlled my life quite nicely until you walked into it and then . . ." He threw his hands up in surrender.

She giggled.

"I'm glad you find this so amusing," he informed her firmly, though a hint of a smile started in the corner of his mouth.

"The easiest way to gain control of one's life is to let go of control."

That brought a generous smile to his face. "There's food for thought."

"Think on it—it makes more sense than you know."

"I know that I love you," he said, his smile turning gentle.

Sarina poured the batter into a loaf pan. "And your love for me will serve me well this day."

A feeling of calm rushed over Dagon and brought an unexpected sigh to his lips. "You know something you're not telling me."

She reached across the table and locked her fingers with his. "Trust me, that's all I ask of you."

"You have all the trust and love I can give, dear heart, but know that I will be at your side through it all, and if you should ever be taken away from me, I would search until my dying day to find you."

"My hero," she said proudly and leaned across the table to give him more than a mere peck on the lips.

"Now," he said standing and pushing up the sleeves of his pale gray sweater, "what other treat does your sister favor?"

"You're going to bake a treat for my sister?" Sarina asked on a laugh.

"Cherry bread," he said with a nod. "If Ali can bake it, so can I."

"Do you mean this, Dagon?" Sarina asked seriously.

He walked around the table, his hands gently claiming

her waist. "A gift made from love for my sister-in-law to be."

His sincerity filled Sarina with joy. "Thank you, Tempest would like that."

"She likes cherry bread?" he asked with a teasing nip to her lips.

She nipped in return. "She respects sincerity."

"I respect fairness." His playful nips softened to a brush of their lips.

"Then you two will certainly get along." Her lips grazed his gently in return.

"I'm counting on it." He kissed her then, full and hard, and they both understood this need to cling, to reinforce their love, their strength, their commitment to each other.

And it was with laughter and teasing that they baked bread together and prepared for nightfall and Tempest's arrival.

Sarina wore all black, Dagon was dressed in complete white. They walked together to a large open area on the castle grounds. Normally one could view the distant hills and the woods in all their splendor, but it was dusk and an eerie gray covered the surrounding area, and the hills and woods appeared large shadows that stared with suspicion at the lone couple.

"I will speak to your sister first, he said, his hand gripping hers tightly. "There is something I wish to say."

She nodded, anxious for her sister's arrival, eager for this to end.

The wind came first, though it did not touch them. It swirled in great fury, a faint light beginning to grow in the center.

"She does love to make an entrance," Dagon said and moved to stand protectively in front of her, their hands remaining joined.

His breath caught when he saw her. He had thought perhaps his memory had played tricks on him, and he had only imagined her stunning beauty. His memory had not proved accurate—she appeared more beautiful than last he saw her.

And the pale yellow of her flowing dress gave her reddish-blond hair the appearance of soft flames that flicked around her. This time her slipper-covered feet touched the earth, and she approached him with confidence.

Sarina stepped out from behind Dagon, to his annoyance, and greeted her sister with a wide smile.

"It is time," Tempest said and waited.

Dagon stepped forward, and Tempest raised an annoyed brow.

"I wish to speak with you first," he said.

"I am not in a hurry, have your say, but—" she said with a tone that warned. "Choose your words wisely."

Dagon smiled then. "That may be difficult, since I find myself deeply in love with your sister and as of late have been more a fool than wise."

He thought he saw a hint of a smile and proceeded with renewed confidence. "First, I owe you an apology. When I requested an introduction to you, my intentions were to see if we would be compatible lifemates. But then I met Sarina and completely lost my heart, my soul, and my sanity to her. My apologies for not making my original intentions clear."

Tempest accepted his apology with a curt nod.

Dagon continued. "I foolishly believed that I could control love, that it was mine for the finding. I never realized that true love found you, that it hit you when you least expected it, and arrived in a package that you thought would never interest you. I learned that you can be blind to love just as love can make you blind. And I learned that a love that is rare is one that should be cherished forever."

Sarina fought to keep her tears from falling, she was so very proud of this man she loved.

Dagon took a deep breath and with authority said, "Sarina belongs to me now as I belong to her. She will not be returning with you."

Her pride for him swelled and her admiration for his courage grew, and she knew Tempest would understand both, though how she would respond was another matter. She did enjoy grandstanding at times.

Lightning split the gray sky so unexpectedly that it caused Sarina and Dagon to jump. Thin crackling spears of light descended in fury on the earth, stabbing the ground around them, causing them to instantly slip into each other's arms.

"A small demonstration of my abilities," Tempest said softly. "And so that you know if my sister fails to satisfy the spell, she will be returning with me."

Dagon moved to step forward, his own anger near to exploding, powerful witch or not.

Sarina's hand on his arm prevented further steps. "It is my turn."

He took her chin firmly in his hand. "I will not surrender you. I love you."

"Trust me," she whispered and kissed him gently before leaving his side and walking over to face her sister.

"You look as beautiful as ever," Sarina said to her sister.

Dagon was surprised by the generous smile that touched her face and kept his distance but lingered nearby.

"You possess a distinct beauty of your own, Sarina," Tempest said, her voice calm and soothing.

"You told me that often enough as I grew."

"I speak the truth."

Sarina smiled. "I know, that is why your words meant so much to me."

"It is time, Sarina, time to complete the spell," Tempest said, her smile reassuring.

Sarina shook her head and Dagon grew upset. Was she about to tell her sister that she had no feat to perform? He waited, his breath caught in his throat.

Sarina spoke with confidence as she circled her sister slowly. "When first you cast the spell, you upset me. I could not understand your anger toward me. I meant no harm in my prediction, I only wished to help you. I foolishly believed you wished to hurt me."

She stepped to the side of Tempest, keeping her sister and Dagon in her sight. "It was only recently I realized the reason for your spell and that my prediction precipitated your reaction. And that your reaction was brought on by your love for me.''

Tempest nodded knowingly. ''I always knew you to be wise.''

''And you knew it was my wisdom that would settle this spell and not my powers—that is why you stripped me of them. Isn't it?''

Again Tempest nodded. ''I knew your wisdom would never fail you.''

''You have that much confidence in me?'' Sarina asked with tearful eyes.

''I have that much love for you,'' Tempest said proudly.

''Then, dear sister, it is time for me to perform my best feat.''

Tempest extended her hands out before her. ''Surpass my powers, Sarina, and demonstrate for me your best feat.''

Sarina looked to Dagon and smiled with delight, then turned to her sister and with tears of joy announced, ''I will give birth to Dagon's son in the summer.''

Dagon felt the breath knocked out of him and rushed to Sarina's side, swinging her up into his arms and holding her tightly to him. ''A son? You're going to have my son?''

She nodded, much too tearful to speak.

He kissed her. ''I love you! Damn, but I love you, witch.''

''My blessings to you both,'' Tempest said sincerely, ''and my blessings to your son.''

Dagon lowered Sarina to the ground, though kept his arm firmly around her waist. ''Thank you. Your blessings mean much to me.''

''You will treat her well.'' It was an order Tempest meant to be obeyed.

Dagon took no offense, for the demand was issued with love. ''Always, I will always love and protect her.''

''I welcome you to our family,'' Tempest said and held her hand out to him.

He accepted her offer of friendship and was startled by the peace, calm, and love that washed over him when their hands embraced.

"Thank you. I am proud to be part of it."

Tempest looked to Sarina and waved her hand over her. "Your powers are now fully restored, and it is time for me to go." She took a step back.

"No, wait," Sarina said anxiously and turned to Dagon. "Please give me a few moments alone with my sister."

He nodded and stepped back into the shadows to wait.

Sarina rushed up to her sister, hugging her, and then taking her hand. "We have a wedding to plan."

"You wish my help?" She seemed surprised.

"Of course! Why wouldn't I? I want it to be special, and only you would be able to help me make it so."

Tempest squeezed her hand. "You were right, my spell was never meant to hurt but to help you. When you told me of *his* return and I remembered how very much I loved him, I realized that you had never allowed yourself to know true love. And I worried that you would forever lock yourself away, and while my own love had brought me pain, it had still left me with joyous memories I would never wish to surrender. I wanted you to experience such a love."

"And the feat—"

Tempest shook her head. "Love, Sarina, simply love, and you even surpassed that with your news of a son created from a rare love. So simple and yet so magical."

"You will be there for his birth? I will have no other tend me," Sarina insisted.

"You'd better not."

Both sisters laughed and hugged.

"Thank you, Tempest, for giving me Dagon."

"I did not give him to you. Love brought both of you together."

"It wasn't until I stopped looking that I found him."

"Then you discovered the secret," she said softly. "You can chase after nothing; it must come freely or you will never find it."

Sarina kissed her sister's cheek. "I'm so glad that you're my sister."

Tempest laughed softly, though a tear filled her eye.

"You have no idea how delighted I was when Mother and Father had you. I had so wanted a sister."

"You didn't mind them plopping me in your care and taking off on their adventures?"

"I hassled Mother and Father until she agreed to let me care for you. After all, they were much too busy on their adventures to give you a proper upbringing. Now go, your witch grows impatient and his body grows needy."

"Tempest!" Sarina said on a giggle.

"He is a good witch, I like him."

"I am so glad to hear you say that and, oh," Sarina said with excitement, "you must stop by the castle before you leave. I have two loaves of apple cinnamon bread I made for you, and Dagon baked you two loaves of cherry bread."

Tempest grinned. "A man that is not afraid to bake! Now I *really* like him."

Sarina squeezed her sister's hand she held. "I want to help you, Tempest, you are going to need it."

Tempest shook her head and slowly withdrew her hand. "It is too late. I knew this time would come, and even you with your tremendous powers of sight cannot tell me of the outcome."

Sarina sadly shook her head. "No, I cannot, but I can tell you that Dagon and I will be there to help you. Sydney, Ali, and Sebastian, too, they are good friends. You are not alone."

"I appreciate that and perhaps—"she faltered in her speech, her sister's love and concern giving her hope— "perhaps all will turn out well. Now give me another hug and go to your lifemate, he is anxious. And I will stop at the castle kitchen and pay a visit with Margaret before I leave and collect my gifts. I will also take time to discuss the wedding with her. The menu is important, and she is an exceptional cook."

They hugged tightly, holding on to each other as if reluctant to let go until finally they separated and with a gush of wind and swirl of light Tempest vanished.

Dagon joined her where she stood looking up at the night sky. "I like my future sister-in-law."

"I'm glad to hear that, because she likes you."

"Really?" he asked as he took her hand and they walked back to the castle.

"She was delighted that you baked her cherry bread."

"The bread came out good, didn't it? She'll like it, won't she?"

Sarina smiled, happiness filling her heart. "She'll love it, and she even talked about our wedding. She's going to help me plan it."

"Whatever you want, dear heart, is fine with me—as long as it is soon."

"I thought February. That will give my sister and me time to plan."

"Ali's going to insist on helping."

"I'd love her help. Actually I was thinking of asking her. Can we call them now?" she asked anxiously, tugging him along toward the castle.

"I had other ideas in mind."

"Will I like them?" she asked teasingly.

"I guarantee it."

"Good," she said and released his hand to run ahead. "Then we'll call Ali and Sebastian first, and then we'll tend to what's on your mind."

He chased after her, taking flight to catch her. He had forgotten her powers were restored, and with a whoosh of wind she disappeared before his eyes. Damn, but this was going to take getting used to.

Later that night after making love slow and easy, they sat in bed sipping hot cider and talking.

"A son," he said, his hand splaying over her naked stomach. "I can't believe we're going to have a son."

"Who will probably have his hands full with Ali and Sebastian's daughter." Sarina giggled.

"Damn," Dagon muttered. "I should have realized that you were pregnant."

"Why?"

"Sydney mentioned to me that our child would grow with Ali and Sebastian's child. When Ali informed us of her pregnancy, I should have known yours would follow."

"Actually," Sarina said, placing her mug of hot cider on the nightstand beside Dagon's, "our son is due before Ali and Sebastian's daughter."

"You kept your pregnancy from me?" he asked, his disappointment evident.

She shook her head. "No, I didn't realize I was pregnant. I didn't even think about it or think about taking precautions." She playfully slapped his naked chest. "You didn't, either."

"What was the point? I knew I loved you and that I wanted you for a lifemate. What difference did it make if you got pregnant? We would wed regardless."

"Positive were you?"

"Absolutely," he insisted with a mushy smack of his lips to hers.

She wiped at the remnants of his wet kiss with the back of her hand. "You do realize our wedding will be attended by many."

"Because of your sister?"

"Yes, there are many who will come to pay their respects and honor her presence and of course request favors."

"What favors?"

"Tempest will be generous with her skills on our wedding to honor our joining."

Dagon shook his head. "I will allow no one to disturb her or make demands of her in my home."

"But—"

He silenced her with a finger to her lips. "No *buts*—that is the way it will be. She is your sister and will enjoy the day, and I will make certain all of the guests are aware of this before they accept the invitation."

Sarina cuddled against him. "I can tell she will favor you."

He hugged her to him. "I heard you ask her to tend you when you deliver our son."

"I would trust no other."

"She will see to your care, then?" he asked, knowing her sister possessed the skills necessary to make her delivery easy and as painless as possible. And he did not want to see her suffer, for he would surely suffer along with her.

"Of course, she would let no other tend me."

"A wedding and a birth," he said joyously. "It will be an exciting year."

Sarina ran her hand over his firm chest. "I told my sister that we'll be there for her if she needed our help."

"You worry about her?"

She nodded, looking up at him. "I don't want to see her hurt. And I fear that *his* return will cause her pain."

"Then we will see that she doesn't suffer," he reassured her.

She smiled and planted a mouthy kiss on his lips. "My hero."

"With your powers restored, you may not require my hero services any longer," he said, sounding disappointed.

She stared at him as if stunned. "You will always be my hero."

"Even though I no longer need to rescue you?"

"You never know," she said with a glint to her eye.

He laughed and gathered her more closely to him.

She snuggled contentedly against him when suddenly she sprang out of his arms. "I almost forgot. I have something for you."

She hurried off the bed, rushing to a wooden oak chest near the window. She retrieved a small tin box and rushed back to the bed with it.

He watched her with curious eyes.

She sat on the bed in front of him and opened the tin box. "I saved these. I searched and collected until I had every last piece."

"Pieces of what?"

The vase I broke when I first began working here. I felt terrible when I realized it was a piece from the reign of James V and a gift at that. I spent hours combing the floor and carpet for every piece, placing them in this tin until my powers were restored and I could then safely restore the vase for you.''

''Sarina,'' he said, reaching out to her, but she pulled back.

''No, this is something that is important to me and that I must do. You have no idea how difficult it was for me without my powers. It wasn't until I came here that things changed and I realized that I could cope if necessary without my energy. After all, I had my sight, not for myself but for others. I learned so much while here—most important, I learned the true meaning of love.''

Dagon leaned over the small tin and kissed her. ''I'm glad you showed up at my doorstep. But I always wondered why you really chose Rasmus Castle.''

Sarina laughed. ''Mrs. MacDougal suggested it to me. She had heard that a position was open and I had created havoc at her castle and I think she was trying to get rid of me in the nicest way possible.''

''So she gave you a glowing recommendation and went on an extended vacation.''

Sarina nodded, still laughing.

''Did she know who your sister was?'' he asked, anxious to make all the pieces of the puzzle fit.

She nodded, ''I was at my wits' end and Tempest instructed me to go to the MacDougals. I am sure she will be relieved to receive an invitation to our wedding.''

''She'll probably take the credit for bringing us together.''

''In a way she did,'' Sarina said. ''Now let me demonstrate a small display of my powers.''

Dagon looked at her with a gleam of suspicion in his eyes.

''What's wrong?'' she asked, surprised by his skeptical response.

He shook his head as if just realizing himself. ''I now know how Sebastian feels around Ali—inadequate and vulnerable.''

Sarina giggled. ''Sebastian does not feel that way. He

has powers over Ali that have nothing to do with magic, and he uses them wisely as a witch would.''

He leaned toward her, his long dark hair spilling down over his shoulders and his handsome face alight with sensuality. "Are you telling me I have powers over you that surpass your own?''

She giggled and pushed at his naked chest, stopping his slow advance. "That is a given.''

"That is a relief,'' he teased and stole a quick kiss.

"Don't you want your present?'' she asked with a petulant pout.

"Is it the gift you wish to give me or your powers you wish to demonstrate?''

"A little of both,'' she admitted.

"Dazzle me,'' he commanded and leaned back against the mound of pillows.

She rubbed her hands together and chewed on her bottom lip in anticipation, then with pointed finger she directed the ceramic pieces to take flight and they did. They swirled up in a circle, round and round, searching for the right connection, the right piece to the massive puzzle, until in a flourish of wonder and magic the antique vase floated intact in the air before Dagon's eyes.

"I'm impressed,'' he told her and reached out and carefully took hold of the floral etched vase, placing it on the nightstand beside the bed. He then pulled her into his arms, and she sighed with the pleasure of being wrapped in his warmth and love.

"I am no longer a clumsy witch.''

Dagon cupped her face in his hands. "I wouldn't have cared if you destroyed this whole castle as long as no harm ever came to you. I could not imagine a life without you, Sarina. I love you so very much.''

She flung herself across him, wanting to throw her arms around his neck and kiss him senseless, but in her haste she misjudged the distance, and her hand sent the newly repaired vase flying through the air to crash into a million pieces on the floor.

She looked at him, stunned speechless, and he began to laugh. "My bumbling witch."

Her laughter joined his, and they spilled into each other's arms, their lips and hands reaching out intimately for each other so they could once again make magic.

TIME PASSAGES

FRIENDS ROMANCE

Can a man come between friends?

❑ **A TASTE OF HONEY**
by DeWanna Pace   0-515-12387-0

❑ **WHERE THE HEART IS**
by Sheridon Smythe   0-515-12412-5

❑ **LONG WAY HOME**
by Wendy Corsi Staub   0-515-12440-0

All books $5.99